YURI NEVSKY

Sardonic and tough, lovable and lovelorn, he's deeply intrigued by the baroque twists of a case that pits him against the brooding, unpredictable Russian soul.

CHARITY DAY

An attorney with a sharp mind behind her classy blonde looks, she's a cool WASP with a warm spot in her heart for her gruff partner Nevsky.

NICHOLAS MARKOV

Young, charismatic, good looking, he's suspected of murder, and he's missing. Some people swear he's innocent; others refuse to discuss him at all.

FATHER ALEXANDER

A great Russian bear of a man, he's a dedicated priest who's sure Nick turned away from a dissolute life... but there's something the Father's not telling.

TATIANA

Fair-skinned, sloe-eyed, voluptuous, she's the kind of woman Nevsky has dreamed about... but his snooping may turn this dream into a lethal nightmare.

**"A HIGHLY PROMISING DEBUT.
I LOOK FORWARD TO MR. GAT'S NEXT."**
Bill Pronzini

NEVSKY'S RETURN

·DIMITRI GAT·

◢ **AVON**
PUBLISHERS OF BARD, CAMELOT, DISCUS AND FLARE BOOKS

NEVSKY'S RETURN is an original publication of Avon Books.
This work has never before appeared in book form.

AVON BOOKS
A division of
The Hearst Corporation
959 Eighth Avenue
New York, New York 10019

First Avon Printing, May, 1982

AVON TRADEMARK REG. U. S. PAT. OFF. AND IN
OTHER COUNTRIES, MARCA REGISTRADA, HECHO EN
U. S. A.

Printed in the U. S. A.

WFH 10 9 8 7 6 5 4 3 2 1

1

Ludmilla Petrovna Markov came to my house at 138 Morlande Street on a day of rain squalls and mid-March winds. I was up on the third floor grimacing and pacing under a spreading wet stain on the ceiling wallpaper. I had put an old pot directly under the drip. OK for the moment. But the tippety-tappety of watery fingers on the thin aluminum was Nature's way of telling me the old 18-room ark needed a new roof. The old one was slate and had been nailed down the year I was born. That made it forty years old. I was getting a little thin on top by now, too. A new roof also ought to be slate. That meant four figures. I didn't have that kind of money right then.

Worse, the leak might be the first in a string of deteriorations. No. 138 had been built in 1860 and well maintained by a string of careful people, the last being my mother, who died two years ago. My not selling the place, choosing to return to and live in Pittsburgh, had been a small risk. I was banking on the house to hold up well. At that moment I was thinking maybe I had made a mistake.

The rain that was vexing me had soaked Ludmilla Markov. I hung her dripping coat on the stand in the small entrance hall. She looked, despite her expensive cloth coat and pillbox hat, like a babushka—a Russian grandmother. Heavy cheekbones, pale blue eyes. Lines branched like webbing across the yellowish parchment of her skin.

She asked me a second time if I was really Yuri Nevsky. When I didn't change my story she abandoned her thickly accented English in favor of rapid-fire Russian. She *was* a Russian grandmother.

I caught most of what she said. I seldom used the language. Hadn't spoken more than a handful of words in years. My father, the old émigré, had made me learn it and use it when I was a boy. Sure way to get me to hate it. I rebelled as well against what I saw of Russian culture. In my early teens I turned against Russian ethnic oddities altogether. People lived in America, they should act like Americans, I thought. In the following years anything Russian was confused by folks with Soviet—read Communist—and so held in contempt. That didn't bother me. I had put my ancestors behind me in getting on with the business of my life.

Ludmilla's grandson was missing, she said. Then followed with something about the police saying he had murdered a man. Impossible! Her eyes burned with loyalty. Nicholas Markov was a good boy.

I asked her—in English—to slow up and start at the beginning—in English.

Her lined face fell. "English for me—hard, Mr. Nevsky."

"Russian is hard for me." I scarcely thought about what I said. So I felt suitably punished for my carelessness when this tough old lady, who looked like she could still bag five hundred pounds of potatoes in a morning, began to leak tears. Not bawl like a schoolgirl or a jilted bride, but *leak*. That was worse somehow. When I asked her to follow me to the kitchen for a cup of tea, it came out in Russian. So did the rest of my conversation with her.

She tended to run on, paying little attention to time, place and connections. I stopped her politely and began to ask ordering questions. The Russian came lumpishly, reluctantly to my lips. I promised myself to keep the conversation short.

"Where do you live, Ludmilla?" I said.

"In Grafton. On the river side. Above the tube works."

"Russian Slope?"

She nodded. I knew it. A couple of square miles of one of the better industrial towns clustered along the Monongahela southeast of the Golden Triangle. Packed with Slavs. Mostly Russians.

"Your grandson, Nicholas Markov, how old is he?"

"Twenty. He's a good boy. A special person. He has high thoughts."

I nodded sympathetically. Show me a babushka who didn't think her grandson had high thoughts. Even if he spent his days shooting pool and his nights beating off. "You said he disappeared. When?"

"Two months ago, almost to the day."

"He in any trouble?"

She shrugged her heavy shoulders. "He was a good boy."

I asked the question again.

6

"I don't know." Her voice was now very small for such a solid lady. I tried a different angle.

"Nicholas have a job?" I said.

"He bowled—sometimes."

I never heard of a bowler living on it, unless he was on the tour. The lad was forging ahead fast in the Yuri Nevsky Ne'er-Do-Well Sweepstakes. "Tell me about the day he disappeared."

"It was a night that it happened, Mr. Nevsky." She sized me up across her teacup. "After dinner he had his regular talk with the priest, Father Alexander. Then he went from St. Basil's to a bad place. A bar called the Eleven-to-Seven. He met two friends—Anya Rok and an Italian girl. I don't know her name. Then Ed Dixon. There was shooting. Dixon got killed. Nicholas ran out the back door. Somebody drove him away in a car. He never came back. The police think *he* killed Dixon." Her face furrowed along the webs of old sorrows. "Because they found a pistol on the floor. Fingerprints." Her tears leaked out again.

I leaned back and tugged thoughtfully on my wiry beard. I felt ready to cry myself—in sympathy. My intuition, which I've learned to trust, was whispering that Nicholas Markov shot Ed Dixon dead. Like Frankie killed Johnny. Worse, that maybe it was a contract. The kid might be taking a paid vacation now. Maybe on a beach in Cozumel, sipping some kind of weird drink out of a pineapple shell. Jumping to conclusions, sure. I'm good at it. I'm right a lot, too.

There were about a hundred questions I could ask. But they would show a commitment I wasn't sure I felt. While I was tugging my beard and thinking carefully about my next words, Ludmilla blurted, "Some people say he ran off with Olga Samnesovich that night. The same night a gold cross was stolen out of a case at St. Basil's—by one of *them*, they say. Mr. Nevsky—"

"Wait a minute!" I got up and raised both palms. The waters were getting deeper by the second. I wasn't nearly ready to swim. "Why'd you come here, to 138?"

She frowned. "I want you to find Nicholas. I have some money—"

"How did you find me, Ludmilla? What I do doesn't get any publicity."

"My son Mikhail says you found some missing money for U.S. Steel. You and a pretty pale lady."

"To be honest, we found out *where* it was. In an account

7

in a Bahaman bank. Somebody else went to get the money. But I—and my pretty partner—got paid just the same."

"You find out where my Nicholas is, *I'll* go and get him."

I shrugged. "I'm not sure I'll be able to help you."

"I know. You want money." She nodded and flashed a glance abrim with Old World cunning. "I have money. Eighteen hundred dollars. To help send Nicholas to college—"

"I'm still not sure—"

"And I'll come clean for you." Her shrewd eyes darted about the disaster area of the kitchen I shared with Charity Day, my tenant and frequent collaborator. I loved to cook—but not clean. Charity didn't like to do either.

"I wouldn't want to take your money."

"Why?" Her peasant's brow furrowed. For her it was simple. There was money to be made by labor. Why say no? "It's not enough money?"

"It's not the money."

"So why, Mr. Nevsky?"

"I don't want to find out things that disappoint you. That make you very unhappy."

"You think—"

"Never mind what I think, Ludmilla Petrovna." God, I had lapsed into using her patronymic! I was annoyed with myself. Why, I really wasn't sure.

I got up and paced, did some more beard stroking. Ludmilla poured us more tea. She held a tea bag up like a rat by the tail and stared at it. "You have no samovar?" she said.

I waved her question away. The Italians have their espresso machines, the Russians their tea-water towers.

"To be Russian and not have a samovar . . ." No mistaking her tone of criticism.

"I don't do Russian things," I said. "I'm not much of a Russian."

" 'To be Russian is to share some secrets with God.' "

My father had used the same proverb. The Russians were great ones for proverbs. I went into my study and got my old spiral-bound notebook with "Harvard Coop" printed in crimson on the cardboard cover. I flipped over a lined sheet that held the preliminary notes for my next consulting job: to find a jewel-encrusted sword called the Sunlight Scimitar that had disappeared from the collection of a Chicago electronics executive. It had been an assault-robbery. He wanted to talk to me after he got out of the hospital. So I had three weeks to kill.

"I want you to tell me something about your grandson, Ludmilla," I said. "That doesn't mean I've decided to find out where he is. I need to know more before I make up my mind. And I'll have to talk it over with my pretty pale lady partner. Understand?"

She nodded her heavy head. I caught a brief gleam in her blue eyes. Triumph? Or hope. "God bless you, Yuri Vladimirovich!"

Hearing and speaking Russian was tiring out my flabby language muscles. Just the same I managed to get down a character sketch of Nicholas Markov largely unshaded by the rose-colored glass of a loving grandmother's biases.

One thing for sure: Nicholas Markov wasn't the typical hood I expected. The obvious facts were that he was born and raised on Russian Slope. Went to school and church there. Lived in the family's big house with father Mikhail, mother Elena, Ludmilla and—until he died eighteen months ago—eighty-seven-year-old Igor Gregorevich Markov, Mikhail's father. Nicholas was thoroughly immersed in the Russian Slope community. Friends, family, social life—even vacation groups—were part of that environment. On the surface he was all wholesome, ordinary and ethnic.

The interesting stuff was underneath. For example, he really didn't have a job, but he had money. He didn't get it from his father. Mikhail was hard on the boy. The disciplinarian type—made even more rigid by his son's brushes with the law. Ludmilla was unclear about the reason for police interest.

Nicholas spent a lot of time reading and thinking—about philosophy and metaphysics. His room—which Ludmilla cleaned regularly—was three-quarters library. I asked her about his books. Turned out to be the great religions and philosophers, writings on Buddhism, Christianity, Hinduism, Kant, Hegel, Spinoza, Sartre. Included the marginal types like Rudolph Steiner, the German nature mystic, Rosicrucianism, others.

Nicholas had some charisma. People liked him. Women in particular. "He has his pick," Ludmilla said with pride. But the expression on her fattish peasant face was guarded. Saying, maybe, while he had his pick, he hadn't picked. And friends! He didn't have an enemy. Everyone liked him—a lot.

To round out my portrait-in-scribbles of a young man with

9

a complex personality I added that he was a superb bowler. Won regularly in the local tourneys. A man named Ray Nevick was after him to go on the tour. Ready to bankroll him the minute he agreed.

I closed my notebook and got up. Ludmilla saw that our conversation was about over. "You'll try to find Nicholas?" she said.

I shook my head. *"If* I decide to help you, I'll try to find out where he is. When I do, my job's over. You—or somebody else—can decide what to do with the information."

"You play with words, Yuri Vladimirovich."

"I know my business, babushka. It's not for you to tell me what I should say."

Her habits of submission to the wishes of men buried the disagreement in her eyes. *"Da,* Yuri Vladimirovich," she said. Yes.

"I'll think hard about your Nicholas," I said. "I'll talk to my friend, the pretty pale lady."

"She isn't Russian."

It was a statement. By God, an accusation! "No, she isn't. But she's a very bright woman. If we decide to help you, she'll probably play a big part." I slid her coat up onto her beefy shoulders. "Anyway, I'm not much of a Russian, either. I've spoken more Russian in the last half hour than over the last six years." I fumbled with the front door, which always stuck in wet weather. "What do you think about that?"

"That you have much to learn about yourself, Yuri Vladimirovich."

I wished her good-bye, an unbidden distance entering my voice.

"I'll be back soon," she said. "To begin cleaning."

"If I agree to help you."

She smiled out of some ancient wisdom. Said nothing.

I watched her black, bearish figure navigate the long downhill walk leading from 138 to puddled Morlande Street. I knew why she had come to me. Not because I had found some small success in my consulting business. Because I had a Russian name.

Maybe the right man. But for sure for the wrong reason.

2

I fussed with Cornish game hens and saffron rice while Charity lamented the poor judgment of the young women attorneys in her law firm. Her main point seemed to be that they put their careers so far ahead of the other elements of their lives that sooner or later they would pay a terrible price. She made some telling points about the shortcomings of day-care compared to good old-fashioned mothering and the tendency of neglected husbands to find other, less ambitious but earthier women.

Charity made her pronouncements from her throne, a library circulation desk chair I had dragged out of the dumpster behind Harvard's Lamont Library into a half-dozen residences over the years. It was upholstered in an ugly institutional-green vinyl and its seat was loose. A heavy tubular steel hoop had been welded above the foot pieces. Charity liked to roll the bottoms of her shapely bare feet across the hoop. She sipped a glass of White Mountain Chablis, her day-to-day drink. To me that wine suited her pale skin and the white-blonde hair braided and piled atop her head.

She also made her pronouncements from the perspective of her thirty-six years—and from the many victories and single great defeat of her life. She had been born and raised on a farm in Iowa. First in a high school class of seventeen, she was admitted to Radcliffe. She married a Harvard Business School graduate student, Walter Day, of wondrously WASPy stock. Over the next five years she bore three children—and earned a degree at Harvard Law. Walter was in banking and was offered a vice-presidency at Pittsburgh National Bank. She joined a downtown law firm and soon was promoted to junior partner. They bought a big house in Fox Chapel . . .

She had overcome challenges like a giant hurdling so many dominoes. I asked her how she had done so much so soon. She said, "I never thought I could fail." And she hadn't.

Two days before her fifteenth anniversary Walter Day and

11

the three children were killed instantly in a head-on collision with a trailer truck on the Pennsylvania Turnpike.

Walter was badly underinsured. There were the expenses of death and related confusion. The house had to be sold. Charity had to start over—in what had to be one of the most painful ways possible.

I met her during an intermission at a Pittsburgh Symphony concert at Heinz Hall. I had been divorced only six months earlier. My ex-wife and two daughters were 800 miles away in New England. My last job, a hush-hush government one, had ended by mutual agreement just as my mother died. Confusion, loss and grief had eaten new lines into my face and whitened wiry strands on my beard. I had come reeling home to the ark of 138 like some latter-day Noah fleeing the Inundation of a crumbling life. Several months of my determined—even compulsive—work had turned the solid old house into two spacious apartments and some shared rooms. Really two houses within one. Charity needed a place to live. I needed a tenant. She was happy to climb aboard the ark with me.

The spark of romance has never burned between us. Our first relationship was landlord-tenant, the second informal partnership. I'm a broad-stroke person, she's small-stroke—precise, suspicious, perpetually questioning. We work well together. It ends there.

I had a hunch my report of Ludmilla's visit would get her mind off the misguided self-absorption of young professional women. I was right.

She frowned. "You know, I remember reading about that murder in the *Press*, Yuri." She covered her eyes to spur recall. "Something to do with drugs. That was it. The police thought the killing was drug-connected. One phrase they used to describe Nicholas Markov stuck in my head. 'Dreamy-eyed and distant.' That was it. Dreamy-eyed and distant."

"Remember anything about the getaway? Maybe planned, mob-connected?"

"Nothing. The paper made a big thing out of it being the scandal of Russian Slope. Those Slavs run a pretty tight ship over there. Stain on their escutcheon it was. There was strong public opinion that Nicholas Markov was a good kid. That he was framed. Or used. Maybe left floating somewhere in the river."

"He'd be down to the Gulf of Mexico by now. Floating on

the surface, twice as big as life. He disappeared two months ago."

Charity nodded and sipped her wine. "Ludmilla's story sounds like such a dreadful hodgepodge. We need facts. First off, did Nicholas Markov kill Ed Dixon? Ludmilla said there were two women friends of Nicholas who were witnesses. What did they see that incriminated him? The police are still looking for him. What do they know that keeps them looking? Sounds like the murder weapon was found. With fingerprints. All that suggests..."

"Yes. And so does Yuri's Notorious Intuition, for what it's worth."

"Which usually isn't very much," Charity said with exaggerated haughtiness. My Notorious Intuition was a heavily argued issue. Not likely to soon be resolved. "If yes, Nicholas did it, then what motive? From motive to getaway. From getaway to hiding place. And so forth. It needs to be lined up and reasoned out. We hardly know anything."

"For Ludmilla, not knowing anything is worse than finding out for sure her grandson is a killer." I studied Charity's pale face, its sturdy nose and generous mouth. "Do we help her?"

Her turn to study me. Blue eyes light years away from dumb-blondeness. "Affirmative. Know why?"

"Why?"

"First, you have three weeks on your hands. Then, Ludmilla got to you some way. So did odd Nicholas. It's not the killing that's hooked you, Yuri. It's the people mixed up in it."

I was indignant. "Who *cares* about another crazy Russian kid, half monk, half terrorist? They're *all* like that! Dime a dozen. Mystics and devils rolled together and no use to God *or* Satan. Beside that, there's not much money in it—and our roof is leaking!"

"I don't think it's smart for us to just start nosing around Russian Slope asking questions."

"Us?"

"I'll admit I'm curious, Yuri," Charity said. "I find mysterious disappearances fascinating. The whole idea of Nicholas intrigues me. 'Dreamy-eyed and distant.' It's all so...*Russian*. I'm not likely to get to Moscow this year. It's not far to Russian Slope. You don't need a visa or a jet. What we *do* need is a convincing story that explains why we're nosing around. I'll work on that angle." She got up and began to set the kitchen table. "I'm very grateful you've gone to all this trouble just to get my mind off women who don't know how to draw the line between independence and responsibility."

"Anything for a friend." I was a bit dazed.

"Now will you sit down and *carve?* I'm starving."

I spent the early evening groping through one of Mozart's easier sonatas on the slightly out-of-tune baby grand in the music room. The piano had been my father's. Educated in the grand style of wealthy landowners in Imperial Russia, he was as comfortable with things cultural as in the U.S. Steel research lab where he earned his living as a chemist. I remembered him sitting on the same bench playing—and stopping to curse when he made errors. He made a lot of errors. Thus my profane Russian vocabulary was developed.

I found it useful to my thinking to play. Notes and thoughts tumbled together like Watson and Crick's double helix to make something in my head greater than their parts. By the time I wobbled through the rondo I had decided helping Ludmilla was a good idea. My primary reason wasn't to do the gallant old peasant a favor. It was to find out about Nicholas and to delve into the riddle of his personality. Charity—as usual—was right.

The next morning I phoned Ludmilla. I told her Charity and I would look around Russian Slope and see what we could find. No promises of information—good or bad.

"God bless you, Yuri Vladimirovich!" she bellowed. "I'll go to the bank, withdraw the—"

"Let's wait about the money. There's really no hurry."

"Then I come to clean next week. I insist!"

I surveyed the kitchen framed by an arching doorway. It hadn't improved. The top of the piano was dusty. The front porch was coated with the cokey grime peculiar to Pittsburgh. The windows were streaked from nature's wintery attentions.

"OK," I said. "One other thing. I think it would be easier if you didn't talk about Charity or me for a while yet. And if you see us around Russian Slope, pretend we're strangers."

"I understand. You'll find many who'll talk about Nicholas. He was friends with everyone. Admired by many . . ."

It took me twenty minutes to tactfully disengage myself.

So I was in business again. A business that had never been part of my life plan. I had started out nearly twenty years ago in a very different kind of business. Odd as it seems, I was a librarian, an "information scientist," they told me. I learned something of the Library of Congress Classification System, named as colleagues some women in sensible shoes, some men who had previously failed in other lines of work. Rewards and challenges among the stacks—even such glorious ones as those of the Harvard University Libraries where I worked for a while—were limited. See one "Germ. Philol." classified book and you've seen them all.

I got another job—electronic information control, this time state-of-the-art in Southern California. From there I moved to a U.S. government agency which I'd rather not name. There I also dealt with information. I learned that the most valuable kind wasn't recorded. It lay largely within individuals' memories. It was also the most difficult to obtain. It demanded the highest prices. In money when that was possible, in human suffering, even lives, if that were necessary.

From the nameless agency I passed to a more formidable one whose existence was not officially admitted. Its business was, again, information. Its methods of obtaining it were as far removed from the dusty shelves of Widener's marble-floored stacks as 138 is from Tranquility Base. In pursuing this information I had to change my beliefs, alter my self-image. I hurt people emotionally and physically in the name of my country, the political system in which I believed.

Something in me—I like to think something higher—wouldn't allow my total immersion in that particular world of information-seeking. In so resisting I couldn't continue to work beside those with total commitment. My marriage was collapsing in part because of what I did for a living. My self-respect would be the next victim. And then very possibly my sanity.

So by means of mutual agreement and many signed and sealed great oaths of silence I returned to the emotional land where men slept through the night. I floundered aboard the ark of 138.

While I arrived largely empty-handed I wasn't without assets. Sure, the house was filled with the quality, durable furnishings of my youth. But my head was packed, too. With methods, techniques, effective approaches in finding information, certainly. But above all, I brandished a profound understanding: *information was people*.

I also brought with me many contacts and friends in government and private business. It was one of them who suggested that a puzzled Gulf executive give me a call. One of his company attorneys had run off with some exceedingly valuable

15

geological survey maps targeting likely locations of crude deposits. I agreed to do what I could. In the middle of it I found I needed confidential legal help. On cue, along came Charity Day. To make it quick: by uncovering an interesting triangle involving a philandering executive, his promiscuous mistress and a novice extortionist we found where the maps were. After that came more jobs.

The trouble was, there was no staying just with information. Keeping clear of the rough stuff, the grease and sweat and fatigue of finding out what people didn't want to tell you was impossible. The words "gumshoe," "private eye," "snoop," "shamus" and "dick" soon began to fit my actions—but never my mouth. I called myself an information specialist, a consultant, a friend. Anything but the usual. I was the first Reluctant Investigator.

3

The next afternoon the sun burned brightly enough to make any self-respecting tulip bulb push a little harder—the first real hint that spring wasn't just something you read about in magazines. The day wasn't any brighter than Charity's grin when she came home about two o'clock.

First thing she did was offer me her long-fingered hand to shake. Which I did. "One veteran *journalist* greets another," she said, grin still in place.

"Huh?"

She whipped out two *Pittsburgh Post-Gazette* press cards and two letters typed on *Post-Gazette* letterhead. The letters were identical. One for each of us to carry. Each informed the reader that the bearer was a journalist—no mere reporter—on the newspaper staff gathering information on the first of a series of long articles on Pittsburgh's many cultural and ethnic enclaves. The purpose of the series was to explore the cultural diversity of the Greater Pittsburgh and tri-state area. Cooperating with us would serve to richen our description of the people and ways of Russian Slope, of the total Slavic community. Signature: Harrison Brightwood, Senior Editor.

"Charity strikes again," I said. "You pull these out of a hat along with a white rabbit?"

"Got them *and* a free lunch at the Pittsburgh Press Club, all in about two hours. Harvey's an old client. Time was when he wanted to apply for the job he has now. He was killing himself doing the work of three for a right-wing paper down in West Virginia. Run by a reactionary, a nearly crazed man, who had tricked him into signing a slave-type contract. Harrison was just a naïve kid then. He got my name somewhere and I helped him break that contract. It wasn't easy. Legal traps on every side. Well, we did it. He got the new job. And I persuaded my firm to allow him to defer the fee for eighteen months. We've been friends ever since."

"I *guess*."

"He's been asking me for years how he could repay me."

"Great time to collect."

Charity frowned. "What about Ludmilla blowing our cover?"

"I talked to her about keeping quiet. She understood. You don't have to tell a Russian peasant how to be cunning."

The next morning we got into my nondescript green Datsun sedan and set off for Russian Slope. I found a chamber-of-commerce map of the area. That and a roadmap Charity rustled about on her lap guided us as we made a preliminary auto tour of the hilly streets.

Russian Slope's area was roughly a square, the contours of the land a shallow S, like a tilted integral sign. One end was the top of the hill; the other led to the riverbank. Or more exactly to the J. T. Elmford Tube Works. Its gray corrugated-steel buildings, storage yards and railroad grid pretty much covered the banks of the Monongahela for a solid half mile or so. Paralleling the river, with the mill on one side, was Commercial Street, once cobblestone and trolley tracks. Now asphalt. Along its other side clustered the businesses common to every western Pennsylvania steel town I'd ever seen. Now noticeably more threadbare than in my younger days. The steel business wasn't good, and never would be again, at least in the way it once was. Bars, sure. Lots of them. They opened at 7 A.M. when the night shift came off. And did a good business. Then came the appliance and furniture dealers who brandished "location" like a hammer. Distant discounters be damned! Credit was really easy. Young couples' moms and dads had probably furnished their first apartments behind one stained storefront window or another. Moving on down, pawnshops, insurance agencies ("*No* one is uninsurable."), used-car lots, smoke shops, a hardware store, a laundromat, old yellow-brick, three-story apartment houses, and too many boarded up storefronts.

Moving uphill, Russian Slope began to show more class. As always, wealthier people sought higher ground. We saw newer apartments with controlled entry, speciality stores featuring Russian and East European foods, a school complex without spray-painted obscenities on its bricks, crowded supermarkets and gas hogs nosed in along the curbs.

Houses appeared, the first with tiny lawns, then just before the hill began to level out at the top of the S, maples and oaks on the lawns, gardeners' trucks, a park. Tasteful signs in English and Russian announced that several of the big stone and brick houses were inhabited by goldsmiths, painters and potters.

Crowning Russian Slope, rising up like a monument at its crest, was St. Basil's Russian Orthodox Church. Its four onion-shaped domes had been recently regilded. They shone on this day of bright March sun. My triggered memory served up a six-year-old Yuri Nevsky, hand-in-hand with his lanky father, asking why the domes came to those funny points. And my father, though not a churchgoer, not a religious man, said, "Those are flames—the flames of the Spirit of God, the flames of souls reaching toward their Maker, the flames of Faith." That memory made me smile.

The street led up to a circular drive around the church and the adjacent building, the priest's home. Buildings, lawn, shrubs were immaculately kept—by the faithful; the work was too loving to have been done by mere professionals.

"What a lovely church!" Charity said. She looked at me. "Russian Orthodox. That's your religion, isn't it?"

"I don't have a religion," I said.

"Oh, come on, Mr. Modern Man! I mean you were baptized as a Russian Orthodox."

"Charity, I'm not baptized."

"You're *not?* Ohmygod. I thought everybody was."

"My father was anticleric."

"He was anti-*sense*." She waved at the modest marvel of red brick, polished wood and gilt. "This could be part of your life."

We circled St. Basil's and coasted down the hill to a nearby park. Below us Russian Slope swept down to the gray ribbon of the Monongahela. Above the river rose the bluffs of Duquesne and beyond, the hills of West Mifflin.

I had been atop Russian Slope years before. The view was familiar. Not Charity. She ogled like a tourist. I found my attention straying to the nearby basketball court behind cyclone fencing erected along the curb. A black kid and a white kid were going one-on-one half court. They were about fifteen— and dead serious. Two six-packs of Coke and two five-dollar bills sitting by the fence were the stakes. The black had the style and the moves. Probably from Rankin, the next town over. Tough town, tough people, hard lives. The white kid had the high Slavic cheekbones seen everywhere on Russian Slope. And the tenacity that went with them. He was a scrambler; the knees of his jeans were torn from diving after loose balls. He played "physical," using his body to keep the other boy boxed out, keeping the left elbow up and out on drives to the basket. He refused to take the lesser percentage outside shot, but kept backing and spinning toward the hoop, his heavy thighs working. He worked hard for his short jumpers and spinning lay-ups. When the black had the ball he was all elegance and deception. Twice he faked the other into a stumbling tangle. Free, he gathered himself for a soaring slam-dunk that exploded down through the chain net with a nasty clatter. The Slav came right back, digging, backing, leaning, patient until he scored. I couldn't see how the shorter, slower kid could win, no matter his determination. Turned out they were playing 25 hoops win-by-two. Ahead 20 to 17, the black kid faded, out of shape. The white kid won by 5.

They staggered off the court. The winner grabbed up the cold Cokes and the money. The loser stood silently, too proud to ask. The Slav shoved a can toward him. Playground ritual refused to allow acknowledgment of skill or stamina, never mind even one-time superiority. "Shee-it, man, you play NFL fouls, not NBA!" the loser growled.

"I foul you, you call it, muthah. And I got news: outclassing ain't a foul!"

They were still making points on each other as we drove away.

We spent the early afternoon driving up and down every street on the slope, Charity working hard to match them up with the chamber-of-commerce map. We both knew how important getting the geography down was. Even I, the native Pittsburgher, had to run a refresher in the face of new buildings, an expanded shopping center, a string of condos, and old stores with new names and merchandise.

The essentials of life in Western Pennsylvania hadn't changed, though. Private industry flourished. People worked here. Tens of thousands of Pittsburghers were up early, beating out the parkway, the turnpike, Ohio River Boulevard, Route 19, the Allegheny Valley Expressway to the mills, the research labs, the trucking companies, the food processors, the printers and the light industries beyond counting. A hard day's work, a good day's pay. Meat and potatoes, kielbasa, polenta, kasha, peroshki and pastrami-on-a-heel filled dinner plates. Plenty of girth on the pedestrians on the downtown Pittsburgh streets. Vacations in the Laurel Highlands, Pymatuning Lake, Tidioute, the West Virginia mountains. When recessions stalked the land they treaded a little lighter around the Golden Triangle.

Still well up on the Slope, but below the park, we found a restaurant lounge called the Black Sea. It was doing a brisk afternoon lunch trade. The customers arrived in big, heavy cars as though the closest gas crisis was on Mars. We got stalled in a hungry crowd in front of a huge color photomural of a southern Black Sea resort. Palm trees and sunbathers. A long way from the traditional white birches and menacing wolves of the steppes. I was reflecting on the diversity of Russian geography when I caught the bullet-headed maitre d's eye. My palmed twenty slid into his hand as smoothly as though we had rehearsed for years.

Besides securing a table, there was another reason for my generosity: I wanted him to *notice* me and Charity. We were going to have to get into the community if we were to find out anything. From the babble of Russian on the lips of roughly half the patrons this seemed like a good place to start.

I ordered my usual Sam Thompson Pennsylvania rye whisky on the rocks. "Buy local" was my motto. Charity remained loyal to White Mountain Chablis. The bullet-headed maitre d' stopped by, gold-capped teeth gleaming with twenty dollars worth of appreciation. Still after adding to the impression I was creating, I forced myself to speak Russian. I told him that Charity and I were on assignment from the *Post-Gazette* to do an article on Russian Slope.

Three minutes later the manager was at our table. Stan Pokora was about fifty. Gray at the temples, spine straight as a plumb line. The blood of horsemen. Cossacks. He divided his attention between trying to extract from me the promise of a plug for the Black Sea and peering down the yoke of Charity's dress. While Charity was in no way a tease, she knew well how to handle men. She could play Stan Pokora like a mandolin.

I asked the maitre d' for a tour of the kitchen. A nod and twitch of the shoulder passed from Stan to the maitre d'. I got the ten-dollar tour and the promise of a grilled striped bass fresh enough to have just flown in seat-belted first class from Boston. When we left the Black Sea there was no bill.

"I hope you didn't make any rash promises, Charity," I said.

She fluttered her lids and smiled radiantly. "Such Old World charm! Such gallantry! Oh, you Russians!"

"Oh, you idiot! Will you level with me?"

"He was a fountain of information. *The* source of information on Russian Slope is a guy who runs a ballet school. He's made a bundle in real estate, so he can afford to be an *artiste*. Name's Ivan 'Volodya' Tschersky." She tapped her purse. "I have his address."

"And what do you owe Mr. Old World Charm?"

"A drink this evening at a place called the Imperial Court. *The* Russian Slope nightspot. *And* also a great place to meet the locals. A certain person was seen regularly there."

I frowned. "Who?"

"Nicholas Markov."

We re-cruised Russian Slope, this time with a focus on Nicholas. We found his home, 1214 Eastmont Road, high up on the Slope, not far from St. Basil's. Big house, red brick, flagstone facing around the lower half. Ten, twelve rooms at least. Three garages. Mikhail Markov, who Ludmilla said worked for U.S. Steel, had to be an exec. Had to have some bucks in his pocket and a heavy commitment to the company way. Maybe that house was a stage set for a classic case of upper-middle-class adolescent rebellion. Starring the "I-gave-you-everything-but-love" father.

We cruised by the Imperial Court. I was expecting a ratty little den. I was wrong. A sizable gouge had been taken out of Russian Slope just below the crest, angled for a western exposure. There someone with taste had built a club with one towering glass wall looking off down the river toward the distant towers of the Golden Triangle. Landscapers had done some work with junipers and hedging. The parking lot was screened nicely from both street and club.

Near blighted Commercial Street, down by the riverside, we got a look at another structural symbol of Nicholas Markov's complex personality. The Eleven-to-Seven didn't even deserve the faint praise of being called a working man's bar. It was cut off from the J. T. Elmford Tube Works by a twenty-foot-high cinderblock wall and stood near the Rankin town line. Two puzzled-looking old men with brown-paper-wrapped bundles on their laps sprawled against the sun-splashed west wall. The Eleven-to-Seven stood on the corner of River and Hope streets. The main entrance was on Hope—a battered wooden door bearing black smears from drunken kicks. The other entrance on River was filled with a dented aluminum door that bore a sign. Meeting Room. Ladies Welcome. A better scene for a murder than most.

"What would a kid from up there"—Charity waved toward the golden domes of St. Basil's far above—"be looking for in a place like this?"

"Trouble," I said. "What else?"

We drove back to 138 for a light dinner, shower and change of clothes. By 8:45 we were face-to-face with the Imperial Court doorman, who wore a spectacular Cossack uniform. "Welcome to the Imperial Court," he said to me in Russian. "The first show is just about to start. There's plenty of time to get a seat and a drink and to make yourselves comfortable." He turned his professional smile on Charity. "Have a pleasant evening, madam," he said in English.

As we walked on, I said, "Had you spotted for a tourist, Charity."

"I *do* feel a little like a foreigner around here."

We went in by the swinging glass doors bearing the Romanov double eagles. The entertainment lounge was to the left. A lettered sign held a photograph of this month's entertainer: Betty Ellen Edwards. That stopped me. I had known a Betty Ellen Edwards. For a while I had *loved* a Betty Ellen Edwards. I took a good look at the photo. Studio shot, pushing for glamor. No mistaking the ski-jump nose. I recognized her even though the small scars from her adolescent acne attacks had been air-brushed off her cheeks. I couldn't tell from the glossy how more than fifteen years had treated her.

In the few minutes before Betty Ellen's performance I rummaged in the grab bag of my good memory. It served her up at our first meeting, in an economics class at Pitt. She wore a madras shirtwaist dress that did just what it was supposed to for her twenty-year-old figure. We talked, we went drinking together. Became friends. One snowy day in February when classes were canceled she phoned and invited me to lunch. I walked from 138 to the small apartment in Wilkinsburg she shared with her mother. She made toasted American cheese sandwiches. There was vanilla custard in the fridge. She led me to the bedroom. A four-by-three-foot picture of the Holy Virgin on the wall above the bed lent an antic, giggling mood to our frolics. She murmured those long-gone words of pre-pill caution. I made dangerous promises beyond my powers of self-control to keep. It was altogether delightful.

Betty Ellen's mother, a diligent worker in an attorney's

23

office, traveled daily to downtown Pittsburgh. "Once she leaves, she doesn't come back till five thirty," Betty Ellen said. But there came an early afternoon when, deep in our passion, we heard the sound of Mrs. Edwards's key in the only door. No more than a tiny click of metal on metal, it chilled our ardor like cold water on hot cats. Up I jumped, witless and pantless. And banished from that day on.

Betty Ellen and I still met from time to time. She was in theater and started to run with the crowd. She told me tales of her new, serious love affairs, her abortion. The last I heard, she went to New York to look for something in show business.

I didn't know what she found in New York, but tonight she was doing improvised topical comedy. She wore a black body suit and slid in and out of suggestions of additional costumes which she donned behind a lacquered screen. She was pushing forty. From the look of her face in the spot the years had been only fair with her. She did a little stand-up comedy before taking scraps of paper from the audience suggesting topics. I had forgotten how quick-witted and amusing she had been. She was getting by on brains. And she was a pro. She milked laughs from a light crowd of salesmen, a few locals, and young girls knee-to-knee with suspiciously older men. She did the energy crisis, the Arabs, the Russians, the Israelis, Reagan and the usual gamut of other political figures.

There had been a local scandal in the papers—a judge and his mistress, a dippy woman right out of *Guys and Dolls*. Her malaprop pronouncements sounded a giddy counterpoint to the somber chords of the judge's crumbling career. I scribbled down her name—Charlene "Choochoo" Chan—on a cocktail napkin beside the Romanov eagles. I took it down to the small stage apron.

Betty Ellen took the napkin, scarcely glancing at me. She grinned. "I was *waiting* for this one . . ." Then she looked down. Her eyes widened. "Yuri!" Her smile brightened for a moment, then faded. Rush of memories of easy, simple times irretrievably lost. Then she got it back. Her capped teeth shone. Her eyes locked on mine. The message: *remember!*

She went back to work—and brought down the house. I was proud of her. When I turned to go back to my table, Charity had company. Stan Pokora, the Cossack-spined gray eagle, had kept his date. No place for me. She would work him for information the way women worked men for anything. All shift and shadow, the hidden promise unmentioned, the spins and

24

bows and postures of that eternal sexual minuet. No one danced it better than my one-time-Iowa-farm-girl lady colleague.

Betty Ellen finished up her first show to a nice hand. Naturally she thought I was waiting for her. She offered me her hand. "Long time, as the sage said." Brown eyes set in the unchanging bony landscape of her face searched my features with muted desperation. I knew for what: *Are you happy?* she wanted to know. Which suggested she wasn't.

She had her own table and her own drink ready for her. Double vodka martini straight up. She drank it like spring water. The waitress saw to it she got a quick refill.

"Nice to see you again, Betty Ellen."

She nodded. "Xerox! That's more up-to-date than 'Ditto!'"

"How's it been with you?" I said.

She shrugged. "I just talked for forty-five minutes. Need to give the pipes a rest."

I filled her in on my side of the missing fifteen years. Editing, of course, offering her a shaped reality useful to her emotional needs and essential to my information business. I finished up with the truth about my divorce and some necessary lies about a journalism career.

She covered from New York to Now. Her version of her life offered me a whole book of lines to read between. I summed it all up for personal consumption: a tough world, enough talent but not enough connections, a knack for forming destructive relationships, and just the slightest tendency to whine about how unfair life was. And worse than these: unlucky.

"So now I'm doing my thing around Pittsburgh and en-vi-rons," Betty Ellen said. "My kind of *shtick*, I tend to get long bookings. I played here a coupla months ago for a month. Then I was out at the Holiday House in Monroeville, couple other decent spots. Now I'm back here. The guy who runs this place, Artie Greenberg, is a hard-assed cheapskate, but he throws in the little studio apartment in the basement. That makes the hair-over-scale he pays look a lot better." She waved one of her fingers for another double.

"This is my first day back on Russian Slope in years," I said. I nodded back toward Charity. "The blonde's my lady colleague. We're starting to dig up information on the Slope."

Betty Ellen looked at Charity and Stan Pokora. "I have a feeling the information passing *there* hasn't got much to do with Russian Slope. Russian *Stand* maybe, but not Russian Slope. Stan chases skirts like greyhounds do rabbits. His wife

25

must be deaf, dumb and blind—or smart. He's got pots of money."

"You sound like you know the Slope, Betty Ellen."

"I pick up a lot just being around."

"And being bright."

"I've never known how to really use it, Yuri."

"Never too late."

"Save it. I'm pushing forty."

I saw which way the conversation would go. Direction change needed. "Charity and I are thinking of hanging our article on the Ed Dixon murder," I said. "Really on the kid who they think did it—who ran off. Nicholas Markov."

"Oh, that. Last time I was booked here people weren't talking about anything else."

"Saying what?"

"Like the answer to any other important question in life— that depends on who you ask."

"Give me some examples."

"The people who knew him say no way he'd kill anybody. Like me. Yuri, here was a kid everybody liked. He came in here with, or to see, a guy named Ray Nevick. I liked him." She looked into her martini, then up at me—sharply. "Don't misunderstand me now, Yuri, when I say I loved him."

I frowned.

"Some kind of intense feeling. Not sexual." She shrugged. "I can't really explain it. Something *about* him. He walked in here and I felt *good*. Crazy, huh?"

"Maybe. What did the cops think?"

"Don't know much about that. Chief is a guy named Boris Polsky. He and the rest of the local fuzz are still looking hard for the kid. That much I do know."

"What about the Slav-on-the-street?"

"The murder upset them. This is a pretty tight community, Yuri. Full of support, full of gossip." Betty Ellen lowered her voice. "Nobody cares that some spade bought it. It was that one of *them* maybe did it. It's the maybe that bothers them. They want the kid found, to settle things one way or the other." She looked at her watch. "It's time for me to go and make myself beautiful for the eleven o'clock. After that I'm through on weekdays. The place is open till one." Her eyes found mine. "Stick around? For old time's sake?"

"Sure."

The eleven o'clock crowd had already enjoyed a few drinks. They would have laughed at cancer. Betty Ellen was a smash.

She had just wet her lips with another double when a man's voice above and behind me said, "B. E., whadaya say you and me go out and get wasted? I got enough coke to open up a drugstore."

I had a feeling I didn't like him. Turning around made me sure. A guy in his mid-forties wearing one of those macho-styled jumpsuits. A brass zipper ring hung at his neck. He was about forty pounds overweight; the costume made it show.

"Ray Nevick, I'd like you to meet an *old* friend, Yuri Nevsky." His handshake reminded me of a small pollock I'd once heaved out of Maine waters. His heavy hair had been styled into a heap of curls. Tiny gray eyes peeked over his thick Slavic bones. He had a receding chin and the shoulders and arms of a defensive tackle. Altogether, both powerful and somehow extremely fragile. Betty Ellen went on: "Ray was one of Nicholas Markov's best friends."

His little eyes narrowed suspiciously. "Who brought Nick up?"

"Yuri did, Ray," Betty Ellen said. "He's a newspaperman doing a feature on Russian Slope. He's going to use the Nick-Dixon thing."

"My ass he is!" He leaned over me. "C'mon, B. E. Ditch this turkey and let's go get wasted."

"I heard the kid was a bum and into dope so deep only the top of his head showed." So I was looking for information *and* trouble at the same time. Not like me.

"*I* heard you stink, Nevsky." Cords stood out in Ray Nevick's thick neck. "And I think you're some kind of snooper that only knows from a newspaper to wipe his ass—"

"For Chrissake, Ray!" Betty Ellen's voice was low and anxious. "I've known Yuri for fifteen years. He's all right."

"Sure." He glowered at me. "Why pick on the kid?"

"Listen, Big Belly. The kid picked on himself when he ventilated Ed Dixon."

"Nobody seen him do it!" Earnestness showed through his anger. He was hanging onto a thin hope.

"I heard two women were with him. An Anya Rok and a P.Q. Antonelli."

"They never pointed the finger, Mr. Big Story. No matter how much the fuzz leaned on them. Anya was his girl. And

27

P.Q. was her best friend. They knew what a class kid, what a *saint* he was."

I laughed. "Saints don't deal dope," I said. Fishing.

"Who told you that?" He grabbed my shoulder and jerked me up and out of my chair. "Who told you Nick Markov was dealing?"

"Hands off!" I gave him a little nudge in the windpipe with my knuckles edged just right.

He stumbled back choking. When I didn't follow up, two huge men with that bouncer look about them decided to hover rather than keep coming.

Ray Nevick lowered his hands. He moved toward me, intent on making his points. He swallowed several times, cooling down more. "Listen, Nevsky. I'll tell you about Nick Markov. He had a hundred friends. The women liked him. Anya wasn't the only one. There was Olga Samnesovich, too. She *loved* his ass. But he was too decent for her. He was religious. He spent time with Father Alexander at St. Basil's. I think he was maybe thinking about being a priest himself. He was a hell of a bowler, too."

Betty Ellen came up beside us. "Ray wanted to put him on the tour."

"Out of my own pocket. I'd have staked him . . ." A dreamy look filmed over the fading anger in Nevick's tiny eyes. "On the lanes he was so *smooth*. Nothing distracted him. He was sealed up like an underwater watch. *Beautiful* approach. *Beautiful* release. *Beautiful* kid all around." His heavy face split into a moony grin, like a lover's.

I was playing Nevick pretty well. I gave another tug on the line. "How beautiful could he be? He killed a guy and probably was a pusher."

Too much. The big man came at me with a howl. A round-house right flew over my ducking head. I got a whiff of armpit and rancid Right Guard. Then the bouncers were on us. We got hustled out a side door that led to the parking lot. Betty Ellen came chirping and scolding after us.

Nevick didn't even wait for the bouncers to retire. He came wading after me, fists up like two big ham hocks.

"How high can you *be*, Ray? You ass!" Betty Ellen shouted. "What good does this do Nick?"

"Gonna teach Mr. Big Story some respect. For me and for Nick."

"Maybe for Nick—but never for you, Big Belly."

Betty Ellen jumped up and down between us. "What happened to *you*, Yuri? You used to sit around and read *po*etry. You never raised your voice. You were nonviolent!" Nevick shoved her out of the way. "Oh, shit!" she wailed.

I'm not really a fighter in the shuffle-and-punch sense. One of the things I learned in that amoral life I had put behind me was a system of self-defense that was ninety percent counters. Left alone I was benign. Attacked, I was able to open up a lethal bag of slashes, chops, stamps, kicks, gouges and knees. Very low on macho. Very effective.

My timing was off. I took a couple of shots to my chest and middle. Nevick paid little mind to my tactics. He kept coming, wading, swinging and panting. I kept retreating. He was tiring fast, and desperate. He reached out, arms spread, looking for a bear hug. I snapped out a very quick kick to his balls. He howled and dove for me. Somehow he got his teeth into my ear. My turn to scream. I chopped him off me. He went down into a groaning heap.

My hand came away from my right ear sticky and black under the light of the mercury-vapor lamps. I cursed and winced.

Betty Ellen ran up. "There's blood all over you!"

"My ear. The sonofabitch bit my ear," I panted.

Her concern turned to laughter.

"Nice way to comfort a wounded warrior," I said.

"Wounded *ass*hole. You got what you deserved." She looked down at Nevick, who was drooling and twitching like a beached fish. "And so did he." She tugged my sleeve. "Let's get *out* of here. Artie Greenberg isn't going to like any of this."

"Runs a class place. Hard to keep out the riffraff, though."

"I'll riffraff *you* if you don't move. I could lose my booking if we don't get *out* of here. Come on down to the apartment and I'll see if you have any ear left."

Nevick was already trying to right himself. Working toward hands and knees. He would end up very sore, but all right. I went with Betty Ellen.

Basement apartment or not, it had wide windows along the front end. Before she turned on the lights I saw she shared the impressive view with the paying customers. I thought I could see the sign atop the distant Gulf Building in the Golden Triangle lit red: fair weather ahead.

She pulled the drapes and turned on the light. I remembered what else I had liked about her: she was a reader. Books and magazines overflowed the two smallish tables, the bureau and the kitchen counter. A lap-size TV and a Zenith radio and tape/record player combo nestled on a kitchen counter.

She sat me in a chair under the kitchen ceiling light. She sponged away the cake and ooze and announced, "Bit right through you, he did. I have some *lovely* earrings if you'd like to try one on for style. I'm really not sure just what suits you. Maybe some feathers..."

"Shut up and operate. If your act was as funny as your bedside manner you'd be playing the Pizza Igloo in Nome, Alaska."

She cracked out two ice cubes and held them to either side of the oozing lobe. Her hand mirror showed me a nasty tear. Nevik's yellow teeth had nearly reduced the ear by thirty percent. When the bleeding slowed she fussed with gauze, cotton wool and adhesive tape. She whistled tunelessly through her teeth as she worked. Finally she stepped back for a critical view. "Of course you'll need cosmetic surgery..." she said.

I squinted into the mirror at her handiwork. "My ear looks like it's being attacked by a giant mold."

"It's those Mexican medical schools." The next moment she was in tears. Her arms went tight around me. "Hold me, Yuri. Just hold me tight!"

And I held her. All men were pushovers for weeping women. Even more so for old lovers whose lives had leveled off or angled down.

She shoved me gently toward the small bedroom. In the corner stood a life-size reinforced cardboard cutout of Ronald McDonald, right hand outthrust. She squirmed out of her bodysuit, peeling it off like a fruit skin to reveal the very white flesh underneath. She hung the Danskin over Ronald's arm. And the while she bantered on, quips and jokes in machine-gun patter. When I kissed her I was dismayed to find it was in part to shut her up.

I worked hard to drive myself to passion. I sank into it at last as into a warm comforter on a cold night. But not until my Betty Ellen of the Imperial Court basement became again the giddy kid with the top of her shirtwaist dress unbuttoned and hanging down from her hips under the infinitely forgiving eyes of the merciful Mother of God.

4

I grunted awake before dawn. I had been about as lucky as Jay Gatsby in trying to recapture the past. All I had was a headache from too little sleep, a throbbing ear and a smarting conscience. I rolled over and studied my friend of fifteen years as she slept, snoring in a low buzzing hum like a light motor with a bad bearing. She lay face up. Age had added half a chin, filled out her well-shaped breasts. Her waist had gone, but her thighs were solid and her calves trim and sturdy.

Recent memories flooded back. She had beaten her heels on my kidneys, battering the small of my back like a street fighter. The lovings of fifteen years had made her a screamer. She keened cries of delight to match my thrusting. I liked screamers. Their noises fell on my ears like blessings.

Past the carnal there wasn't much. I wondered when the romantic in me would finally roll over, four feet straight up. Until it did, this sort of coupling would invariably depress me. I was never sure whether that side of my thinking reflected the maturity of rejecting sex without love—or the impossible idealism of an adolescent. That it had to be good *and* meaningful. What I needed was to quit caring so much.

I shifted around to slide out of bed, planning a discreet exit to eliminate the need for kind lies. Betty Ellen snuffled awake and sat up. Even though this was probably the earliest she had been up in five years she insisted on making me a cup of coffee. Instant Brim.

Her show-biz life habits left her sluggish and bleary-eyed. She clutched her robe at her chest and mumbled in monosyllables. Gathering herself, she rose and began to redress my ear.

"Maybe a rabies shot," I mumbled.

"I'll tell you this: nobody's going to ask you who your ear piercer is. Nasty hole."

While she worked I tried the waters of gossip. "Nevick mentioned a girl being mixed up with Nick Markov. Never heard her name before. Olga something."

"Olga Samnesovich. About nineteen. She came in upstairs a lot. Looking for Nick. Looking for trouble anyhow. A confused young lady, I heard. A tramp, I heard. She's right in the middle of all the Dixon murder talk."

"How come?"

"She disappeared the same night the kid did."

I took a deep breath swallowing that one. "Together?"

She grinned, capped teeth lighting up her fatigue-lined face. "Dot iss ze qvestion."

"Vot iss de *anzer?*"

"Olga and Nick sometimes hung around together. They say she had the hots for him. That it was a coincidence they both scrammed the same night is too much for this cynical old brain to buy."

"You think they planned their exit and it was tied in with the murder?"

Betty Ellen's terry-clothed shoulders rose and fell. "Why not?"

I got dressed and dug my Harvard Coop notebook out of a pocket. I wrote down the name Olga Samnesovich under those of Anya Rok and P.Q. Antonelli. One thing was sure: Nicholas Markov was a busy young man so far as the ladies went. What wasn't so clear was the exact nature of his relationship with any of them.

A faint, diffused gray showed around the edge of the drapes. I ordered Betty Ellen back to her slumbers with a chaste kiss and assurances that I'd be around town for a while. I closed the apartment door behind me and strolled slowly out into the empty parking lot. I took a deep breath of the damp morning air. The taste of coke dust touched the back of my tongue. I hadn't been back in Pittsburgh long enough not to notice it.

I walked over to the edge of the asphalt. Below the chain link fence was a drop of eighty to a hundred feet. Beyond the Slope the Monongahela gleamed like a faint silver ribbon in the early light. A barge, yellow glow in the pilot house, pushed upriver, the V of its wake on the deserted water reaching from shore to shore. To my right, further east, the Rankin Bridge carried light traffic, and beyond it the illuminated stick of the Homestead High Level Bridge linked other early-rising men and women with their responsibilities. Maybe a guy going to get a restaurant ready for a 6 A.M. opening, a waitress on her way to relieve the night shift, or a store owner heading to a couple of undisturbed hours with the books.

Just then a gentle swell of melancholy washed over me. I saw the lives of those in the cars and trucks as simple, rewarding and fruitful. I saw my life as jagged, unfinished, like a piece of wood torn from a tree by lightning. My twelve-year marriage, finally ruptured after long years of disintegration. Jane and Clara, my daughters, tear-stained and shattered alongside the metal detector at Logan. They planned to visit me at some time in the future—in a strange city where my life-style had no place for them. The years in the grosser side of the information trade . . . the bad taste it left. I had improved on that—to become an honest, cunning snoop. Erratic, not greatly profitable work. Not like that of those who drove their cars in straight lines to definite destinations this early morning and the ones to come. And my roof leaked . . .

I touched my lightly throbbing ear, then went on to knead a sore calf and flex a stiff chest, reminders of Ray Nevick, he of the loglike forearms and volatile emotions. At the same time I decided I was just beginning to feel sorry for myself. That's a company I don't buy stock in. No way. Two things a person can do: first, act to get rid of the reasons for the blues and keep acting till they're whipped; second, if the reasons aren't vulnerable to immediate change, then act—period. On whatever *can* be changed. Or on anything. Get moving! For me it works.

My reason to get moving was Nicholas Markov, saint and devil. Or as was more likely, a confused kid who performed one of those many irreversible actions with which life challenges even the most reluctant and cautious of us. Yes, the lucky come to a time of testing and decision. The kid wasn't able to deal with the consequences of his acts. Too, there was something unfinished about it all which was raising my interest and starting to demand my increasingly focused attention. I didn't have time for gloom.

I heard shouting from the side of the Imperial Court. The manager, Artie Greenberg, was bellowing angrily at the garbage men. The two massive blacks, hands gauntleted by thick leather gloves, and their huge dumpster-gobbling truck boasted enough raw power to toss him into the rear maw and devour him like another salami end or used Bunn-o-matic coffee filter. But the social system, habit and confidence were on Artie's side. The blacks trudged into the interior to return the four plastic garbage cans they had at first refused to replace. Like so many relationships: one to dominate, another to allow it.

Just the same—I didn't like Manager Greenberg. Always a sucker for the underdog, that's me.

When I got home to 138, Charity was already in the kitchen having coffee, warming her hands around her own mug with the Gothic C on the side. She was wearing an ice-blue dressing gown and matching slippers.

"What? Both slippers on?" I teased. "Not one brimming with champagne at the lips of a certain handsome Cossack with graying temples?"

Women like Charity with blonde hair, pale blue eyes and fair skin—particularly those wearing light blue gowns—can give *very* cold stares. "Stan Pokora is a gentleman, Yuri. Very gallant. He saw me only as far as the door." She waved toward the distant slab of polished oak.

"So you said no, huh?"

"Remember the old high school joke?" She giggled. "The one about Roman hands and Russian fingers?"

"Sure."

"Well?"

I poured coffee. "I see. Learn anything useful?"

"Some original Old World compliments and how to say 'Hands off my tits!' in Russian."

"A great language—filled with color and precision."

"We parted friends. Promises to meet again."

For her that was possible. From time to time I had to remind myself that Charity was a WASP. To me that meant not giving in to impulse or emotion. Not taking risks. Being conservative and safe. Security above all else. My lovely colleague was a weigher and measurer.

She also knew herself. Fresh from a crushing personal disaster, the death of all her loved ones, she needed time for the wound to knit. Practicing her profession, along with her natural toughness, had kept her afloat. Helping me find information forced her to focus on problems not her own. Kept her attention, kept her moving. An affair with a graying wolf of a Cossack was close to the last thing she needed.

"How did *you* do last night?" she said. "After you and your hulking friend were thrown bodily out of the Imperial Court."

"That was Ray Nevick. We had differences of opinion about Nicholas's character."

"Spent the night in jail, did you?"

"With the lady comedian."

"That's the hard way to bring laughter into your life. For

a few dollars you could buy a Monty Python record. Lot simpler."

"She's an old college friend. Full of information. For example, a girl of uneven reputation—one Olga Samnesovich—disappeared the same night our Nicholas did. Back to Nevick. He seems to have been close to the kid. Said he was a saint. Loved by everybody. Specially the ladies. Very sensitive on the dope issue—as you saw. Wanted to put the kid on the bowling tour. Nevick's mental processes reminded me of a short-circuiting fuse box."

"He the one who bit your ear? Or was the comedienne really passionate?"

"He bit it. We finished our brawling in the parking lot."

"Hardly the way to ingratiate yourself with the Russian community." Charity got up. "I think right away we ought to get to Mr. Information—the ballet teacher, Ivan Tschersky—before your friend Nevick gets going bad-mouthing you."

The Petrograd School of Ballet Arts was a low wooden building filling a large corner lot about halfway up Russian Slope. It had been faced in cedar and carefully maintained. Shutters gleamed with fresh red paint. In the parking lot a Lincoln, an Olds, a Cadillac and a Mercedes lay like big fish in the small pond of compact imports. The big cars came from Mount Lebanon, Sewickley Heights, Edgewood, Squirrel Hill, where a few more dollars for gas meant nothing. Where the elite lived, the folks who could afford to give their children the best—as near as they could figure out what it was.

Ivan "Volodya" Tschersky was standing in a pulpitlike observation platform set above one of the studios. Girls nine and ten lifted left legs at the barre like a string of marionettes. The secretary introduced us. Volodya Tschersky was a burly, bullet-headed sixty-year-old. He was bald and wore rimless, square-lensed glasses and a turtleneck. His handshake was powerful. He bowed and beamed at Charity. I was fast tiring of charming Russian men.

I couldn't help smiling at his thick accent. It echoed those I heard on long-ago Sunday afternoons when my father entertained. When the house was filled with Russian men and women who, no matter how many years spent on American soil, spoke English as they might wrestle boa constrictors.

Volodya scanned Charity's letter from Harrison Brightwood of the *Post-Gazette* and beamed. His grin widened further to show gold-capped eyeteeth when we told him we had heard

35

no one knew more about Russian Slope than he. He hustled us into his office. Its walls were chock-a-block with autographed and framed 8 x 10s of the world's ballet greats. Seven feet of a highly polished barre cut from the long original had been set into the wall. Its plaque's Cyrillic letters read: Temporarily removed from the Petrograd Ballet Corps Studio, November 28, 1918.

Volodya fixed his steel-blue eyes on me. "Yuri Nevsky," he said. "That is Russian. That is name with a ring of the Motherland."

"My father left in 1918." I nodded toward the length of barre. "An interesting year. I was born here, though. I'm not much of a Russian. I speak the language seldom and not well."

Volodya's upthrown arms nearly toppled him from his perch atop a high stool. "Is not language that makes Russian. Is *blood!*"

I mumbled some polite nonsense and looked to Charity for help.

"While we're interested in *all* of Russian Slope, Mr. Tschersky—"

"Please, my little apricot. Volodya. *Al*ways Volodya."

"Vol-odya," Charity said.

"*Da.* And you are Charity." It came out "*Zha*rity."

"We want to write about all of Russian Slope. But we want to start with the Nicholas Markov mystery."

Volodya's face fell, but he quickly recovered. "So much else there is, little apricot. So much better here."

"You understand newspapers, I'm sure, Volodya. It's not sweetness and light that keeps up circulation."

"This I know..." He frowned. "What from me do you want?"

I pulled out my Harvard Coop notebook. "Anything you know about Nicholas Markov. Anything about the shooting. His disappearance. Anything about the gold cross stolen from St. Basil's—"

"Yes, that! We must find it! A reward I am giving for finding it. Ten thousand dollars. Cash money." He slapped the heavy leather purse over his shoulder. "My money. Volodya's money."

He explained that the Slavic cross was nearly solid gold, as long as a man's forearm, drilled at the top of the upright so it could be hung around the neck. How it came to be in the

36

case where it had lain for sixty years was not known. The cross was very old, its history a puzzle. Nonetheless he insisted it was of enough importance to be listed among historical art treasures. I took notes.

"And Nicholas Markov?"

"To many he's been a great disappointment. To his father, Mikhail, for one."

"Why?"

"Mikhail Igorevich had high practical goals for his oldest son. Connected with the science and business. But Nicholas Mikhailovich was a dreamer. Spirit, values, hopes for—ah, *revelations* occupied him. He was a seeker. A reckless one. It is for this reason, I think, that he turned to the drugs."

"So he *was* involved in drugs," Charity said.

Volodya shrugged his thick shoulders. "This is what I heard. Gossip, rumor. But true, I think. I was told he believed in drugs—for a while—as a way to secrets of the soul. He was enthusiastic. As only those sixteen-seventeen can be. He spread word of what the drugs had shown him. He began to provide them to the curious."

"Where did he get them?" I said.

The Russian smiled grimly. "You work for the papers. You must know that the drugs are sold all along the river. The business is organized. Mostly they sell to the blacks, to others who have no hope, no perspective, ugly pasts and frightening futures. Here, we are *Slavs*. We do not have much problem. Church, home, family, society very close. Yet there are some—as always—who fly in the face of our values. They say one of these provided the boy with drugs to sell."

"Maybe a guy named Nevick? Ray Nevick?" I focused hard on Volodya's red moon face.

"Rodino Nevikorovich became a friend to Nicholas. Were he my son I would have wished another choice. Rodino is badly tormented man. Even for Russian."

"And he bites." Charity pointed to my ear.

"You've met." Volodya grinned.

"You think Nevick is connected with the people who push drugs in the Mon Valley?"

"I do not wish to be quoted. I do not wish libel."

"Nevick's really broken up by the whole business with Nicholas. About his being in trouble. About his disappearing."

"He acted wildly, now repents deeply," Volodya said, dis-

37

missing Nevick's Slavic approach to misbehavior with a toss of his shoulders.

"What else can you tell us about Nicholas?" Charity said.

"That his whole life was changing for better until he ran away. About this I know. Both his grandmother, Ludmilla Petrovna, and his mother, Elena Dmitrievna, spoke to me with hope in their hearts." Volodya turned to Charity. "Ms. Day, when a Russian is troubled in spirit, when his life is confused and full of error, from early times he has gone for help, for purification. Gone to the church, to the confession, to the monastery—or to the starets. The holy man. To receive from him counsel and guidance in meditation."

"There's a holy man, a starets, on Russian Slope?" Charity said.

"There came one, so far as Nicholas Mikhailovich was concerned. Some nineteen months ago the church replaced our former priest with a new one. A priest with great spiritual and physical strength. Father Alexander. No one can say who or how one becomes a starets for another. In fact a starets is not often a priest."

"But somehow Nicholas and Father Alexander got together?" I said.

Volodya nodded. "What passed between them—who knows? But both mother and grandmother saw their loved one rebuilding his spirit." He pointed his finger at me. "*This* you will write about. Russian *spirit*. Russian growth in *soul!*"

I bent to my notebook to hide my smile.

"We've been told a young girl disappeared the same night. Olga Samnesovich. Can you tell us anything about her?" Charity leaned forward and flashed her most disarming smile. "And do you think she and Nicholas ran off together?" She made a convincing reporter.

"Olga was not—what you say?—flower of Russian-American youth," Volodya said stiffly. "She was young, but mixed with many men beside Nicholas. Her father, Lev, the widower, is also an unfortunate man. He drinks, fights and lusts. He curses God and man. Ran off together? Who knows? Let us speak of something sweeter."

"Do you think Nicholas Markov is alive or dead?" I said.

"Alive. And in great difficulty far from here." Volodya changed the subject then, with no coaxing him back on it. He leaned back on his stool and gave us a verbal grand tour of Russian Slope and Russian-American culture. With side forays into Imperial Russian history, Orthodoxy and the Byzantine nature of the Russian personality. I learned more from him in the two hours than I had in thirty years from my close-mouthed father.

Volodya finished his impromptu lecture with a vocal rendition of "White Birches," the famous folk song. I should have guessed he sang in a passable patented Russian bass.

We culled out the names of three men who clearly would be a help in adding to our store of Nicholas/Olga information. Vince DeTempo, an attorney, Tom "Trackman" Tolovitch, the reporter-editor of the local Russian-language newspaper, and Boris Polsky, whom Betty Ellen Edwards had mentioned, the police chief within whose jurisdiction the Slope fell.

"As to others to whom you must speak—everyone knows Volodya." He sprang off his stool and dug into his pants pocket. "And everybody knows about Volodya's kopeks. Give everybody one of these. They will know you are a friend of Volodya. And so a friend of theirs." He thrust at us each a handful of the coppery coins.

We thanked him and slipped on our coats. He rushed over and pinched Charity's cheek. "This Saturday night I will have a *great* party at my house. You will come, my little apricot. And I will toast your beauty with iced vodka. And you, too, Yuri Nevsky—Russian who says he is not a Russian. We will match drink for drink. How else can men become true friends?" He scribbled his address on the back of his business card, dropped it into Charity's purse, and showed us out.

Charity stopped dead in the parking lot and took a deep breath which she let out slowly. "My God, talk about a forceful personality!" She looked at me. "How did we do—as reporters, I mean?"

"Well, my little apricot . . ."

"Yes?" Her voice was acid.

"We did just fine. Thanks to him we're going to keep on doing just fine all over Russian Slope." I rattled my pocketful of kopeks. "I'm off to see the fuzz—Chief Polsky."

"I'll try DeTempo, the attorney," Charity said. "And hope he doesn't spot me for a colleague."

"I'll walk. To get the true savor of the Slope."

"And your tools. I'll drive. Because I'm lazy."

A lie if she ever told one.

5

The police headquarters was over the crest of Russian Slope, inside the borders of a blighted bedroom town called Oakdale. New, modern and faced in white stone, the building gleamed like a diamond on the wrinkled finger of the run-down neighborhood. The well-groomed public park nestled against the rear wall added a touch of class. Parking was provided in an underground garage.

When I told the sergeant at the desk that I was a reporter, he waved me to a chair to wait for Chief Boris Polsky. I was starting to get some idea about the chief. The scattered magazines on the waiting area table sharpened my focus on the man. Among the expected *Time*s and *Police Gazette*s lay weightier journals: *Law Enforcement Theory and Practice*, *Psychology of the Offender*, and *Federal Funding for Law Enforcement and Corrections*. A subscription to this last, small type said, cost $120 a year.

Chief Polsky had a slow but steady stream of visitors. None wore uniforms—unless one considered conservative suits and stylish ties as kinds of uniforms. Those favored by folks working for the mayor, the alderman, the judge and the chamber of commerce—the political power holders of any of the medium-sized towns like Oakdale nestled in and around Pittsburgh's hills. So Chief Polsky was a political animal, probably the grant-getter who had forged a community alliance that lasted at least long enough to get a long proposal for funds together and off to the feds. What I couldn't tell was—how did he do at solving crimes?

A woman officer waved me up and toward her. I followed her into the building's innards. The unintentional tour helped to partially answer my crook-buster question. The place was packed with the latest electronic information and communication hardware. It looked sophisticated enough to belong aboard Air Force One. Our destination was an underground target range. Two female officers were squeezing off rounds from .38 Police Specials. A tall man wearing sound-protection earmuffs and a salt-and-pepper goatee was firing a huge Magnum pistol just a few calibers short of a light artillery piece. The woman said that was the chief.

Chief Polsky shook my hand and led me to the elevator. We got off outside his office. We went in and his secretary brought us coffee—in china cups. His office was spare, but sneakily elegant: top-of-the-line desk and a leather-covered executive-style desk chair, a Miró numbered lithograph on one wall, on the other a four-by-four-foot black and white blowup of the assembled Oakdale finest, c. 1912.

"Nice place you have here. I mean all of it."

"Built a year-and-some ago. Took me five years to get my ducks in line. Community input, political support, digging hard for matching funds or other in-kind." He spooned sugar into his cup. "Not to mention playing the mediator, the peacemaker, wriggling clear of kickbacks and payoffs. Let me tell you something, Nevsky, the federal grant chase is the last outpost of the entrepreneur."

I smiled. "You find any time to play the TV kind of cop?"

"I manage." He slipped a sheet of paper out of a folder and passed it across the desk. "List of felonious crimes. Each column is a year. Since I took the job five years ago we've gone down every year in every category." He smiled thinly. "I think that answers the question."

I swung into my bogus rap about the Russian Slope feature article, the Dixon murder hook. I put one of Volodya's kopeks on the edge of the chief's desk.

He grinned and shook his head in mock weariness. "So you have the blessing of our social gadfly."

"Quite a guy. Got the energy of two men half his age. And history books in his head."

Polsky nodded and glanced at the grandfather clock in the corner. "We better get to it. How can I help you?"

"I wonder how you've done trying to find Nicholas Markov. And did he have reason to run?"

"This has all been in the papers."

"I've been out of town on assignment. I didn't have time to read them."

Polsky frowned and looked sharply at me. Then he shrugged. "Take it in a nutshell then. Ed Dixon and Nick Markov met at the Eleven-to-Seven. Probably to make a drug deal. Nick selling. Dixon buying."

41

"The kid really dealt, then?"

"I had him picked up a couple times. To scare him. To do his family a favor. They're lovely people. He was carrying enough pills, powders and weeds to be called a dealer, I suppose. I talked tough to him." Muscles marched along between the bones of his heavy jaw. "And I can *be* tough, Nevsky."

I believed him. This guy was a supercop: modern, effective—and human. "Where'd the kid get the stuff?"

"I'm not prepared to say anything about that for publication."

"Maybe a flake named Ray Nevick."

"Maybe." Not an eyelid fluttered.

"Since I came to Russian Slope I heard the murder weapon had Nicholas's fingerprints on it."

"A reporter made a good guess. I never said so. Nobody's asked since, but the ballistics show the slug matches the .33 caliber Bearcat automatic with the prints."

"Two girls were with him . . ."

Polsky nodded wearily. "Anya Rok and P.Q. Antonelli. The beauty and the brain. This isn't for publication—I don't need a libel suit—but sure as cops wear brass buttons they both saw the kid waste Dixon. I *leaned* on both of them. I separated them and did every trick I know short of rubber hoses on the bottoms of their feet to get them to tell me what they saw. Couldn't budge them. Tears enough to float this desk down to the Mon. But they stuck by their story."

"Maybe Nicholas didn't do it."

Polsky waved that possibility away. He pressed his fingertips to his sizable nose. "The nose knows—yes, he did."

"What was the ladies' version?"

"Said they were in the bar just outside the room where Dixon and Nick Markov were talking. They weren't looking toward them when the pistol fired. There was a ratty curtain between the two rooms, but it was only half drawn. Neither Anya nor P.Q.—nor any of the barflies—were in a hurry to charge toward gunfire. So it was some seconds before anybody went in. Dixon was still in his chair, head down on the table. Hole in his forehead. The automatic, one cartridge ejected from the magazine, was on the floor. The girls both ran out the ladies' entrance. A car was pulling away. Two people in it. Maybe Nick was one of them, because he wasn't anywhere around. We had a car down there in minutes. Then three cars. Combed the sidewalks. No dice. No Nick."

"What about the car?"

Polsky shrugged. "Neither woman could—or would—identify it. Some kind of dark sedan. Million of 'em." He looked at the clock again. "You asked me how I was doing trying to find Nick. I never answered you."

I frowned. "I assumed the answer was lousy."

"Answer is *good*—and bad." Chief Polsky pulled a file and jerked out a hand-addressed envelope. "You can write about this if you want. The writing's Nicholas's—no question. I had it checked against his school papers, the prayers he was writing for Father Alexander. It's his, all right."

The postmark was New York. Dated January 8. Two days after his disappearance. I slid out the single sheet and scanned the lines.

Dear Chief Polsky:

This letter is to tell you that I didn't kill Ed Dixon on the night of January 6. I know everything points to me, but there's another explanation. You have to believe that. You're probably not looking for the murderer in the right place. When you do you'll be surprised. Until you solve the case I'm staying somewhere in New York. Don't bother to try to find me. You can't. When the Dixon business is cleared up I'll come home. Good luck and may God bless us all. Ask Father Alexander to beg God's mercy for my cowardice, as I beg Him: *O Lord, Jesus Christ, Son of God, have mercy on me, a sinner.*

Nicholas Mikhailovich Markov

I looked at Polsky. "How you read this? There another angle? Another suspect?"

He shook his head. "Damn near open and shut, Nevsky."

"How about there was a third party? How about Dixon shot himself? How about they struggled over the Bearcat? A manslaughter deal?"

"Not likely."

There were twenty years of police work and an IQ probably somewhere around 130 behind that "not likely." It took a less bright amateur snooper to half-believe Nicholas. Me. I said, "You send somebody from here to New York to look for him?"

Polsky's laughter was dry as blowing leaves. "Can't really

43

afford to send a man. Too big a job anyhow. Like drinking Lake Superior. We sent NYPD all the paper, photo of the kid."

"You gonna let it go at that?"

"Would have, except Gregory Ogalkov has a bug up his ass. He's the insurance impresario of Russian Slope. I heard from him there's a big policy on Nicholas. Big enough that the insurance company is going to send a man to New York to look for him. The chief's eyes narrowed. "Seems he was insured against . . . disappearance."

"Disappearance?"

"It's something a company will do. Hardly anybody ever disappears. Ogalkov told me that if Nick doesn't show inside of six months, the company has to pay. And pay big enough they'll send a man to the Apple to try to find the kid. And maybe pay the expenses of one of my cops to go along."

"Funny thing he should be insured against an unlikely disappearance—then disappear. Who's the beneficiary?"

"You'll have to talk to Ogalkov about that."

I looked in my Coop notebook. "What about Olga Samnesovich? Volodya Tschersky said she and Nicholas were seen around together. She blew town the same night he did."

"What about her?" Polsky's voice turned somber. "You mean did I ever make her a guest here for a misdemeanor or a felony?" He shook his head. "She wasn't a criminal in the commonly understood sense, Nevsky. Like so many of us, she was a closet criminal, doing subtle harm—to her friends, to the people who were supposed to love her. Crimes against the heart, against decency, good taste and style. And most of all, against herself." The chief's expression turned grim and wise. "She wasn't a bad kid. Just . . . not the best."

"She go off with Nicholas?"

"I don't believe in coincidences. Here's a girl with a lousy home life. Probably mooning after Nick and maybe a halfdozen other guys of varying ages and sizes. Maybe they didn't plan it. Maybe Nick shot Dixon, got away, somehow met her. And off they went on the spur of the moment—into the purple sunset."

I gave him the 138 address and phone. "If your cop or you find out anything more about Nicholas, I hope you'll call me. Public info or not. My curiosity's up."

"I see you don't print anything I don't want, maybe I will."

"How about a copy of the letter?"

"You can use it, but I'll decide when you can print it."

44

I was about to get up, then I remembered the theft of the cross. I asked Polsky about it. Another non-coincidence?

"If everything Nick and Olga did was spur of the moment, the way I think, the cross bit fits fine. I checked Nick's savings account. No withdrawals just before the murder. Olga didn't have any accounts. Her father didn't give her any money. In fact he ripped her off whenever he could. Lev is a scum. I think they realized they were running away broke. One of them thought of the cross and broke in and stole it."

"Worth much?"

"Better believe it. Weighed about fifteen pounds. Just enough alloy in it to keep it from bending and denting easy. Rest, pure gold."

"At maybe 600 an ounce. My God."

"I figured it out. Worth around 150,000 balloons."

"Turn up anywhere? New York pawnshop? Jewelers?"

"Not yet. Father Alexander isn't sure which is worse. Not having it turn up, or having it turn up—in chunks here and there. Maybe Olga and Nick figured they just couldn't unload it without trouble."

"Volodya said it was an art treasure of obscure origins," I said.

The chief pursed his lips. "That's not my line. You might want to ask Father Alexander. He might know something. He's been all in a tizzy since Nick disappeared. The kid was a major reclamation project for him—until the night of January 6. He was up here the next day as soon as he heard about the murder. Asking hadn't we notified all bus companies, airlines, trains, to stop Nick from getting away. I told him they did that mostly in the movies. There's more ways to get out of Pittsburgh than into trouble. He was surprised. By the end of the next day we did get a photo of Nick to the major stations and airports. Long odds, though, and nothing ever came of it. Father Alexander called me just about every day since, asking after Nick."

"Don't tell me he loved Nicholas, too. *Everybody* loved him, Nevick said."

The chief got up; my interview was finished. "Nevsky, I'm a pretty hard-assed fact man. Not much for charisma and touching the spirit. But—this is no lie—Nicholas Markov had something. Don't ask me what it was. I'll start saying stupid things and blame you. Get out." At the door he flashed his first real grin. "I hope you don't plan to get into another brawl. Word is you don't fight 'right.'"

Never mind age and experience—I blushed. "Word travels fast on Russian Slope," I said.

"We know couples are having affairs before they do."

I touched my ear. "Anyway, Nevick doesn't fight fair either. He bites."

6

I got to the Black Sea first. Charity was right behind me. She had arranged a lunch meeting with Trackman Tolovitch, the local newspaperman. Her call to Stan Pokora got us a good table off to the side. Clever Charity. She and the Cossack were still friends.

She had time only to remind me Trackman's first name was Tom before Pokora escorted him to our table. The Cossack politely withdrew after a restrained leer at Charity's chest. Tolovitch looked a track man—distance. Storklike, with a long, pointed nose. Once a gangling kid, he was slipping into his thirties with a little gut slung around his hips. Gut and all, he couldn't have weighed 130 pounds.

We ordered a drink. The yammer of the locals bolting down cod and lobsters was just distant enough to let us talk comfortably without being overheard. Charity said, "Tom, I heard you know almost as much about Russian Slope as Volodya Tschersky."

"Born and bred. Speak the language. The *Russian Voice* isn't *Pravda*, but it keeps my ear to the ground—and crusts on the table. By the way, Trackman's my handle these days."

We trotted out our *Post-Gazette* dodge. Some risk. Newspapermen were clubby. Our letter from Harrison Brightwood seemed to convince him.

"Good idea, starting with Nick and Ed Dixon. An unsolved murder makes a good hook," he said. "Sure, my *Voice* ran a few articles on it, but it's yesterday's news. Even for a weekly. Anyway, my boss is antisensational. An optimist. There're a few left. We cover mostly the good news—from the Russo-American angle. Kids who leave the Slope and make good. Locals who do the same. Lot of nonpolitical articles about the Soviet Union. Tourist stuff. About as controversial as sunrise." Trackman grinned. His teeth were very white. "For me it's great. I'm curious, don't want to get rich—and I love the Slope. I believe in its values. Family, community, roots. And

I believe in God the Father, too. I seek His mercy. 'O Lord, Jesus Christ, Son of God, have mercy on me, a sinner.'" He eyed us both. "I know religion and faith are out of fashion. My feelings won't be hurt if you laugh."

"Who's laughing?" My voice was thick as custard. Nicholas had sent Polsky the same well-used prayer.

"Sounds to me like you're a lucky man," Charity said.

The waitress came, took our orders. When she left I asked Trackman what he knew about the murder. His version was much the same as Chief Polsky's.

"What about the kid himself? Nick Markov."

"He came from good—if eccentric—stock. Good if you believe in aristocracy, class and the elite. He came from the landed people of Imperial Russia. The ones with summer estates and private railway cars."

"I can't knock it too much," I said. "My father was one of them."

In Russian Trackman said, "Are you Russian enough to be able to speak the language?"

"Only when forced to," I said—in Russian. I was being forced to a lot lately.

"Nick's grandfather, Igor Gregorevich Markov, was one of the old emigrés. I couldn't help but meet him," Trackman said. "He used to write angry letters to the editor about the *Voice* being 'pro-Bolshevik.'" He chuckled. "The Bolsheviks walked off history's stage sixty-five years ago. Sometimes Igor Gregorevich would stroll over to the paper swinging his ebony walking cane. To complain in person about our editorial policies. He was tall and pale, with a little white moustache. Chin up. Eyes clear. Didn't even need glasses. Clothes years out of style—but the best. Full of odd ideas, a lot of them as out-of-date as hoopskirts. Ludmilla and her daughter-in-law Elena—Nick's mother—would always fret when he went walking."

"Afraid he'd get lost or hurt, I suppose," Charity said.

"No. Afraid he'd shoot somebody. He carried a pistol. License and all. Mikhail told them Igor had owned it as long as he could remember. The old man finally did shoot somebody about a year-and-a-half ago."

"Who?"

"Himself. He was cleaning the pistol in his room. Elena heard the shot and found him. The slug caught the side of his throat going up. Rode up through his brain. Messy."

Charity sipped her Chablis with eyes closed.

"No health problems?"

Trackman shook his head. "Nope. And at eighty-seven you've seen it all. If you're healthy you don't have troubles. Just being *alive* is a trip."

"Any of the grandfather in Nicholas?" I said. "People been talking about his charisma. About his spiritual strengths. But sure as sugar he dealt dope."

Trackman frowned. "He wasn't a simple kid. I knew him. I could make some guesses. The dope was a chance to break down some of the walls of reality. He was hungry for mind-expanding experiences. The rest was rebellion. Mike Markov is an authoritarian. Nevsky, Charity, if I were you I wouldn't try to make any more out of it. Mystical-smishtical."

I turned a page in my notebook. "You know Olga Samnesovich, Trackman?"

"Went out with her." The thin man grinned again. This time less openly, with a touch of the feral. Masculine code. Word translation begins: "Men have certain basic needs . . . and there are certain women . . ." Damned Russian men—praying one minute and gloating over fornication the next!

"They say she was in love with Nicholas," Charity said.

Trackman pondered that, looked up at the painted dolphins arching across the ceiling. "Wouldn't say that. More like . . . she wanted his *attention*. Not quite the same."

"What about Anya Rok, P.Q. Antonelli? They want 'attention,' too?"

"Anya was interested in him, Nevsky. But who knows in what way? P.Q.? She was Anya's sidekick. A bright woman, but for some reason nobody takes her very seriously. Anya's been called the 'Ice Queen.' I guess that makes P.Q. her lady-in-waiting. You oughta talk to both of them. You know, Anya and Olga were pretty good friends. You could maybe find out some stuff from Anya."

"You think Olga went off with Nicholas?"

"I think she *wanted* to."

"But you don't think he'd buy it?"

"No."

Something was bothering me, had been for a while. Niggling at the flaps of my mental tent. "Since I came to town I've heard how the ladies liked Nick. What I want to know is—did Nick like the ladies?"

"He enjoyed their company. He wasn't shy—"

"Trackman—let's be frank. Did he chase tail?"

"People didn't talk about it if he did. And neither did he."

"Even here on the Slope? Where Ivan knows how much lint is in Boris's pocket?"

Lunch arrived. The waitress had that graduate-student look. She was testing entry into the real world with some snappy chatter and just a hair of condescension for us working peasants. By the time she had served us all, Trackman had gathered his thoughts about Nick. "This may sound crazy, Yuri, Charity, but Nicholas Markov was a very moral kid. You ask, did he sleep around? From his point of view that's the same as saying—did he steal? Did he cheat and lie? He really was on a higher plane than most of the rest of us." The thin man got busy with his broiled whitefish. He took nourishing his gut seriously. Charity and I picked at our food. In a while he surfaced with a mouth only half-filled with sour-cream-and-chives baked potato. "See, except for the dope business, except for getting mixed up with a few bad apples—"

"Ray Nevick?"

"Him, Dixon and another guy I just heard the name of. A higher up, tugged on Nevick like a puppet master. Guy named Houle." Trackman held up his fork to halt my question. "That's *all* I know about him. He's in drugs. His name's Houle. Nevick mentioned to me one night when he was stoned that he had introduced Nick to 'Houle.'"

Houle. The name rang a faint bell. But I was too Nicholas-centered at the moment to rummage in my memory.

"So what I'm saying," Trackman went on, "is that if you look at the rest of Nick Markov's life, he was Mr. Clean. Good student, good friend, good bowler, all around nice kid that everybody liked. Like the pols say: look at the record. Based on the record, I have some opinions about what happened." He paused, waiting for encouragement. His pointed nose aimed at each of us in turn.

I smiled. Here was a man who was as born to gossip as Ali was to punch. "You're dying to tell us, Trackman," I said. "I hate to see you suffer. Shoot."

Trackman put his fork down and slid his napkin off his lap onto the table. "Let me say a little about Ed Dixon first. He was a hophead. He'd lost his cool years ago. He had junkie myopia: he could see only as far as his next fix. A torn fishnet of nerves. He set it up to score some dope from Nick. Something went wrong. Either he or Nick pulled a gun—the cops never could trace it. Dixon caught a slug. Nick panicked and ran out—"

"There was a car waiting," I said.

"Sure. With some drug-connected creep at the wheel." Trackman waved a long finger at Charity and me. "Here's the thing that I mean about his record. Everything points to his facing the music. Getting an attorney. Standing fast. Standing moral. His disappearing, dodging responsibility, just doesn't fit. I think the folks who run the drug business in the tri-state area didn't want a trial. Didn't want cops digging around. Had to cause them problems. So they either sent Nick out to Arizona or . . ." He drew his finger across his throat.

"Maybe New York," I said, thinking about Chief Polsky's letter.

Trackman shrugged. "Why not? Let me recommend the chocolate mousse."

Diners going in and out had been pausing to exchange greetings and bits of information with Trackman. His eyes lit up and he brimmed with smiles. He was living the life he liked, doing what he wanted. He was a lucky man.

"One person you really oughta talk to, if you're interested in Nick Markov and the Slope, is Father Alexander," Trackman said. "If there was a positive force in the kid's life, he was it."

"So we heard. His confessor-adviser. Starets, I guess, is the word."

Trackman nodded. "Father Alexander's been an asset to Russian Slope altogether. At first people were kind of set against him. His predecessor, Father Gregory, was very popular. The decision to transfer him came from the archbishop's office in New York. Some of the paperwork carried the signature of the metropolitan himself. The bishop of Pittsburgh and West Virginia had to obey the directions for the good of the church. Once Father Alexander arrived at St. Basil's he started winning people over. Father Gregory was rather aloof, very patriarchal. Father Alexander didn't mind getting out in the community. In fact, one of the first things he did was set up rap sessions for teenagers and young adults. He sprang for the cost to fix up a lounge down in the old Moskva Hotel—a real roach ranch—just for the sessions. He talked old Anton Rastokov, the relic who owns the place, into donating the space."

"How'd he get anybody to go?" Charity said. "Play disco music?"

51

"He played music all right. He can play just about any wind instrument any way you want. Flute, clarinet, all kinds of horns. Rock, jazz, Schubert, you name it. And he can *do* it on the violin, too. He's a real showman. Small wonder kids went. And he looks—well, *impressive*. He's about six-four, maybe fifty years old. Black wiry beard shot through with gray. Big voice." Tolovitch's white teeth gleamed. "Makes God look good. And he has this *commanding* personality. The kids and the y.a.'s love him.

"And he's always ready to go out and visit the old folks, the shut-ins. The hospital and the slammer are on his regular route. He *performed* in the liturgy, too. Satan himself would run from Father Alexander reciting: 'O God of the spirits of all flesh, who hast destroyed death and trodden down the devil...' Very moving in the liturgy."

"Must be pretty energetic," I said.

"He is. And he isn't married. No family. He has a house-keeper who takes care of him. So he has plenty of time to minister to his flock." Trackman pushed back his chair.

"This is on the *Post-Gazette*," I lied, picking up the check.

"You know, with the exception of Nick's family, nobody was more upset about his disappearance than Father Alexander," Trackman said. "He worked hard with the kid, really helped him. Personal counseling. And the longer Nick is gone, the worse he gets. I talked to him the other day, and he seemed about to cry over him. He must think the kid's dead. If you haven't heard enough about Nick, go have a chat with his starets."

"We want to thank you for your help," Charity said. "You're a wealth of information."

"Anytime. Just stop by the *Russian Voice*. I can be identified by the melon-sized pencil callous, middle finger right hand. And you're welcome to check back issues of my rag."

We shook hands and Trackman left the restaurant, tossing off greetings and cheerful farewells on all sides. A happy man.

Charity and I each ordered a Cointreau and sat a while. I brought her up to speed on my visit to Chief Polsky and showed her a copy of Nicholas's letter.

"All we have to do is go find him," she said.

"The odds are only thirteen million to one. Maybe you could take over that part of our search."

"Nothing sexist about you—not afraid to give me a *real* challenge. On the serious side, if you don't mind, I talked to

52

Attorney DeTempo about the Markovs. He was pretty open for an attorney. I slipped him one of Volodya's kopeks and promised 'not to print anything.' He told me Mikhail Markov had paid him a small retainer relative to negotiating with an insurance company about a policy claim. He was mysterious about just what kind of claim."

"I know that piece of the jigsaw puzzle. It was a *big* policy, Polsky said. So big the insurance company would rather not pay. It's going to send a man to New York to nose around for Nick. Seems the policy specifically covers *disappearance*. Curious coincidence."

"My turn now," Charity bubbled. "DeTempo told me who the beneficiaries of the policy are."

"Who?"

"All the members of the immediate Markov family. Elena, Sasha—a younger son—and Mikhail."

I had a sip of Cointreau on that. "Who took out the policy? Who paid the premiums?"

Charity looked carefully at me, to make sure I was paying attention. "Nicholas's grandfather, Igor Gregorevich Markov. He took it out when the boy turned ten."

"Now he's dead. An accident. And Nick's disappeared. Hmmmm . . ."

"DeTempo handled Igor's will. He didn't leave much, but enough to pay off the policy until about the year 2000. And that's what the will said to do with the money."

I fiddled with my beard. My Unusually Puzzled Stroke. Little twirls of my index finger against the hidden dimple on my chin. "What won't go down easy is disappearance being named specifically in the policy," I said.

"As if the old guy knew disappearance was a strong possibilty."

"*What* is going on here? What's been going on? The more we find out, the less clear anything is. Nicholas Markov looks like he's too much for us."

"To quote the sage: It's always darkest before the dawn."

I scowled. "Leave it to the Princess of Platitudes to console a puzzled soul."

Charity got up and adjusted her coiled blonde braids. "Here's more bad news. This half of the dynamic duo has to go and work for a living. The law firm beckons. What're you up to this afternoon?"

"Talk to Anya Rok and P.Q. Antonelli."

"I'm sure you'll charm them to death. Ooops! Bad word to use."

"See you tonight. Tomorrow if I'm lucky."

7

I went looking for Jaschekoff's Discount Sales. I asked directions, but a couple of twisting streets and a one-way confused me. I had to nose my Datsun in low gear up what seemed a seventy-degree, cobblestone grade. I had forgotten just how hilly some parts of Pittsburgh are. Over the crest I horsed the brakes and eased slowly down toward the river. On a sidestreet not far above slummy Commercial Street was Jaschekoff's Discount Sales, six storefronts run together. Their plate glass was plastered with white banner posters. Red block letters screamed SALE, SALE! 3 PRICES HERE: LOW, LOWER, LOWEST! NAME BRANDS—NO FRILLS!!

This last was true with a vengeance. As near as I could tell, the only frill was the door on the single bathroom. Appliances and electronics were stacked on bolted metal shelving. Green paint glowed under neon units so powerful they made me want to confess to crimes I hadn't committed.

No one had ever described Anya Rok—the Ice Queen—to me. No matter. I had a feeling I had spotted her first thing. A snow blonde wearing a clean, recently ironed, store-issue smock stood idly by a couple arguing over the merits of two available models of hot-air corn poppers. Yes, she was the Ice Queen. I could see the Finnish blood in her Russian stock. Beneath that hair and her so-pale skin her naturally red lips and bright blue eyes burned out in contrast. Not the Ice Queen just for her looks. I saw in the planes of her lovely face and in the cast of her eyes a distancing, a cool reserve. And caution rather than intelligence.

"Pardon me, are you Anya Rok?" I said.

Her eyes moved over my face and upper body. Making certain basic evaluations. "That's me." Her voice was low and mollow. Nice in the ear.

"My name's Yuri Nevsky. I'm with the *Post-Gazette*. I wonder if I could talk to you?"

Her slender, long-boned hand stroked her hair with grooming motions. She heard distant sounds of stardom. "About what?"

The corn popper couple had begun to trade sharp personal insults. I had to raise my voice. "About Nicholas Markov."

Her face fell. "I don't really want to do that. I've talked about him *enough*."

I gave her my rap about the Russian Slope article and slipped her one of Volodya's kopeks. She frowned and nibbled an already decimated thumbnail. "I get out for coffee in about ten minutes. I'll meet you in the diner down the block."

"Anya, that's *not* a customer!" A shout from the front of the store. More shouts from the corn popper couple, now close to blows.

"Ungh! Jaschekoff should be running a *gulag*." She waved toward the shouting couple. "And they should be *in* it. See you in ten. Red Lion Diner."

The Red Lion Diner was right out of *Blondie*. The counterman had hairy arms improved with Korean-War tattoos. Flies strolled across the pie slices. I sat in a corner booth, nursed a mug of coffee, and studied the notes in my Coop spiral notebook. Soon Anya settled in with a swirl of stirring white hair and the fetchingly faint scent of Night Call. Nineteen! I thought, when life was endless and the future's a piece of cake.

"So what you want to know, Mr. Nevsky?"

"Try 'Yuri.'"

"Sure."

"I guess I want to know about you and Nicholas Markov. People said you ran together sometimes."

"He was a class guy. I liked being around him."

"The paper's always looking for a romantic angle. You his girlfriend? Now—or then?"

She tossed her head. Her blue eyes narrowed. "I was closer to him than any other woman."

"Closer than Olga Samnesovich?"

Anya snorted and her perfect lower lip twisted. "Her! She wasn't good enough to sweep up his fingernail clippings. That one! She'd drop her drawers for a joint or a bottle of booze. She didn't mean *anything* to him. Even if she did stick herself in front of him every chance she got."

"I was told you and Olga were friends."

"You were told wrong." Her blue eyes slid away. "At one time we could've been called friends. B.N. Before Nicholas."

"Some people on the Slope say they ran off together."

"That's bullshit! A carload. They *weren't* that close. What would a class guy like Nick want with a scumbag like Olga?"

Color Anya green. What did Nicholas *have* that drew such interest from the ladies? "Then it's a funny thing they disappeared the same night," I said.

Anya sipped her tea. "Coincidence."

I closed my notebook. "Off the record now, OK?"

"Maybe you lie?" Her eyes challenged mine.

"No way."

"I want you to know where I'm coming from," Anya said. "Whatever you write, I don't want you to badmouth Nicholas. He's taken enough shit."

"One of the things that's come up is drugs. On the Slope. What I've heard makes me think I have to write something about Nicholas Markov. He dealt."

"Off the record now?" She stared at me suspiciously.

"My word."

"A little—nothing heavy duty. Drugs were a tool for Nick. He thought he could see things better—understand better— when he got high. So he wanted to spread the wealth."

"I didn't hear anybody say he gave dope away, Anya."

"He didn't make that many big sales. I saw all of them, so I should know."

"You gotta explain that," I said.

She did and I got a quick character sketch. Not of Nicholas, which I could have used, but of a slightly spoiled and immature young lady named Anya Rok. Shortened from Rokalsachefsky. She had been drawn to Nick because she expected to get him, as she had most things she wanted—to make him her lover and then husband. She found him a very emotional young man. As near as I could read her somewhat embarrassed rush of words on the subject, those emotions ran on a higher plane than the fleshly. Or at least—as I had begun to notice—not toward female flesh in any case.

Still hopeful, she continued to spend time with him. She admitted she had been bored and hungry for excitement. So she somehow talked him into letting her be on the scene for his few larger sales. Usually she took P.Q. Antonelli with her. The two women would hover in the vicinity of the transaction, gleaning cheap thrills from the illegality of it all, and from the characters who bought the dope.

"Why'd P.Q. want to be there?"

"She was my main lady. Where I went, she went. At least

that's the way it was then." She smiled happily. Here was a woman who liked any kind of attention.

"Where'd Nicholas get the dope?"

Her eyes wavered. "I don't know."

"I heard it was Ray Nevick."

"You been really busy," Anya said. "I'm not saying he was or he wasn't, understand. But he's a crazy, mixed-up guy. He liked Nick a lot. Helped him in all the wrong ways."

"And he bites."

"Huh?"

"Tell me about the night Ed Dixon got killed."

"I already told the cops. And the reporters. I feel like an LP."

"Play it again, Anya."

She was right. She sounded like a record. All automatic. The story all pre-planned, packaged and delivered. And likely not true. I recognized the same information Chief Polsky and Trackman Tolovitch had shared, based on the two women's story. Anya and P.Q. looking the other way, the shot, the hesitation and Nicholas's flight. I knew there was no sense challenging the version. She and P.Q. had put it together to protect Nick—a man immune to the charms of shapely blondes who hung around him starry-eyed. A man who seemed to live in the priestly land beyond carnality.

"The car that drove away. You see it?"

"Yeah. Not very good, though. Some kind of dark four-door. Maybe gray, green, dark blue. Light down in the flats is lousy at night."

"License plate?"

She shook her head. "Didn't have my glasses on. And I'm nearsighted." Her eyes were steady. No lies now.

"Driver?"

"Couldn't tell. Maybe Nick. Maybe not. A man, a woman? Young, old? Beats me." She grinned sheepishly. "Another reason I couldn't see so well—I was hysterical. That scummy bar, that big spade Dixon dead. The shot, the *blood*. And the *fear*. I was screaming out there on the street. Still screaming five minutes later when the cops came."

"Must have been a tough few hours," I said.

"Was. Woulda been worse if P.Q.'s attorney hadn't showed up."

"What happened? He chase ambulances?"

"P.Q. called him. While I was bawling, she was dialing."

"She didn't call her folks?"

"I thought she was. Then she said, 'One hysterical woman at a time's enough. I'll deal with my mother *later*.'"

Anya drained her tea. Her pale face set itself, hinting at lines that age would etch. "I was *scared*, Yuri. I was scared worse than I ever was in my life." I followed her eyes as they angled toward the diner door. "Oh!" She smiled.

A young man came up to our booth. He was maybe twenty-nine and wore a cheap three-piece suit. He smelled of Brut and self-importance. I looked higher and saw the flushed face of a born bureaucrat, insurance drummer, family businessman— a safe face, one without a risk in it to take.

"Yuri Nevsky, this is Ron Sakinoff, a *very* good friend." Her white hand reached up to tightly clutch his forearm. In that circling of slender fingers I saw just how badly Anya Rok had been scared. She had glimpsed some of the danger in life. She had whiffed the spent powder of the cartridge of capriciousness, the hazard from which none of us can hide. Her reaction: to scamper for security. And Ron Sakinoff was what she thought it was. I heard wedding bells pealing amid the Commercial Street traffic. Babies screaming. Another marriage for the wrong reasons. "He sometimes meets me here on my coffee break."

She rattled on into a complete introduction. From the moment of Ron's arrival I didn't exist any longer in Anya Rok's self-centered world. For a moment she tore her eyes from her lover's pudgy face and glanced at me. "You oughta talk to P.Q. about all that stuff for your article, Yuri. She's really *freaky* sometimes about remembering things."

P.Q. Antonelli wore a white dental jacket and an alert expression. She was manning the reception desk and phone console in the offices of the orthodontist group practice where she worked as a receptionist. So many phone lights were flashing that every kid in the Mon Valley must have lost his retainer. She handled each call with a few polite words. Used the intercom and message pads with similar economy. At the same time she made me feel welcome and saw that I found my way to the crowded waiting area and a coverless copy of the *Twisted Tooth Journal*, or some such. She said she'd be happy to talk to me as soon as she had a chance.

I kept an eye on her as she went about doing the work of two. She was about five-eight; her black hair piled high made her look even taller. Her movements were rapid, efficient—and graceful. She made filling out appointment cards nice to watch.

Five middle-class kids in jeans, sneakers and properly tattered tops talked about beer, community colleges and the Moody Blues. Their teeth—surrounded with enough wire to fence a concentration camp—were already the envy of most of the children in the world. Such white, hard teeth didn't need realigning any more than I needed flawless skin or an unlined face. A portly lady on my left who should *not* have been wearing yellow stretch pants assumed I was a father paying the freight. She wanted me to know right away how much her Dr. Jorstedt charged. And had I had to take out a bank loan to perfect my kid, too? I wondered what it was in the American middle class that made its parents want physical perfection in their children. I supposed because it was the easiest kind of perfection to understand. And the least valuable. Also the easiest to buy. Better they should work toward developing perfection of heart and spirit. The stuff that really mattered. If Yuri Nevsky were in charge of helping a child toward perfection, the only thing he'd pay would be close, personal attention, and the only accounts kept would be those of lines of communication held open. Leave it to a divorced man in the middle of a determined mid-life crisis to know all the answers.

It took P.Q. Antonelli, efficient as she was, the better part of half an hour to get straightened away. By that time the hour hand on the lifetime, set-in-acrylic wall clock had nudged past four. The crowd in the waiting area had thinned to one lonely-looking black kid with an unfortunate snaggle of front teeth. His right ear was pressed to the side of a massive portable tape/radio console, his own electronic empire. Lost in a transistor world of soul.

I expanded my initial introduction, dropped a few names, including the *Post-Gazette* and Anya Rok. Through it all she kept her attentive dark-brown eyes on my face. When I mentioned Nicholas a bright, almost beatific light sparked in those dark pools that the poet said were the windows to the soul. Simple message: she loved him. *Really* loved him.

I must have hit her unawares. Quickly her face tightened up and her eyes again mirrored only intelligence.

I flashed my most disarming smile. "First big question from the press—what's P.Q. stand for?"

"Pasqualena. That's Italian. Something to do with Easter. Can you blame me?"

"Nope." I sat back and stuck out my size 12s. "Anya said I should talk to you about Nicholas."

"Why Nicholas? There's a lot more to Russian Slope than an ugly shooting in an ugly bar."

"The more I find out about him, the more interesting he seems to be."

"I think you're a cop," she said.

A sharp lady, sure enough. "I'm not. I'm not into guilt or innocence. I'm into information." I met her glance. "That's all. And I need help."

"I don't want to talk about that night. It was ugly."

"What *will* you talk about? Nick himself?"

She nodded. "I'm not the kind of woman who runs on, Yuri. I'm not a waster of words or anything else. I'll tell you some things about him. Five years I've known him. Sometimes from a distance. Sometimes up close. I'll boil it down for you." She drew a deep breath. "Nicholas Markov had something magic about him. Something that put him—not *above* other men, just...apart from them." She cocked her head and her bright eyes raked my face. "Sounds crazy, huh?"

"People been telling me something like that since I hit Russian Slope. I'm getting tired of hearing it. Because it doesn't go anywhere."

"He had two things I never saw in one person: charisma and spirituality. I could talk for hours about him, but that sums up what I know that's important about him. No, wait. I can be even briefer. He was a born leader."

I nodded. A spiritual leader. A kid maybe interested in being an Orthodox priest. There was some kind of thread here. Making anything out of it was something else again. "You want to talk about your relationship with Nicholas? You go out with him?"

"Anya did."

"And you two were friends."

"Yeah. More then than now. Now it's Ron for her. Growing up a little more for me. Anya used to tell me all about Nicholas. And the three of us used to go out a lot together."

"Didn't either Nick or Anya object to that?"

P.Q. smiled nervously. She had good teeth. Maybe free orthodontic treatment was a fringe benefit. "At first Anya did a little, but Nicholas kept inviting me."

61

"He interested in you?" I watched her carefully, looking for that love light.

"Only as another human being, another soul worth some attention." She was closed up tighter than a hatch on an atomic sub. "Then after a while Anya didn't care either if I was around."

"Why?"

"She saw it wasn't going to go anywhere with Nicholas. I mean go the way she figured it would. He wasn't the physical type."

"Meaning?"

"Have to draw you a *picture?* She kept waiting for him to close and he didn't. She tried providing the occasion and hinting like mad. No way. Finally she told him what she wanted. He said he liked her, but . . ."

Not interested. I knew that was significant. But not why. "But she kept seeing him. *You* kept seeing him."

"He was that kind of guy. He was exciting to be around. Anya and I stuck around him for thrills."

"For Anya the thrills ended the night he shot Ed Dixon."

P.Q.'s dark eyes widened and she rushed to Nicholas's defense. "Who said—"

"Save it!" I held up my palm toward her. "I know what you're gonna say. I already heard the recording. Anya's got it down pat. Listen, P.Q., the cops know Nick wasted Ed Dixon, half the folks on the Slope know it. You and Anya know it. Even *I* know it."

"I said I didn't want to talk about it, then you brought it up." Her face darkened with sadness. "Oh, it's all so . . . rotten."

I touched her shoulder. "Sorry."

The phone buzzed and P.Q. did her job. When she turned back to me she had herself under control. Tough young lady. "For sure Anya and I shouldn't have been there that night. Because we were chasing the wrong kind of thrills for one reason. For another because Father Alexander had asked Anya to stop seeing Nicholas altogether."

"I heard he was working with Nicholas to get him out of the drug scene and straight again."

"It wasn't just that. He was working with him on his Orthodox prayers and responses. And old church history. 'Doing the whole man,' Nicholas used to say."

"His starets. Counselor, seer, monk, lay therapist, adviser.

No exact translation. And Father Alexander plays Ann Landers, too. No Anya for Nick, he said."

"He was Anya's confessor," P.Q. said. "I'm sure she told him about her and Nicholas. Maybe he figured it was better for her not to see Nicholas. She wasn't getting anywhere with him, that's for sure. So I guess it was good advice. Too bad she didn't take it."

"You know Father Alexander?"

P.Q. grinned. "'The Widow's Heartthrob,' they call him. Big hunk of man. Big spirit. Great guy. I met him at the rap sessions he runs down in the old Moskva Hotel. He didn't care if I was an R. C. He was a true ecumenical. I liked him. And not just because he was a big, hairy man. Nicholas wasn't the only person he helped. He counseled anyone from the groups who wanted it. Some harder cases he'd refer to Western Psychiatric Hospital. He was pretty hip for a guy who'd only been in the country a couple years."

"Where was his last church?" I said.

She shrugged. "Over in Europe somewhere, I think. You oughta ask him."

A scowling dentist came out of one of the pain rooms. My interview with P.Q. was about over.

"One last thing," I said. "The night Dixon was killed. And Nick drove off with somebody. You see the other person?"

"Didn't even see Nick."

"You see anything else?"

A flicker of hesitation. "No." She was lying.

Real, useful information about Nicholas Markov was tougher to find than eyeglasses at a pilots' convention. "You could think about telling me the truth, P.Q. Who knows—it might end up helping Nick."

"I wouldn't mind helping *him*. The problem is I don't trust *you!*" She got up.

I didn't want to let her get away. I wanted a chance to build up some of that trust. And find out what she held back. "Volodya Tschersky's having one of his parties this Saturday night," I said. "Half the folks on the Slope will be there. Come as my guest."

"I'll think about it."

She showed me her back.

8

The next afternoon, Saturday, my destination was 1214 East-mont Road, the Markov's 12-room castle. I stopped only long enough to phone ahead. Elena Markov's voice was stiff and anxious. Turned out I had nothing to do with it. Her natural state. The inside of her house was even more elegant than the outside—but it spelled prison just the same.

I knew the general story, if not the details. Elena was one of those unlucky women who went from her father's house to her husband's. No chance for her to test her non-domestic talents, develop her independence and self-confidence. Her face—a handsome one of smoldering brown eyes and good bones—told me she now had reached that testing slope between thirty-five and forty. The strains were there—resentment at her husband's domination and her own dependency. The dilemma: to find herself amid the spice racks and soap operas after the last carpool had been driven, or to strike out on her own with few skills and no place to go.

She offered me a light handshake. Her fingertips were nicotine-stained, her voice husky from what must have been a three-pack-a-day habit. "My mother-in-law told me she went to see you, Mr. Nevsky." Elena swallowed. "Mikhail, my husband, doesn't approve. But he's promised not to say anything outside these walls. And of course I have, too."

Thundering footsteps down the stairs. A boy burst into the living-room. I recognized him. The Slav who had gone round-ball one-on-one with the black kid and worn him out. He pulled up short at seeing me. "Sorry, Mom," he said.

"Nice game the other day, fella."

"Huh?"

"On the park court. You passed him on about the twentieth hoop."

Understanding, then a grin of triumph. "'Downtown' Brown! A tough dude, but I *own* him." He frowned. "Where were you?"

"In a car. Just happened to be sitting there."

He feigned disappointment. "Geez, I thought maybe you were a scout for *NBA on CBS.*"

"Sorry."

"Mr. Nevsky, this is Sasha, my other son. Sasha, Mr. Nevsky is a newspaperman who's doing an article on Russian Slope."

We shook hands. "You're gonna write about my *moves*, huh?"

I grinned. *"Sure."* I liked Sasha.

"Catch you later, Coach," he said. He dashed off.

"Nice kid," I said to Elena.

"Yes. So different from Nicholas." Her face shadowed. In that sadness she grew more comely. "Rough and practical. Feet on the ground..."

"But Nicholas is your favorite."

She snapped a glance at me. "How do you know that?"

"Not so hard. First son. All alone with you for maybe five years till Sasha came along. A lot of strong bonds develop in five years."

Elena Markov lit a cigarette. Pack, lighter, hands moved with that economy of the practiced addict. Melancholy deepened, intensifying her brown-eyed gaze. "I invested too heavily in my children, Mr. Nevsky. I was a properly raised daughter. I *did* for my children. I did and did and did. And they're both fine boys. I wish I had done for myself from time to time. I wish I had known how necessary, how *healthy* measured selfishness can be."

"It's not too late." .

She stared at me as though I was the Russian Slope idiot. "I'll be thirty-eight next week."

I thought of Betty Ellen. Almost the same words. With any kind of luck there was a lot of life left for both women past forty. But they had to believe it from the gut. They couldn't be convinced. What they saw was what they got. That sneaky street profundity held true again.

"Tell me about Nicholas," I said. "Tell me anything that might help me find out where he is."

She painted me a mother's picture. Surely not the most reliable reporting on earth. Still, by holding up my own filter to the stream of her bias, I got to know Nicholas a little better. He had grown up a withdrawn dreamer. When he chose to leave his introspection and compete, he excelled—in Russian-language studies and bowling, to take two examples. The commanding aura that others had reported was not an exaggeration. From his earliest years, young Nicholas had a way of being listened to, admired, and even obeyed. By everyone except his father. To Mikhail his son was womanly and indoorsy. Unforgivable traits in the eyes of one who defined masculinity as lying within the narrowest boundaries.

Not surprisingly Nicholas turned for a model—and companionship—to his paternal grandfather, eccentric Igor Gregorevich Markov. "He came around to really *loving* my father-in-law," Elena said. "He had his own name for him—Gory—that only he used. He would spend hours in Gory's room. The old man told him old stories about old Russia." She put out her cigarette and lit another. "In a lot of ways the clock stopped for Igor in February of 1918 when he left Russia forever."

"Where in Russia did he live?"

"His family—and was he proud of it!—came from the Caucasus Mountains. Southwestern Russia. A valley way up in a remote area. His people were landed aristocracy. They sort of ruled over the region, as near as I could understand. Had since before the fall of Constantinople—in 1453."

"That's a while." I couldn't help but remember my own father's genealogical chart. My roots, too, went back to the fifteenth century.

"I think Igor Gregorevich knew every one of his ancestors—personally." Elena's smile was sincere and warm. She should have used it more often. "He filled Nicholas's head with his legends and stories. He also filled the gap that Mikhail left." She closed her mouth quickly, as though to bite off the trickle of spousely criticism. "My husband is very committed to his work, Yuri. He doesn't have time for much else. He's a *good* provider."

"Sure."

She made us coffee. The kitchen was ominously spotless, as was the whole first floor. Clean was about all Elena had to do. And buried deep was the certain knowledge that she wasn't cut out to be only a cleaner, a housewife, a mother. She had played those roles; her soul asked for more. And that desperate wish deepened the lines about her mouth and tightened the screw of tension a little every day.

"It's been a tough year," she said. "Of course Nicholas's disappearing, the whole murder business, was just awful. Still is. But Igor Gregorevich was a trial, too, before he died. Ludmilla wasn't much help. Mikhail was going through a trying period at the steel company. Most of the burden fell on me. Senility, I guess it was. The old man started to imagine things. Imagined people were after him. Imagined that he was back in his family's home in the mountains again—the Valley of Promise."

"I'm sorry."

"We had terrible set-tos about his pistol. You know about it? Mikhail tried to keep it away from him. But he'd scream and shout so we simply couldn't live with him." Elena's deep gaze swept my face. "He was a headstrong, half-crazy, proud old fool. And strong and devious on top of it."

"Why'd he carry the pistol?"

"He said he would shoot them if they came after him."

"Who?"

Her sad smile was all the answer she had. I said, "Tom Tolovitch, the local newspaper guy, told me Igor's carried the pistol a long time. For years. When he had all his wits."

"Yuri, no one was after him. Not ever. He was imagining it all along." Elena shook her head. "He started losing his marbles all across the board. He was never religious. In fact, he loathed the Church. But the last year he would shout and scream about priests and churches. Some of them were from his days in Russia. Long dead or destroyed. Some of them were imaginary. And some—like poor, patient Father Alexander and St. Basil's—were definitely in the here and now."

"They didn't get along? The priest and your father-in-law?"

"Not from the first pastoral visit, a courtesy call by Father Alexander. Igor Gregorevich hardly ever came out of his room for company. He sort of held court. I was embarrassed that he wouldn't change his custom even for the *priest*. So Father Alexander climbed the stairs. And pretty soon the old man started shouting at him. Ordered him out."

"No way to treat a priest," I said. "How did he take it?"

"Pretty much with a smile." Elena shook her head with the memory of embarrassment. "Father Alexander said the Church could survive a little abuse. That Igor was worth returning to the sacraments. Father Alexander came back twice more—but there wasn't any improvement. They screamed at each other in old Russian. And I'm not really that good at new Russian. I'm just as glad as far as those shouting matches were concerned." She got up and poured more coffee. Her movements were jerky and hurried. Heavy thoughts were weighing on her.

"In the end Father Alexander turned out to be the better man. And a better friend to the family than we deserved."

"You mean because he counseled Nicholas—never mind Igor?"

"No. That was a favor, sure, but..." Her voice was tight. "I probably shouldn't say this. Mikhail and I agreed not to mention the possibility. And Father Alexander cooperated."

"What possibility?"

"That Igor Gregorevich might have killed himself." She couldn't look at me. Her eyes plundered the spice rack. "He *had* been cleaning his pistol, but... The way things were, the way the bullet went up into his throat..." She shook her head.

"You found him?"

"Everyone else was gone when the pistol went off."

"He leave a note?"

Elena walked away from me, down the length of the kitchen. Keeping her back to me. At the far end she whirled around. Her hair danced over her shoulders. "Not a suicide note, if that's what you mean. He'd been doing some doodling and writing on a pad. About half a sheet. I—I was a coward. When I found him lying dead, his head a ruin, I thought—suicide! The most wicked act of all. I tore off the sheet and hid it. No one has seen it. Even though"—she grinned thinly—"there's really *nothing* about suicide on it. Do you read Russian, Yuri? Yes?. Then I'd like to give you the paper. Everything should be done that has even the remotest chance of helping you find out where Nicholas is. If it's no help, then at least I didn't hold back." She went into another room and came back with an envelope.

I tucked it away into my notebook just as a door slammed in the basement. I happened to be looking at Elena, so saw her stiffen. "Mikhail's home. He was working this morning. They're so busy at the company now. All that foreign steel..."

A thundering stream of Russian sounded from the basement stairs. Shouted orders to Ludmilla, who was somewhere off in one of the upstairs rooms. Something about making his drink and taking it to the library. Overhead I heard the old woman's slow footfalls.

Elena introduced me to her husband. Mikhail Igorevich Markov wore a 600-dollar suit and a permanent expression of impatience. His handshake could have cracked Brazil nuts. His heavy voice demanded obedience. As to standing up to him—only the strong need apply. His autumn-gray eyes appraised me, weighing my worth like a U.S. Steel foreman sizing up a shipment of billets. "To speak frankly to you from the go, Mr. Nevsky, I don't approve of your presence here," he said. "I only condone it."

Here was a guy it wasn't hard to dislike. But unlike Ray Nevick, the druggie troublemaker, Mikhail Markov projected strength and strong opinions, not weakness.

"Don't see how you can quarrel with maybe finding out where your son is," I said.

"Wherever my son is, he deserves to be." Mikhail led me to the library and offered me an armchair. "If I had to characterize my eldest son, I'd say: a disappointment. He didn't have the family fiber, Mr. Nevsky."

I was one down with Mikhail Igorevich. He was about to offer me a minimum of courtesy, then expect me to stay out of his house and life. And I had an inkling that valuable information lay under his red Florentine-tile roof. I needed some kind of modest coup. So I said—in Russian—the proverb: "The son is mirror to the father."

This let loose a torrent of Russian from Mikhail. I got most of it, which pushed up my stock. And encouraged him to list the ways Nicholas had been a disappointment. Ludmilla arrived with drinks. Her greeting to me was brief. As was her stay in the library. Not so short as not to get the drift of her son's words. The lined web of her face deepened in sorrow. She rushed out on heavy, peasant feet.

"He never faced his responsibilities directly, Yuri Vladimirovich. He was an evader, a confidence man."

"I've heard some things about him. He seemed to have a good side."

"By whose standards? Not by mine. Not by anyone's who knew the quality of the Markov family. What we're capable of." He leaned forward and tapped the rim of his glass to make his point. "He wasn't aggressive. He wasn't ambitious. He spent too much time dreaming. And he used people—used his smile—to get what he wanted. He didn't face the world straight ahead—like a man. He showed no interest in intimacy with women. And there were some interested." He raised his chin with just the hint of preening. "And the Markovs are attractive to the opposite sex. Nicholas was . . . unmanly in that way. And don't think I didn't tell him about it!"

"I'm sure you did." I had heard about as much about this particular father-son relationship as I needed. Mikhail Markov

69

sounded like a heavy out of Dickens's London—or a psychiatrist's textbook. "I'd like to offer my sympathies on the passing last year of your father, Igor Gregorevich."

Mikhail thanked me, nodding the while. "*There* was a Markov. The blood of Imperial Russian boyars was rich in his veins. He's in my prayers every week. Even so, I can't believe he's gone. I go to his room, look at his empty chair." He smiled sheepishly. "I've allowed nothing to be disturbed. Of course some day . . . But he was my *father*."

"Elena said he and Nicholas were close."

"Igor Gregorevich never could see through the boy the way I could. Sometimes I think he even encouraged his dreaminess."

"Since coming to Russian Slope I've heard Nicholas called 'spiritual.' You think your father encouraged that rather than what you call 'dreaminess'?"

Mikhail waved his slabby hand impatiently. "I'm sure he talked some nonsense to the boy. The right of the grandparent. I didn't deny it to him. What was important to me was that Nicholas learn about Russia as it was. That, Igor Gregorevich knew well. Past that, God knows what nonsense, what 'spiritual' discussions they had."

I sipped my bourbon. "What about Nicholas and Father Alexander?"

"To little and too late. The priest did his best, but Nicholas was too far gone into what I found out too late was drugs. If *I* had known—"

"Mikhail Gregorevich, where do you think Nicholas is?"

"Off with his dope-dealer friends. Turning his back on responsibility. On family. On everything decent in his life."

"Suppose he isn't. Suppose the drugs had nothing to do with his disappearance. Maybe he ran for other reasons. Maybe he ran away from his life. Maybe away from you."

"Yuri—"

"Wait! I'm just supposing."

"I don't give a damn for your supposing!" Mikhail jumped to his feet, bowling over the coffee table. Drinks emptied into the thick Kerman rug nap. "Don't shove him at me! I've washed my hands of him. Understand? *Washed my hands* of my own son. My murderer son. I don't care whether he's alive or dead!"

"*Mikhail!*" Elena stood in the doorway. Horror and shock twisted her face like a blow. "What kind of man *are* you? What did I marry? *What did I marry?*"

70

"You married a Markov! And you couldn't live up to the name any more than your son could!" Mikhail's face was red.

"Excuse me!" I shouted. "I have to leave." That quieted them down for the moment. Elena got me my coat and showed me to the door.

"I'm sorry," she said.

"I'm sorry, too—about you and him. I want to come back, check out your son's room. Igor Gregorevich's, too."

"Whenever you like, Yuri. Really. I'm home almost every day. Just call first. *Please* call." Naked desperation and loneliness colored her face like dye.

"See you later."

"Good-bye."

I let myself out. I glimpsed Elena as the door swung closed, turning toward her husband, as grim-faced as if he were an executioner. I knew what would happen. I knew such marriages too well. They would quarrel. He would lean on her, work on her guilt, on her poor self-image. Maybe she would end up apologizing. She would eat her resentment and jam it down into her emotional gunnysack to fester with the rest of the load. And pay him back in dark, devious ways.

Sasha Markov was waiting by my car. Practicing tricky dribbling between his legs. "How'd it go, man?" he said.

"So-so. I'll be back."

The ball seemed attached to his fingertips with invisible elastics as he worked it around and between his legs. "I know you're not a reporter." His eyes were on the ball.

"Oh?"

"Babushka told me. Said you were looking for Nick."

"More or less. Don't let it get around, OK?"

"No problem, Mr. N. One thing you oughta do, though. I wanted to tell you. You oughta go see Father Alexander."

"I plan to."

"When you do, ask him what he and Grandpa used to argue about so loud."

"You must have heard," I said.

"They were screaming and shouting in Russian. I don't know it that good. Drives my dad crazy when I don't understand him a lot of the time. And I heard them through the ceiling of my room. Think. So all I can tell you was that all three times the argument was something about Grandpa breaking a promise."

"About what? Who to?"

71

Sasha shrugged and dribbled off.

"What's any of that have to do with your brother?" I called after him.

"Probably nothing. But you oughta talk to Father Alexander just in case. Stay cool, Mr. N."

The closer I got to 138 the more stretched and drained I felt. The sloping lawn and giant horse chestnut trees failed to do their usual pep-up job. I thought about jogging around the high school track, but the idea left me flat. No messages from Charity or anyone else on the phone tape recorder.

I played doctor to my ear. I've never been fond of mirrors. As I struggled with a Band-Aid disc and a stiff lobe, I was treated to a close-up of my receding hairline and washboard brow. Lines on each side of my mouth marked the paths of my frequent smiles and laughter. A large nose and long-lashed brown eyes finished off the package. Fortyish I was. Fortyish I looked.

Not many months ago I had paid the high price of divorce to set myself emotionally free and to open up options which had grown to be of value to me. As I and my wife, Ann, passed through the inevitable changes of anger, bitterness, quarrels, resentment and grudging acceptance, I sensed that what the future offered would be worth it. I was guided by that hope like a returning mariner in a gale is by the home-port light buoy. Well, I had made it to port, to 138 and a new life. Opportunity? The chance to chase memories of a missing saint-sinner up and down Russian Slope. Emotional freedom? Getting tangled up with the Slavic temperament in all its Byzantine glory—and finding it striking all-too-many chords on the puzzling instrument of my own heart.

I had planned to spend the early evening at home, but my memory seemed determined to serve up nothing better than another rendition of those Shattered-Family Blues. And the action *was* on Russian Slope. I left a note for Charity, showered and jumped into a suit and tie.

I edged my way into the Imperial Court's packed house just as Betty Ellen Edwards was swinging into her nine-o'clock act. The gallant Cossack, Stan Pokora, surfaced at my elbow. He was leaving his ringside table. It was mine if I wanted it. I said I did. "Will the lovely Ms. Day be joining you this evening?" he said.

"Maybe."

"I'll be back later."

"I hope you'll join us," I said.

"A *pleasure*."

I settled down with a Sam Thompson and soda. At least Pokora the Cossack knew what he wanted. Straight-ahead sex. He offered a refreshing directness amid the horde of oblique Slavs strung throughout the events of the last five days.

Betty Ellen saw me at ringside. She gave me a big smile. Her routine drifted away from political satire into some sophisticated material on love—the second time around. The gist of the one-liners, quips and set jokes seemed to be that bloodied, scarred souls knew better what love was, and how to appreciate it.

Betty Ellen. The lady from my distant—and not so distant—past sat on a stool under a soft, flattering spot and beamed at me. Love was on her mind. Love for me, for goodness' sake. Blossoming again a little too fast for my sense of security. At the break she pushed through the crowd toward my table.

"You could keep on leaving when the milkman comes, Yuri—if you'd come back the next night. I hoped I'd see you last night."

"Well . . ."

"You be the swallow; I'll be Capistrano."

"It was nice seeing you, Betty Ellen. But I'm really wrapped up in this article I'm doing. Flat out with no time."

She plunged on, not really listening. Her mascaraed eyes devoured my face like creatures from outer space. "Yuri, I had forgotten how gentle you are with a woman. How tender and truly loving. I . . . haven't known many men like that lately. Most of them think *Joy of Sex* is the favorite in the third at Meadowlands Raceway."

I was feeling *very* uncomfortable. "I do the best I can," I said.

She rested her hand on my forearm and gave it a possessive squeeze. She leaned forward, eyes still on my face. Her left breast nudged my elbow like a soft puppy wanting a petting. "Hot in here," I said.

"I've been hot all day, thinking about *you*. Your strength. Your wanting. Wondering why we let it all fly apart years ago. Full of regret—and hope."

"But not patience? Listen, Betty Ellen. I told you I just got finished going through a divorce. My emotions are about as reliable as a Corvair at high speed."

73

"I under*stand*." She didn't. "But you're going to meet me after the last show anyway, aren't you?" Soft puppy got to work again.

"Excuse me, Yuri. I have to talk to you *right away*." I looked up. Charity! A couple of wings and she'd have been a bona fide angel of mercy. "It's important," she added.

Betty Ellen remembered Charity was my partner, a "fellow reporter," not a rival. "Excuse me. I'll talk to you later, Yuri." She gave me a look of smoldering lust, then got up and moved into the burly arms of half-a-dozen star-struck Slavs. She would do OK. Charity slid into Betty Ellen's empty seat.

"What's up?" I said. "Finally got a lead we can get our aging teeth into?"

"Speak for your *own* teeth, buster. Mine are as white and sharp as Mack the Knife's. Ageless, that's Charity Day. White Mountain Chablis, please," she said to the waiter.

"So what did my lovely attorney-lady friend find out that made her chase off the entertainer?"

Charity grinned. "Nothing. I saw you under some heavy emotional pressure that you obviously didn't want. That's all. Safety valve."

I sat back with a relieved chuckle. "Evelyn Wood couldn't have read that any faster—or better. Thanks."

"*De nada*. What's a partner for?"

I filled Charity in on that fun family, the Markovs. When I finished she sipped her wine and looked at the ceiling. "One thing. I wish you'd asked the family about Olga Samnesovich and Nicholas. I can't get by their having disappeared the same night. What did she mean to him? If anything. Maybe Elena knows."

"I'm gonna go back. I'll check."

"Ask about the insurance policy, too. That fits in somewhere. And we have to get around to seeing Father Alexander. I want us both to go."

"Sure."

"Next, I'm *dying* of curiosity. How have you waited so long?"

"Huh?"

"The scribbles that Igor left on the pad. Big excitement!"

"Elena said they didn't amount to much."

"Have the sheet with you? Yes? Translate it *this minute!*" Charity was bouncing in her chair in anticipation.

"There's not that much. Already glanced at it."

Charity pulled a little notebook out of her purse with a stub of pencil. "Sock it to me!"

I shrugged. In the reflected stagelight I read off the words written in a flowing Cyrillic script flush with the frills favored by French tutors in a long-dead age.

"'. . . to see the Valley of Promise again . . . Sister Katerina . . . the Markovs shook the earth . . . Vladimir the Lion. . . Boris . . . the first Katerina . . . I curse Father One-Leg . . . Soiler of Mount Volzna . . . I curse the Holy Order of the Caucasus . . . Not Mikhail. Nicholas. No, not Mikhail . . . I curse the Holy Order of the Caucasus . . . Nicholas! . . . 70 years and half a world away! . . . to find a Wonder of Holiness . . . Father Alexander . . . the holy man . . .' That's it, Charity."

She copied out the last words, looked up at me. "Maybe you should read it to me in Russian. It might've made more sense."

"I can make a little out of it. The Valley of Promise is where the Markov family lived since way back. The names I guess are historical. Mikhail—Nicholas's father. And Nicholas. We know Father Alexander."

"What's the 'Holy Order of the Caucasus'?"

"Beats me. Never heard of it."

"That's one of the things we'll have to ask Father Alexander when we see him. We should show these scribbles to him, too."

"I'm not sure it's worth the trouble. Elena Markov said Igor was losing his marbles. Talking about the old days and hating religion. This sounds like more of the same."

Betty Ellen had started her second act. The Imperial Court was packed. Day after payday at the tube works. I turned toward the bar and saw Ray Nevick bellied up to a beer. His torn jumpsuit had been replaced by Western wear, square-toed boots, embroidered shirt and jeans jacket. A string tie with a steer's head on the slide rounded out the fashion plate.

Beside Nevick stood three men in their thirties with thick necks and guts. About seventeen years past hearing their last play called in their last huddle. You could see them in the football stadiums all up and down the river towns of western Pennsylvania and eastern Ohio. Haunting the sites of the only small triumphs life had given them. Glorifying their first-division finishing teams, maybe Western Pennsylvania Interscholastic Athletic League Class I Championships. Trophies tarnishing in the back corners of cases in high school corridors. They had the names of the starting seniors of half a dozen of this year's teams on their tongue tips. Couldn't put the trappings of adolescence behind them. The *splack* of pad-on-pad echoed in their heads down the hallways of years. Besides football they didn't know very much. They had failed to grow. They took solace in the Steelers and booze, kept their women down, and nourished their ill-understood resentments as though they were hothouse plants. Socially they were slobs. Politically they were just to the right of stupid.

A word from Nevick and all three joined him at trying to stare me down. "There's my friend Nevick with his compadres at the bar," I said to Charity.

"He looks like an angry cowpoke whose pony got run off by Paiutes."

"With three left defensive tackles in search of a blitz. After the other night I've got this *real* strong feeling his head is put together like a house of cards. One good *poof* and . . ."

"I hope you're on better behavior yourself, Mr. Glass House."

"I am. Have to be. Only have one ear to go."

"You better stick to that. He wants words."

At least his pals were staying behind. I didn't want trouble. Two-time losers with the bouncers didn't get back in the Imperial Court. Nevick plodded as he came. He put one foot carefully ahead of the other as though they both belonged to somebody else. He eyed me this way and that. He stood so close I could see, even in the imperfect light, his dilated pupils.

"You, reporter, narc, whatever you are."

I tensed. Damned if I was going to have my other ear pierced. "Me?"

"I don't give a flying fart what you think of me, get it?" Nevick said. "But you gotta know Nick Markov was a class kid. A saint."

"If you say so," I said.

"Everybody loved him. *I* loved him. I tried to help him." Nevick leaned over. His dilated eyes were brimming. "He was good—*great* on the alleys. He coulda been on *Pro Bowlers' Tour!*"

"Maybe he would have been, if you hadn't turned him onto dope," I said.

Nevick began to cry. He stood blubbering and sputtering. "I wouldn't have hurt him. I loved him. *I loved him!*" Tears dribbled down his beefy cheeks. He turned and right-foot-left-footed it back to his cronies. Then past them and into the crowd waiting for tables. A burst of laughter from the audience turned my head toward Betty Ellen on stage. When I looked back, Nevick was gone. Another mad, melancholy Russian.

A guy about twenty-eight wearing an elegant handlebar moustache turned to me. "Don't you be too hard on Ray, fella. I got to tell you the kid meant a hell of a lot to him. You think he was bad just then? Shee-it. Couple years back he was such a head you wouldna believed. He did uppers, downers, speed, LSD, angel dust and smack once in a while."

"You're saying he's Mr. Clean compared to what he was."

"You got it, chief. Like in the flicks, the kid, Nicholas, gave him something to believe in. Straightened him out for a couple years. Pulled him together. Then I guess you heard about what happened to the kid?"

"The Dixon thing. The scramola."

"Yeah. Well it hit Ray real hard. Like it was his own son that let him down. Now he's starting to slip back down again." Moustache shook his head. "His liver, his *brain* can't last if he's doing the kind of shit he was."

"They say he deals. Is hooked up with the mob."

"He deals. He had the kid dealing, too. People know that, but they mostly sit on it. Because they're both Russky." Moustache lowered his voice. "Russky don't cut no ice with me either way. My name's Ticky Green. That ain't Russky, dig. Irish. *Sen*sible people. The kid had some fancy idea about what dope could do. Maybe Ray shoulda slapped him upside the head and told him to get bowling. Instead he got him different kinds of shit. And pretty soon the kid was turning on his friends."

"Where you think the kid is now?"

Ticky Green grinned mirthlessly down into his glass of Sombrero. "At the bottom of the Mon. Wearing cement shoes."

"How do you square that with Nevick wanting to do the best for the kid?" Charity said. "Being his main man?"

"Lady, that's the way life is. You start out every morning walking toward the sunrise. Then after twenty years you find out you've been traveling west all along!"

"You sure you don't have some Russian blood?" I said.

Ticky Green snorted. "No way, man. I've lived too long around the Slope to *want* any."

I felt my face color. I was about to ask Ticky Green to

account for those words. He turned back to his Sombrero before I had a chance to make a fool of myself again.

Charity studied my face. "What is *wrong* with you? You look ready to pick another fight."

"Forget it, OK? Keep your mouth shut. You're not my wife, remember?"

"Oh, now come *on*, Yuri. Pick a fight with *me*? You, the lover of peace and harmony. The Libra in the crowd."

"Just shut up. All right?"

"What's with you, sourpuss?"

I had to clutch the sides of my chair to keep from slapping her quiet. Slap Charity! I leaned back and closed my eyes. A wave of laughter from one of Betty Ellen's lines broke over the Imperial Court. I cooled some. "Who knows what's wrong? I feel an onset of the Sickness Unto Death. A fever caused by too much human condition. I need a couple weeks on the sand at Cancun. Alone. I can't hook my head into this goddamn Russian kid. This saint-sinner who everybody loved. Who killed a guy over a drug deal. I can't get used to people who want the best of Russian Slope in the paper. Then they go ahead and turn over another rock and something else ugly squirms out of the Slavic soul. I don't like tyrannical husbands, young women who lose their nerve and marry for the wrong reasons. Then turn around twenty years later with ruined lives. And right up on stage there's a woman from Yuri Nevsky's college years who wants to parlay nostalgia and a one-night stand into an ominously long-lasting relationship—complete with ring and bless-this-mess wall plaques."

"Listen to *you*," Charity said.

"P.Q. Antonelli, a bright woman who should know better, is still in love with Nicholas Markov. And knows something important she won't tell me. Even though it might help us find him." I closed my eyes and sighed. "What's wrong with me?"

"If I had to guess I'd say you're afflicted with a serious roots disease. Sort of like a houseplant. You've been so busy growing, like one of those horse chestnuts in front of 138, that you haven't thought about where you've come from. Historically. Genetically."

"All these Russians with their strong sense of community. Charity, I don't belong here."

"That's not what I said. It's questions of *roots* that're eating at you. Not geography. Not language. Remember what Volodya said: it's *blood* that counts."

78

"All this ethnic stuff is crap!" Charity was annoying me. "My father was as much an Imperial Russian as Igor. His family had summer and winter estates. Gardeners. Tutors. All that. I wasn't raised the way Mikhail was. The way Nicholas was. With all that Cyrillic, Byzantine world jammed down my throat. I don't belong with these people."

"Don't be so sure."

"I'm an *American*. Not a Russian."

Charity giggled. I wanted to throttle her. "You *are* Russian, Yuri Nevsky. Don't you know that? Can't you see it in yourself? *I* can. And I'm hardly an authority on the Russian soul. I'll give you one fast example. Remember what you told me about the love affair you had when your marriage was breaking up? One of those hotel/motel relationships?"

"I remember. A lovely lady. Her husband didn't understand her. Went to bed eight thirty at night and to work at six."

"And what did you do? Besides the expected, I mean? Remember? You told me you read the Gideon Bible to her."

"Ecclesiastes. A very special book. My favorite. Attributed to Solomon."

"Now *that* is being a Russian, you nit. Screwing *and* Bible reading. *Together*." Charity giggled wildly and clapped her hands.

I couldn't help grinning, but I didn't feel any better. "All the people on the Slope seem to have a *place* they belong. Friends, family, someone. Even Nevick hangs out where he wants."

"And you started comparing yourself with them."

"Sure. Natural thing to do. And it's started me thinking about Pittsburgh, growing up here." I gestured broadly, taking in Betty Ellen, Russian Slope and Greater Pittsburgh with a twitch of the forearm. "There's a lot of memories floating around this town for me, Charity."

"I think you're in the middle of reckoning up accounts, Yuri. The debits and credits of your life."

"Charity, I think I'm in the red."

"Nonsense!" She aimed her cool gaze on me. That level WASP look. No nonsense. Abrim with rational. "You're going through a hard time. Divorce, new career, loneliness. It hurts, but it's all normal. I've tasted a little of it myself lately."

"I've always known life doesn't disclose its meaning easily,

Charity," I said. "But this is ridiculous. Nothing makes any sense. And on top of that there's all this *Russianness* around."

"And the question of where you fit into it."

I opened my mouth for a reflexive protest. And closed it. At that moment I realized she was right. Where *did* I fit into my heritage? Into that genetic pool of the twenty-eight generations of Russians my father had pinned down like specimens on his genealogy chart. From 1410 to now. Me and the Markovs. No, my ancestors couldn't buy me even one cup of coffee without coin. But they meant . . . something. I mumbled vague agreement and signaled for the check. I wanted to get out of the Imperial Court before Betty Ellen finished her act. And we had a destination. Tonight Volodya Tschersky was holding his big bash. I scribbled a kind note for the entertainer and practically dragged Charity out of the place.

In the parking lot, though, I found myself drifting over to the edge of the bluff. To the typical Pittsburgh view—bridges, rivers, hills and mercury-vapor streetlights. I felt Charity at my side.

"Something else about you before we pack in the Where-Is-Yuri-Nevsky-in-Life Seminar . . ." I felt her hand rest on my shoulder. The encouraging touch of a good friend. "The things you've told me about your marriage, the bad way the last couple years have gone for you with relationships. Your wife's gone. Your kids are miles away. Your mother just died. You're emotionally isolated. Starved. You need some emotional nourishment."

That was Charity. Ms. Rational. Ms. Controlled. Ms. Right Again! I looked out across the Mon. Cars like bright-eyed bugs moved along unseen roads. "Pills. I'll take pills," I said. "Emotional supplements. One-a-days."

"I'm not sure that'll do it."

"What do you have in mind, doctor?"

"Some kind of emotional commitment."

"Volunteer work? Computer-match dating service?"

"Something like that."

"Adopt a child."

"Well . . . you could overdo it." She strolled away a few steps. On heels, shadowed face, hands warming in opposite coatsleeves, she could pass as an oracle. "It's time for a big change for you, Yuri. A hard time. But you're *alive*. You're not a guy holed up in himself. One of the ones who's so sure of himself that he's terrified to be uncertain. You know you're not always right. You know your acts are sometimes off-base. You have the capacity to retool. I don't want to reduce your situation to a couple of platitudes, fella. I think too much of you for that. But two apply to you now, and where you're going. *No growth without pain.* And *no gain without risk.*"

"Well, I'm hurting. I seem to be questioning everything about myself."

"How healthy!"

"Charity, come on!"

"I'm serious. You're showing the signs of a living, viable personality. You're coping with change. You're in the middle of working through some heavy shifts in the essential Yuri Nevsky."

"Pollyanna."

"Enough! Counseling session is *over*. Time to get going to Volodya's party. All those passionate, intense Russian men just *waiting* to charm little old me, the lady attorney."

"Christ!"

"I know it's a big party. But I don't think He'll be there."

9

Surely I was going to die. No one could feel this bad and live—even five minutes, never mind years. I stared over my coffee cup at a pair of blue eyes so bloodshot it would have been easier to count the white spaces than the red threads.

"Ten minutes have passed," Charity said. "I'm going to move my head again."

"I always had you figured for gutsy," I said.

"This is the *worst* hangover of my life. A whale. All that came before were minnows." She dropped an Alka-Seltzer—her third— into a glass of water.

"Goddamn Russians and their vodka toasts!" My throat was drier than a Maine man's wit. And tasted of—was it asphalt?

"And we got there late. Volodya and half of Russian Slope had started a couple hours before." Charity made a face—carefully.

"Oh, how *could* they?"

"What didn't we toast?"

"I remember five toasts just to Mother Russia."

"I tried to keep up with them," I said. "My competitive spirit was aroused."

"They kept toasting you," Charity said. "I had to drink to that."

"And to your beauty. How could I say no?"

Like a horse to a cruel master, my memory resisted returning to last night. "Anything happen useful to what we're about?" I said. "Nicholas Markov, I think his name is."

"You realize I only remember up to a point," Charity said. "After that I remember very little."

"You were the belle of the ball. You had a panting coterie up to when *I* stopped remembering."

"I remember women having words over you. Your entertainer friend from the past . . ."

"Betty Ellen."

82

"Uh huh. And a handsome woman with dark hair. Always had a cigarette in her hand."

"Elena Markov. Nicholas's mother. What a charmer I am!"

"The two of them hung around you waiting for each other to leave. And there was another woman who kept trying to get you off alone. Fat chance. Youngish. Tall, hair piled up."

"Oh, God. P.Q. Antonelli. Anya's and Nicholas's friend. The woman I told you was still in love with him. Who's holding out information. *I* invited her." I frowned with what felt like someone else's face. "I talk to her?"

"Not hardly at all, from what I noticed. And never alone. Your friend Betty Ellen wasn't happy either. You wouldn't get rid of Elena. So she stalked off and out. Then a rather unsmiling fellow came up and jerked Elena away. So tactless it could only have been her husband."

"The one-and-only Mikhail."

"One thing's for sure. We're well known to just about everybody on the Slope. Volodya introduced us all around."

I held my head. "They kept saying that only after you get completely drunk with someone are you truly friends."

"Friends we have, then, Yuri. Friends we have."

I called a faculty member I knew at Pitt and talked him into a game of squash. Charity and I had planned to talk to Father Alexander that afternoon. But I couldn't face a five-year-old the way I felt. I needed Sunday to recover. Chasing a black ball around a white windowless room was part of the price I knew I had to pay to become a human being again. For the first five minutes I had trouble focusing on the ball, and even more going after it. Later my agony subsided to mere pain. A hot shower, a massage and a quart of orange juice put me on the road to recovery.

The next morning I nosed my Datsun up the steep streets of the Slope toward the gleaming onion turrets of St. Basil's. I pulled into the wide parking lot, where Charity and I got out. Father Alexander lived in the split-level, brown wood-and-brick home built hard by the church. A wide strip of grass grew between the two buildings.

I knocked at the door on which hung a wrought-iron Slavic cross. A woman eased open the heavy oak. Her hands were white. Flour. Her fingers were long and delicate. It was with a tiny burst of anticipation that I raised my eyes to her face.

She had dark hair, deep black eyes with the slightest Oriental tilt, a delicate nose, arching nostrils and a full, inviting mouth.

A face so truly Russian that I spoke the language to her without thought, saying who we were, what we wanted.

She smiled and opened the door wide. "I'm really quite fluent in English, too, Mr. Nevsky." She offered us her hand to shake, forgetting about the flour. "I'm Tatiana Tamanov. I'm Father Alexander's housekeeper. Come in, please. She led us into the dim interior. She had good legs and a nice in-and-out flare at the hips. I guessed her to be in her early thirties. I was altogether impressed.

She said Father Alexander had someone with him. Would we like to join her in the kitchen for tea? The kitchen was spacious and only slightly untidy. In its air hung a familiar odor that greeted me like a long-lost friend. The rich, yeasty smell of blini batter. Blini, the small raised pancakes that long ago we used to gobble down with sour cream and smoked fish around the lenten season.

A samovar had been set up in a corner of the kitchen. No doubt to provide refreshment to the steady flow of socializers, penitents and the pious. Tatiana washed her hands and served the tea Russian-style, in clear glass with lemon slices.

"Are you finding Russian Slope interesting?" she said.

"I am," Charity said. "I'm not a Pittsburgher. It's all new to me."

"And you, Mr. Nevsky?" Her dark eyes were flecked with gold.

"Yuri Vladimirovich, please."

She nodded. Her gaze appraised me lightly.

"Born and bred in Pittsburgh," I said. "And I've been on the Slope before. But we've got a bit of local history caught in our craws that won't come up or go down. Until it does I don't really think we're going to make much progress with our article. It's the Dixon shooting. And Nicholas Markov's involvement." That wasn't too far from the truth, but I didn't like lying to this lovely lady.

Tatiana nodded grimly. "If you've been around town any time at all you must know Father Alexander invested a lot of time and care in the boy. He told me Nicholas was his Major Reclamation Project for his first two years here at St. Basil's."

I nodded. "How did he take Nicholas's disappearance?"

"At first not bad. He was sure the boy would give himself up or be found. Something. And—somehow explain that he didn't murder Dixon." Tatiana sipped her tea. "Then six, seven weeks ago I guess it dawned on him that Nicholas wasn't going to come back and might never be found. He had a couple of really gloomy days." She lowered her voice. "I'm not sure he's over it yet. Just the opposite, maybe."

"I'm sorry," Charity said. "He's done so much good, from what I've heard."

"And Easter's coming up in a few weeks. The holiest season of the Orthodox year. It's really the busiest time for St. Basil's," Tatiana said. "There are enough strains and responsibilities for him as it is, without Nicholas Markov still weighing him down."

Tatiana told us Father Alexander ought to be free in a minute or two. We ought to get out to his study before somebody walked in and aced us out.

Father Alexander had the ideal voice for an Orthodox priest. I remembered Trackman Tolovitch saying it was a voice to chase the Devil. I heard its barrellike rumble as he opened his study door. ". . . so then Ms. Antonelli's tiny bit of information, I think, is better kept to herself. Do what you can, Anya Petrovna, to convince her—"

Anya Rok came out of the study first. Behind her Father Alexander loomed up, a bear in black, brown and gray. Anya introduced us. He bowed to Charity. He took my hand in both his. His grip was firm, but not punishing. His beard was brown wires shot through with gray, like mine. Unlike mine it bristled and spread as far out as his ears and down to his black vest. Above the beard burned gray eyes. The intensity of their light, its purity, was that of the committed believer. A formidable man. Physically, certainly, but emotionally and spiritually, too. Yes, priest and Nicholas's starets in one man.

Anya cast an odd—was it frightened?—look at me. She wasn't the Ice Queen as she pushed by on her way to the door. She was flushed and nervous.

Father Alexander's study was surprisingly Spartan. I had expected book-lined walls, but the yards of shelves were largely empty. A half-dozen missals, prayerbooks and Gospels lay about on the desk and tables. Two bottom shelves of the enormous central bookcase were filled with old books, their leather bindings yellowed and gone powdery.

Lying on the floor or propped against the walls were at least a dozen wind instruments. Saxes, clarinets, flutes, basset horns, pennywhistles—even an oboe—gave the study the look of a conservatory practice room.

In the customary corner of the room on a low table stood

Father Alexander's personal ikons. No mistaking their antiquity. Their wood had mellowed with age. Their paint had dulled and faded. Yes, prayers enshrined in painted wood that sang of Old Russia. Christ and the Theotokos—His Mother. I was stunned by the sternness of their expressions, the almost repellent savagery of the pictured piety. Father Alexander's God knew we were all sinners, that life was short and that we would be judged.

Even so, sinner that I was, I kept lying. I told Father Alexander that Charity and I had been fascinated by Nicholas Markov and were gradually abandoning our plan to do an article on the Slope. Instead we thought we might do one on Nicholas. The priest paced the study as Charity and I filled him in on the general impression we had gleaned of the young man. We finished up by saying that in the last months before Nicholas disappeared, Father Alexander seemed to have known him better than anyone else. Through it all the big man placed one black shoe before the other, a lurching, hairy bear. Then he turned and faced us, gray eyes burning. "No!" he said. His expression softened. "By 'no' I mean I can't help you if it means an article about Nicholas Mikhailovich." His accent was thick, like those of my father's friends at long-gone Sunday afternoon gatherings.

"Might I ask why not, Father Alexander?" Charity said.

"I don't want attention put on his . . . situation. Whatever it is, still more publicity I believe would hurt him."

Tatiana came in with tea. China, silver, linen napkins. She took care. Nice thing in a woman.

"What do you think his situation is?" I said.

"Difficult. Maybe unfortunate."

"Could you be more specific?"

"I am guessing. I do not know. I think he killed the black man. I think he ran away. I think he is in another city. All guesses." He shook his craggy head. Lines of sorrow and pain gripped his ruddy face. In Russian he said, "God is cruel to his servants. Tests and defeats come in armies to try our souls."

"You're saying you don't want him to face justice," Charity said.

"Justice! Whose justice?" he bellowed. His deep voice boomed like a cannon in the small room. His pale eyes flashed. "Who will pay for the injustice of a life of the greatest potential gone wrong? Answer that!"

Tatiana's soft Russian: "Don't excite yourself again, dear Father. You've said you must accept God's will."

He grunted, nodded, sat and sipped his tea. Tatiana closed the door quietly behind her. The priest looked at Charity and me in turn. "Forgive my crying out. I lament the loss and waste when such a man as Nicholas Mikhailovich is dealt with so harshly by fate. I lament so much of my work is lost. That his growing and maturing should be swept away by one unfortunate act. So much of a future of the greatest value to—" He broke off with an angry gesture of disgust. "Yuri Vladimirovich, let me have your word as a Russian that there will be no articles on Nicholas Mikhailovich Markov. Ms. Day, the same promise from you. Go back to your original purpose—a story about this community. Then I will tell you what I know of him. For you it can be unwritten background."

We both nodded. Giving away a straw man was easy.

Father Alexander eased his big body back in his desk chair, cup on saucer resting in his lap. "I first met Nicholas shortly after I came to St. Basil's. I met him at a gathering of youth I had arranged. I must tell you the state he was in. He was on a—what is the youths' word?—'bummer.' Yes, his whole life was a bummer. He was closed in on himself. Full of dreams. Passive. Beaten. On the edge of a fall into fatal addiction to the most dangerous drugs. Yet, yet . . ." The priest's face opened into a wide smile. Almost beatific in its radiance. ". . . I knew *there* was a young man with the spirit, the soul of *ten* ordinary men. I knew that he was a leader. Even then I hoped he might one day become a spiritual leader."

"A priest?" I said. "An orthodox priest?"

"Possibly. Or to lead pious men in other ways. So I made his acquaintance, began to talk with him."

"How'd you get his confidence?" Charity said.

"He had great interest in the philosophical, in the spiritual, in tradition. As I do. From his grandfather, the unfortunate Igor Gregorevich, he had learned to love Old Russia. Imperial Russia. *Mother* Russia." Again the glorious smile. "Our country. Which cannot ever really change. Whose people are eternal. Whose ways—no matter the trappings of the moment—never change."

"You said Igor was unfortunate," Charity said. "Why? You two didn't get along, I understand."

The priest cocked an eyebrow. "You know this? How?"

"Elena Markov told me you two fought," I said.

87

"The disputes of two old men firmly set in their ways. Healthy disputes. It was my wish to return him to the church of his fathers and forefathers. It was his wish not to do this."

"But you allowed him to be buried through the Church," I said.

"Christ Our Lord urged us to forgive. Urged us to compassion."

"One other thing about you and Igor Gregorevich, Father. I understand you fought as well over his broken promise."

His bushy brows shot up in surprise. "Who said this?"

"Sasha Markov."

The priest chuckled. "The boy does not know Russian well. He misunderstood. The promise broken was that made with his baptism—to live a life as an Orthodox Christian."

"I see." Or did I?

Father Alexander finished his tea with a hearty *slurp* and put cup and saucer on the desk. "Igor Gregorevich went so far as to tell young Nicholas not to talk to me. Not to allow me to counsel him."

"I'm sorry. That must have made it hard for you," Charity said.

"I made it clear to the boy that his soul was crying out for help. That I would give it, if he chose. The decision to meet with me was his. I was also able to make Nicholas Mikhailovich aware of his special ways. His power to command others to follow him."

"That was real, then?" Charity said. "People have told us about that."

"I assure you, Ms. Day, he was a leader—even a *savior* of men. The future before him was"—the smile!—"glorious."

Tatiana knocked and entered with round butter cookies rolled in powdered sugar. Tea balls. Fixtures of my youth. Stirred up memories of covies of Russians in their summer cottages in Murraysville outside of Pittsburgh. Yuri the child gobbled tea balls by the dozen while the July breeze stirred old maples and the sun blazed like a kept promise.

I found my eyes on the back of Tatiana's head. She wore her black hair up in a braided bun held in place with a silver comb. She turned suddenly and our eyes met. A thrill of desire and embarrassment quivered through my chest. Spots of color rose in her cheeks as she hurried out.

Father Alexander went on: "So I began to invest much time in Nicholas Mikhailovich. I drew him out. I helped him to grow stronger. I stood by his confession. I heard his fear and hate of his father, his love of his grandfather. I grew fond of him. I, who have never married, came to think of him as my son—in spirit. My hopes for him grew. And he grew, too, as a person. Grew stronger. Even so, he refused to take my advice about the drugs."

"You couldn't get *any*where?" Charity was leaning forward in her chair. She was fascinated with Father Alexander's raw personality. Her forgotten tea cooled on a corner of the desk.

"Not at first. He grasped onto them so tightly. To those who sold them to him."

I promised myself to spit in Ray Nevick's face.

"I saw that only when Nicholas grew stronger still would he throw the drugs back to the Devil where they belong. And slowly that day came close. I gave him more and more moral instruction—"

"And you told Anya Rok not to distract him," I said.

The priest flashed me a sharp glance of annoyance. "It was an important point in Nicholas's life! His whole future hung in the balance." His voice was rising. "It was not fit that a woman intrude. That he be turned aside from the future. Do you *criticize* me?"

"I was only commenting—"

"I do not need such comments!" Father Alexander heaved to his feet. His thigh brushed the china cup and saucer. They clattered to the uncarpeted floor and flew to pieces. "What does your newspaper matter beside such a grand soul as Nicholas Mikhailovich Markov?" The shouted question was thrown in my face like a gauntlet.

"I don't see him as grand," I said stubbornly. "He was a drug pusher and probably a murderer."

"He had finally renounced the drugs!" Father Alexander shouted. "That man Dixon, he was the last buyer. Nicholas *swore* to me that he was through. A commitment had already been made. Money paid. I begged him not to keep that appointment. He insisted. 'A loose end,' he said. He was, in fact, through. Through! Do you hear me, Yuri Vladimirovich? *Do you hear me?*" Flecks of spit darted white from his lips.

"I hear. Explain away the murder, then, while you're at it."

"An accident. A cruel joke of fate. A joke so cruel you cannot imagine!"

The study door opened and Tatiana rushed in. She held a wet cloth and a glass of water. She spoke Russian: "You mustn't

89

excite yourself again, Holy One." She put her white hands on his black shoulders and guided his bulk back into the chair. The wet cloth went on his forehead. She snapped at me: "You shouldn't excite him!"

"I'm sorry. I said what I thought, that's all."

"Maybe you should watch your tongue." From the desk drawer she pulled a pill bottle. She wrestled off the childproof cap and slid the capsule into the priest's panting mouth. She held the glass to his lips. Her eyes were on me. "Better yet— maybe you should *leave*."

"No, no, Tatya. It was I who lost control—again." The red of rage drained slowly from the priest's face. Tatiana adjusted the wet cloth. The hot light in his eyes cooled.

"Maybe we should leave," Charity said.

"No, but—please—no more about Nicholas Mikhailovich." Father Alexander gestured for Tatiana to refill our cups. She did his bidding. She scooped up the shards of broken cup and set out a new one. She removed the cloth from his forehead. Her eyes found Charity, then me, with looks of accusation. She slammed the door behind her.

The priest smiled. "She mothers and protects me. Such a jewel!"

Charity nosed in her notebook. "Father Alexander, there's someone else we could talk about. And something else that happened the same night Nicholas disappeared. Would you mind if we wrote about Olga Samnesovich? And about the stolen cross?"

The priest nodded. He drew a deep breath. "Here is at last an easy matter: Olga stole the cross that night. A separate matter from the other."

"You don't think she and Nicholas ran off together?" I said.

Father Alexander chuckled. "No, no. A separate matter. A separate matter altogether." He waved our budding questions away. "For many *months* Olga planned to leave home. To leave her scum of a father, Lev Alexandrovich. Whenever she put a little money aside from her small pay as a maid, he would beat her and take it away. I knew these things because she brought them to her confession." His heavy face turned down in regret. "Having no mother—she ran off—and a pig of a father, Olga herself did not grow to be a whole young woman. She was very limited. She hated herself."

"She did spend time with Nicholas," I said.

He shrugged. "True, true. She worshipped him, followed

90

him like a faithful dog. I warned her that this was senseless, purposeless. She failed to listen. To him she meant nothing. Of course he treated her with respect..."

"Why are you so sure she stole the cross? And alone?"

"She came to me alone that evening around nine o'clock. Nicholas was not mentioned. She said she had decided to leave home. No matter that she had little money. She begged me for money. For me it was a hard decision. In the end I saw that she would not survive at home. She had to get away. I offered her what cash I had here. She took it and asked for more. I had no more. She screamed and shouted. Abused me. Then she left. It was about nine fifteen."

"How was she traveling?" I said. "Bus, car, dogsled?"

Father Alexander shrugged. "She didn't say. I failed to ask her. In any case, about a half an hour later, the church's safety alarm rang. I hurried over. A window had been smashed, a door opened. In time I found the broken case and the cross missing."

"Could you say something about the cross? We don't know much about it," Charity said.

"Very old. Of Russian origin. From where in the Motherland, who knows? It was given to St. Basil's in the nineteen-twenties by an anonymous donor who brought it from the Motherland. You couldn't put a price to it these days. So much gold!"

"You think Olga could sell it?" I said.

"Not whole. But to cut a piece off such soft gold would be easy."

I winced. "Do you have a picture of it? I'd like to know what it looks like."

"Such a picture was in your paper, the *Post-Gazette*. With a small article about the misfortune."

"I was out of state, on assignment, when it was stolen."

"The cross is a sore point with me, Yuri Vladimirovich. Its insurance had lapsed. I failed to renew it."

"I'm sorry, but I'd like a look at the photo anyway."

"You are persistent. As though you think I have something to hide." I saw the light brighten in his eyes. Another fit of anger bubbled just below the surface.

"I only want information," I said.

The priest rose slowly and opened his desk drawer. He turned to me with a photo in hand. His eyes burned. "I smell deceit in you, Yuri Vladimirovich. I smell some of the rot that oozes from this hillside." He walked toward me. For the first time he seemed menacing. *"Da,* rot. Against which I have fought—"

"We've *heard* of your good work with everyone." Charity sensed the rising tension. "And how well everyone thinks of you."

"The Devil is busy here in this town, this city, this America. Everywhere I see spirit and good in retreat."

"No more than anywhere else in the world," I said. "A little *less* than in a lot of places." It would be easier to agree with him. But I have this stubborn side.

"The young are not the only ones afflicted by the rot," Father Alexander said. "The adults, too, are steeped in vice and error." He gave me the photo. "Their behaviors are shameless. And I cannot exclude you both."

"What's that mean?"

"That I visited the gathering at the home of Volodya Tschersky Saturday night. I saw you both in the grip of drunkenness and lust."

"Oh." Charity's face reddened.

That primal guilt that lives deep in the heart of even the best of us thrust its nasty head out of its cave. I blushed and looked away, even as my rationality rushed forward with explanations.

"So badly was I taken with the weak, undisciplined souls of what you call Russian Slope that I began to surrender. Seven weeks ago I lost heart. I felt alone, isolated, defeated. I bought an airplane ticket to Europe."

"But you didn't leave," I said.

"I was prepared to. Only Tatiana stood between me and my own shaming. Blessed woman, she argued with me. Persuaded me, over a week, not to desert my spiritual charges." He turned his hot eyes onto my face. "No matter how much rot I saw among them."

"She must be quite a woman—to stand up to you," Charity said.

"She is. Sent by God to aid His poor servant." He smiled and sat down again.

I slid the photo into my notebook, then thumbed to the page I wanted. "Father Alexander, what do you know about a group called . . . the Holy Order of the Caucasus?"

The priest's face turned stony. "I'm surprised you even know of it," he said. "Even I who was raised in the Caucasus have heard little. And that mostly hearsay. Now of course that order is no more."

"Oh?"

"The revolution. All such splinter sects were burned away. The Church was an enemy of the state. The small eccentric sects were without protection of the great Church—itself in the gravest danger. So they were easy victims to misguided revolutionary zeal."

"What was the order?"

"A small, close-knit group of holy men who lived in a remote valley in the Caucasus Mountains. And had for many years." Father Alexander shrugged; that was the extent of his knowledge. "Do you mind if I ask where you even *heard* of it?"

"Some scribbles left by Igor Gregorevich."

"That one!" The priest's face twisted into a scowl. With his great beard he looked like a vengeful patriarch. "What abuse did he heap on that trivial order? Hater of holy things that he was."

"Nothing, really. Just a few words scribbled on a piece of paper. By the way, he was a good grandfather, whatever else he was." My repressed annoyance was surfacing fast. "He loved Russia and its old ways. He was a strong man, and as far as I can tell, a good one."

"He was a coward! A breaker of promises!"

"What promises? You said there were none."

"They concerned matters of the Church, as I said. Igor Gregorevich agreed with nothing that came from me."

"So he didn't like you. Maybe he had good taste. It's hard to like somebody who finds fault on all sides. Who takes basically OK people and says they're rotten."

"What do *you* know of discipline and obligation?" Father Alexander heaved himself out of his chair.

"Maybe not much. What I do know is that you have to love people before you can help them. Whether you're a nurse—or a priest."

"You insult me!"

"Yuri, stop it!" Charity jumped up and stood between us. She looked angrily at me. "You are no help at all."

I exchanged glances with Father Alexander. "Priest or not, he gets under my skin."

"Then go out into the hall and *I'll* finish talking to him."

She put her hands on my chest and shoved me none-too-gently toward the door. I went out and closed it behind me. I put my back to it and felt my face. Cold sweat stood out on my forehead.

10

The house was very still. Cooling, I wandered the first floor. I heard whispers from the airy parlor. Tatiana was kneeling before her own ikons. Christ and Theotokos shone radiant and compassionate. She crossed herself. Now I heard her words. The much-used prayer: "'O Lord, Jesus Christ, Son of God, have mercy on me, a sinner. O Lord, Jesus Christ, Son of God...'" The same one Nicholas had written in his letter from New York. That Trackman Tolovitch had used at lunch.

Private moment. I turned around to leave. A floor board imported from a haunted house creaked like the voice of a lost soul. Tatiana's head turned and she saw me.

"Sorry to disturb you," I said.

"That's all right. I'm finished." She rose quickly and blessed herself.

I explained why I was wandering. She nodded and said we should go out and walk on the church grounds. We went out.

"I think I might have misled you earlier." She held up a white hand to shade her gold-flecked Oriental eyes from the afternoon sun. "You asked how Father Alexander had taken Nicholas's disappearance. I told you the last six weeks had been tough and he wasn't over it yet. Really, he's been *more* upset, rather than less. He's not in any way getting over it. Just wishful thinking on my part."

A circular cement walk led us around the ornate, round church. We ambled slowly, in step. "You've missed seeing the best of him, Yuri. Up to the time Dixon got killed he was all over the Slope. An active, involved priest. The youth groups, the pastoral visits. The concern for the community. There just couldn't have been a better shepherd for our flock. Now the youth group is the only one he really keeps up..." She shook her head and sighed. I put my arm lightly across her shoulders. "...he's become critical—even cynical. And his temper! Whew!"

"I saw. I heard. I almost felt."

"I made him go to Dr. Petrarsky. He prescribed those strong tranquilizers I gave him. Still, little things that wouldn't have bothered him a while back get under his skin now." She looked up at me. "You really shouldn't have dug at him the way you said you did."

"It was his down view of people."

"When I was in the study you made me mad doing that. You didn't know how good he had been," Tatiana said.

"You hid your anger well."

"I thought . . . uncharitable thoughts about you. And . . . other thoughts as well." Her black eyes mirrored that ambiguity patented by Eve at the dawn of mankind. "That's why I had a small chat with God." Her right hand curved around my back and rested lightly on my hip. "Now I'm not sure I should talk to you. I have a feeling you're somehow against Father Alexander. Maybe even against me."

"I'm not. I swear it. I'll tell you the truth about me and Charity. Listen." I looked closely at her face. "I want you to know me. Know what I am. I'm not a reporter. I'm an information specialist."

"What's that?"

"People want to know. I find out for them."

"You find things?"

"I don't deal in hard goods or people. For me it's: how, where, when, why. After I do my work I get paid. Then I step back. Others take over. Can you guess what I'm trying to find out?"

We walked four in-step strides. "What happened to Nicholas?"

"Where he is. Same thing."

"Why? Who's paying you?"

"Nick's grandmother."

"Ludmilla? She doesn't have anything."

"She has small money in the bank. And she's going to clean for Charity and me twice a week."

Tatiana grinned. It was a bright, vital grin. "You softie!"

"I've been all over the Slope. I've been finding out things left and right. Most of them about Nicholas. Some of them about myself. But none answer any of the big questions about him. Bits and pieces are all I've got. I was hoping Father Alexander could put it all together."

Tatiana skipped out from under my arm and turned toward a stone bench. I saw how long her neck was, and how long

96

her hair must be, braided and piled as it was. Dress her in the clothing of the 1800s and she would look a fixture on a summer estate outside St. Petersburg—or a heroine of Count Tolstoi.

"So when your tact fails, your lover takes over the questioning."

"Charity's not my lover." I explained our relationship.

Tatiana frowned from the depth of her womanhood. "Platonic friendships don't work."

"This one does."

"Yuri, you're coming on like some kind of Robin Hood. Working for little old ladies for next to nothing. You must steal from the rich or something."

"Volodya's offered ten grand for the recovery of the stolen cross. Maybe I'll find out where it is."

"Come into the church. I'll show you where it was."

She led me around toward a rear door. She pointed to a ground-level window. "New glass in that. Whoever stole the cross broke it and got in that way." She unlocked a side door and led me in. The church was cool but its air was alive with the sweetness of old incense. I had been inside an Orthodox church only once. When I was ten and an aunt, who knew nothing of my father's aversion to religion, took me to a service. I remember standing and standing. And everyone walking around.

She led me behind the altar to an old empty glass case once used for display and storage. The case top was a hinged metal framework into which four glass panels fit. One panel was smashed. She told me only the cross had been taken. The remaining valuables had been transferred for safe keeping. The cross had been in there a long time. I could see its outline on the cloth lining the case bottom. Two cross pieces and a hole at the top.

I asked her if she had been in the house the night Nicholas disappeared. She had been. For months Nicholas had regular meeting times scheduled Mondays and Wednesdays, seven in the evening. The sessions lasted an hour. The study door was sometimes open. She didn't pry, but she knew most of the time was spent in religious instruction, Russian history and prayers.

Tatiana agreed that Father Alexander's virtual adoption of Nicholas had brought around a slow but dramatic change in the young man. The two had grown very close. She was surprised to hear them through the open door shouting at each other the Wednesday night of Dixon's murder. Nick had promised to meet a man named Nolan at the Eleven-to-Seven. The priest didn't want him to keep the appointment. That tallied—except for the name—with what Father Alexander and Chief Polsky had told me: Nick wrapping up his career as a dealer by a final delivery of some prepaid dope.

Finally things quieted down and Nick left about 7:45. About 8:10 Father Alexander told Tatiana he was still angry about what the boy was doing, so he was going for a short walk to calm his temper. She was sure he went walking, too, because she had taken a plastic bag of garbage to the cans in the garage. The priest's car was in its usual bay. By 8:45 Father Alexander was back in his study.

"What time did Olga Samnesovich arrive?" I said.

Tatiana's brow furrowed. "She didn't. I mean I didn't let her in."

"There another way she could get to Father Alexander?"

"Well, you saw the study. There're ground level windows..."

"She could have used them. Father Alexander said she was here that night."

"I'll ask him about it."

"Don't think you should." I led her out into the sunlight. "He'd know the question came from me."

"That's not the only reason."

I looked sharply into her almond eyes. "What's that supposed to mean, Tatiana?"

"That maybe he had something to do with Nicholas's disappearing."

I started to deny it. Then I saw I really couldn't rule out that possibility either. "I am *very* confused about everything. Got no reason to think Father A. was—or wasn't—mixed up in it. Unless Charity comes up with a pearl from him, that's not going to change. I'm starting to think Nicholas is alive and well in New York after all."

"What?"

"Chief Polsky got a letter from Nicholas two days after he scrammed."

"What did he say?"

"That he didn't do it."

"Sharp one, that cop. He was up here after Nick disappeared. Asked Father over and over about when he last saw Nicholas and where he was going. He asked about ten different ways. He asked for samples of his writing. Father was so patient.

Good thing he's not asking around *now*. Father would lose his temper in five minutes." She shook her head. "Poor, dear man."

"You take good care of him."

She nodded. "I do my best." We walked back around the church toward the house.

"Don't hit me, Tatiana, but you seem an awfully classy lady to be a servant."

She laughed and threw back her head, exposing her long white neck to my covetous eyes. "This really *isn't* my regular line of work. Spend a minute and I'll tell you all." She waved me toward the kitchen door. "Let's have some good old coffee. This Russian tea thing can get out of hand."

"OK. What *is* your regular line?"

"Foreign service." She glanced sidelong at me. "State Department."

"The D.C. scene. My God! I was there myself."

Tatiana put on the pot and told me about herself. She had been born right here on the Slope, not a quarter-mile from where we sat. She proved to be a focused and determined young girl. Doubly so after her father was killed when a crane malfunctioned in the tube works and her mother sank into depression and ill health. She won a scholarship to Pitt. Double major: Russian and international relations. On to Georgetown for additional foreign language training. A contact helped her land a translator's job in the State Department.

She plunged into Washington's work and social worlds. Shared an apartment in Georgetown with another State Department woman translator. She dated widely, spent time running with groups of bright young-and-hopefuls. For the first three years it was all new and challenging. The ambitions, goals and ways of thinking were very modern, very contemporary. Trendy. From time to time she began to pierce the mask of the life she led. First through heartbreaks. Men who, behind their sincere smiles and earnest repartee, played fast and loose with her trust. Then she began to scrutinize her work, saw herself exploited and cheapened in the name of some ill-defined service to democracy. Worse, she saw her values under steady assault, her religion, in the eyes of her peers, a quaint curiosity. At the end of her fifth year in Washington her mother died. She felt her spirit in disarray. She went to her priest. He suggested a solution in the grand Russian tradition—a length of time dwelling among the holy. A period of cleansing thought spent in an atmosphere largely free of distraction. Monasteries or convents were the frequent choice, for weekends, weeks, months or even longer.

Tatiana asked for a leave from her job and returned to Russian Slope, planning to go from there to a holy place of retreat. The arrival of Father Alexander coincidently allowed her to strike a bargain. She would serve as his housekeeper and largely confine herself to the house and church grounds. He would give her what religious instruction she wanted and would guide her confessions. She would have time to pray and center herself again. After two months at St. Basil's, she resigned from the State Department and sent a friend to retrieve her possessions.

"There're so many things about myself I don't know." Tatiana cleared away mugs and uneaten tea balls. "One I do know is that for a while, this is still where I belong. Close to my roots. With time to look over the past and plan the future."

She reached for the last spoon lying on the table. I stood up and gently took her wrist. Her bones were delicate but not fragile. She didn't pull away. Her black eyes searched my face. "Any previews being released on what your future plans might be?" I said.

She flashed her bright smile. "A major studio is still working on the final editing. The rushes have been above average, but not wholly impressive." The slender fingers of her free hand brushed unseen debris from my jacket lapels. "The *very* latest gossip says the female lead is thinking about more of a romantic angle . . ." She freed her wrist and spun away. I got a long look at her back. When she again turned to me, her smile had been frowned out. "On the other hand, that might complicate the film beyond salvage."

"If the leading lady is going to have a hand in the casting, I might just be between commitments," I said.

She made a nervous, brushing-away gesture. She was looking to change the subject. And did. "You know, the Nicholas business. What you've told me and all. I've been thinking . . . I guess I know the key to it all."

"Should I take you seriously?"

"Sure. The key is Olga Samnesovich."

"The same thought's occurred to me, but . . ."

We sat down. Tatiana nibbled the end of her index finger, then said, "I'm going to be judgmental, Yuri. That's not my usual style. But you have to understand that young lady was no good. The ladies of the church love a good gossip. I heard about her without half trying. She was a classic case of flat heels. I think about every third guy on the Slope—not excluding grandfathers and hairless striplings—got a taste."

"You exaggerate."

"But you get the idea." Tatiana chased table crumbs with the edge of her palm. "And she was very hostile. I think she hated men—except for Nicholas. He was her unattainable white knight. If I had Lev Samnesovich for a father I'd hate men, too."

"Heard a little about him. No chance of his being Chamber of Commerce Man of the Year."

"The best thing I can say about him is he's a good mechanic—when he's sober. The rest of the time he's an abusive, selfish, lecherous and probably dangerous little man. He used to beat his wife. Folks on the Slope used to tell her to leave him. She kept going back for more. And Lev was heard to say—with pride—that she liked being hit."

"Ugh!"

"Fyodora Petrovna went back once too often. She did finally leave him, though—too late. She fell down one day in the aisle at Jaschekoff's Discount. Brain hemorrhage. Her head had lots of 'soft spots,' thanks to Lev. She woke up once and Chief Polsky asked her to press charges. She wouldn't. Died three hours later on the operating table. After that, Olga started showing up with black eyes and bruises. People said she made jokes about them. She had never been a teetotaler, but after Fyodora died, she really went to the juice. Did drugs, too. Guess who I heard she got them from?"

"Nicholas."

Tatiana nodded. She adjusted her elaborate braids.

"I've been asking people about the two of them. The consensus is she wanted to and Nick didn't. Fits in with what you said."

"Sure. Point is, *there* was a woman who would do anything. Traveled light, in the moral sense."

"You think she stole the cross?"

"Why not?" Tatiana strolled around behind me. She put her hands on my shoulders. "Know what you oughta do, Mr. Information?"

"Uh?"

"Find her. Look for her, maybe you'll find Nick."

"Look where?"

"Maybe New York. It's just too much of a coincidence for

101

her to split the same night Nick did. I'd talk to Lev, too. Go in the morning. You'll have a better chance of finding him half human. That's the best you can hope for."

"You want to take over? You sound like you'd do better than Charity and me."

"No, thanks."

"What do I owe you for the advice, then?"

She kneaded my shoulders. Slender fingers with surprising strength. "Small favor?"

"Sure."

"Try to lay off Father Alexander. I am *so* worried about him. I see what's happening. He's slipping mentally. He just can't *take* pressure anymore, Yuri. That damned Nicholas!"

"I'll try."

"If that's the best I can get, I'll take it."

We had come to the end of our day. Before I had a chance to feel down I said, "I'd like to have you and Father Alexander come over for tea Sunday afternoon. Just a social visit. I really want to see you again."

Her fingertips worked gently into the pits of my collarbones. "I'll talk to Father about it. But no inquisition for him. OK?"

"I promise."

She kept her position, her fingers busy. They moved up to the cords of my neck. And somewhere in that short journey crossed the line from friendliness to desire. I reached up to touch her hands. A brush of thin bones under warm skin. She gasped and pulled back. "I'm sorry!" she said.

I turned slowly in my chair. I glimpsed brimming eyes before her glance fell away in shame. Her cheeks reddened as she crossed herself. Her voice was rushed, breathless: "'O Lord, Jesus Christ, Son of God, have mercy on me, a sinner. O Lord, Jesus Christ...'"

I got up, embarrassed myself. Like so many folks nowadays I had trouble dealing with piety. "I didn't know a little touch on the neck rated whole prayers," I said.

Tatiana's eyes were still down. "It was a dishonest act," she said. "Dishonest to you. Dishonest to me."

"I don't know what's dishonest about a little affection."

"I hardly know you. And I wasn't just touching you. I was having . . . thoughts."

"I've been having 'thoughts' since I laid eyes on you. You're a lovely woman."

She shook her head frantically. "No, no, I'm not ready, Yuri. I'm not centered."

I started to argue when Father Alexander and Charity came laughing into the kitchen. The priest embraced me, a gentle bear hug. "My apologies, Yuri Vladimirovich, for my behavior. I am under much strain. The great day of Pascha—Easter— comes. All are reminded of their faith. And the—waste of Nicholas Mikhailovich holds me like a leech." He shook his head.

"Forget it. I apologize for egging you on. I've invited you and Tatiana to come for tea Sunday afternoon. I hope you'll be able to."

Father Alexander smiled and nodded with delight. "Of course. It will be a pleasure." He turned to Tatiana. "Tatya, a few blini for our guests. To remind us of the holiest season. To correct our inhospitality."

I began to beg off, but he silenced me with a wave of his huge hand.

With the batter ready, it took only a few minutes for Tatiana to prepare a modest feast. I hadn't tasted a single buckwheat pancake since boyhood. Charity had never enjoyed their yeasty goodness wrapped around a dollop of sour cream and a tender bit of smoked whitefish. We both made up for lost time.

When we had all eaten our way to mellowness Father Alexander took me aside. "With your permission, to speak again of Nicholas Mikhailovich."

"Sure. Go ahead. If you want to."

"Where he is I do not know. But in my heart I know it is those who deal in the drugs who hold the answer."

"You think the shooting, the getaway were planned?"

"I told you an agreement had been struck. Nicholas Mikhailovich was to complete it—and swear off all dealing with drugs. He gave me his oath on the Gospels to truly do this. Possibly those with whom he dealt were unhappy over his resolve. Or they deluded him into joining them in plotting to murder that Dixon. Or made him a scapegoat."

It was a possibility. Explained the getaway car. The letter from New York would fit, too. Nick now tucked away in some cop-proof nook until the heat was long off, I'd give it some thought. By now I had lots of pieces that needed putting together.

We said good-bye about six and headed back toward 138.

"What're you grinning about, Yuri Nevsky?" Charity said.

"Was I grinning?"

"Not any more than the Cheshire Cat. What happened to the gloomy Russian? The one with no roots and bushels of self-doubt?"

"Beats me. All of a sudden I feel great."

"The old Yuri. The one I like working with. Thank God!"

"Why 'thank God'?"

"Because I'm an upbeat person. And so are you. You believe in a positive attitude and some control over your destiny. Seeing you wallow in doubt and turned every which way made me nervous. So, it's nice to have you back on the track again."

"It's still a tough time of life for me."

"Sure it is, but now you're coming around to dealing with it."

"I wonder what changed my attitude?"

Charity shrieked with laughter. "Listen to you, fishing for attention. Nothing like an exotic-looking woman to cure *your* ills." She eased index fingers into the corners of her eyes and shoved lightly upward. With a thick quasi-Slavic accent she said, "I em Ruzzian, too. Led us supper *togeder*."

"Stop."

"She seems like a wonderful woman. Altogether too good for you."

"Thanks."

"Yuri?"

"What?"

"You're fun to tease."

11

Charity was up early and at an English muffin before eight the next morning. She wore her Research Outfit—a khaki jump suit sneakily styled and impervious to the grit from the tops of the pages of long-shelved books. She planned to spend the day in the Dewey 200 Class, Religion, at Carnegie Library in Oakland, trying to find out something about the Holy Order of the Caucasus. She had another idea. To check the art division to see what was there about the origins of the stolen cross.

Five minutes after she left I decided to go jogging. I slipped into tattered sneakers and my Playboy Resorts International sweat pants and chugged up the street. The only pedestrians these days were kids under driver age, and they were in school. I had the sidewalk to myself.

Two blocks from the house I heard a car behind me. It was moving slowly, sounding like it was going to turn off into a driveway. But it didn't.

I glanced back over my shoulder, saw a big gray Imperial, three male faces within. Car and men totally unfamiliar. I kept jogging. I was getting loose and starting to break into a sweat. I felt good and speeded up.

When I came to the wide empty lot at the end of Weldon Street, the Imperial finally passed me. It stopped about twenty yards ahead. A man got out. He wore a Ben Hogan–style white linen golf cap and a knitted yellow short-sleeved shirt that showed off the biggest shoulders and thickest neck this side of the Highland Park Zoo gorilla cage.

As I jogged by he said, "Hold it, Nevsky." I stopped. He waved a meaty hand toward the Imperial. "Get in."

"Why should I?"

"The man wants to see you."

"Which man?"

"Houle."

My memory sparked distantly, but the connections slipped

105

away among the synapses. Not enough to get me to climb in. "Have him call for an appointment," I said.

"Don't get wise! Get *in*." Hogan Hat stepped out to block my path.

"Sorry."

His heavy lips moved toward a smile. I had a feeling he liked rough stuff. Liked to keep in practice smashing smaller, weaker people—like me.

"Let me by. I'll talk to your 'man' when I know who he is and what he wants."

"Huh uh. *Now*."

I heard the car door open. Reinforcements were on the way. Hogan Hat made a move to collar me. I backed away. He rushed me and I ducked aside.

The human knee is a complicated joint. It can take a lot of abuse. But when there's weight on the foot, it's vulnerable to blows from the side. As Hogan Hat lunged by I kicked the side of his left knee as hard as I could. I heard snaps, crackles and pops. And knew he was out of the rough stuff before he did.

I whirled just as the guy out of the car was swinging a skullduster at my head. I grabbed his arm, did some fast footwork that walked him around into a half nelson. "Drop it!" I said.

"My knee! My fuckin' *knee*." Hogan Hat was dancing and discovering he could put no weight on his left leg.

I was feeling cocky about things. Instead I should have been counting men. I figured there was still one in the car. I was wrong. My first inkling of this was another skullduster making brutal contact with my noggin. They had dropped off a man behind me before pulling up ahead. He stood behind me now, waiting for me to fall. Red waves and roaring washed through my brain, but I was too dumb to fall. The second konk finished the job.

I woke up on the floor of the Imperial. Somebody was using my back as a footrest. Hogan Hat was talking seriously of castrating me. The other two were warning him that Houle could see to it that he got far worse than a busted up knee if they didn't do just as he ordered: Get Nevsky, no rough stuff.

The Imperial stopped indoors. I was dragged out onto a concrete floor smelling of spilled oil. Somebody poured a bucket of water on my head. I sat up. My head throbbed and my stomach did flip-flops. I lay back down slowly. I knew I was in trouble now. Made worse because I didn't know what was going on.

The third member of the trio, who I unfortunately hadn't seen, was pointing a small automatic pistol at my head. "You didn't look like trouble, Nevsky. But you are," he said. "It's the bald and the beard throws a person off. But you luck out. The man said, 'No squeeza da peach.'" The speaker was small and dapper. Neat moustache, thin nose and eyebrows. "You gonna behave now?"

"I gave back what I got. King Kong there started it."

Hogan Hat only cursed and glowered from the passenger's seat. He had rolled up his pants leg above the knee. Now he was mesmerized by the massive swelling and the understanding that cloth would have to be cut away at the hospital. "I'm gonna take you up to see Houle," the dapper man said. "You gonna behave?"

"Me make trouble?"

"My name's Pete. Your name is Boot Hill, you try anything. This little piece gonna be in my pocket all the way. We gonna walk some and ride some. I'm gonna be right behind you all the way."

We walked out of the building. I saw we were at the foot of Mount Washington. "Houle lives up there." Pete pointed toward some luxury apartments atop the bluff.

Mount Washington reared up on the south shore of the Monongahela right above the Golden Triangle. The road that ran along the top of the high bluff was called Grandview Avenue. And that about described how the city looked below. Tourists could see all thirteen bridges leading into the heart of downtown Pittsburgh. They could see Three Rivers Stadium, Point Park, the Civic Arena—the jutting stone and metal landscape of the Pittsburgh skyline. The U. S. Steel Building thrust up above it all like a triangular finger raised to remind us of what had made this town.

"We walk on account of cars are maybe spotted by the fuzz. Houle draws attention."

"What line of work Houle in?" I said.

Pete snorted. "He knits doilies for little old ladies to put on the arms of their couches."

We walked up to the Monongahela Inclined Railway—"the Incline," the locals say—up to Grandview Avenue. As the Incline ticked up I struggled to place the name "Houle." Then it came to me! TDK. My frat brother at Pitt. Doug "Hothead"

Houle had been a fast-talking magnet for every kind of trouble twenty years ago. I remembered his being a brawler, a guy with a temper an axe murderer would envy. I also recalled his being a flowering alcoholic. He needed four fingers of scotch in the morning before he could shave.

I took deep breaths trying to put the worst of the after-effects of my trip on the Dreamland Express behind me. Atop the bluff Pete led me to the most luxurious of the cluster of apartments. By now it couldn't have been clearer that Houle was in the rackets. That understanding brought with it a triggered memory. Trackman Tolovitch had told me a guy named Houle was pulling Ray Nevick's strings. My old frat buddy was a drug baron!

Pete ushered me into the penthouse suite. It was done in white. Actually interior decorated—white rugs, white furniture, drapes, telephone. Houle sat at a big white desk in a room with a glass wall. Heights don't bother me, but it looked like a person could fall through the glass right into the Golden Triangle. Houle had lost the boyish leanness I remembered. The journey to middle age had filled him out too generously. He battled the weight. I guessed at regular health club workouts, carefully tailored clothes, and chef's-salads-hold-the-dressing for lunch. He wore a pair of imported racing-style glasses with thick lenses.

He came around the desk. "I want to apologize for the rough stuff," he said.

"Don't apologize to me. It's your gorilla who's going to the hospital."

"Jocko's needed a lesson in self-control." There was something tight, wound up in Houle. "I forget the secret handshake," he said.

"TDK didn't have one." We shook hands.

"Drink?" The long, white liquor cabinet was open. "Too early for me," I said. "Help yourself." I remembered him wining out of a juice pitcher.

"I don't use it. It almost killed me."

I studied his face. Yes, the control. Teetotaling would be a big part of it. "The booze can do that," I said.

Houle waved me to a white, vinyl, body-shaped chair. When I was as close to comfortable as I was going to get, he said, "I want to know what you want out of Russian Slope." Before I could open my mouth, he held up his palm. "I mean what you *really* want."

I was a bit puzzled. "I'm doing a job for the *Post-Gazette*. With another reporter." I dug out my Coop notebook and gave him the letter from Harrison Brightwood.

He read it and nodded. "This is what I heard you were doing." He held the paper and mimed wiping his ass with it. Then he threw it on the floor. "That's all that letter's good for, Nevsky, and you know it."

"Look, Houle, I don't—"

"I got friends in funny places, Nevsky. In my business people like to do me favors. I got a friend at the *Post-Gazette*. You aren't on the payroll, old frat buddy. Never have been. Congrats on the letter, though. Fool anybody halfway honest."

"But not you, huh, Houle?"

"Not me. So you're not in the newspaper business. What business you in?"

I looked right into his glasses. Behind them his eyes looked tiny, like dangerous gimlets. I said nothing.

"You know what worries me?" Houle asked. "What really worries me about you? I'll level. First, you gotta know I got gadgets in the walls here that sniff out electronic bugs like terriers after rats. You got no bugs on you. So I'll deny what I'm gonna say, if it comes to my word against yours. Nevsky, I'm worried you're a narc."

"So that's it."

"That's it. Are you or aren't you?"

"I aren't."

"A cop."

"No way."

"And you're not a reporter, either. What *are* you? Why all the goddamned questions? I heard you talked to about half the Russkies on the Slope. Questions, questions. So many questions about Dixon and that kid Markov." Houle walked to the glass wall and looked down at the Golden Triangle. "Questions I figured only a narc would ask. Questions that're making a lot of people real nervous."

"People like Ray Nevick."

"Maybe people like him. Maybe other people who buy and sell—unless they think there's a bust in the wind. And I don't mean Bo Derek bare-tit either." He swung away from the glass.

"I'm rocking your boat, Houle."

"Like a goddamned tidal wave."

"I don't give a shit," I said. "Your business stinks. Nevick stinks. Maybe even *you* stink."

Two white spots formed high on Houle's cheeks. Tight when I walked in, he was tighter now. Some day he wouldn't be able to hold in all the evil, destructive energies. I hoped I wouldn't be around when he let loose.

"I want to hear preaching, I'll go to church, Nevsky. Lay off. Show some style." With deliberately slow movements he drew a round case a little larger than a pillbox from his pocket. It gleamed and glittered in the morning light. Gold-and-diamond snuff box. He snorted a pinch and enjoyed two explosive sneezes. "Let's say you're leveling with me—you're not a narc," he went on. "You're not a cop. You're something else. You want to find out about Dixon and Markov." He snapped a glance at me. "Why?"

"I'm getting paid to find out where the kid is."

"Private eyes are as with it as high-button shoes."

"I sell information, Houle. That's *damn* trendy."

"OK. I'm hip to what you want. I figure the thing to do is help you out. Tell you what you want to know."

"Why should you tell me the truth?"

Houle flashed his tight grin. "Maybe because we were TDKs together."

"Sure."

"Maybe I tell you what you want to know, you'll go away."

"Maybe. Let's try it, Houle. What I want to know is, is Nicholas Markov really in New York City? Or is he somewhere else?"

A shadow of disappointment colored Houle's professionally shaven face. "I don't know where he is."

"You leveling with me?" It was a stupid question. He was a death merchant. What good was his word? But what other choice did I have?

He held up a curved hand in a shrug. "Gospel, Nevsky."

"What the hell good are you?"

"Damn good. I don't know where he is, but I know what happened that night. You want to know, I'll tell you."

"I already know some things. This better be good."

"Good or not, it's right on, Nevsky. First off, the kid Markov didn't do any heavy dealing. No smack. Just uppers, downers, pills and grass. I don't know why Nevick bothered with him. Except he was a pretty boy and Nevsky likes pretty boys. Anyhow, the kid gets a rep as a real straight shooter. Customers started going to him for their shit."

"He did tend to draw crowds."

"The fuzz were real interested in Nevick. They didn't have anything on him, but they were curious. Sometimes they tailed him."

"I talked to Polsky, the cop. They went easy because he was a hometown boy. Same with Nicholas. Tried to scare him a little was all."

"We figured that in a pinch the kid was a better bet. Less likely to draw heavy attention from the fuzz." Houle began to pace in front of the glass. "That brings me to Noodlehead Nolan." He looked at me. "Heard of him?"

"I heard the name Nolan just yesterday. When I expected to hear the name Ed Dixon."

Houle nodded. "Noodlehead's a man in the trade. Does business in Rankin and Braddock. He's not our man, but we deal with him. A while back Nolan needed big smack quick. He had the cash up front. He gave us half, held the other half until he got the goods.

"I had some problems with my people around then. Narcs, poor health, sudden winter vacations." Houle glanced sidelong at me. "Got me? I had a little emergency. The shipment comes in and I want to move it right on to the noodle man. So I listen to Nevick and decide to use the kid. We set the time and place."

"Eight o'clock. The Eleven-to-Seven," I said. "Nicholas delivers the dope and collects the other half of the money. He has to show because Nolan already paid half up front."

"You got it. Ten K is ten K. The kid looks to get the five K before he turns over the goods."

"So what went wrong?"

"Ed Dixon was the nigger in the woodpile—excuse the racism." Houle's tiny eyes were masked by the morning light reflecting off his racing glasses. "Know anything about him?"

"What a local newspaper man told me. That's all."

"You do get around, TDK brother."

"Tolovitch said he had a real habit."

Houle's smooth face twisted into a scowl. "He used to deal for Noodlehead. Used to be his gofer, too. Used to be good—before he started sampling his own shit. Then he started doing smack and PCB. Over about three months he turned into a wild and crazy guy. Noodlehead tried to cut him loose, but he kept hanging around.

"Then the deal went down. Nevick got the goods to the kid. He also gave him a piece. A Bearcat. I told him he was crazy, but Nevick had this thing about the kid. Wanted him 'to be safe' carrying the five K. The kid doesn't know a pistol from a popsicle. The Bearcat has a hair trigger. Goes off if you friggin' *breathe* on it." He glanced sharply at me. The lenses of his glasses freed themselves of glare. His eyes were like awls. "With me so far, Nevsky?"

"Right on, loyal frat brother." A leaden feeling gripped my chest. A hair-trigger pistol . . . for the first time I was absolutely certain Nick had killed Dixon.

"Here's the zinger. And I heard this from the noodle man—when I visited him in the hospital. So I know this is real true. Ed Dixon was wandering around with half a brain and a habit Rockefeller couldn't feed. Some way he heard about the deal. He knew where and when. But he only heard half right. He thought *all* the dough had been paid. So he jumped Noodlehead with a fungo bat and tried to knock his head all the way to Three Rivers' outfield. Then he took his place at the Eleven-to-Seven." Houle pointed a neatly manicured finger at me. "You used to be pretty smart, Nevsky. You fill in the rest."

"Don't have to be Herman Kahn to write that scenario, Hothead. Dixon met the kid at eight o'clock. He had to talk him into believing he was Nolan's proxy. The kid maybe bought it, but smelled something. Dixon said give me the goods. The kid wanted to see the money first. Dixon maybe argued and lied, but the kid had been around the trade long enough to know—no dough, no snow. About then Dixon maybe lost his cool and got heavy. The kid pulled his Bearcat and—"

"Bango!" Houle's pistol-fingered hand was pointed toward the center of my forehead. "He touched the trigger and wished he hadn't. Might even call it an accident. Just about was."

"How'd you know he'd have to get out of there quick?" I said.

Houle frowned. "I didn't know nothing like that, man. You just heard *all* I know about the whole deal."

"Somebody drove him off in a car. I figured one of your people, one of Noodlehead's maybe."

"I heard that, but no way. Had nothing to do with it. Neither did Noodlehead."

I got up and walked over close to Houle. I invaded his personal space, as they say. I made myself look into his piggish eyes. I tried to look into his soul—to see if there was any truth left in it. "You being straight with me?"

"Why would I lie? I want you off my back, off the Slope. The kid means nothing to me. He didn't rate a ride. We figured all he had to do was walk four blocks and give the dough to Nevick."

I believed him. Hated to ... I wanted things simplified. Wanted it all easy. I got up to leave. "The kid contact Nevick since he split?" I said.

"No. And that's hit him bad." Houle shook his head. "He's making the same mistake Dixon did. Sampling too much. The kid meant a lot to him. Not hearing, not knowing's messing his head around. Right now I wouldn't trust him to wipe his own ass. Christ, Nevsky, it's hard to find good men." He leered at me. "You aren't by any chance interested in taking some goods on consignment, are you?"

"Up yours, good frat buddy."

Houle flashed his tight, mirthless smile. "You get enough from me to stop you asking questions?"

"To stop asking some questions of some people."

"I don't think that's enough," Houle said.

"It'll have to be."

"Nevsky—"

"Relax, why don't you, Houle? You found out I'm no narc. No cop. I don't give a fart in a whirlwind about your stinking line of work. I'm trying to find out where Nicholas Markov is. Period. Get the word to your goons that I march to a different drummer. And I'll probably be out of everybody's hair in a week or so, whether I find out what I want or not. That's the best you're gonna get out of me. OK?"

Houle shrugged. He lifted some papers off his desk and shoved them at me. "Listen, Nevsky, I'm working with some other TDK alums to boost Pitt football. The Golden Panthers. We each ante up one thousand bucks for permanent scholarships. We want to keep the Panthers in national prominence." Houle was serious.

"I'm a little short right now. The roof of my house leaks. Guess I'm not in the thousand-dollar league."

"No? We'll accept any kind of contribution. It's a good cause."

"I'm really short, Houle."

He shrugged. "OK. Here, take some of our literature just in case." He flashed his first real smile. "Go Panthers!" he said.

From the lobby payphone I called the St. Basil's number. The sound of Tatiana's soft voice brought a pleasant ache to

113

my chest—and a pleasant surprise. "I was hoping I'd hear from you," she said. "Our little time together seemed to demand . . . more, I thought."

"I *was* wondering if there were more tea balls."

"That wasn't quite what I was thinking. But maybe I can find some. Can you come over?"

I headed home to shower and change first, and then while driving too fast to the Slope I remembered what Charity had said about my needing some emotional commitment to steady my life. That advice in the abstract hadn't made a lot of sense. Packed into Tatiana's trim shape it took on potent meaning. My response to her voice and earlier brief touch cued me to something else—how vulnerable I was. At the least we all needed attention. At best, to be loved. Lately only Charity had nourished me at all, and on a platonic level at that. I told myself I ought to be careful about Tatiana. But I didn't want to be.

In my first ten minutes with her I counted her five smiles—and seven frowns. In her way she had been kicked around, too. Like me, she was looking toward building a new life. With God's help, in her case. I shook my head and grinned over my tea glass. "We *are* a pair, aren't we?" I said.

"Oh?"

"Half happy, half unhappy. A bit tortured. Isn't that in the great Russian tradition?"

"A stereotype." Her grin showed white, even teeth. She sat across a small diningroom table set for tea with the care I had noticed and appreciated earlier. No flour on her hands today, and no apron. She wore a plaid jacket and skirt and a white blouse with a bow at the neck. "At least I'd like to think so."

She poured more tea. Her almond-shaped eyes found my face. "I said I hoped you'd call. When we met I had the feeling there was too much left unsaid, too much room for misunderstanding."

"That business about your feeling guilty about touching me."

She nodded. "That was just part of it. It was what I deserved for not telling the whole truth about myself."

"You have a past?"

"In a way, yes. When I was first in Washington I . . ." She paused. Her long hands fluttered below her chin as she groped for words. ". . . fell into the hands of—there really *aren't* any other words to describe my bad luck—a wicked man."

"'Wicked.'"

114

"Not a fashionable word, is it, Yuri? Francisco De Nolte *was* wicked. He was one of those too sick, too amoral people who seem to gravitate to Washington. In my way I was very innocent. He was very much the opposite." Her voice began to shake.

"Hey, Tatya, you don't have to tell me if—"

"I *do* have to. I want you in my life, Yuri. I do. But you have to know about me." She drew a deep breath, then raced on. "He spoke to the dark side of my soul. He drew out of me ugly desires and appetites I didn't know were there. He was older, jaded . . . sick. His world was distorted. He made me— no, that's not right! He *drew out of me* my willingness to join him in my degradation. To join him in my sexual exploitation."

"Oh, God." My voice was dry with dread and disgust with my own minuscule arousal.

"The details aren't important," she went on. "We went past all those acts that could even remotely be considered 'normal.' I stood back and saw myself becoming little by little his slave— but I couldn't, or wouldn't, help myself. There were groups of lovers that we joined, then, and devices for pain. There were sharp needles . . ." The rising ragged edge of her voice finally tore into a near choke. Her hands were clenched together, strained tendons and bloodless knuckles. "I was being destroyed emotionally. All the values and framework I grew up with here on the Slope were being mocked and destroyed. Francisco filled up my life, crowded everything else out. His evil moon eclipsed the sun of my soul. I was an instrument he played on—and with. I knew I was doomed . . ." She shuddered and broke her determined eye contact.

I hurried around her tidy table and hugged her where she sat. It was an awkward embrace, my arms down over her shoulders, my cheek against the piled braids. I smelled her shampoo and her dread.

"Then God chose to spare me. I know it was He who ordained that Francisco be a victim in a dreadful, senseless auto accident."

"He died?"

"Broken spine. He ended up a vegetable. Family members had him returned to Switzerland."

"And you?"

"I had a breakdown. I had a great deal of therapy. It didn't seem to work. So, as I said, I came here instead of staying on in Washington. I hope God can heal what man cannot."

I drew her up out of her chair and hugged her. "You were brave to say all that."

"There've been no men in my life—at all—since Francisco. Except for Father Alexander, who *is* my father now. I'm not sure I can have a normal relationship with a man. But if I can, I want him to be somebody a lot like you."

"Tatya—"

"I'm . . . half crazy, Yuri."

"No, you're—"

She looked up suddenly, her eyes more than a bit wild. "Oh, I am. I *am*."

I hugged her harder. "Even so, will you spend time with me?"

"Oh, yes. *Yes*. I will." Her weeping discharged the tensions tightening her spine. She blubbered on and on as I held her. After a long while the noon whistle blew down at the tube works. She gently pulled away. "Father will be home from the youth group soon and wanting lunch."

I opened my mouth and began to say something obvious and probably stupid about her courage in being honest with me. She smothered my lips with white fingers. "It wasn't just a confession," she said. "It was a warning."

I left, promising to call her and meet quickly. She wiped away tears with the back of one slender hand, and closed the door with the other. I didn't like what I saw in her drying eyes. But I was drawn to her all the more for it.

It was just after twelve when I pulled into the flats of Russian Slope. The seamier side, down near the main drag and the tube works. I stopped at a state store and bought a quart of Four Roses. Lev Samnesovich lived on the third floor of a sulfur-darkened yellow-brick walk-up. Odors of barbecue and incontinent cats hovered in the hallways.

Lev was in. He needed a bath and a barber. His straight blond hair protruded from his skull in long bristles. Below a vein-blasted nose a wispy moustache grew down into his mouth. His watery blue eyes leaked mucus. My *Post-Gazette* letter and Volodya's kopek got me in the door. The Four Roses got me an unupholstered chair by the kitchen table.

"You want to know about Olga for the newspaper?" He had a whisky baritone voice.

"Sure."

"Cost you two hundred bucks for her story."

I didn't answer. Just looked him in the eye. My will against his. Before long his glance fell away. "That's ridiculous," I said. "If you're selling an exposé, call *Midnite*."

"She was no good to me when she was here. What's wrong with trying to make a few bucks off her now?" He turned to his glass on the stained oilcloth table cover.

"Why don't you tell me about Olga," I said.

Like most self-pitying people, the only story he could tell was his own. But I listened to it. Prelude to information about his daughter. I listened to Lev Samnesovich's trite litany of the injustices done him—the failure of the world to grasp his fine qualities. The insensitivity of his wife whom, as I remembered, he beat and indirectly murdered. The whisky he tossed down three fingers at a time fueled his righteousness. He was in full cry when I managed to steer him back to his daughter.

"Like her mother. No good! Needed beating." He looked at me, eyes bold with liquid courage. "I hated to do it. But the strap was the only thing Olga paid attention to. I thought when the old lady keeled over, things would be different. Thought Olga'd cooperate in helping me make a bundle."

"How were you going to do that?"

"Pictures. Pictures of her. I was gonna sell 'em. C'mere." He lurched toward the flat's bedroom. Lev Samnesovich had turned it into a photolitho Sodom. Pornographic pictures had been glued chock-a-block to the spotted wallpaper. Skin magazines lay in heaps around the bed. More female genitalia hit my eyes than a gynecologist sees in a lifetime. An Instamatic and a pair of cheap floodlights gathered dust on a cluttered bureau.

"These kinda pictures," he said, waving at the walls. "Olga didn't want no part of it. She'd give it to any guy who came down the pike. But she wouldn't show it to her own father to help him make a few bucks and maybe get us off relief."

"Kids these days." My memory flashed the image of Tatya's lewd bondage master. He and Lev were cut from the same rank, coarse cloth. Wanting to spit in his face, I turned back to the living room. He followed me. "I heard she ran off," I said.

"She kept saying she was gonna. Said she was gonna go to New York. I told her that was crazy. That was a sick town. She should stay home where she was safe."

"Nothing like a healthy home environment."

"Huh?"

"She said she was going to run away."

"Twice I had to take her money. For her own good, get it. It was the only way to keep her from doing something crazy." He poured himself another strong one.

"But she ran off anyhow."

Lev pointed a shaking index finger at me. "She ran off *with* somebody."

I drew a deep breath. "Who?"

"I don't know."

"Was it Nicholas Markov?"

"Nick? Don't know. Mighta been. Somebody come to the door that night. She answered it. She went out in the hall for maybe a coupla minutes."

"You see who it was?"

"No."

"What time was this?"

"Not sure I remember. Oh, yeah, the TV program was just changing. Right close to eight thirty."

That way maybe twenty minutes after Dixon had been shot. Plenty of time for Nicholas to get over here from the Eleven-to-Seven, get his driver to park the car, come upstairs. Question was, though, why did he want her to go along? "She came back in here after being out in the hall?" I said.

"Yeah. Like she was gonna stay. Then she picked up her purse and said she was going out for some milk. She was gone before quarter to nine. Ain't seen her since." His shaking hands made washing motions. "Good riddance! She was a slut and a tramp." Lev was well into the safety of his alcoholic haze.

"The night she left. She take a suitcase?"

"Nah. Just her purse."

"You check her clothes later?"

"Yeah. She didn't take any. I pawned them." Lev grinned cryptically. "Maybe she didn't need any clothes. Maybe she had somebody to buy them for her. Somebody who liked to throw money around."

"Like who?"

"Whoever she ran off with." He laboriously dug out his wallet. He pulled out a folded length of blue tissue. It was the nonnegotiable carbon of a bank check. The check had been made out to Olga. The names were typed: Olga Samnesovich and "John Smith." Dated the day Nicholas and she disappeared. Five hundred dollars. Getaway money . . .

I went down the stairs talking to myself. The more I learned, the more confused I got. One strong feeling I was getting: Olga fit in somewhere, just as Tatiana said. Finding out where she was would be almost as good as finding Nicholas.

A woman was standing by my car. It was P.Q. Antonelli. She gestured toward her yellow VW bug. "I was running a lunch errand and spotted your car."

"How'd you know it?"

"I checked it out when you drove out of the medical-center parking lot. I don't miss a trick."

I remembered this was a smart young lady. She was trying to frown. "You owe me two apologies," she said.

"Oh?"

"The first for inviting me to a party—and hardly even talking to me! Standing around toasting 'Mother Russia,' for God's sake."

"I'm sorry. Really. And you weren't the only person I made angry."

"I *noticed*. Popular guy. Or you *were*. Second, for giving me that *Post-Gazette* reporter jive. You're no reporter."

"Where'd you get that idea?"

"Ludmilla Markov's been having dental problems. You know, Nick's grandmother. I got to know her in the waiting room. We talked yesterday. She was in a good mood. Asked her why. She tried not to give too much away, but because you had already been around, I put her 'someone special is going to find Nicholas' and 'a handsome man of Russian blood' together with you." She grinned. "It really wasn't very hard."

I nodded. "Apologies, apologies. Yeah, I'm trying to find out where Nicholas is."

Her eyes glowed at mention of his name, as they had for a moment during our first meeting. "OK, so you know about me. I know about *you*, too. I know you're so much in love with Nicholas Markov you light up like a TV quiz-show scoreboard whenever you hear his name."

"Is it that obvious? No one's noticed."

"Noticing things is useful in my business."

"You're not a cop, are you? Or the much-glorified private eye?"

I told her what Charity and I did.

P.Q. nodded and relaxed. "If you know how I feel about Nick, you'll understand why I didn't tell the cops—or even Anya—what I saw the night Dixon was shot." Her dark eyes burned into mine. "You know what it's like to be totally *gone*

119

on someone? To want them so much nothing else matters? To toss out all the dumb rules and routines we hide our lives behind? To know what it's like to hear your own emotions freed up and shouting? Do you, Yuri?"

"Never been that lucky. Until yesterday."

"And it was crazy for me, too. Because Nicholas was...distant. I told him how I felt. I mean I poured it out to him. He turned those *electric* eyes of his on me. And said *something*—Christ knows what—full of generalities, ifs, maybes. If I talked to the cops, I thought it would help them find him when he didn't want to be found. No way would I do anything to hurt him." She looked appraisingly at me. "Now I want to tell you."

"Why? What made you change your mind?"

"Two things, Yuri. The first is wrapped up in intuition. For the first couple of weeks I was sure Nicholas had got away. That he was hiding on account of the murder—alive and well, like Jacques Brel was. Now my gut feeling is that he's in bad trouble. Maybe dead. I was so sure, I decided to tell Anya what I had seen. That was just a couple days ago. That brings me to the second reason. I did tell Anya. She went to confess with Father Alexander. He gave her advice to give to me."

"Which was?"

"Eat what I know. That made me suspicious." P.Q.'s appraising glance swept my face.

I remembered Anya leaving the priest's study, his cautioning words, her haste to beat it when she saw I was there. "Father Alexander told Anya that by now Nicholas should be treated like a sleeping dog. Yuri, you think he knows where Nicholas went?"

I laid out the highlights of my talk with the priest—that it was hard to imagine someone more upset about Nicholas being gone.

"Then maybe we can settle Nick's situation one way or the other. One thing's for sure—I can't live much longer the way I am. All tangled up with hopes for Nick and me. Knowing I should know better. So I'll give the license-plate number to you—instead of to the cops—and step back and see what happens."

P.Q. explained that she had rushed past the slumped corpse of Ed Dixon out the side entrance of the Eleven-to-Seven. Anya was right with her, but she was Ms. Myopia. As the car sped away with Nicholas in the back seat, P.Q. memorized the license-plate number. She gave it to me and I wrote it down in my Coop notebook.

She got into her VW. "Yuri, I'm tired of being bewildered by love," she said and drove off.

I had time to kill before my rendezvous with Charity at the Imperial Court. My notebook had the address of the Moskva Hotel, where Father Alexander held his rap sessions with adolescents and young adults. It was a block and a half away. About two blocks up from the river. I decided to walk over. On the way I stopped for a burger in an old storefront snack bar. By the time I got to the hotel entrance it was nearly two.

The near-the-river location should have tipped me off about the Moskva's condition, even before I saw the decaying facade with its keystone dated 1923. Soot-blackened brick spaced off the first-floor windows, half of them broken and patched with tape and newspaper. A lumpishly lettered sign screwed onto the broken revolving door promised rates by the day, week or month. Two down-and-outers sprawled against the brick banisters with brown paper bags on their laps. I had a real strong feeling the Moskva Hotel wasn't in the *AAA Travel Guide* this year.

I hadn't taken two steps into the dusty lobby when a gangling stick of an old man with a fright wig of white hair came rushing around from behind the main desk. "Who are you? What you want?" His Russian accent made his words nearly unintelligible.

I spoke Russian—there was no other way. I trotted out the *Post-Gazette* story and one of Volodya's kopeks.

The old man wasn't impressed. He *was* an old man. Skin gone thin and yellow. Liver-spotted hands. My father—another tall, thin old man—had gone white and sere, too, before cancer finished him. Same generation. Here was yet one more tough old Imperial Russian, one more emigré tottering down to the end of the road.

His name was Anton Rastokov. Trackman Tolovitch had told me he owned the hotel, had turned over one of his rooms for Father Alexander's use. He was more than a little crazy. But when a person broke through the age barrier to, say seventy, he earned the right to have his oddities accepted.

Rastokov's voice, like his skin, was dry. Just the same, he fairly shrieked at a geezer shambling in with the uncertain footfalls of the alcoholic—trying to sneak past him for a night's free flop.

121

"You pay me! Or you get out!" He rushed at the bum like a great crane. His styleless suit, two sizes too large, flapped around his arms and legs as he dragged the offender toward the door. For a few moments his eighty years meant nothing.

He came back scowling. The Russian, rich with contempt, poured out. "They are scum! The worst of what is bad to start. There was a day when the Moskva Hotel was the gathering place for some of the finest people in Pittsburgh. People of a quality nearly that of my countrymen in Mother Russia—in those days when we lived in the embrace of our father, the czar. Deep in the mountains of our beloved Caucasus. There in the Valley of Promise God gave us saints and heroes to lead us generation after generation."

"The Valley of Promise? The place Igor Gregorevich Markov came from?" I said. "You're from there, too?"

Rastokov blinked. His old man's eyelids squished. He nodded. "Yes, but we were not friends. What a place our valley was, Yuri Vladimirovich! Such grain we grew! Streams and lakes sweeter than a virgin's kiss. Our men were strong, our women flames of beauty. We prospered in lives close to the earth. We had strong guidance in our spiritual lives. Holy men and a great family of noblemen who looked after us . . ."

Poor old guy. We were pushing to the year 2000 and zany Rastokov still lived long ago, half a world away—another emigré whose clock stopped in 1917. I interrupted. "You were talking about the hotel."

"Yes. I built it and ran it. And the best people came for dining and entertainment. All the furnishings, the food, the service, the *style* was Russian. In those days there was an appreciation of finer things. The Moskva's style drew travelers from all over this country. Then the trains ran. And the station was close by. Such parties were given! Such eating! And such drinking! It was said only at the Hotel Moskva did wine flow as it had in the court of the czar!" He blinked his squishing eyelids. "Why did you say you came here, Yuri Vladimirovich?"

"I really didn't quite say. Father Alexander holds regular youth meetings here—"

"Yes, the holy man. I know him well. He is a saint, Yuri Vladimirovich."

"And I wanted to ask you if you knew anything about Nicholas Markov."

"That boy, his destiny is a great one." He nodded and paced, his manner agitated. "He will one day reach that destiny. It is God's will."

The old man for sure had a screw loose. "What do you think his destiny is?" I couldn't help but think: the bottom of a river or a life as a wanted man.

"A destiny with no connection with you, Yuri Vladimirovich. No connection with this grimy town without glory. This town far removed from the earth and its simple holy ways. Such earth we had back in the Valley of Promise where I was born and lived . . ."

He was off again. The senility switch going off and on.

I urged him to show me the youth meeting room. He took me up the stairs to the second floor. The room had been painted by the group. They had hung two fluorescent fixtures. A half-dozen card tables, several folding chairs and a wheeled blackboard were the only furnishings. The chalked message announced the next meeting. This coming Thursday at 4 P.M. "Bring guitars, banjos, etc."

"They sing here. Play here," Rastokov said. "And there is laughter. The Devil hides when men and women laugh."

"Father Alexander does well with the group, I understand."

Rastokov shrugged. "He does as he wishes."

Down in the lobby someone palmed the desk bell. We went down the stairs. Chief Polsky and two of his men stood by the desk. "Time for another comb-through, Anton Alexandrovich." The chief's Russian was good. "Old guy uptown used a sash weight as a wife persuader. Then beat it."

"My pleasure to again be of service." Rastokov dug in a desk drawer and came up with the Moskva master key strung through a hole in the end of a sawed-down tennis racket handle.

The chief gave it to one of his officers. He waved toward the antique elevator. "Every room, sergeants. Hold your noses."

The chief joined his men. "No search warrants?" I said.

"We come through this dump so often half the winos think we live here. No one's called us on it yet."

"Rastokov doesn't care?"

"He doesn't want trouble. This place has almost as many residential violations as Buchenwald. I do what I can to keep public health off his back. One of those scratch-my-back deals."

"Ever find who you want?"

"Sure. Or I wouldn't bother. The Moskva draws people on the run. They think a phony name on the register is all they need." The chief nodded at me. "I'm surprised you're still around here, Nevsky. How long's it take to write an article?"

"I've got hooked on Nick Markov. Trying to find out where he is."

"Then that's why you're in this pit. To see if the kid's squirreled away in one of the rooms?"

"Not really."

"Well, he isn't. We've been through here twice since the kid disappeared. Every room. Plus a hot attic and damp basement." He smoothed his salt-and-pepper goatee, weighing a hard comment. "You know, Nevsky, something about you really doesn't square with me." He wouldn't let me forget he was a sharp cop. "I heard you been all over the Slope asking about Nick. Asking the kind of questions that're hard to answer. Almost like you were playing cop. I'll let that go for now. What I want to know is—you find out anything?"

"This and that—not pieced together yet. Nick's gone. Everybody's upset for different reasons." I shrugged. "I really think he might be in New York after all."

Polsky nodded. "Maybe we'll score soon. Ogalkov got his insurance company moving. Kept their word. They're sending a man to the Apple and paying one of my cop's travel to go with him. They're leaving this afternoon."

"I'd like to know if they find him."

"We'll see." The chief wrinkled his large nose. "Sometime I want to sit down and talk to you—straight, Nevsky." His eyes raked my face. "I don't like being deceived. I don't even like being *misdirected*."

I nodded. "I wonder if your cop could dig around for another Russian Sloper in New York. Maybe another handle to the same pot."

"Who?"

"Olga Samnesovich."

The chief nodded. "I hadn't forgotten about her. But thanks for the reminder. You can't check the King, sometimes the Queen is the next best thing. One more thing: my man is going to work through NYPD on pawnshops and jewelers. The cross. Another handle."

"I wish your man good luck," I said.

"I got a young sergeant up for lieutenant. Went to an Ivy League school. But shrewd anyway. For some reason he wants to devote himself to law enforcement. *Likes* people. Could be a classic good cop. He does this job, he goes up to lieutenant."

"Motivate your workers," I said.

"The only way to effective management," Chief Polsky said.

On the short flight of concrete steps leading down to the sidewalk I found a coincidence lodged in my mind that refused to be digested—like a tough piece of beef. Rastokov and Igor both came from the Caucasus Mountains, from the Valley of Promise. They were countrymen of the same generation, social dinosaurs breathing their last. What of it? Why did it hang in my head when it was so far removed from Nick and now?

I swung into a brisk walk. I drew a deep breath and tasted Pittsburgh's coke dust on the back of my tongue. The scenery? Not much. Storefronts dating from the '20s and '30s. Some boarded up. Others filled with dusty lampshades and used clothes gone yellow after months in sunlight. I counted two derelicts and one woman carrying a full shopping bag and mumbling loudly about Jesus. Above the shingled roofs the massive profile of the tube works gorged the near horizon.

I smiled. One of my big, beaming, Cheshire Cat jobs. Why should a little local off-color bring me down? L'affaire Markov had changed direction today. Away from drugs and syndicates and cement overcoats toward . . . something else. That was reason to smile. I had one other. Tall, with black braids piled high. Eyes shaped with a hint of almond. Tatiana!

12

Elena Markov was too glad to see me. She had hung by my side at Volodya's party trying to get me alone. Now she had me. Her smoldering eyes were set in good bones. She had dabbed on a bit of Moonlight Nocturne just after I arrived unannounced at 3:15. I hadn't come to see her, though. I came to see her father-in-law's room.

Her man-charming skills were rusted by years of kids and domesticity. That didn't make her any less dangerous. Maybe more so. She had the wrong idea that years of housewifery had made her less of a person. That idea weakened what was already a poor self-image. In the worst way she needed to validate herself. And for her it would have to be in a man's eyes, the only coin in which she knew how to trade.

I felt compassion for her desperation. She insisted we have a cup of coffee. As we sat together I saw in her eyes and her relentless sucking on her Pall Mall Lights her feeling of betrayal. She had played the game of life by somebody else's rules. She had a house with double doors, sons, a providing husband, financial security. And she was miserable. I guessed she saw now what the wise know from the go—that self-commitment, loving attention and sharing are the heart's nourishment. The other stuff is just dressy facade.

She brimmed with hints and double entendres. Her husky voice tried to raise my lustful temperatures as we made our way up the stairs. She told me in what direction *her* bedroom was. She had already let me know nobody would be home for at least two hours. Just the same I maneuvered to Igor Markov's locked room. She had the key on a brass hoop. When I reached for it she put it behind her back. Held it with both hands, offering a challenge and handsomely matured breasts at the same time.

I was in a bad position. I needed her cooperation, but had too many scruples to turn the energies of her dissatisfaction to serve my personal ends. Because I didn't dare spurn her—only the worst fool shoved that in a woman's face—I played my only trump.

"I'm trying to find your son, Elena. I need all my attention on that job. All my imagination."

"Yuri—"

"And you're just too powerful a temptation for me to deal with. I can't find your son *and* fall in love with you at the same time."

"You're like President Ford was? You can't do both?"

I stared into her eyes. "Could you?"

She shook her head. "If you find him—or you don't, after that?" The keys came around to the front.

"I'm a newly divorced man. I'm looking to explore new relationships." Saying everything—and nothing.

"Mikhail is a pig!" The resentment boiled like lethal acid in the dark caldrons of her eyes.

My good sense whispered: it takes two to maintain a bad relationship. My mouth said, "Nicholas, Elena! He comes before anything."

"Y—yes . . ." I saw her picking up her motherhood again, like a resentful beggar shouldering his heavy pack.

I convinced her that it would be better if I had some time alone in Igor's room. She unlocked the door and snapped on the overhead light. As she slid past me, her warm lips brushed my ear. "I want you in my life!" she whispered.

I closed the door behind me and drew a deep breath. I savored it with my eyes closed. So doing put Elena behind me. The smell of slowly drying leather bindings evoked familiar surroundings. I grinned at the heaps of yellowing Russian emigré papers that I knew were cranked out by old men in New York City walkups. Men whose attentions, whose very lives, were sealed in the past like insects in amber. I saw one of the old Russian-English typewriters, its type on raised rubberoid half-circles struck by a hammer with the paper in between.

Igor Markov's room was like my dead father's study.

A bed, a small bureau, a solid, carved chair with heavy baronial arms crouched like mahogany-colored beasts in an old tapestry. I sat in that huge chair before the solid desk. Bric a brac and small objects lay about on it like sediment on the dry lake bed of a spent lifetime: an ornate brass key, a paperweight barrel dated Chicago 1919, a gold-filled mechanical pencil without lead, a half-dozen coins from as many countries, a low dish brimming with rust-spotted paperclips and razor blades.

I imagined a link between my father, fleeing everything he owned and knew as a stoker on a ship brimming with beet seeds, and Igor Markov, he of the dated clothes and angry letters to the editor, who had seduced his grandson with the past glories of Mother Russia. My eyes were drawn toward the edge of the bed where I sensed Igor had killed himself. I thought of my father's place of death—a hospital room. Tubes ran into his arms and out under the sheets. With an electric razor I had shaved around his mouth gaping open in an O of weakness and confusion. He died at night; a well-meaning nurse with a vulture's instinct for the final moment hovered over him. She reported, "He talked crazy in some kind of funny language up to the last." Russian—which he had called "that jewel lying on the tongues of lucky men."

The tears oozed out of my eyes, unbidden and unexpected. I had wept often in the long months of my father's decline, but not once since his death—until that moment. Long overdue. I wallowed in my unscheduled few minutes of mourning. I was grateful for the privacy and for crying at last for the dear dead man.

In time I wiped my eyes clear and prowled the lengths of unmatched, irregularly shaped bookcases. Many titles were the same my father had owned. Crumbling leather bindings carried Cyrillic letters embossed in gold leaf. Unbound booklets were stacked in careful piles. I saw works of writers popular in a tottering Imperial Russia in editions identical to those on my father's shelves. I smiled. As there, none published after 1917.

My eye caught a familiar binding in tin. A short-lived experiment by the Petrograd publisher, Dimishkin, my father told me when I was ten. The book was by Ronchersky, a writer fond of the most intricate plots, verbal mazes, riddles and other secrets and surprises. He stuffed them by the dozens into his works. His popularity had been a short-lived craze, but a profitable one for Dimishkin. In the spirit of the writer, my father had explained, Dimishkin had fabricated these thick, intricately embossed tin covers. And before my wondering eyes he pressed a hidden catch on the back cover. A hinged door swung open. In the shallow compartment the owner could keep his own secrets. I had opened that hidden panel a hundred times as a boy. By habit my fingers found the catch. The panel sprang open to disclose several yellowed sheets folded together.

It took a less curious person than I to leave them undisturbed. I unfolded them carefully. They made up a letter written in rolling Russian script.

July 14, 1928

To Mikhail Igorevich Markov, my son born today:

This letter finding your hands means that I am gone. I speak to you from the grave. These are my last words to you. So you must read carefully and believe what I say

The manner of my death will tell you how to read these words. If I died smiling with you at my bedside, then my message will be a footnote to the unique genealogy of a special family. If I died in some ugly fashion or you have been contacted by men with fanatical ideas, you will already know much or all of what follows—or some twisted, distorted version of it. What I write here is the *truth*. Mark it carefully. Your life and future may depend on it.

If ill fortune prevails you will one day hear from those who call themselves the Holy Order of the Caucasus. They and their predecessors and the family Markov were intertwined for centuries, almost as long as men have kept sheep on the heights of southwest Russia. Make no mistake: our family ruled over men before there was a Holy Order, before there was a Russian church, because the rich lands, the pastures of the Valley of Promise belonged to us. Long, long ago all prospered through the wisdom and goodness of our forefathers, in the isolation of the mountains.

As you may someday learn, when you are grown, in the 1200s the Tatars advanced into western Russia. In the 1300s they ruled everywhere. It was their wish to rule in the Caucasus Mountains as well. In early battles the Tatars prevailed against all who tried to stand against them. As always the mountain people withdrew after their defeats into the remote heights where none before dared follow. The Tatars, however, pursued them.

In panic their leaders and holy men came to the Valley of Promise, begging for deliverance of the family Markov. It was then that Vladimir, to be called "the Lion," a giant man whose blood is in your veins, became their leader. After many battles, wounds and great losses on both sides, the Tatars were driven back to the foothills.

It was written that in all these glorious battles wonders and miracles of God's making took place. These were said to have been worked on account of Vladimir the Lion's holiness. In time pious men and hermits said he was a saint. And though there was no Russian church, only the Greek one, in the mountains he was sainted and died so.

In the middle of the fifteenth century, plague or some other hideous disease came to the mountains of the Caucasus. Many died in the Valley of Promise. A Markov—Katerina Ivanovna, a simple young woman—answered the desperate cries of the people. She passed among the sick and dying, healing them. She was given to trances, fits and wisdom visions. In time she, too, was seen as a saint. Her grave was a holy place where flowers bloomed in winter.

In the sixteenth century Ivan IV, known as "the Terrible," subdued his boyars with ruthlessness and cruelty. An armed force said by its leaders to represent the wishes of Ivan moved south from Tsaritsyn. In fact they may have been little better than bandits with pretensions. Again a Markov rallied the men of the mountains and repulsed the intruders. This took many years. Repenting his life of violence, Boris became a monk, a starets to many, and another saint of the Caucasus.

After all this, in 1750 a holy hermit came to the Valley of Promise from God-knew-where and built his hut on a spare and windswept height. Father One-Leg he was called. He walked with an ivory crutch, his empty pants leg pinned up. He possessed great powers of persuasion. In time he drew to his side priests of the Russian Church. He guided their confessions, gave them penance and shared thoughts he said came from God. It was these priests, acting on "divine" commands from Father One-Leg, who founded the Holy Order and Monastery of the Caucasus on Mount Volzna.

And it was Father One-Leg—I curse him before God—who in his last weeks on earth delivered his Prophecies, written down by priests of the order. In it he declared the everlasting holiness of the family Markov—our family—and tied it to the people of our remote Valley of Promise. He prophesied further events, dangers and troubles to come to the Valley. But in such-and-such generations of the family Markov, individuals would be born who would see the valley and its people through those black times. He died vomiting blood, shouting, "God bless the family Markov!"

Blind chance found some of his Prophecies fit further events. Men's imaginations and priests' fanaticism did the rest. The parchments were pored over in the great vault of the Monastery of the Holy Order of the Caucasus. There, too, the lives of the family Markov were recorded. Each new generation was set down like a diamond into its mounting.

Other members of our family were made saints as time moved on. My great-grandfather for one. My generation was spared the murky speculations of the one-legged one. So long as our family remained in the Valley of Promise, all was well with priest, landowner and peasant. Their fanaticism, our vanity, and the common people's piety . . .

Then came Comrade Lenin and his revolution. The lands of Markov, ours since there was a race of Slavs, were taken. We fled for our lives. Your grandfather stayed to fight for our heritage through law. He was killed for his trouble. My older brother fought in the so-called White Russian Army. He died under arms. My two sisters, Alexya and Anya, ages 10 and 12, were ordered to flee into exile in far eastern Russia. Alexya was raped and murdered by roaming Evenks. Her personal effects were later seen by priests of the Holy Order who traveled to the banks of the River Chunya—halfway across Russia—to see the bloodied rags. Anya was to drown childless twelve years later, in safety, while boating with her husband.

My father, seeing well the direction the wind blew, booked my passage on a freighter bound for America. Utmost secrecy. It was a time of unimaginable disarray, and both bribes and enemies were everywhere. The night before I was to sail, a priest of the Holy Order came to my shabby hotel room in Petrograd! I cannot conceive of *how* he found me. So they might well find *you*, Mikhail. Maybe there are no barriers of time and space to stop the truly fanatical. The priest tried to persuade me to stay in Russia, as the others of my generation were doing. I well understood his reason. Father One-Leg had prophesied that your generation, or conceivably the next—the Prophecies were marvels of ambiguity—was to sire a "Wonder of Holiness" whose life would be "as an earthquake" in the Valley of Promise. Among all the true saints of the family Markov, he was to be a giant of giants.

I told him I wouldn't stay. Mother, father, brother and sisters were on Russian soil. I was not needed. It was a long argument, but in the end he understood my determination. He then took a heavy crucifix from under his robes—a great relic of the order's monastery. It was nearly solid gold. Through the hole in the upright had been strung a leather thong circling his neck. He made me kneel and kiss the icy gold and swear that no matter where I went I would honor my "obligation" to God, the Holy Order of the Caucasus and the Valley of Promise. I did not tell him I thought he—and his fellows—were mad. He also made me swear, on pain of "loss of my immortal soul," that I would raise all my children in the Russian Church and tell them of *their* obligations. Should one of my offspring prove to be the Wonder of Holiness, he was to be returned to the Valley of Promise.

Had we grasped the totality of the revolution we were experiencing, he would never have allowed me to leave. We all thought that after a few months things in Mother Russia would be set right again.

So I felt I had escaped from both the revolution and the Holy Order of the Caucasus in America, a modern country with modern ideas—where superstition and fanaticism do not flourish as they do in the dark pits of Slavic souls. Ten years have passed since my feet touched American soil. No one has called or contacted me. No matter. I bought a pistol. I will kill anyone who talks to me of the Valley of Promise and my "obligation." If there are too many, I shall kill myself. Should any ghost from the past try to lay a hand on *you*, my firstborn, I needn't spell out my response.

So then years have passed. Do not think, then, that I will relax my vigilance. What is ten years in the sweep of hundreds? I do not underestimate the mad fanatics of the Holy Order. They have survived hundreds of years and practiced their austere beliefs in the country of the commissars where everything possible has been done to discourage religion. I know that they still flourish. They are as patient as the mountains and determined as a river is to seek the sea.

I finish this letter with a warning. They may yet come, my dearest Mikhail, to take you back to the Valley of Promise, to rule over them in the fastness of the Caucasus Mountains where the rein of the Bolsheviks is thin and strained. That would be madness, I know. From another age, another country, a senseless doomed attempt to fly in the face of time and history.

Just the same, they will do it if they can.

Guard against them! Go to the police, the law. Expose them! *Fanatics!*

My firstborn son, I bless you a thousand times and hope that you walk in the light of the Almighty.

You are the last Markov.

Your father,
Igor

Scrawled at a later date across the lower half of the last page: "Through the grace of the Almighty, not needed and hidden."

I wandered out of the old man's room and found a note from Elena. Sasha had twisted an ankle going one-on-one with Downtown Brown. She had to take him to the hospital for X rays. I was relieved. My thoughts tumbled around like rapids.

Hairs stood up on the back of my neck.

13

I rendezvoused with Charity that evening at the Imperial Court. Business was booming as usual. I saw Betty Ellen off in a corner having dinner with Ray Nevick. I'd have to talk to her about her taste. She saw me, but made no gesture of recognition—fallout from Volodya's vodka-logged party.

When I had a Sam Thompson and soda in front of me, Charity filled me in on her day's research. The resources of the Carnegie Library were unequal to uncovering the details of the Holy Order of the Caucasus. Hardly surprising. I managed to contain myself, bubbling over as I was with information.

When it came to the missing cross she had better luck. The reference librarian had sent her to a Russian Orthodox monastery in Ligonier, about fifty miles out of town. It had an extensive library of Eastern religious art.

"I had the newspaper photo with me," Charity said. "That made it a lot easier. The priest in charge of the library pointed me toward the right shelves. Of course all the books were in Russian or Greek. I had to go by pictures, plates." She pulled some sheets from her sack purse. "I Xeroxed the three that looked close. And the text that went with each one." She pointed to one of the sheets. "This looks like the one. Here's the copy."

I scanned the paragraph of Russian text.

Ceremonial Cross (c. 1490). Uncovered by A. Atnonovich during his methodical surveys of the monastery art of southwestern Russia. Size: 50cm. vertical. Upper crosspiece 12cm. Lower crosspiece 16cm. Material: Lightly alloyed gold. Artist unknown. Location: Monastery of the Holy Order of the Caucasus, 160km. northwest of the town of Volzna. Atnonovich noted that, despite its value, the primitive masterpiece was worn by the local patron during socio-religious ceremonies.

I translated for Charity, my hackles stirring again. Then I told her about Igor-Markov's letter to Mikhail. I watched her eyes widen. I sensed the chill breeze blowing from ancient Russia touching her WASP soul. Staid and ladylike, she nonetheless said, "What the *hell?* . . . The cross *belongs* to the Holy Order of the Caucasus? The Wonder of Holiness? That nasty Mikhail Markov?"

I shook my head. "Remember the scribbles left by Igor. What did he say?—'Not Mikhail . . . Nicholas.'"

"Nicholas!" Charity shook her head. "Can't be. A dope pusher and a murderer?"

"Don't be so sure. Isn't he the charismatic one that everybody loves? Isn't he the leader? The guy with 'something special'?"

Charity took a stiff swallow of her Chablis. "Let's get hold of ourselves, Yuri. All that Russian mumbo-jumbo is just muddying the waters. What do you think? Some *Moonstone* fanatic slipped out of Russia, traveled five or six thousand miles, got to Russian Slope and nabbed Nicholas—on the *same* night he happened to shoot Ed Dixon? Come *on!*"

"Took him back to the Valley of Promise," I said, not sure I was serious.

"What about the letter from New York?"

"Still works. He was made to write it, mailed it between flights. From the international terminal of J.F.K. Before the flight to Moscow, or more likely to Constantinople or northern Pakistan."

"Yuri, why *now?* After all, he was 20 years old."

"Don't know."

"I don't buy it. Somebody would have to finger him for the order. No other way they would know who he was and where he lived after all those years. Again, same question, Yuri. Why *now,* not before? Why the night of the shooting?"

I couldn't answer that. My initial enthusiasm was fading before Charity's Anglo-Saxon skepticism. A letter more than fifty years old, no matter how dramatic, shouldn't carry too much—if any—weight. It was fascinating, though, intriguing. I was starting to get a hunch about that big insurance policy. Promised myself to go see Gregory Ogalkov before long.

Betty Ellen walked by, purse on arm. She leveled a look at me that would have blackened grapes on the vine. I understood that glance of hate. My behavior at Volodya's do had sent her several direct messages. That she wasn't the only woman in my life was the first one. The second was that making love in middle age lacked both the significance and emotional trappings it did at twenty. And that trying to turn back the clock remained a feat that needed more talent and imagination than the team of Betty Ellen Edwards and Yuri Nevsky could muster. The final message was, I supposed, that Yuri Nevsky had become emotionally independent. I had grown unevenly, in fits and starts, staggering, weaving, but just the same making it on down the road. The tall kid with lots of hair and white teeth was gone—along with the lovely lass in shirtwaist dresses. My behavior spelled the death of her unspoken illusions about us. By now such disappointments for her, as for others middle-aged, were surely a familiar experience.

Being disappointed had driven to the surface the darker sides of her nature. Reminded her of aging, the loss of physical beauty, the loss of love, without which none of us can flourish. Out of it all grew intimidation for even the toughest person—the specter of a life alone.

Maybe she was too hard on me. I had loved her when I was twenty-two. When life was simple linearity—free of the ornate twists and ambiguities of the adult world. She might be surprised to know that I treasured those days, too. I just knew better than to try to go back. Just the same the persistence of memory posed real questions for me about the meaning of time passing. To me she was still the shirtwaisted girl ordering lemon Cokes or cooing at the edge of passion for me to be careful with her.

I owed her something and she thought I didn't know that. What I owed her was the chance to feel good about herself. I turned in my chair. She had found her way into a familiar pocket of Imperial Court regulars. A handful of leering Slavs with some bucks in their pockets were paying casual, habitual attention to her femininity. The reflexive desire that went before all our masculine folly. I promised myself to find a way to remind her she was a very intelligent, still-attractive woman with a bright future.

"Pardon me!" Charity's voice carried a waspish tone.

"What?"

"I didn't know you were in love with the comedienne, too. I thought you were running a special on housekeepers this week."

"I told you—we're old friends. We went to college together."

"I *know* that. I was saying what else did you find out today?"

I told her about getting KO'ed by Houle's honeys, and about P.Q.'s license plate, Olga's father and Olga's mystery visitor. Just skimmed the surface. I left out Tatiana's confession.

She beamed. "Now *that* is more like it. To hell with Russian mumbo-jumbo. License plate number. Times and places! Some things you can see and count. I'll check the number tomorrow. We get an owner's name and it'll be all downhill from then on."

"Somehow I doubt it." My mind swung back to Nicholas. I told Charity about Anton Rastokov and the fleabag Moskva Hotel. And the coincidence I couldn't digest: Rastokov and Igor Markov both being from the Valley of Promise.

"Don't you think you've pushed that Old Russian stuff as far as you can for now?" Charity said.

"OK. OK. Here's another down-to-earther for you. Polsky was in the Moskva. He told me the insurance company's sending a man and paying one of his cop's way to New York. To try to find the kid—or Olga, *or* the cross."

"Lots of luck. How many people in the Apple? Twelve million?"

"You are *hard* to please, little lady."

"I like facts. That wasn't a fact. That was a faint hope."

We ordered dinner. I wasn't hungry despite a hard day's work. While we waited for the meal I detailed my visit to my college classmate, Houle, the drug baron Pitt booster. Charity listened closely. When I finished, she said, "You believed him?"

I thought for a second. "Yeah, I did."

"Then that means Nick disappeared on his own. No drug connection."

"Nope."

"Too bad." Charity emptied her wine glass. "I wanted things simplified."

"So did I."

She slid glasses and silverware around on the table. "No mob members to muddy the water. Nobody else disappeared except Olga. Let's think about it a minute, even if we don't know whose car was used.

"This ash tray is the Eleven-to-Seven. This glass is St. Basil's. This one is Olga's apartment." She tore four matches out of a book. "Olga, Nicholas, Father Alexander and X. At seven o'clock Nicholas is with Father Alexander." She put the matches side by side. "Olga is with Lev in their apartment. At a quarter to eight Father Alexander and Nicholas have a shouting match, then Nicholas leaves. Fifteen-minute walk, just enough time to get him to the Eleven-to-Seven. He meets Dixon. P.Q. and Anya are there reaping cheap thrills. At eight ten Father Alexander goes for a walk. Or does he jump into another car?"

"He doesn't use *his* car," I said. "That we know."

"Mr. or Ms. X . . ." She slid a match. ". . . pulls up outside the bar. Not Olga. Probably not Father Alexander."

"Ray Nevick maybe." I glanced across the room where Nevick was standing with his hand on Betty Ellen's ass. Then I remembered how upset he got about Nick being missing. And that Houle said the paunchy one was waiting for Nick to bring him the five thousand. "No, not Nevick."

"Nick kills Dixon and gets in the car with X."

"About eight fifteen," I said.

"Then X drives Nicholas to Olga's apartment." Adjustment of match sticks. "They pick up Olga—"

"Hold it, Charity. Two small problems. First, it's about two minutes by car from the Eleven-to-Seven to Olga's place. Second, Lev didn't really see who was at the door. It might not have been Nicholas."

"It had to be Nicholas or X. And there had to be a car." Charity's slender index finger shoved the Olga match all the way across the table to the St. Basil's glass. "Because she had to get all the way up here to beg money from Father Alexander by nine o'clock. And to steal the cross—if she did it."

I grunted with surprise. I saw some crumbling in the hard stone of our Slope Puzzle. My voice was dry when I said, "Olga didn't need money to get away from home, Charity. She had just cashed a check for five hundred dollars. Lev showed me the carbon."

Charity shrugged. "She could have needed more."

"But she never had anything. Five hundred would look like a fortune. Maybe she never went to Father Alexander."

Charity looked doubtful. "A lying priest?"

"Another Rasputin, maybe. Oh, well, for now let's say Olga did meet Father A. That means she was driven up to St. Basil's by X or Nicholas." I sat back. "Another point. Don't forget, anything could have happened in the half hour between the

138

getaway from the Eleven-to-Seven and the knock on Olga's door. Could have been a change of cars, change of drivers, anything."

"Let's finish up here before we angle off." Charity moved the Olga and Nicholas matchsticks to the St. Basil's glass.

"Better put X up there, too."

"One or more of them had to be there, Yuri. To steal the cross." Charity's light blue eyes searched my face. "Right?"

"Yes. To send it with Nicholas out of the country."

"Oh, will you *stop* that. It doesn't work. Olga or Nicholas stole the cross to sell."

"They—or X. I'm not committing myself as to who—or why."

"You *do* hold onto an idea." Charity cocked her index finger. With her other hand she shoved the Olga and Nicholas matches together. The waiter brought the meal. "Anyway, off they flew, Nicholas to New York, X and Olga to who-knows-where." She snapped the matches off onto the shadowy floor. She attacked her stuffed shrimp with unnecessary vigor. "That all didn't prove much, did it?"

"Don't sell us short, partner. You made us realize some things. First, that there's a half an hour unaccounted for before Olga got picked up. Second, that maybe she didn't visit Father Alexander *or* steal the cross. Best of all, everything's getting mixed up. Chinks in the armor of people's stories. Tips of the wedges and all that. When we track the license plate I really *do* think the pieces are going to rearrange themselves."

Charity nodded. "I want to make a bet. That Nicholas Markov is in New York."

"I don't bet against that."

"And that Olga Samnesovich is right along with him."

"A dinner. You're on." I stirred the last of my stuffed filet of sole. "We've got to deal with Father Alexander before long."

"Say more."

"See how, where he fits in. I'd like to pin him down on his movements that night."

Charity rested her fork on an empty plate. Never wanting for appetite, my colleague. "The poor man. He adored Nicholas just like everybody else. I agree. He fits in. But his head is all messed up with Nick being gone." She picked up the dessert menu. "I'm going to have the parfait. How about you?"

I still had no appetite. I had left half my dinner on the plate. Betty Ellen's act had begun again with an upbeat "No Business

139

Like Show Business" from the house piano. An old love. Now I had a new one. Almond eyes abrim with piety. Facial bones angled to point to the most ancient strains of the race of Slavs. An intriguing shape hidden under her conservative but stylish clothes. A sense of purpose and great serenity flourishing among the troubled, betrayed women of Russian Slope. Tatiana. I wanted to see her. "Don't forget, I issued an invitation to 138. Father Alexander and Tatiana. For Sunday afternoon tea. An old Russian custom."

"At least you're admitting you *are* one. For you that's a big step forward."

"I hope you'll play hostess."

"Cook and clean for them?" Charity looked me in the eye. "You know they haven't *made* an apron that'll fit Charity Day. Never will. I've *done* my domestic time." Sorrow behind her stubbornness.

"I meant just be there."

"A cup of tea is pretty lean rations."

"I'll handle that part."

"She must mean a lot to you, Yuri."

"Who?"

"Oh, come *on*." Charity's eyes rolled ceilingward. She giggled. "I'll be there. Keeping the holy man's attention while you exercise your aging seduction skills."

"With friends like you, Charity . . ."

On a whim I excused myself and went to a payphone. I dialed St. Basil's. "I couldn't wait till Sunday to hear your voice," I said when Tatiana answered. "Wake you up?"

"Couldn't sleep. I was thinking about you. And how unfair I was to you."

"How unfair, Tatya?"

"Pouring out my ugliness on you."

"Tatya, you're not—"

"And making it seem as though Father Alexander wasn't important to me."

Jealousy bloomed. "You're not lovers?"

"We care for each other. I support his earthly needs. He nourishes my spirit. It's not romantic love, Yuri, but it *is* love. And respect. And loyalty."

"There's room for me in there somewhere."

"I don't . . . know. I feel I've somehow deceived you. I want a man's love, but I'm all tangled and sharp inside. Like barbed

140

wire. I don't know if I can give anything. But I'm selfish just the same. I want you in my life. I want you to . . . love me."

"I'm well on my way," I said.

"That sounded awfully quick and flip."

"The truth comes out fast."

"Oh, Yuri, Yuri, I want to love you. You must teach me how. Sleep, my darling, with a kiss." She hung up.

For a moment I thought of re-dialing. I thought better of it. She had given me what I hadn't known I wanted: hope.

I went back by the table to pick up Charity.

We had to pass Ray Nevick's bunch on the way out. He stepped out to block our way. He was wearing one of his jump suits. His protruding gut touched my hip.

"You're a lying fucker, Nevsky."

"And you're a toilet-mouthed creep. So we're even. Let the lady and me by, please."

"Betty Ellen tipped me off about you. About your being a Kojak with hair." He scowled at my emerging dome through widely dilated pupils. "Some hair, anyhow."

"I'm not a cop."

"Narc scumbag!"

"Betty Ellen didn't tell you that."

"She shit!"

"Watch your mouth! We got thrown out of here once. You're heading us for time two."

"I don't like snoopers. I don't like people nosing in after Nick Markov."

"I don't care what you like. My friend Charity and I want to go home. We want you out of the way."

"You've had it here on the Slope, Nevsky. Your name is mud. Nick Markov was ten times the man you are."

"And a hundred times what you are!"

The bouncers appeared like djinns from a flask. Nevick turned his wild eyes on them and stepped aside.

"You seem to like rough stuff in the parking lot, Nevick," I said. "Come on out if you want round two."

"You've bought it, Kojakoff! And all your cute, slant-eye combat tricks ain't gonna save you."

I pushed past the gut with Charity behind. She lectured me in a low voice all the way to the parking lot. The thrust of her remarks was that men in their forties made lousy hooligans. Out on the asphalt I took a few deep breaths and looked down-river toward the distant lights of the City of Pittsburgh. The view would never be lovely. But at night it did have some charm.

Charity stood at my side. "You love this smelly old town."

"I swore I'd never come back."

"Never say 'never,'" Charity said.

My eyes moved up and down the river, darting from light to light like moths. I thought about my return to Pittsburgh. All in all it was going well. The life of Reluctant Investigator suited me. Possibly more important, things were also improving down in the wheelhouse of my heart. I was feeling better about myself and wasn't lonely. Much of the credit for my mental health went to the classy lady on my right.

I looked down at Charity's head and face, smears of white and gold in the river valley lights. I hadn't trusted my relaxation and ease in her company; my failed relationship with Ann had made it impossible for me to rely on my own intuition. Charity had seemed too amiable and comfortable. Slowly those worries were fading like fog under sun to reveal that she really had supported and nourished me. Nothing flashy, of course—not from Charity. No, all laid back without the hot, short-lived sparks of overdone enthusiasm and temporary commitment. She was there, steady and unflappable, across her cups of coffee and glasses of Chablis.

How I helped her deal with the tragedy of losing her family was less clear. My just being there in her life helped. In a sense we had a home and certainly a degree of companionship. We could exercise the healthy adult need to nurture by being mutually attentive and sharing the essentially trivial events that made up so much of our lives. All that sounded a lot like a marriage . . .

I turned and saw Nevick hurrying down the concrete steps. His hand traced the railing. His feet were unsure. But he kept moving, running through his stumbles.

"He's drunk," Charity said.

"Stoned. On heroin, I think."

We strolled back toward my Datsun. A door slammed. Nevick had gotten into his Mustang. Its engine roared. Its lights winked on. It jerked out of its space like a three-year-old leaving the Aqueduct starting gate and came barreling across the open asphalt.

Nevick was going to run us down.

I gave Charity a shove toward the nearest line of cars, then darted the other way. The Mustang veered toward me. Charity would have time to reach safety. Where I was heading, there was no place to hide: flat asphalt lit by mercury spotlights. Like a bullring. Or a Cretan arena where men and women once tumbled in acrobatics across the horns of wild bulls.

I was an experienced tumbler—handsprings, somersaults—and had pretty fair body control. I didn't have the spring and reach that I had fifteen years ago. But I wouldn't need them. Just timing—and luck.

I turned and faced the onrushing car. I squinted past the glare of headlights at a spot about a third of the way up the hood. The Mustang was doing about thirty-five. Nevick's face was a shadowy smear behind the streaked windshield. I took three short running strides toward the onrushing chrome. I got my feet together, cocked my legs and sprang up and forward, spread hands reaching for the flat of the hood.

I got my hands down on the still-cold metal, legs above my head. The rush of the car and my straightening arms brought my feet over. My rear hit the back end of the trunk and I bounced hard. The rear bumper grazed my back. I hit the asphalt in a tangle of arms and legs. Those bumps hurt, but nowhere near as bad as a couple tons of onrushing Mustang.

Had Nevick thrown it into reverse and hit the gas, my brief career as information specialist would have been over. Instead he jammed on the brakes, opened the driver-side door, and leaned out to look back. By then I was on my feet and sprinting for the line of parked cars. Charity's screams hurried me on.

Nevick whipped the Mustang in a tight turn and cut toward my direction line. My brain did some rough cut calculations that told me that the race would end in a dead heat—with me the dead part. I had to change direction. Back out onto the empty asphalt but still inside the box of cyclone fence. This time there wouldn't be any chance for cute vaulting tricks. Nevick would be looking to upset my timing. Then to crush me for my error.

I headed for the fence. The Yuri Nevsky Monkey Act—never rehearsed and never performed—was really my only chance. A shriek of laying rubber told me Nevick had floored it. The asphalt hummed with the vibrations of the onrushing Ford as it ate up the yards in a sudden gulp of velocity.

My driving toes carried me across dark wet patches on the asphalt. Then I was at the fence. I leaped high, arms reaching, fingers spread like a raptor's claws. I caught the mesh and drove my shoe tips into the wire. Some purchase let me scramble to the top crossbar. I got a poor grip on it. I threw a quick glance over my shoulder. The Mustang was fifteen yards away and traveling fast.

Nevick saw I was too high to hit. The best he could do was knock me off. He hit the brakes hard. Locked them. That and hitting a puddle of oil added two big mistakes to that column in his life. The last two entries.

The Mustang hit the wire a little to the left and below me. The impact tore the vertical poles out of their cement footings. The tons of wheeled weight rolling over the wire knocked me off like a bug. I tumbled to the asphalt right beside the rear wheel. That lethal round of rubber rolled past my skull. The Mustang flattened the fence and crept out over the edge of the bluff. For a moment it teetered on the bed of wire. Dazed, I still heard thumps and scrapings as Nevick tried to bail out. But the dope had wrapped him up like a shroud. With a dreadful grating thump the Mustang went over.

Charity's screams drilled through the fog in my head. I got up on hands and knees. Her hands were on my face. "My God! You all right?"

"Bloody but unbowed." I staggered to my feet using, needing, her arms around my waist. I knew I was badly scraped and bruised. But the fleshy clockwork was intact.

"Nevick." I walked under my own power to the edge of the bluff. About 150 feet down and two or three heavy bounces farther the Mustang lay driver's side up. Fire bloomed in a garland of bright flames around the rear chassis.

"Charity, call the ambulance."

"For you?"

"Nevick. I'm going down and see if he made it."

She headed back toward the sound of excited voices. I found a steep gully that angled down into the darkness off to the right. It was littered with bits of thick shale and empty soda and beer cans. I slipped and scrambled my way down, collecting a gouged knee and a gashed hand.

The car had landed in a copse of stunted sumac trees. I shoved the thin trunks aside. The fire had spread, casting a weak light that let me peer through the webbed windshield. Nevick was jammed against the down door. His body was facing the dashboard. But his face was looking into the back seat.

I scrambled away just as the fuel tank went off with a small *phooph*. Leave it to Nevick to be driving on fumes. Just the same, the small fire kept me away. I paced around the flaming vehicle feeling more tired and beat-up by the minute. After a while I sat on a rock.

I heard sirens. Then Charity called out my name in the littered darkness. She rushed up with the big first-aid kit I kept in the back seat of the Datsun, and the eight-cell flashlight. She shushed my protests and busied herself with the damaged patches on my hands and face. She didn't spare alcohol, tape or criticism of my exposing myself to danger. "You could have handled all that *much* more safely," she said. But didn't suggest how.

Firemen and then cops came crashing around the sumacs. I felt drained. There would be questions. Portable lights were dragged in and the fire foamed out. Two firemen with shoulders like the Budweiser Clydesdales tipped the Mustang upright. By now it looked like a battered sardine can.

A medic appeared and peered in at Nevick. What he saw in the smoke made him shrug. He waved up the two stretcher men. The firemen and cops went to work on the least damaged door. It took about twenty minutes to open it. The medic crawled in and right out again.

"Dead at scene," he said to no one special.

Charity gasped and hid her face for a long moment. The stretcher men dragged Nevick's body out. His head was lolling like a spring-necked toy's. The blanket went right over his face. The stretcher men had some trouble working their load out through the sumacs.

I got up and looked back up the bluff. Flashlights moved around the flattened cyclone fence. A cop rode us back up to the Imperial Court. I went looking for Betty Ellen and found her with the rubbernecks in the parking lot. I grabbed her neck and looked down into her face. The mercury lights were unkind to both of us: every year showed. "Thanks!" I said.

"I don't want to talk to you."

"Thanks for siccing Nevick on me."

"I didn't—"

"What did you tell him?"

"Nothing."

"Nothing? So much 'nothing' he tried to run me down with his Mustang. No lie! I had to do unlikely things with my body to get out of the way." I jerked a thumb toward the bluff edge. "That's his car down there. He's already gone—to the morgue. He skidded on some oil and went through the fence. More than

145

a hundred feet straight down. Not counting the bounces. Broke his neck."

"He's *dead?*" Her eyes widened with shock.

"Very. And *you* put the words of death in his ear."

In the merciless light, her acne scars showed livid. She tried to meet my gaze, then her eyes fell. She looked away. Her head was cocked at an angle that accented her ski-jump nose, made her seem vulnerable. "I didn't! I didn't at all. I told him I didn't really think you were a reporter. That you were probably after Nick, and that was all. Anybody after Nick gets him crazy. I wanted him to beat the shit out of you this time. I never *dreamed* he'd...oh, oh, shit!"

She started bawling.

I gave her a small hug. "I know you were pissed about Elena Markov and P.Q. Antonelli."

"You didn't even *care* about me."

"It just seemed that way. Neither of those women means anything to me. I was just being sociable. And I was drunk."

"I can't get over Ray. The poor *slob.* How am I gonna do my second act? God, Yuri, I wish I'd never *met* you. You weren't good for me when we were kids. You're not good for me now. Get away from me!"

Charity made it a threesome. "A real charmer with the ladies. You should excuse him, Ms. Edwards. Born couthless. Die the same way."

Betty Ellen wailed and ran off.

"Too many women in your life, Nevsky," Charity said.

"We better hang around. The cops are gonna want to talk to us."

Right on cue, another cruiser, blue lights circling, nosed into the parking lot. A sergeant was driving. Chief Polsky was its passenger. He flashed an icy smile and crooked an index finger toward Charity and me.

14

The chief made me tell my story from the beginning when we shoved by Nevick's gut to where he saw us from his squad car. He made me tell it slowly—and provide a guided tour, too. *Here* was where Nevick almost stumbled. These rubber marks came from his jackrabbiting out of his parking slot. About *here* on the asphalt I had done my improvised tumbling act.

"You jumped *over* the Mustang, Superman?" Polsky's voice was icy with disbelief.

"I vaulted it. Just got up above it and it went under me."

"That's impossible."

"I *saw* him do it." Charity's chilliness caused the chief to move on.

As we wandered, Polsky's team of photographers, notetakers, counters and measurers tagged along like a silent chorus to the dreary tragedy of Nevick's end. The chief was relentless in his search for exact details. We stood forever by the wire while the electronic flashes winked like fireworks on the Fourth. Down the cliff we went to the flattened sumacs and the smoldering Mustang. It was ringed with enough police lights to make it look like a filming sequence from a hoods-behind-the-hoods, Grade B drive-in movie.

The chief wasn't nearly through. By now it was pushing two in the morning, chilly, and way past time for Yuri Nevsky to be tucked into his beddy-bye. My thumps and lumps were throbbing like the bass section in the *Rite of Spring*. I was bone tired.

"Nevsky, I just asked you a question!" Polsky growled.

"Ask it again. I can't remember whether it was the sixteen- or the thirty-two-thousand-dollar one."

The chief moved fast for a big man. He grabbed me by the shirt and shook me around like a man trying to make an eight the hard way. "This is fucking *serious* business, Nevsky. A guy has died ugly—and you're up to your ass in it all. Don't wise-mouth me, fella."

"You leave him alone!" Charity shouted. "Ray Nevick tried to murder him. And what you're doing is unnecessary, illegal and plain *nasty*. And *I'm* his attorney."

"That ain't all you are, lady," the chief said. But he put me down.

There were more questions, measurements and photographs. Around 3:30 the chief looked to be winding down. The chorus packed up its gear—except for one eager-looking sergeant.

"We finished?" I said.

"Some of us. *You* have to give the sergeant a detailed deposition."

"What's he been *doing*?" Charity said.

"This is the *official* one. Start talking, Nevsky. Sergeant Locatelli is Police Shorthand Champion of the Middle Atlantic States."

"Does he ever get writer's cramp?"

"Hand like a claw in a penny-arcade machine."

"And when I finish with him, I go bye-bye—right?"

"*Wrong*, Nevsky, wrong. You and Ms. Day come up to the club. I want to ask you some *hard* questions."

Even as I bitched to him I understood that the last three hours and the one or more to come of testimony to Sergeant Shorthand had been used mostly to soften me up. The *real* questions were still to come. I wasn't looking forward to them.

An hour and forty-five minutes later Polsky took Charity and me to one of the small function rooms on the second floor of the Imperial Court. He stationed one of his men outside the door, refused my pleas for coffee, ignored Charity's legalese complaints, and started in on me.

My condition, the hour, his vitality—maybe even his looking a little like the popular version of the Devil in the weak light—didn't auger well for my answers. His questions reminded me of a long piece of modern music. Soft followed by loud. Short bursts then long pauses. Lots of surprise blasts from different angles. He started with the day I was born. A few easy questions, then a zinger. He got real personal. Considering my condition, I would've crumbled into a heap of self-contradiction if it wasn't for Charity. She stood up to the tough, smart cop. "Yuri doesn't *have* to talk to you, Chief Polsky," she said. "He's well within his rights to refuse."

"I can *get* the papers, Lady Attorney," the chief said. "I can *make* him come to headquarters. We can *stop* being friends."

This exchange—or variations on it—was repeated at least

a dozen times. Each time the chief angled off a bit—but later came twisting back to the same sensitive area. My past work life and my week on the Slope took most of our time. I tried to leave blanks; he tried to fill them in. Neither of us was completely effective. Neither of us was happy with that. Both of us were getting pissed.

"Polsky, that is asking for self-*incrimination*." Charity's voice was like an ice pick in our ears—deliberately, I was sure. When I glanced up wearily I noticed dawn was inching through the window.

"All right. All right!" Polsky's meaty hand thumped down on his Panasonic's lever. "You two could handle a couple of Spanish Inquisitors before breakfast and the SS before tea. You're almost enough to fool a determined cop."

"You think we're playing games?" I said.

"I know you're playing games."

We started to protest.

"Your newspaper friend—what's his name? Brightwood? Harrison Brightwood has been 'in conference' or 'out of the office' for the last five days. And he isn't returning my calls. You don't by any chance think he's dodging a chance to vouch for those hokey carte blanche letters he wrote for you?" Polsky's face was puffed a bit from fatigue, but his eyes were as sharp as ever. "I ran checks on both of you." He glowered at Charity. "You're a widow. And a bona fide member of the Pennsylvania bar. You're with Wellman, Thorne and King down in Gateway Center. How come you have time to be running all over the Slope day and night?"

"Senior Partner Thorne is a great believer in public service," Charity said. "He figures we all should contribute to the community. And he's an old criminal lawyer. When I told him there was a missing person—Nick—on the Slope, he gave me a little nudge to do an article for the *Post-Gazette*. Legal angles on disappearance. Then later I could rewrite it for a law journal."

The chief snorted, even though what Charity said was largely true. Senior Partner Thorne was in love with the kind of work I did and liked to see her help me out "for the greater good of the firm."

"So you and I are both public servants," Polsky said sarcastically. He waved away her start at further explanation. "Bad enough, but *you*, Nevsky. Living in an eighteen-room house with no visible means of support. I had some *good* people try

149

to check back on your work history. Talk about being *stone-walled*. They found out you were in D.C. for a long time—and didn't leave a single goddamned trace! I don't get it. I don't get it at all. You didn't officially *exist*, near as I can figure out. So that means some kind of superduper top-secret crap. MX missile, CIA, Dirty Tricks, Inc. Something. For all I know you're Mission Impossible No. 1."

"What's your point, chief?"

Polsky rubbed his eyes and loosened his tie. "I told you before, Nevsky. I don't like people who think they can do end runs around a dumb local cop. I don't like to be used or deceived. I do a great job. You saw my stats. The big thorn in my side is the drug business. Drugs are poison to cops, too. Even getting them under control—never mind wiping them out—is what they call 'labor-intensive.' Just the same I've been making slow but steady progress. But a lot of folks who call themselves agents of some kind have been wandering around—city people, state people, even a few feds. They don't give me the time of day. They don't *lower* themselves to check in with me. To tell this old steel-town cop what in hell they're doing. They sure don't care what *I'm* doing. The Dixon murder brought in a bunch of the worst ones. So you are looking at one *pissed* chief of police. I have five empty cells in my shiny new slammer. I'm gonna put some of these people in. And I think I'm gonna start with *you*, Nevsky. If you're some kind of heavyweight drug buster with a James Bond briefcase, you're gonna have to use it, pal. You are *in trouble.*"

"I'm flattered, but your guessing machine is programmed about two levels too high."

"You are not leveling with me! Either of you. I *know* it. I been questioning everybody from bums to bankers for twenty years. I know jive when I hear it."

I shrugged. "So hear the truth. It'll disappoint you, I think. Ludmilla Markov—a little old babushka—hired me to find her grandson, Nick Markov."

"What? I got a *pair* of attorneys here?"

"No," Charity said.

"Then, Nevsky, you're..." Chief Polsky howled with laughter. It shook the chandelier hanging above. He wheezed and heaved and clutched his sides. "You're a...a *gumshoe,*" he howled. "A private dick. You! Nevsky. Christ, Sam Spade, where are you now that we really need you?"

I was tired, impatient and now insulted. "Listen, Polsky,

I'm doing her a favor for small money. Since I started, Nick Markov's got further under my skin than an IV needle."

The chief puffed down like the Little Engine That Could. "How come she asked you?"

"Because I have a Russian name."

"Lots of people have Russian names. She didn't ask *me.*"

"I have some luck at finding things. She heard about it. She wouldn't come to you because if *you* found Nick, he'd be up for first degree." I thought we were about through. The birds were singing and I was relaxing.

Right into the trap—as usual. "I want the goddamned truth out of you, you bastard!" His clutching hands almost tore pieces out of my shoulders. "What were you doing talking to the biggest dope dealer in western Pennsylvania? What were you doing in Doug Houle's penthouse suite? The narcotics squad has his phone bugged and films everybody who goes in and out. A friend of mine heard 'Russian Slope' on the phone and gave me a buzz. And you better talk *straight* this time or I'll—"

"*I'll* speak for him, Chief Polsky." Charity's voice was icy and professional. Her attorney-in-court voice. She explained everything—the hoods who had grabbed me and bought me a ticket on the Slumberland Express, frat buddy Houle, his paranoia and my being no closer to the drug business than to the Berlin Wall. She spoke firmly and precisely—convincingly.

Finally the chief nodded, sat back. He took off his tie. "So you're just doing an old lady a favor. You're a goddamn boy scout." He frowned and shook his head. "You must have *some* other angle. Something."

"There's the stolen cross. We think it's mixed up with the murder and the getaway," Charity said. "Volodya Tschersky's offered a sizable reward."

The chief stretched and stroked his goatee. "Far as I'm concerned the Markov kid's in New York. The insurance guy and my Ivy League Sergeant, Whitcomb, are there now, looking for him." He looked at me. "You got any reason to think different?"

I had to say no.

"You find out, I want to hear. I wouldn't want you to, say, go to New York or Las Vegas, or some damn place, find the kid and help him get up to Canada. Got that, Nevsky, Attorney Lady?"

"Sure."

The chief got up, stretched and walked to the window. "It's good for everybody to see the sun rise from time to time. Strengthens the character. Reminds us of our links with natural cycles."

I groaned.

"First day in quite a while our friend Nevick won't see," the chief said. "Always a shock when somebody goes down for the long count. Even a poor turkey like Ray. I'll tell you two something. Since the kid disappeared, it was all downhill for him."

"So we heard," I said.

"Maybe you heard. But I don't think you heard how bad and how hard he slid. After the kid disappeared, Ray became a very reckless and careless man. And when you deal, that's a very serious shortcoming. He floundered around the Slope like a dinosaur in a tar pit. He started selling anything to anybody. Like he *wanted* to be busted hard. And he started using his own wares. My office set up a little sting just for him, and he swallowed it all. End of the week we were going to bust him. I have a pile of hard evidence six inches thick. One way or another he wanted to destroy himself. And he did." The chief turned back from the window. "Know why? 'Cause he really *loved* Nick Markov. More I think about it, more it makes sense." He paused for effect. "I think the kid was gay. And Nevick brought him out. Then he fell in love with him."

The same thought had been rubbing around the edges of my mind.

"Nevick knew we were tailing him. That some of his ugly would rub off on the kid. That the kid—sooner or later— would end up in bad trouble. Because he loved him so much, he arranged for him to be driven off to some place safe—like New York—far away. He made a personal sacrifice, then couldn't live with it. That's why the kid disappeared right *after* the drug deal. Nevick had to deliver or he'd be in trouble."

I saw the chief's idea holding some water. Nick gay and Nevick his lover. All the time people had been telling me what a saint the kid was. But he never touched a woman, even though they were lined up like he was selling tickets to *The Empire Strikes Back*.

Charity, on the other hand, was cranking up her skeptical machine. "What about the cross? How's that being stolen fit in?"

The chief waved it away. "With gold better than six hundred an ounce it's a wonder it wasn't ripped off sooner. No connection. One of those coincidences that seems to fit right in—but doesn't. Think through it. Who knew where Nick would be between eight and eight fifteen that night? Nevick, P.Q. Antonelli and Anya Rok. All of them are still around."

I thought aloud: "Olga Samnesovich didn't know. She was home watching TV."

"Father Alexander knew. Didn't want Nick to meet Dixon," Charity said. "But he never left town."

"You think about it." Polsky gathered up his tape recorder and briefcase. "The more you think about it, the more sense it makes. The kid's gone to New York. And we're never going to find him."

Outside, Charity and I decided for the moment we were past being sleepy, and were ravenous. Sure enough, the Black Sea served breakfast. If I needed evidence that lechers have a special early warning system, Stan Pokora's swooping down on our table would have provided it. Didn't this guy *ever* sleep? He leered at Charity with an intensity that Groucho would have envied. "No check for this table," he said to the waiter.

Instead of chasing him away Charity spouted a stream of small talk and insisted the Cossack join us. Effects of sleep deprivation, I decided. Fatigue had brought out the lines around her eyes and on her forehead. Made her look fragile, in need of protection. She could have fed Pokora his scrambled eggs right out of her hand.

Toward the end of the meal the Cossack tore himself away for a few moments of business. Charity looked at me. "Today's license plate day. My firm has a friend at the Allegheny County Bureau of Motor Vehicles. I'm not going to bother going to sleep, Yuri. I'm on a high." Her eyes were sparkling. When Stan came back she said, "I'm going to run some errands. Want to come along for company?"

The Cossack beamed. "I would accompany you if it were only to the town dump—and we had to walk all the way on our hands!"

"Today we're using a car." She smiled prettily at me. "I need a change of face for a while."

They swept off, leaving me to soiled napkins and coffee dregs. Change of face indeed! What had happened to Charity's taste?

I sat alone with a red face and a pounding heart. It bothered me that she had left with someone else. It couldn't be jealousy. I knew she spent a lot of time in the company of eligible men into their years of prosperity. And why not? She was an adult emotionally. I hadn't met many such women. And she was professional, self-sufficient and independent as well. I had found her to be a source of strength as I struggled to reassemble myself. She always had time for me, even though she wrestled with her own demons of dead children and husband—loss and pain so deep that I couldn't begin to fathom them. Yes, she was tough. Like the best of womankind, she would prevail.

Her physical attractions weighed against her strength of character were insignificant. A twenty-five-year-old Yuri wouldn't have grasped that. It took middle age and a number of lady friends, both close and less so, spread back over the years, to really understand: the looks went, and if nothing accompanied them, ladies' lives failed. Some failed dramatically—drink or gunshot—more failed slowly. Like drops falling in Chinese water torture, days passed in which no risks were taken and no wholehearted commitments made. At life's end the landscape of spent years lay in a jumble of untaken roads not unlike a wasteland. Charity wasn't in that club. She was rebuilding and prospering. For the right man she was surely a great find. Pokora wasn't the right man. And I wasn't jealous. After all, I had Tatiana . . .

I drove to 138 for a couple lousy hours of sleep. I woke up in the sweat I always get from daylight slumber. I showered and felt a little better. I wandered downstairs to the piano. I wasn't in the mood to murder the masters. I did some nasty little finger exercises. Made plenty of the mistakes that seemed to fit right into them.

The door chimes rang. Ludmilla, here to do the cleaning she promised. She eyed my various bandages and plasters. "Do you know yet where my beloved grandson is?"

I bent my tongue around Russian again. "I've been working hard. I know a lot I didn't know before. But just where Nicholas is, I don't know—yet."

"You will find out. I know it. You're a blessed man in God's eyes. He will give you to know what my heart wants. And at the same time He will give you some of those things which are yours, but you do not see."

"What?"

She drew a huge apron from her shopping bag. Its heavy canvas around her lumpy figure made her look like a sack of potatoes. Her shrewd peasant's eyes swept my face. Within that seemingly simple glance I thought I saw a deeper light of—was it the mystical? "Your face is not the same one I saw on that day of rain and wind," she said. "God has begun to give you to see."

"Oh."

"Where are the cleaning things? Such a nice house and you live like pigs."

"A little dust, a few dishes unwashed is all. That's not so bad." I told her where the cleaning closet was.

She emerged armed with a heap of rags. "You must let my daughter-in-law, Elena, go her way, Yuri Vladimirovich."

My face reddened. Elena. She of the keys in back and the bust—and lust—in front. Nicholas's mother. Here I was, at forty, getting my hands slapped like a little boy, for something I hadn't done. "I'm not interested," I said.

"'If the fox is hungry, he will eat a frog.'"

I had just begun a long protest when Charity came bustling into the house. I was glad for the relief. Lecturing mothers make for awkward conversation. "I invited Stan to our Sunday afternoon do," Charity said.

"You *what?*"

"You are having guests?" Ludmilla said in her uneven English. "For tea, yes?"

"Sure. It's just Father Alexander and his house—"

"To have the priest come is an *honor*. To eat you are giving him . . . ?"

"Well . . ."

Ludmilla looked at Charity. "What will you bake?"

"I *don't* bake. I *don't* cook."

"Then *I* will do it." Ludmilla turned to me and spoke Russian. "To have the priest and an *empty* table . . ." The reproach dripped like whipped cream from a sundae. "I will make zakuski."

I drew Charity to the music room. "What're we doing? Turning Sunday into a circus? We were hoping to get some information out of Father Alexander—"

"We'll get it. Stan won't be able to be here until more than an hour after the others."

"Probably has to spend some time with his wife."

"Since when have *you* harped on details?"

"Details!"

"I look after my *own* social life, Yuri. And you've always stayed out of it. Why change now?"

"I haven't changed. It's just Pokora is—"

"You're going off with Ms. Almond Eyes. You think *I'm* comfortable pussyfooting around that zany priest? I have a right to provide some entertainment for myself!" Those red smears were rising in her cheeks. Signs that she was *well* past mere vexation. "OK. So six won't be a crowd."

"Six—"

"Ludmilla's in charge of munchies. We can't have her slave away, then all of a sudden send her home."

Charity's eyes widened. "My God, here we are bickering about our little tea—and you haven't even asked me about the license plate. Our friend at motor vehicles was right on the ball. Guess who owned the car?"

I took a deep breath. "Father Alexander," I said, my throat tight.

"Couldn't be *more* wrong. Little outfit called Avis."

"They try harder."

"You should try harder—at thinking, instead of guessing. Stan and I went to Avis's Pittsburgh headquarters. My dear Cossack was happy to wait outside. I told him—and the co-operative Avis fellow—that this was confidential legal business. They were happy to help. They have one of those *won*derful computers. Great printouts and displays of all kinds. That car—a dark blue Chevy Nova by the way—was rented the day of the Dixon murder—"

"At an Avis lot close to Russian Slope."

"Wrong again, Sherlock. At an Avis beside the South Hills Plaza shopping center. All the way across the city."

I scratched my head. "I ought to get with it," I said.

"More questions to come. You can redeem yourself. Pay close attention and *think*. We drove out to the South Hills, found the place. They checked their files. Sure enough, the Nova transaction was down in black and white. Cash deal. Question: "Who rented it?"

My mind was tangled up in the tar baby of a fifty-year-old letter about a fanatical religious order and an old Russian family. So I named the only priest I knew. "Father Alexander!" I crowed.

"Wrong again! Sex?"

"Now?"

"Idiot! What sex was the renter?"

156

"Male."

"Female! Olga Samnesovich. For a trip to . . . ?"

"New York City."

"Right! Knew you had a decent answer in you. I paid for the long-distance calls to Avis, New York. Took a while, but I got on the line to the clerk who was on duty when the Nova turned up. It was left out in the street the morning after Dixon was killed. The papers were on the front seat. There was a big bill tucked under the sun visor. More than enough for the charges."

"It didn't have to be Olga who ended up in New York," I said.

"Didn't *have* to be . . ."

"One little problem . . . when the Nova drove Nick away from the Eleven-to-Seven, Olga Samnesovich was home watching TV."

"Do muddy the waters, don't it?" Charity said.

"Yeah."

She frowned. "I'm going to say something maybe you won't like, Yuri. Something that's not kidding around."

"You *are* the serious one."

"And you're not!" There was snap in her tone. "And that's what's bothering me. I don't think you're giving the Nicholas problem your full attention. I think you're more interested in the ladies and in wisecracking with me than in getting the job done."

"I'm falling in love with Tatiana."

Charity cast a sidelong glance at me. "You are, huh? I didn't think exotic hothouse flowers were your type."

"She's not—"

"And what about the comedienne?"

"You were there the other night. It was never good. Now it's worse—or better. Anyhow, she's out of my life. What's bugging you, Charity? Jealous?"

Her cheeks colored. "That was irrelevant, a change of direction—and a cheap shot. What I'm *talking* about is our having about a week and a half before you have to go to Chicago to chase that Sunlight Scimitar. A week and a half to find out where Nicholas Markov is hiding. And you're just hacking around." She made a fist—index finger out—and punched my upper arm hard. "So get busy!"

157

"Ouch! Yes, ma'am!"

"Promise me you'll get serious."

"I've *been* serious."

"Prove it!" And out she walked.

15

After a light dinner Charity wandered off to her side of 138 "to think." Translation: Do Not Disturb. It wasn't just Nick Markov on her mind. Stan Pokora was in there somewhere. And so were Tatiana and I. Since hitting the Slope I found myself having to try to deal with my Russianness. I thought Charity's problem was trying to come to life emotionally after the dreadful loss of her family. Like many a valued machine her emotions weren't reviving smoothly, but in exasperating and testing fits and starts.

I checked my scrapes and gashes, stepping down to a mere Band-Aid where possible. Then I decided to do some thinking of my own. I poured myself a small Benedictine and slid onto the piano bench. Playing oiled my thinking. I had put a lot of two-and-twos together over uncertain right-hand runs and occasionally accurate left-hand chords. I was going to get some bumper stickers made up. *Mozart Motivates!* or *Vivaldi Vivifies!*

But it turned out that, while I was motivated, I was not vivified. A blue Chevy Nova and a bunch of Russians raced around in my head with the randomness of droplets in a cloud chamber. About all I knew new was that Olga Samnesovich had rented a car that ended up taking someone—or ones—to New York City. One very likely being Nicholas. Last night's ugly circus and poor sleep were still with me. Fatigue and sluggish thoughts sent me to bed before ten.

I slept the sleep of the just and woke up to a gray and windy morning. By the time I had breakfast and checked the Pirate spring training box score I felt housebound and in need of— of all things—a Bloody Mary. A curious and unusual craving. For that reason not to be ignored.

I opened the bar at the Imperial Court. The bartender was sliding stemware upside down into overhead slotted racks. He looked at me with the controlled interest of a man happy to recognize yet another problem drinker. I carried my Bloody

Mary out of the bar and into the closed dining-room. I found the best table by the glass wall and stared down into the windswept Mon Valley. I retreated into what a poet would call reverie.

"This section is *closed*." Artie Greenberg wore soft-soled shoes. The manager who had hassled the garbage men and intimidated Betty Ellen Edwards had arrived to do both to me.

"Oh."

"You'll have to move."

"I like it here."

Artie Greenberg's midwinter Miami Beach tan had almost faded back to his natural pallor. His lips were thick, his nose thin. His black eyes, which now brightened in recognition, bulged slightly. "You're Nevsky. That Yuri Nevsky."

"Good morning. Have a seat. A drink, coffee. It's on the house."

Artie remained standing. "You're not funny and I'm not sitting here—and neither are you!"

"I am sitting here. Look, me, sitting."

His scowl was unusually ugly. "You *are* a troublemaker, aren't you, Nevsky? Just looking for it all the time."

"What I am looking for this morning is either to be left alone or some polite conversation."

"As long as you're here, I *do* have some things to say to you."

"I figured you for a conversationalist, Artie."

Artie held up a thick index finger. "Item One. You started brawling in here the other night. We had to have you thrown out. Item Two. You finished your brawl on Imperial Court property—"

"To wit—the parking lot."

Three fingers were up. "Item Three. Two nights ago you played a part in the destruction of Imperial Court property—"

"To wit—the Cyclone fence."

"There was a hell of a lot of confusion. We lost customers."

"Sirens, police, burning cars, ambulances, fire engines. An eight-year-old boy's idea of heaven. Except for one ugly death."

"Item Five . . ."

"Item Four, Artie."

"Betty Ellen was so upset she couldn't finish—"

"Yes. Ms. Edwards," I said with what I thought was just

160

the right tone of deep respect. "She has the gift of being in touch with her emotions." Quite casually I pulled out my Coop notebook and opened it on the table beside my glass. I pulled out my Rapidograph pen.

"I had to can her," Artie said. "She was so 'in touch with her emotions' she couldn't go on for her second show. And the show must go on. That's what all these show business people *tell* us anyway. Tonight's her last performance."

I wrote.

"What the hell you writing, Nevsky?"

"How long have you been managing the Imperial Court, Mr. Greenberg?"

"Six years. And it's a damn nice job, if you want to know the truth. Why the notes?"

"They're for Ms. Edwards's counselors."

"What? She's in therapy?" Artie was waffling between contempt and uncertainty.

I cocked an eyebrow. "Her financial counselors."

The dollar, even in these inflated times, still commanded Artie's attention. "What's she need financial counseling for on what I pay?"

I put my Rapidograph down and flashed an expression of mild surprise. "I see you don't know."

"What? Don't know what?"

"About Ms. Edwards's financial situation. Not surprising, really. There are so many truly wealthy families these days who are able to keep low profiles. I think of them as the Thingamajig Rich—"

"What the hell you babbling about, Nevsky?"

"—meaning a grandfather, a father comes up with a gadget, a part, a *trick* that the world finds it can't do without. Little twist of plastic or metal. Don't amount to a damn. Only one ends up in *every* car, *every* artillery shell or every other backyard in the world. It sounds like you're not aware of what Ms. Edwards likes to call the 'Resin du Richesse'—the source of her family's sizable fortune."

Artie sat down. His mouth was open.

"Just a powder and a solvent mixed together under the right conditions. *Very* high-viscosity resin—for a while. Then after it dries it's just about inert. And *very* hard. Just the thing to anchor those delicate electronic components going into inertial guidance systems for aircraft, rockets and missiles..." I shrugged and grinned sheepishly.

161

"Betty Ellen is . . . rich?"

"Fabulously. And eccentric. Strong ideas about living a normal life. Self-sufficient on her own talent. Happy to let others manage her share of the family's wealth—the counselors I mentioned. Right now they're looking into the financial wisdom of her wanting to buy the Imperial Court. That way she could make an investment and perform indefinitely."

"Buy—" Artie's mouth was now all the way open.

"The counselors asked me if I'd spend some time here now and then. Check out the crowd, volume of trade . . ." Pause. ". . . quality of management. So on."

Artie sank back, spaghetti-spined. "I didn't know the Imperial Court was for sale."

I gave him a patronizing smile. *"Everything* is for sale, Artie. The only question is price."

"You're right, Nevsky. God knows you're right." He groaned and hid his face in his hands. "How could I *fire* her? Jesus, the rich are such problems for the rest of us shmucks. My job is gonzo." He tried a glance of sincerity—neither an easy nor a successful effort. "I don't suppose you could put in a word for me, could you? I saw you sitting with her."

"Betty Ellen is very sensitive to concessions to her wealth."

Artie groaned. "I am fried. Fucking *fried.*"

I sipped my Bloody Mary. Tasting better every moment, it was. Across psychic distances I heard the applause of two massive black garbage men, beating their gauntleted hands together. I turned my back to Manager Greenberg and stared down into the gray, windswept river valley. I waited a good while before I opened my mouth. "Maybe . . . a mild apology . . ."

"You think it would *work?"*

"No mention of wealth, that you know her secret. Maybe if you said you spoke in haste, under pressure . . ." I turned and leveled a double-barreled gaze into his bulging eyes. "Maybe you didn't understand how upset she was. How close she and Ray Nevick were. I think offering her a meaningful raise in pay *might* convey your sincerity. Meaningless as it might be financially."

Artie scrambled out of his chair. His face was alight with hope of reprieve. He saw my back. "I'd wait till at least noon if I were you," I added. "Show people sleep late."

"Oh! Sure. Nevsky, hey, no check for you. Drinks on the house."

"Thanks." I smiled out into the late March morning. I

guessed Artie was just about out of the room. I called: "I'd like another Bloody Mary, please. Make that a double."

"Thanks, Nevsky. Thanks so much."

I let my smile broaden into a grin so wide it could only be described in vulgar terms. Sure, there was some justice on this blue marble spinning through space. Cropped up in unlikely places, and never enough. Like mushrooms after a rainy spell. So I sat, sipped and thought. Manager Greenberg would give Betty Ellen a better deal all around, and would look on me in a different light. Respect, they called it. And anyone lied who said he didn't want it.

Somewhere up and behind me Tatiana was nourishing her starved spirit. How she did it while cooking, cleaning and managing the erratic priest's affairs was beyond my understanding. She had run from assaults on her spiritual values— only to find new testing in what were to be retreat and meditation. Usually I wasn't attracted to the weaker women. I liked the fighters, the bareknuckle broads. They could be soft-spoken or hide their determination behind tweeds and thick glasses. I saw value in will and the guts to slug it out down in the mud pits of life.

It was always testing to admit someone you were growing to love wasn't perfect by your standards. Healthy as it was, the descent from illusion to reality never took place without a sense of loss. No, this one, that one or the next wasn't ideal. Neither was I. Neither was anyone. All we could do was eat the imperfections and carry on.

Still, her eyes, her gentle voice, her spirituality made me very much want to share with her some of my life's favorites, like Renoir's portrait of Madame Henriot in Room 17 of the National Gallery, the sweet reek of basil growing in a summer garden, body surfing at Nauset Beach on Cape Cod. I would tell Tatiana to break away from pious meditation and accept life: even the best water contained some impurities. I would say, pick up the jewels along the way. To hell with waiting for complete peace of mind.

Thinking about her wasn't enough. I drove up to St. Basil's. I wanted to take her to lunch. She answered the door. The sight of her white face with its luminous almond eyes made my chest ache. How vulnerable to her I was! How much I wanted her!

The Church ladies were coming for lunch. She was busy, aproned and damp-browed to prove it. She had time for only one circuit of the onion-domed church. When the building was between us and the house I put my arms around her and kissed her. Her mouth was cool at first. Our lips clung. Her whimper of desire became a soft growl. In an instant she was squirming against me. Her teeth and tongue attacking my lips were only a hair on the soft side of savagery. Her hands slid up to the back of my neck. Her nails, driven by her flaring desire, sank like awls into my skin. We swayed in a stew of pain and pleasure.

She pulled away. Her eyes were hooded, smoky, devilish. "You don't know what I *am,*" she said.

"I don't care what you are. I'm falling in love with you."

She shook her head. Her breasts heaved under her gray work dress. "You don't *listen* to me. You're as mad as I am."

"I don't want to hear any more of that!" I grabbed her chin in the V of my thumb and forefinger. "You've had a tough few years. Your head's still shaky—oow!" She had rolled her chin and bitten my finger. She ran away down the walk, skirt held up in front.

She shouted back at me. "I *do* want to love you, Yuri. But I don't know *how* . . ." The door slammed behind her and I heard the metallic *snik* of the lock.

I wanted to tell her she was doing fine. She just had to give herself half a chance. The back of my neck itched. I put my hand up. It came back bloody streaked. Like the inside of my mouth.

I shuddered before my glimpse of the deep, dangerous lake of her polluted sexuality. I felt myself drawn to her all the more powerfully. As she had been drawn to decadent Francisco . . .

I drove around the Slope till I calmed down. Then I ate a fish sandwich and drank a cup of coffee.

After lunch I headed for Ogalkov Insurance. Ogalkov's secretary was a young man with a neat beard. A quick look up and down showed me the rest of Lucas Vokoffsky—the desk placard said—was neat, too. So was his desk. So was the whole office. I didn't see a paper out of place. Lucas Vokoffsky was good at his job. He looked me over. "You're Yuri Nevsky," he said.

I had never seen him before. At least I didn't remember seeing him. My memory for faces is excellent. Unless I'm . . . "Ohmygod, you were at Volodya's party."

He grinned and nodded. "I see you don't remember me— even though you did me a favor."

"I don't remember much of anything. Except being surrounded by women. All of them ended up hating me and each other."

"Drunker I've never seen," he said. "Or gamer. You were actually trying to keep up with those old men and their toasts. If you'd grown up on the Slope you'd know our seniors have had a lifetime of practice. Their body fluid is half-and-half, blood and vodka. Livers like the armor plate on tanks."

I groaned at the memory of my hangover.

"Drunk or not, you were trying to slide out of your situation with some style. Playing matchmaker, you were. Recruiting eligible—and not so eligible men—to thin your coterie."

"Like you, maybe?"

He winked. "Like me. And you didn't do badly, either. I like her."

"Which one?"

"P.Q. Antonelli."

"That's a bright young lady, Lucas. You want to handle her as well as you can."

"I intend to. We've been out once since. Altogether a great time." He nodded toward his boss's office. "Shopping for insurance?"

"Information."

"He's talking to a Main Office Man. Sit down for a minute." Lucas sat in silent council with his memories for a moment—then burst into snickers.

"What?"

"For all your matchmaking, you showed a streak of possessiveness and healthy male competitiveness."

"I did?"

"You shouted after P.Q. as she and I were leaving together. You said—I remember your last words. Too vivid to forget—'Don't you know, the older the stag, the harder the horn?'"

I covered my face. "Apologies, apologies."

Ogalkov's door opened. The Main Office Man, a fast-moving fellow wearing a 700-dollar Brooks Brothers and carrying an attaché case thin as a wallet, was soon out the door and gone.

Lucas said, "Mr. Ogalkov, this is Yuri Nevsky. He wants to talk to you."

Ogalkov stood beaming in his office doorway. He shook my hand and greeted me in Russian. "I've heard about you from a half dozen folks. Very pleased to meet you."

"English is OK," I said.

"Sure." Ogalkov was Russian-American to the core. He had the Slavic bones, the burliness. I sensed in him the Russian's peculiar aptitude for close and meaningful friendships. His office walls were decorated with 8 × 10s of him posing with groups of civic, religious and political leaders. I saw Rotarians, Boy Scouts, Russian Culture clubbers, Friends of Russian Music, members of the Social Committee of St. Basil's, Young Republicans. He was plugged in completely to Russian Slope. That was directly connected with the rest of his wall decorations—plaques from a half-dozen companies awarded him for selling millions of dollars worth of insurance. The framed needlepoint centered behind the desk and likely produced by a loving wife's hands summed it all up—in Russian, of course: The Slope Spells Insurance "Ogalkov."

He offered me a seat and more of that big sincere grin. "Saw you talking to the newspaperman over at the Black Sea last week. Our Trackman Tolovitch."

"Meeting of newspapermen." I pulled out Harrison Brightwood's letter, now just a bit worn-looking, despite the expensive *Post-Gazette* bond. I also slipped him one of Volodya's kopeks. "I came up to the Slope to write a catch-all article, but I've got hung up on one of your town's unhappy episodes. Ed Dixon's murder. And Nicholas Markov's running away."

Ogalkov frowned and nodded. "Not typical," he muttered, "of the people or our community."

"It's generally understood there was a large life policy covering Nicholas. You wrote it. It covers disappearance, too. I wonder if you could tell me something about the history of that policy."

For a moment Ogalkov's quick glance of surprise exposed the shrewdness, the skills of insight beneath his straight-on exterior. "You must be quite a reporter."

"This isn't confidential information we're talking about?"

"No, not precisely. Just the exact sums. You came at a good time, Yuri Vladimirovich. The guy who just left just came back from New York." Ogalkov heaved his prosperity-paunched frame back in his expensive chair. "Sort of wrapped it all up as far as Ogalkov Insurance goes."

He laced blunt fingers behind his head and told me a lot I already knew: that Igor Markov had taken out the policy when Nicholas was ten. There had been some initial problems defining disappearance in a way that satisfied both the old man

166

and Great Northern Life Insurance Company. More about that later, Ogalkov said. About every year Igor would come in and raise the coverage another fifty K. He had some kind of small pension and no living expenses. His son gave him money. He always paid cash. Never missed a payment. Funny thing, there wasn't a dime of coverage on him.

"He didn't come in maybe a week before he died and try to take out insurance, did he?" I sensed that the question of suicide or accident bore on Nicholas.

"He did come in a week or two before that ugly pistol accident," Ogalkov said. "But it was to triple coverage on Nicholas. He had a wad of bills in his hand to pay the increased premium. I called the GNL central office and they agreed to the additional coverage."

"Did it occur to you that Nicholas might be in danger? From hanging around Ray Nevick, drugs, whatever? This is a small town."

"I'm an actuary, Yuri Vladimirovich. Not a moralist or a fortune-teller. The numbers said it wasn't likely. I'd sell the same policy tomorrow."

"You didn't mention who the beneficiary was." I tried to keep the eagerness out of my voice. I badly needed a big stone to hurry the slow-rising arch of my understanding.

"There were five."

"Five?" I was looking for help, not confusion.

"The other Markovs: Igor, Mikhail, Sasha and Elena, and Ludmilla Markov. The total sum—which was quite large—was to be divided equally among them. With Igor gone, the remaining shares are of course larger."

My mind served up a quick vision of family members scheming to eliminate Nicholas, then one another—the survivor to eat the whole cake. Surely that couldn't be.

"When Nicholas first disappeared in connection with the murder, GNL wasn't greatly concerned," Ogalkov went on. "First, they had six months for Nicholas to be found. Second, the police were looking for the lad, too. But as the weeks passed and the police seemed ineffective, the company realized it might have to pay."

"What could they do, really?"

"Not much. In effect they had been outsmarted by an eighty-five-year-old man and the randomness of statistics. They contacted Boris Polsky, who had reason to believe Nicholas was in New York. It was the only lead there was. Considering the amount of money involved, I thought they ought to have started earlier. Got a man or two to New York. I told them so on the phone." Ogalkov grinned. "And they told *me* some things. But I was right. GNL wasn't good, as they say, but they sure came up lucky."

"They *found* Nicholas?"

Ogalkov opened the folder lying in the middle of his desk. "That guy who rushed out of here works for GNL. High level investigator. Name of Prospere Garrick. As I said, he and one of Polsky's men, a Sergeant Whitcomb, just got back from New York. Garrick works fast. He's already written this report." He riffled the half-dozen pages. "Too bad. I was rooting for the Markovs to collect. It was a legitimate policy. It's not easy to lose an eldest son. Cash is no replacement. But you can turn your attention to spending it. That helps."

"Garrick found Nicholas?"

"Yes and no."

"What the hell!" My heart was pounding. *"What happened in New York, Ogalkov?"*

"I'm coming to that. Garrick carried some weight with him—thanks to GNL's big New York office. The company had ways to kind of stir New York's finest around. And *they* started stirring other people. The word went out—got anything on a Nicholas Markov of Pittsburgh, Pa. And—as I said—Garrick and Whitcomb came up lucky. Lucky for GNL, that is."

"Then he did find Nick."

"Call came in to NYPD from Kennedy International Lost and Found. A conscientious kid took the bulletin seriously. Went through his collection and found a paper bag. Stamped as found the morning after the murder. Right by the International Departures gate. In the bag were Nick's wallet and the clothes he wore that night."

"He left the country." Headed for Russia. And the Valley of Promise.

"Seems so."

I frowned. "Then how did Garrick come up lucky? The kid's still missing. Probably forever."

"That comes back to how the policy was modified, Nevsky. GNL had to do something to protect itself. The language was so much in favor of the policyholder that when Igor came in to triple the coverage, they added a clause saying their liability was limited to disappearance within the contiguous forty-eight states. That is, there had to be *some* chance of finding the insured. The existence of evidence of the insured leaving the country voided any claims on the "missing" part of the policy. Of course it didn't affect death coverage. Igor fought that change like mad. But I had to tell him: if he wouldn't agree, there'd be no policy at all."

"So the family gets not one red cent."

"Prospere Garrick is good at his job."

"Jesus." I sat back. "It's not ironclad. Not by any stretch."

"The family could go to court." Ogalkov's face took on its jovial patina, as though he were speaking to the Markovs now. "I'd have to advise them against that, though. Honest advice for honest people in a close community."

"Oh."

"David was a one-shot freak. The smart money still goes with Goliath."

I was numb, weak and spent. Nick was gone. The fifty-year-old letter lay behind it all. The Holy Order of the Caucasus had come and nabbed him. He was ruling in the Valley of Promise, muzhiks at his feet, priests his to command. Yuri Nevsky, information man, had come to the end of this road. I was without resource, just about without compensation. The Markovs would never see their eldest son again—or a penny of insurance money.

I got up from my chair like a heavyweight after taking a mandatory eight-count. That old-world-is-a-rotten-place tango was throbbing in my ears. My face must have showed my state of mind.

"You're close to the family?"

"In a sense."

"There's no finding Nicholas now."

"I know."

Ogalkov opened the door. The phone rang in the outer office. Lucas answered. "For you, Mr. Ogalkov."

Ogalkov took the receiver, listened a moment. "No, he just left. He's a fast man on a fast track. A happy man after what he found in New York... Why won't he be happy?... uh huh... uh huh... So the door's still open... a crack. Damn thin crack if you ask me... Garrick, GNL aren't going to like that... Well, you can watch your language, chief... I'm just telling you how they'll feel... All right... sure. Chief, listen, you're on my list for a call to review your life coverage. This inflation is playing havoc with trying to get decent protection for a man's loved ones . . . Sure you're busy. Remember, Boris, you're not valuable *just* to the department. But to Natya and the kids . . . Saturday? Saturday, Sunday. Anytime. I'm never too busy to help a man find peace of mind. Especially a man in a dangerous line of work like yours . . . So we'll see you Saturday." Ogalkov hung up beaming. "The chief is a hard cop, Lucas. But a pussycat at handling insurance salesmen."

"What did he want? Something about Garrick?"

"He doesn't feel things are quite settled about Nick Markov yet. Whitcomb came across somebody the chief thinks might make a difference."

"Who?"

"Olga Samnesovich."

Sergeant Whitcomb was bright and articulate. He sat relaxed smoking a Vantage under the chief's Miró lithograph. The chief had heard his story, but was sitting in to hear the retelling. Charity and I were as intent as cats outside a mousehole.

". . . so Garrick and I were on the elevator in the courthouse-cum-precinct-station-cum-God-knows-what. The building was very multi-purpose. Very New York. Attorneys coming and going. Felons, witnesses, jurors, cops, detectives, everyone going every which way. Real New York scene. You know, *controlled* chaos. We were going upstairs to see a lieutenant who knew missing persons and runaways. We stopped at the floor and a matron got on with a young woman. I caught just a glimpse of her face. Her hair was longer than in the photo I had seen. Just the same I was sure it was Olga Samnesovich. I told Garrick I'd see him later and followed Olga and the matron off. Followed them into an office. I showed my I.D. and did some fast talking. The lady lieutenant in charge gave me five minutes with Olga." Whitcomb shook his head apologetically. "Made a big mistake. I told her I was from Russian Slope. You shoulda seen her eyes. Wider than Orphan Annie's—but turning hard. 'I don't want to talk to you,' she said. 'My friend says I don't have to talk to anybody till my attorney gets here.' 'Who's your friend?' 'Snakeman.' 'Where is he?' 'Downstairs. Waiting for my attorney.' I begged her to talk to me. But she was tight as a clam. I told her I didn't want to hassle her. I wanted to know about Nicholas Markov. She said she didn't have to talk to anybody about anything unless they had the right papers. This was America where everybody had some rights. Snakeman had told her most people

170

misunderstood the Constitution. She shouldn't. She had rights and she should stand by them." Whitcomb got up and paced. He was tall, lean—and clean. He threw up his hands in exasperation. "If I had had more *time* . . . Before my five minutes were up, this shyster came busting in smelling of Parodi cigars and bar whisky. He knew every in and out of the law. He paid the fine and had her outside in forty-five minutes." He looked sheepishly at Polsky. "I felt like a rookie again."

"A hard-assed New York street lawyer can do that," Polsky said.

"I managed to weasel address and phone out of her. Even though her friend Snakeman 'told me not even to give my age until I had counsel.' I said I'd call her that night. 'Far out,' she said . . . To come to the embarrassing part right away," Whitcomb went on, "I phoned—no such number. I grabbed a cab to the address. It was a MacDonald's. And, no, she wasn't behind the counter salting fries. She did a job on me. Her friend Snakeman must've taught her how to lie to dumb out-of-town cops."

"Forget it, Whitcomb. You did the best you could," Polsky said.

"Who was this guy Snakeman?" I shouted. "What was she doing in the station house? What was going on?"

"For a guy with a lotta brains, you can be dumb, Nevsky. You any faster on the uptake, attorney lady?"

Charity's face was stony. "Olga's become a whore. Snakeman is her pimp."

Polsky sent Whitcomb back to duty. While I gathered my wits, Charity filled Polsky in on Olga renting the car. When she finished, Polsky went on: "She'd been picked up twice before. Prostitution both times. Whitcomb checked. She worked the streets. Picked up around Eighth Avenue and Forty-eighth Street both times. Spent the night in the slammer, paid the fine and went out and did it again." The chief waved his hand disgustedly. "And now she got away clean." Now it was his turn to pace. "Deep down I know she knows when and if the Markov kid flew off in the big international bird, or if he ditched his I.D. and clothes to make it look like he became a foreign traveler. Then squirreled himself away in the city,"

I thought he was gone, to Russia, to the Caucasus, that I was closer to New York than Nicholas Markov ever would be again.

Polsky was still talking. "This department *hates* to give up.

This department hates to rest, to call it quits, when there's *one more stone* to turn over to see if Nicholas Markov squirms out from under." He stroked his goatee with fast, almost feverish fingers. "But this department cannot print money. In fact, it's committed to discouraging the practice." He looked pointedly at us. "You have every right to say no to what I'm gonna suggest. I gave it to you both pretty good the other night—"

"Amen!" Charity said.

"—for all the good it did. Mr. and Ms. Brazil Nut." He waved the past away. "I can't afford to send Whitcomb back—"

"Does he make lieutenant based on his New York performance?" I said.

Polsky grimaced. "Jury's still out. Depends on how the Markov thing ends."

"I'd say it's about ended," I said.

The chief cocked his head. "Not if you two go back there and find Olga."

"There might not be that much time in the world," I said.

"The senior partner indulges me," Charity said, "but he's not crazy. A couple, three days is the best I could do. And I couldn't go until early next week. I'm helping wrap up one of those corporate litigations. Like Godzilla versus Rodan."

"I don't know..." I said. "I think we're months late and maybe six thousand miles from doing any good."

"You said you wanted to find the kid. Look, Nevsky. I've been around this case *months*. I thought it was all over a couple times. For the last time a couple hours ago when that robot in his Brooks Brothers came in here and crowed. Now I *know* it's all over—unless we chat with Olga and maybe find something." He paused, his ruddy face grim. "There's nothing else left."

I felt tired and unmotivated, like a ten-year veteran shortstop trying to get up for a game with an expansion team. I turned and looked at Charity. "Whadaya think?"

"There are lives and money riding on Olga's little white shoulders." There was an edge in her voice. Olga whoring wasn't sitting well with the former mother of two daughters. "We catch the first flight out Monday morning."

Polsky and Charity were right. There wasn't any other way to go.

16

Nature must have known we were having Sunday guests. She set out her own late-March feast. Blue skies, no wind and what the KDKA weather person called "unseasonably warm temperatures." By whose standards? I grinned from the vantage point of the wide wooden porch that edges around about a third of 138.

The open door behind me filled the fresh air with the sweet odors of the last of Ludmilla's baking. She had worked late into last evening and had returned with the dawn. She sang and hummed—and flour came to life beneath her solid, wrinkled hands. Balls, crescents and twist cookies, sweetmeats. These zakuski made after ancient family recipes were piling up into small mountains. She had brought a gift "from my house to your house"—a charcoal-burning samovar pulled down from the Markov attic. Stamped on its bottom: Tsaritsyn 1893. She insisted on polishing it even though it was already shiny enough to dazzle the blind. She had also brought charcoal to heat it.

Close to one o'clock the door chimes sounded. I greeted Tatiana and Father Alexander—with a bandage around his head. Tatiana helped him into the house. Despite his unsteady feet he shook off her arm with the sudden vexation of the strong with the assistance they've never before needed.

"What happened?" I said.

"We were *attacked*." Tatiana slid the black coat off the priest's big shoulders. "By a *giant*."

Father Alexander burst into voluble Russian that rang like a drum inside the small entrance hall. "Shortly after the morning service we were strolling by the church. I was hearing Tatya's prayers—"

"We usually do that in his study. It's a ritual. But it was such a lovely morning that father wanted to get out."

"Sunlight and the smell of the changing season shows God's hand better than gloom and stale air. We had paused to look down at the community and—"

173

"He came rushing around from behind the church."

"Who?" I heard Charity's footsteps behind me.

"A huge man with a hairless head, Yuri Vladimirovich. Nearly seven feet tall. Waving a broken limb as a club. He rushed at us with senseless shouts."

"What did he say?"

"His Russian had no accent." Tatiana's mellow voice carried the rough edge of fear. "He shouted, 'Death to the anti-priest, enemy of God! Death to an enemy of the Holy Order of the Caucasus!'"

Igor's letter! The family Markov. The holy order. There *was* something to it. I had known it all along! Or told myself I had.

"It was God's inspiration only that made me do what I feared most." Father Alexander's wild grin was skewed, his eyes bright. "I met his rush with my own! Only after I had closed with him did I realize I had made the club of little use to him."

"He gave you a pretty good whack with it anyway," Charity said.

"When I was younger I wrestled for many years. I struggled for a hold. I took what he gave me. I encircled his waist with my arms and squeezed."

"And I screamed and screamed." Tatiana's delicate face twisted and cords rose in the front of her neck. "It was *horrible*. 'Anti-priest! Enemy of God!' he kept shouting. 'Soiler of the future of the family Markov! Death to your black soul!'" She blessed herself.

"It was then that he struck me. A cramped and glancing blow, but it loosened my hold and he broke away."

"Who was he?" I said.

"A creature from hell." Father Alexander closed his eyes at the memory.

"A huge, thick head, face all bone and thick white eyebrows." Tatiana's voice was a near whisper.

"Seen him before?" Charity led us out into the living room.

"Never."

"What happened when he broke loose?" I said.

"He stood shaking, wondering whether to strike me again or flee," the priest said. "He was unsure."

"There were some people on the street who heard me scream. They came running toward us. He ran off the other way."

"You called the police?"

"They came. We talked. They asked a lot of questions and took notes. They said they'd watch for him." Tatiana shuddered. She wore a pink blouse and an ankle-length dark skirt. How long her neck was! A breathless feeling eased into my chest, sending me basic messages about the immorality and immediacy of the nature of desire. "I was so *happy* to drive away from there," she said. I put my arm over her shoulders. That she should have been put in danger seemed to me an unthinkable stupidity of fate.

We all sat down. Father Alexander waved his hand. "What I do not understand was why did he—whoever he was—call *me* an enemy of the family Markov? I, who resurrected Nicholas, a magnificent soul shackled by drugs and hate for his father. Who gave Christian burial to Igor Gregorevich, a scoffer before the face of God?" He adjusted his long beard in his chest. "Clearly a madman." He pointed a finger skyward. "And he may return. In which case I am prepared now to defend myself." He slid aside his black coat and vest to expose an ornate knife handle. He grabbed it with his right hand and jerked out a gleaming blade nearly a foot long.

"Father! . . ." Tatiana's almond eyes turned away from the weapon.

"As an attorney I recommend you don't ever use that," Charity said.

"I am a man of peace. I would never lift my hand against sane men. To say that *I* am an enemy of the Markovs *and* God Almighty . . ." He grunted and thrust the gleaming blade at the air. His black eyes shone with the wild, icy light that preceded his earlier rage at me.

It seemed the moment to tell him about Igor's 1928 letter. So I spilled out the stuff about the Holy Order of the Caucasus, the fanatical priests and followers, all ruled over by the Markov family. When I finished, Father Alexander shook his head. "You think the giant somehow came from this Valley of Promise? No, no. I spent many years in the Caucasus. The order is long gone, dead, burned away in the fires of revolution. A curious story. One that catches like a burr on the imagination." He waved the tale away. "But a fable from a Russia that is no more. Even if the order still exists—through some unlikely joke of God, and they have kidnapped Nicholas and taken him back to Mother Russia—why do they now attack me? And shout to Heaven about their order?"

Good questions. Too good to answer. I had a question for

him that needed asking now. "P.Q. Antonelli saw the license plate of the car that drove Nicholas away. Father Alexander, why didn't you want that known?"

"God forgive me, Yuri Vladimirovich." The priest looked down in shame. "I wished only to keep Nicholas safe wherever he was. With the number the police might have found him." He shook his shaggy head. "I do not think clearly when I think of Nicholas. I loved the boy as though he were my own son."

"I think Ray Nevick loved him, too," I said. "I thought for a while he sent him out of town that night. In a car rented by Olga Samnesovich. We found out she paid a visit to Avis Rent-a-Car that morning. The car was found in New York the next morning. I'm not sure whether she drove it there or someone else."

"Now you don't think Rodino Nevikorovich—Nevick—did this?" the priest said.

"Nick's clothes and identification were found at Kennedy International," I said. "It doesn't seem likely that Nevick would see the need to send Nick out of the country. Or, if the clothes were a decoy, why had Nevick bothered? New York was far enough away for Nicholas to be safe. Why advertise that he had ever been there? To completely finish off that possibility, it's not likely Nevick would have got so depressed and doped up if he knew Nick were safe and they would eventually get together again."

"Rodino Nevikorovich was an unhappy soul who went to an unhappy end." Father Alexander signed the cross in the air.

"He tried to run Yuri down," Charity said. "I don't feel so sorry for him."

Tatiana gasped. "Yuri, you didn't *tell* me." She made a sour face. "Because of Nicholas! *Must* we talk more about him?" She flashed me a weary glance. Beneath it I saw a deep sadness over Nicholas indirectly putting me in danger. And over what his absence had done to the priest. Now her beloved Father carried a knife and was threatening violence.

"Tatya, the boy means so much to me. I welcome *any* news." His bushy brows rose quizzically. "Has any *real* trace of him been found? Or of the golden cross?"

"Not yet. The police found Olga Samnesovich in New York, but she got away before they could talk to her about Nicholas."

Father Alexander grunted in surprise.

"Pretty obvious they went there together," I said. "But it *wasn't* Olga who picked him up outside the Eleven-to-Seven."

176

I sketched in my visit with Lev, her gross toad of a father, the movement of people and the vehicle between eight and nine thirty the night of the murder. Then I stopped talking. I wanted to hear what the priest had to say.

"I respect your analysis of the situation, Yuri Vladimirovich." He folded his hands over his solid middle and the ugly blade. "But I must say again—as I did the first time we met—that the boy had little use for Olga. He was cut from dear cloth, she from rough. I do not think they went to New York together."

"Then maybe they went separately. Or we're back to the remote possibility that Nevick paid Olga or a friend to drive Nick to safety. Nevick knew about the drug deal. It wouldn't have been hard to manage a getaway, planned in advance. That there was a murder was really beside the point. As I said a minute ago, I have a feeling Nevick loved Nicholas. I didn't make myself clear. I'm talking about a homosexual love. A physically consummated one. And I have a feeling Nicholas became a practicing homosexual with Nevick's encouragement."

"No! This is an obscenity!" Father Alexander heaved out of his chair with surprising agility. He looked about to rush me. So I jumped up. So did Charity and Tatiana. Charity stepped in front of me. Tatiana cooed soothing Russian into an ear hidden in a thicket of beard and hair. "Apologize!" the priest screamed. Tatiana hung on his heaving arm like a parrot. "Apologize for your slander!"

"The tea is ready!" Ludmilla stood in the doorway. She had gussied herself up for Sunday afternoon with the priest. She wore a sacky blue dress, a golden brooch on her Everest of bosom, and shoes with suggestions of heels. She took two steps forward and knelt. "Your blessing, please, Father."

The priest looked confused. "I—didn't know you would be here, Ludmilla Petrovna. I thought only Yuri Vladimirovich and Ms. Day . . ."

"Your blessing, Father," she said again. Her head was down, but her voice—no, her presence—brought order and calm into the room.

He blessed her generously. That act and the return to his role cooled the bright coals of his eyes.

"We're having another guest later, too," Charity said. "Stan Pokora. Do you know him?"

"Of course! A true gentleman of a *most* interesting Imperial Russian family. Let me tell you about them . . ." The priest

177

offered Charity his arm and off they walked toward the dining room, the samovar and the zakuski.

What lay behind the priest's anger at my suspicions Nicholas was gay? Or was it Nevick's possible conquest of the boy that galled him so? The anger might well have its roots in jealousy—if priest were courting boy, too. I thought of the many hours they spent together. The man they called The Widows' Heartthrob seemed to have no doings with any women except Tatiana. Their relationship swung between father-daughter and nurse-patient. Sexual jealousy would go a long way toward explaining why the priest had grown so upset after Nicholas exited—possibly with Nevick's help. Nicholas Markov, adored by women, loved by men. What kind of guy was he? *Where* was he? I sensed that one day I would meet him. And Olga would show the way.

During a tour of the house Father Alexander saw the piano. In moments he bulldozed me into joining him for "music making." He proposed a duo—his clarinet and my piano. Tatiana and Charity—taking leave of their senses—encouraged this. Tatiana got his clarinet and music out of their car. So we started in on a Clementi duo. My hands turned spastic before an audience and an unfamiliar score. Father Alexander was inspired to Benny Goodman–like heights. Or so it seemed to me.

As we bent our B-flat way in the music room, another voice was raised in a different time and key. Ludmilla, in the kitchen, had chosen to sing loudly in Russian, a lascivious old folksong. I didn't have to hear too much of it to get the general drift.

> . . . Said the brave burly soldier walking with the sweet
>   shy maid:
> Three years I fought. Three years I marched. At last I
>   have been paid.
> I've hiked in rain ten versts to meet you here upon the
>   grass.
> Think I've dreamed of your natural sex? No! It's been
>   your ass.
> And then he rolled her over,
> And then he rolled her over . . .

It took her ten slow verses to totally disintegrate our little jaunt into the classical period. Giggling, we assaulted the food again.

Father Alexander took my hand and Tatiana's. "Such

178

glances you two trade! As though you were alone. You *should* be alone. I think you should go off together. Outside. Take a ride. Spend some time together alone."

Tatiana frowned and lowered her eyes. "Holy One, I don't like to leave you—"

"Nonsense! Am I not your starets? Do I not know what's best for you? Your eyes tell me I'm right."

"It's what's best for *you* that worries me."

The priest beamed and preened. "To be left in the presence of this fair, blonde and beautiful woman is far from a hardship." With his bandaged brow he looked as dashing as a good-natured brigand. I glimpsed the presence that, months ago, had endeared him to everyone on the Slope. He had been a good priest. "We were speaking of the beauty of the Russian language."

"He said he'd start to teach me the basics of pronunciation," Charity said. "You and Tatiana should go out for a while."

I looked at Tatiana. Her eyes were on me. I read in her expression that long-time feminine posture: if you want me, do something. That made it easy. "I have a little cottage out in Murraysville. Up on a hill. Let's drive out and see it. It won't take long."

Her smile was nice to see, after all her frowns over Father Alexander. "Let's take Father's car. It's right out front."

"Of course. With my blessing," the priest said.

"Be gone an hour and a half at the most," I said.

"You're both very kind." Tatiana embraced Charity and then the priest.

As we pulled away in the St. Basil's Buick, a Cadillac coming the other way was slowing in front of 138. Stan Pokora, the Cossack, was early. Of course. I could almost hear his lustful pants over Charity.

On the way out the Parkway East, Tatiana ignored our last meeting and its passion. She poured out her concern for the priest. "I came to St. Basil's to mend my soul, Yuri. And for a while I did. Now already its new strength is being tested. The man who gave me that strength—who *truly* helped me— is now demanding that I use it to help him."

"He's slipping worse?" I said.

"The dear man. He tries so hard, but . . ." Her voice nearly cracked. She let the car buzz on in silence while she swallowed for control. "He really hasn't been able to prepare for Easter. The deacon, the church committees are after him to help plan the celebrations. He doesn't return their calls. When they show up at the door he makes some lame excuse. He doesn't make the pastoral calls he used to, either. I've been doing as much of his job as I can. Covering for him, doing correspondence, handling social obligations while he goes off for walks to clear his head. The only things he still handles are the youth and y.a. groups at the Moskva. They're like the last fingerholds he has on his responsibilities." She sighed. "I'm not sure how long he can hold on to even those." Her tone turned venomous and bitter. "That goddamned Nicholas Markov!"

I reached out and gently touched her cheek. "The reason he got so upset when I said Nevick loved Nicholas was that *he* loved him, too," I said.

"That's hard for me to accept," she said. "But all the hours Father devoted to him, the intensity of the relationship . . ." She said nothing for a long while. "I think you're right," she said finally. "I'm pretty conservative, Yuri. So that really drags Father down in my eyes. And *now* he has that knife." She turned her puzzled face to me. "And the letter you found. That crazy stuff about the Markov family. And that huge bald man shouting some of the *same* craziness. It's all a dreadful, dreadful mess."

"That big guy showing up means the Holy Order of the Caucasus definitely isn't dead, no matter what Father A. says. That possibility's been in the back of my mind ever since I found the letter."

"And Father Alexander is mixed up in it some way?"

"Very likely. Willingly or unwillingly, who knows? Just how, who knows? Maybe somehow as a victim. Maybe as a participant in a kidnapping."

"Oh, God!" Tatiana shook her head slowly. "I don't want to have to believe that. I want to help him out of this. I want to help get it cleared up. Maybe I should really look around the house, see if I can find anything."

"If you do, be very careful. They probably won't find the crazy with the club. And now Father Alexander has that knife."

"Yuri!"

"I'm just saying don't take chances."

Tatiana, following my directions, swung the car off the Parkway East extension onto old Route 22 at Miracle Mile in Monroeville, then headed east. We drove on in silence for three or four minutes. Then she said, "Father Alexander found out you're not a reporter."

"He did?"

"He hears a lot. Gossip, confessions, small talk. He told me what he heard last week. I didn't know what to say. So all I said was I didn't *think* you were the lying type." No mistaking her accusing tone. I had been lying; she didn't like it.

The deception she once accepted now for some reason stuck in her craw. I knew I had somehow lost ground with her. In an effort to recover it I told her about my recent struggles with my past and gropings with the essentials of being Yuri Nevsky. I did not spare details of my life's disappointments or my failed marriage. Nor did I mask my successes with false modesty. I knew I was doing more than hitting the high points. I was digging down and disclosing myself to her. I was offering myself with the warts, the somber shadows in my soul, the sores and beauty spots of weaknesses and strengths. Something I had never dared to do before another human being. I wanted her to know who I *really* was at that moment. And more than that—I wanted her to accept me.

She listened with limited response. "You're giving me a lot to think about, Yuri. You've lived so much more . . . healthily than I have . . ."

By the time I rushed through the last of my confession we were bumping up the hill toward the low one-story house and acreage my parents had bought just after World War II. The land sat amid high fields and looked down on the slopes and folds of western Pennsylvania's rolling hills. I rented the house; the tenant was a gentleman farmer with a few large plots. He was enjoying his annual trip to the Everglades just then. I told Tatiana to pull the car up by the old orchard my father had planted. Peach, nectarine and apple trees marched in two rows away from the house.

I told Tatiana about the summer colony of Russians who had gathered in the other cottages nearby, about being a child here in those endless summers of the late '40s.

"This was your father's dacha," she said. "His get-away-from-it place. How very Russian to buy such a place and come here on weekends and in the summer. Did you ever think of it as his dacha?"

We were among the trees of the small orchard. We found a knoll of dry ground and sat. I told her about the trees, then, and how they hadn't really worked out. They had needed early spraying. My father, showing the worst side of his aristocratic streak, never learned to drive. My mother, the family driver, was busy with job and house. He had trouble getting out here in the early spring. About now, it would have been.

I remembered autumns with the fruit laying about on the grass where we sat: peaches bigger than my fist ruined by cancerous smears of brown rot, plums soft to the touch exploding in the mouth with juice—and worms. So much effort—ordering the trees all the way from Missouri's Stark Brothers, the planting, the pruning, the shaping—for nothing. Eventually the trees grew past best bearing. At this moment, years later, I swelled with sadness for my father's failure here, then for him, though his life was a success, and finally for his death. Tears dribbled down my cheeks.

Tatiana saw them and took my leaking head in her white hands. She kissed and licked away my tears like a friendly puppy, whispering the while, "My poor man. My poor sad man." My arms went around her and we rocked together atop our dry nest of dormant grass under a still-warm sun. How different than her near savagery of our last meeting.

Soon her comforting turned to desire and my sadness—a legitimate one, a world away from any con or carney—was swept away by sweet intrusions of her tongue.

Long minutes later her breasts lay within the dacron parenthesis of her half-unbuttoned blouse. For all her seeming conservatism she wore no bra to bar the eager attentions of my hands, nibbling teeth and busy tongue. I heard the muted growl of her growing desire rumbling in her white neck.

Then for reasons maybe dating back to the illicit sex of my '50s adolescence, the long hours in cars parked in public places, I raised my nuzzling head to look around. My half-closed eyes followed the line of trees back toward the cottage and car.

The trunk of the Buick was opening.

A man was scrambling out—huge, bald, white eyebrows. The man Father Alexander had called a devil!

"Tatya!"

She took my tone of alarm for one of passion. "My love!" she said. She wrapped her white arms around my neck and pulled me down to nurse on her again. An ugly suspicion reared in the back of my mind. I tore free of her arms and began to scramble up. "Yuri, what's—"

"Look!"

The hairless giant jerked his club out of the trunk and lumbered toward us. Fear welled up in my heart. With it more of the hot acid of suspicion.

Tatiana gasped and whimpered. "Him! Oh, dear God protect us. It's *him*."

My eyes bored into her frightened gaze. "I think you knew he was there! I think you set me up. You and Father Alexander."

She stared at me with dazed, uncomprehending eyes. "Oh, no, I *didn't*. Yuri!"

The giant was running at us now, club cocked for a right-handed cut like a cricket batsman out of an LSD trip. His eyes were on me. Tatiana scrambled up, jerked off her low heels and ran, long skirt hitched up above her knees.

For whatever reason, I decided she had the right idea. To stand successfully weaponless before a giant with a club called for divine assistance. Considering my spiritual track record to date, I decided it wasn't wise to expect it. Ogalkov had reminded me: David was a one-shot long shot. And he had a sling. I turned and ran like hell.

There was more than the reflexive scamper of the wild rabbit behind my flight. Men over six-five tend to tire in long runs. Maybe this guy was one of them.

So I churned off away from the orchard, across a fallow corn field. I wasn't in bad shape. I tried to set my pace to running without haste, like a miler working his race plan.

Behind me rose the litany Father Alexander and Tatiana had already described. Guttural Russian: "You will die, enemy of God. Betrayer of the family Markov! Blasphemer before the eyes of the Holy Order of the Caucasus!"

I wanted mightily to know who he was and where he came from. I wanted to know if Father Alexander and my dearest Tatya had betrayed me.

I crossed a fence and took off across another field, heading in a wide circle around the cottage. There was no place to which I could run; the nearby cottages were for summer use and deserted.

From somewhere in the distance I heard Tatiana screaming my name. In glee, terror or concern I couldn't guess. I had been set up. I was sure of it. But I had no real time to be angry. And possibly would never live to avenge that betrayal.

I was starting to get an idea about where the giant lumbering after me had come from—an Olympic Games training camp. He was gaining and I was tiring. "Death to enemies of the family Markov!" he was bellowing as loudly as ever. "Death to enemies of God and the Holy Order of the Caucasus!"

I felt like a turtle trying to outrun a locomotive. So like a turtle I headed toward a thicket—this one of saplings growing thickly together. Oak, ash, poplars stuck up their thin fingers toward the sun. Among them the giant couldn't swing his club very effectively. I could dodge and duck around them.

The giant stalked me through the thicket. Closer he was more menacing. His eyes under their white, tufted brows gleamed with the bright light of total commitment. Worse than that of any airport Moonie. That he was out of synch with time and history was of no more concern or relevance to him than the asteroid count between Jupiter and Venus. I remembered Igor's letter—about no barriers of time and space to the truly fanatical.

He lunged forward and swung the length of tree branch in a ponderous arc. I dodged and wood met sapling. A thin tree was sheared off. Stringy fibers white with new sap twisted up from the sudden stump.

"This is crazy," I said in Russian. "Why do you want to kill me?"

His answer was to rush at me all the harder. He grunted and flailed—and struck my right arm a grazing, nearly paralyzing blow. All the while his eyes burned wildly in their bony pits.

"Yuri, Yureee!" Tatiana screaming. Lover or traitor? The latter, I thought. I didn't answer. The giant didn't need any reinforcements. I did. I rubbed my arm back to life and kept backing away.

He tried a few more swinging attacks which the saplings deflected. "The last Markov lives despite you, coward!" he grunted.

"Where?" I wanted to know before I died.

"In safety. Soon he will complete his journey to the Valley of Promise."

"You came from there?"

He grunted and threw down his club. He would take me bare-handed. I would do my best with my array of counters. But he was really too huge to damage badly enough. I would hurt him a lot. In the end, though, I would die.

"Yureeee! Yure-e-e-e!" Tatiana wandering in the field nearby. "For the love of God, where are you? Yuri. Yureeee!" I had nothing to lose. I was doomed. I shouted to her just as the giant rushed me full tilt. I threw him over my hip. I felt the great thickness of his bones, the heaped muscle. He hit the ground hard. He shook his head and sprang up. He rushed at me again, arms outstretched.

I made an error then that brought around the inevitable a little faster than necessary. I tried to chop him down with palm-edge blows to unguarded nerve clusters at his neck and shoulders. My hands met great knots of muscle and flesh. I would have had as much luck trying to KO a 747. He clubbed me down with fists like sledges and leaped on me. His weight was immovable, like a piece of heavy road equipment. His gross hands filled my field of vision as they moved toward my throat.

Crashing in the underbrush. The hands dug into my flesh as though it were so much dough. My fingers groped for the giant's little fingers, to break them or his grip. I couldn't pry them free. I was done. The giant's huge face filled my vision like a moon. His sunken eyes under riots of eyebrow were squinting with loathing and concentration, like a man tromping a particularly ugly bug.

The crashing came closer. I heard bare feet on last year's leaves. I struggled to see, but my world was choked with those murderous eyes. Suddenly they widened, flashing blue in great pain. The giant let go of my throat. He screamed and cursed in coarse Russian.

He scrambled up. Now I could see Tatiana—and the pitchfork. Its long rustless tines had been polished and sharpened by my gentleman-farmer tenant. Never had the routines of agriculture made more sense: sharpen tools in the winter.

I jumped to my feet, coughing and sucking in air. Tatiana, holding the monster at bay, stood like Eternal Russian Woman in some tableau. Hair half-unbraided—my handiwork—hung below her shoulders. Her blouse was still open. She was panting and pouring sweat. Her delicate face was twisted into a mask of savagery. Her hands showed white from her grip on the pitchfork.

She tossed the tool to me, tines up. "I should have let you die!" she screamed. Her eyes flashed wildly. "I should have let you *die* for thinking what you thought!" The Russian words fell on my ears like hot lead.

I tore my attention back to the giant. Mr. Rough-and-Ready should have seen the wisdom of retreat. Instead he readied himself to rush again. I shortened up on the pitchfork handle. I couldn't believe he'd charge me. Finesse and maneuver were absolutely necessary.

Fanatics—at least this one—had neither. He kept coming

over the next ten minutes. And paid the price. I ripped up his arms, skewered one of his shoulders, and got in what I thought were fatal thrusts between the ribs of his right side. But he was too big and tough to go down. Just the same he was pouring blood and hurting.

I was at a dangerous psychological point, one which big leaguers trying to go four-for-four in their last at bat and professional hit men don't reach. I was in peril of feeling sorry for my opponent. Bloody and slowed, running on only one program, he was surely to be pitied.

Just then he rushed me again. I defended and one of the tines ran through the meaty part of his left palm. He howled. Instead of trying to dislodge the gleaming tine, he caught the tine base with his right hand and drove the dreadful needle further in—until the base was flush against his pierced palm. Thus he had a grip of sorts on the tormenting tool, a grip that cost him an acre of agony. Made worse when he tried to heave the fork out of my hands. His arms swung in arcs high and low, back and forth. I clung to the pole, praying the ash would hold against his strength. Now I was terrified far worse than before. I understood how the *Wehrmacht* soldier felt on the Eastern Front: "Let me fight anyone but the Russians."

Adrenaline flooded me afresh—a basic fight-for-your-life jolt. So when the tine finally tore through the ruined meat of his hand I stuck the fork with all my strength behind it into his neck. I tore up his carotid artery and his trachea and God-knew-what-all.

Tatiana screamed. I jerked out the fork and blood spurted in bright fountains into the sunlight. Self-preservation and the risen killer instinct left no room for niceties. I had done the job too well: bleeding we couldn't staunch and vocal cords torn to tatters.

He died with my hands above the pad made of Tatiana's blouse pressed against his spurting neck. The mad light in his eyes never softened. It just winked out like a flashlight bulb over rundown batteries. Even as he died under my hands I spouted questions in a nervous spray. Who? How? Why? But his throat gave out only raspings and pathetic tweets—and a great deal of blood.

Tatiana leaned both palms against a nearby oak and vomited. Some of the stuff fell on her swaying white breasts. I wiped my gory hands on the dried stalks of last year's weeds. I searched the fallen giant. He carried no wallet, no identification. There was nothing in the pockets of his dark slacks or his white-collared shirt.

I noticed both shirt and slacks were a mediocre fit. Mass produced with indifference to the consumer.

I was ready when the labels in both were printed in Russian. He had come from Russia.

17

I wanted to leave the giant behind where he was. Tatiana didn't, for religious reasons. I explained my motive: more trouble from the police, more delays in my finding Nicholas. We could see to him later. We left him.

In her tense face I saw how severely our relationship was damaged by the reckless accusation I had flung at her. It had hurt her deeply, striking at the very heart of my trust—and so hers. Nor could I now explain it away. It was too late. Now I understood that the giant had hidden from the police in a most unlikely spot. Father Alexander and I were his "enemies." Through great luck he got chances at both of us. And had come up very empty.

I put the pitchfork in the trunk of the Buick.

"You want that?"

"Maybe I'll start a memories room. This'll be my first collectible."

The ride home, not long in distance, seemed endless. As we swung down Morlande Street Tatiana said, "It would be better if we didn't see each other for a while, Yuri."

"Why?"

"I think you know. I don't want to go into it." She gathered my jacket more tightly around her.

"I think you have to say more than that." I pulled over to the curb well before 138. "If you don't want to see me, I have to hear why. I have to hear the words."

She turned to me. I expected to see the heat of anger blossoming red in her cheeks. Instead her face was drained of color. I saw fear in her eyes. *"Please."* It was a choked cry. Like the peep of a weak cornered animal.

"You don't like being confronted, do you? You don't like being shoved up against tough moments, do you, Tatya?"

She made a dive for the passenger-side door. I grabbed her arm and pulled her back toward me. She clutched the jacket to hide her exposed breasts. "You can't be afraid of *me*," I said.

"It's not easy to tell someone they've had unworthy, vicious and destructive thoughts."

"Why not?—if that's what you really think."

"How could you *think* I'd conspire to kill you, Yuri?"

"Normally I wouldn't—*couldn't*. But the situation..." I held her shoulders and looked down into her eyes. "I was afraid, Tatya. So were you. I thought Father Alexander was mixed up in Nicholas's disappearance. Maybe you were, too. How could I *know* one way or the other?"

"Those are just excuses."

"Tatya!"

"If that's how little trust you have in me, how can *I* trust your love for me?"

"The two are different."

"No."

I lifted my hands from her shoulders. "You're too hard a judge, Tatya. Too unforgiving. As though you *wanted* me to be found wanting. Maybe that's a pattern in your life. Setting standards only saints can meet."

"I will *not* be psychoanalyzed. I had enough of that in Washington." She pointed toward 138 in the distance. "Do we ride, or do I walk?" The subject was about closed.

"You won't change your mind?"

"In a way I have changed it. I think now we should wait even a little while *after* the Nicholas business is settled to see each other."

"Tatya!"

"There're things about you I'll have to think about, have to pray about."

"There's something monstrously unfair here somewhere."

"I think you need time, too."

"Tatya, I *love* you! I want to see you."

She touched my cheek with her cool white fingertips. "You're a wonderful, charming man, Yuri. My feelings for you are...strong. Let's leave it there, please. Let some time pass. All right?"

I agreed. The resentful voice within consumed I had been tossed the merest crumb. But my real voice said, "All right."

She told me Father Alexander had a youth group meeting that evening and, thanks to our country troubles, she and he were running late.

As we got out of the car I asked her to offer my apologies. I "wasn't feeling well." Then to tell only the priest and Charity what had happened. I left the pitchfork by the garage and went in the upstairs door and right to the shower. I put all my gory clothing and shoes in a paper bag. When I raised my blood-caked hand to slide open the shower-stall door, I saw my fingers were shaking. I saw *I* was shaking. The excitement and now the letdown. I hung onto the towel rack waiting for my nerves to finish dancing.

I heard Father Alexander's and Stan Pokora's cars start out front. Moments later there was a knock on the bathroom door. "What?" I said.

"Open," Charity said.

I inched open the door. In thrust her white arm like the Lady of the Lake's. Instead of Excalibur she held a double Sam Thompson rye, neat. "We need to have a talk," she said. "Right after you finish."

The house was empty. Left behind were enough pastries and sweetmeats to last us till the time of the fusion engine. We sat over coffee.

While she didn't lecture me, she made a couple of good points; again her general theme was that I hadn't been aggressive enough in handling the Nicholas disappearance. We needed to take charge of things.

"We're going to New York tomorrow," I said. "You forget?"

"You should go and talk to Father Alexander *tonight* about what happened."

"Now you think he's mixed up in all this, too."

"Yes, I do. Somehow. Maybe unwillingly."

"Even though he's almost gone 'round the bend because Nicholas has been gone? Even though Tatiana told me he can hardly cope any more on account of the kid? Even though he was in love with the kid?"

"That business today was... funny," she said. "Suppose... just suppose the attack on Father A. was staged."

"Staged?"

"Sure. The lump he took on the head was just to make it look good. Maybe the bald Hulk crawling into the trunk of the car was by prearrangement, too. Father A. knew he'd be coming over here. He also knew you'd be going off somewhere with Tatiana. Wherever you went, the stooge was going to

190

finish you. Even if you just went for a walk, he'd get you on the way back."

I told her about my accusing Tatiana, how she had reacted.

Charity looked coldly at me. "Her anger could have been an act, Yuri," she said. "You could be too much in love to sort anything out where she's concerned. Women can be fanatics, too."

I sipped my coffee and thought a long time about it all. "If you want to talk crazy, I'll talk crazy, too. The shove-around with the giant was also staged so Father A. could openly carry that big pigsticker without any one of us wondering too much." I paused. "He planned to kill *you* while the stooge was killing me. Tatiana told me he had heard what we were really trying to find out right after we first talked to him. A week in these jet times is just about long enough to get anyone from anywhere to anywhere—including Russia."

Charity shivered and closed her eyes for a moment. "Well, it's all maybe and suppose. You maybe made a serious error making assumptions about Tatiana. Let's not make the same mistake with Father A.—unless we can prove it. We don't have much in the way of hard data, either. And motives don't work too well. Just the same I'm glad Stan the Anxious got here early."

I poured more coffee. "About motives. If Nicholas is safely out of the country, or on his way—what the giant implied—getting the two of us out of the way would seal it all up for the order. I'll bet Igor's letter is already gone out of its book cover. We're the last folks who are close enough to know and care about what's going on."

"Really, though, we're just *guessing*, Yuri. That's why we've got to be more active. There's so much ambiguity. By the way, the Orthodox Church of North America returned my call."

"And?"

"Father Alexander escaped from Russia about three years ago. The government refused to let his papers follow him out of the country. The church fathers here, as part of a special arrangement, examined him and found him 'a man of extraordinary talent, piety and commitment.'"

"How'd he get assigned to Russian Slope?"

"'That was decided at a very high level,' I was told."

"Hmmmm." I finished my coffee and got up. "You're right. It's time to beard the lion. I'm going to see Father A."

191

"Watch out for the knife."

"I'm going to catch him at his youth group meeting. I'm gonna stay on his good side."

"Just don't relax . . ."

In the alley behind the Moskva I found a rusty fire escape ladder that had a better than fifty-percent chance of not collapsing. I scrambled up, the grit and oxide rasping at my palms. I slid into a window on the second floor. I was avoiding zany Anton Rastokov, the tottering emigré. I didn't want him dogging at my heels. I didn't want him nosing after what I was doing.

Most of the bulbs in the hallway's fixtures had surrendered to age or theft. Shadows were thick enough to cut out and sell by the pound. From the small rooms on either side came grunts, coughs, hushed whispers and odd pantings. The hallway reeked of urine, cheap wine and broken lives.

I didn't know the layout of the hotel, so I took it slow, working my way by trial and error over to the youth group meeting room with the blackboard and fluorescent lights. I listened for loud voices, maybe singing. Heard nothing. Finally I found the room—dark, deserted, silent. I prowled around, glanced at my luminous watch dial. Meeting time, but there was no meeting.

Across the room behind me I heard an unmistakable sound: the squishing of Anton Rastokov's eyelids. Before I could turn, gunfire cracked and a hot bee snapped by my ear. The lights went on. I whirled and saw Rastokov with a huge old revolver in his two hands. White hair flying above his fleshless limbs, he looked like a hit man from a geriatric ward.

"It's me, Yuri Vladimirovich!" I shouted in Russian.

He fired again and the pistol barrel exploded. Bits of blued metal embedded themselves in the wall like shrapnel. None of them found Anton or me. His sleeves, however, were on fire, and some powder had stung his cheek. "Thief!" he shouted weakly through his shock. "Sneaking around!" I had no idea if he recognized me or not. He rushed at me, cocked his arm and threw what was left of the pistol by my ear. "You not steal from me, from my Moskva!"

I couldn't believe it. Old and rickety as an antique cane chair, he came flying at me. I had to try to collar his flailing, smoldering arms. Right then the information business seemed even less glamorous than usual. Here I was, duking it out with an eighty-six-year-old man.

"Calm *down*. I was here before. I'm Yuri Vladimirovich Nevsky. Don't you *remember* me?"

He stopped struggling and stared at me. He blinked and squished. His mouth, close to my face, reeked of the uncertain digestion of old age. He slapped at his smoldering sleeves.

"Why are you sneaking around my Moskva?" The Russian heaved through the wheeze from his exertions. "I have a permit to shoot trespassers."

"Your armaments need to be updated."

"That was a fine revolver. Made by Ulchensky Arms, St. Petersburg, eighteen ninety-four.The ammunition was at fault. Too modern, too powerful."

"You were lucky. You could've lost half your head."

"At my age, my whole life is in the hands of God."

"I came here looking for Father Alexander." My voice came out tough. He might well have recognized me—and fired a second shot anyway.

He looked at me oddly. "Why should he be here?"

I jerked a thumb at the room. "Youth group tonight."

"Ah!" He nodded. "Yes. I remember. It was canceled. The holy one phoned me and said he was involved in an emergency out-of-state. The group would not be meeting."

"'Out-of-state?'" New York. "Where out-of-state?"

Anton shrugged. "The holy one didn't share that information with me."

In the lobby someone was vigorously palming the desk bell. "Anton Rastokov! These are your friends, the police." Chief Polsky's Russian. "Time for another comb-through."

This was where I had come in. I didn't want to see the chief. I didn't have the time or inclination to bring him up-to-date on the day's adventures. I grabbed Rastokov's bony shoulder. "He's not to know I was here." I caught a glance of defiance in his eyes. "Attempted murder is a serious charge," I hissed. "I could make trouble for you." Half bluff, but it worked. "As you wish, Yuri Vladimirovich."

I hurried away down the hall and slipped out, down the fire escape. I went to a pay phone and called St. Basil's. Tatiana's voice. My heart thumped like a teenager's. "This is Yuri. I'd like to speak with Father Alexander."

"He's not here, Yuri."

"When will he be back?"

"I don't know. Whenever the youth meeting's over, I guess."

"I was at the Moskva. He canceled the youth group."

"Yuri, he didn't tell me." How soft her voice was! How much I regretted my accusation. That it was spurred by fear and suspicion was no excuse. I should have been a better man.

"Tatya, I'd like a favor."

"As long as it's not personal."

"I have reason to think Father Alexander might not be back tonight—"

"What?"

"But I'm not sure. I want you to phone me if he comes home."

"Where is he?"

"Will you do me that favor? Please. Anytime tonight. I mean it. Tomorrow I have to go to New York. You can get word to me there through Charity's law firm." I gave her the name and number. "OK?"

"Sure."

"One more thing. Stay out of everybody's way. And be very careful. You might even want to spend a few days with a friend. Away from St. Basil's."

"I can't do that, Yuri. Father Alexander needs my support. I'm the only person he has."

"Then watch yourself. He may well be mixed up in it all."

I went home, threw some stuff into a suitcase, and had a glass of sherry while briefing Charity. When I finished, she said, "Things are happening now. And we're right in the middle of them. And we're gonna push, push, *push* it all right through Nicholas's front door." She beamed. "Sweet dreams."

I didn't dream. Can't dream if you don't sleep. At 4 A.M. the phone rang. I pounced on it before the second ring. Tatiana—on the edge of hysteria. "Father called from New York. He said he was in trouble! He said he might never be back—"

"Where in New York?"

"He didn't say. There was some shouting—a man shouting at him in Russian. Then the receiver hit the floor and someone broke the connection. Oh, Yuri, *Yuri.* What's happening?"

"Sounds like somebody might be trying to get Nicholas out of the country at last. Out of New York —headed for Russia."

"What about *Father?"*

"I don't know. Tomorrow maybe we'll find out where they all are from Olga—if we can find her."

"Yuri, I am so *worried."*

194

"Then you won't have trouble remembering to be careful."

Her voice turned cold as a polar bear's paw pad. "Your concern is touching—considering you thought I was a co-conspirator."

"I can only ask you. Because I care that much about you."

"All right. I'll be careful." She hung up.

I stood with the phone in my hand. I began to dial her number. I wanted to pour out how much I loved her, how I regretted my thoughtless accusation. Her decision not to see me now was eating at my gut. In my guilt and sorrow I felt I had to face her to say the things I felt. A machine just wouldn't do. I tottered off to bed, where I swam in remorse toward dawn light as gray as my hopes.

We flew to J.F.K., rented a car and checked in at the Lombardy. We grabbed a chopped-chicken-liver-on-rye and coffee and started cruising the streets. We knew there wouldn't be much action. People in Olga's trade treated daylight like Count Dracula. But some were sunlight workers.

We didn't find her. At six we gobbled burgers, fries and coffees-to go. This go-round Charity drove. New York streets at night . . . Rome and Sodom in one. Again and again we patrolled the area around Eighth Avenue and the Port Authority Terminal and up to Olga's favorite haunt around Eighth Avenue and 48th Street. We averaged about a hundred glances apiece at our Olga photo. And reminded each other several dozen times that her hair was now longer.

As the evening wore on, both headlights and neon and the traffic's jerking uncertainty rankled our nerves. My eyes ached from studying the shapes and faces of the women behind shadows and heavy make-up. We motioned two likely hustlers to the driver's side window. Their resemblance to Olga decreased with the distance to our itching eyes. We asked them if they knew Olga. "You want information," one said, "call the operator."

About 4 A.M. we cruised down 42nd Street by the world's Gold Coast of pornography. Peep shows big as Vegas hotels, live sex extravaganzas, magazines, books, paraphernalia. If Lev Samnesovich ever got here, he'd OD on pudenda. This bright sun of sin and its planets scattered in cities from Denver to Dallas to Des Moines shined bright light on an odd trait in the American middle-class male's sexuality: sex as an observer activity. For whom else did the porno masters grind out their stuff? There weren't enough stereotyped shifty-eyed perverts in raincoats to consume one percent of the flood. No, it was mostly for those middle-aged men who lived lives of quiet sexual desperation. Why fantasies instead of involvement I didn't know. Blame it on lack of good father image, poor mother image, repression, too much TV, lack of prayer in public schools, the decadence of the West. One thing was for sure: if you asked that vast army of respectable consumers if they occasionally indulged, most would indignantly deny it.

We saw dawn peek over the eastern skyline. No Olga.

Charity's indulgent senior partner had given her permission for three days max away from the firm. And the hard truth was we couldn't afford to stay very long in New York anyway—for reasons as simple as dollars and cents. Ludmilla's cleaning my kitchen didn't go far toward defraying plane fare or hotel bills. I was short of money anyway. And of course my roof leaked.

Day Two. We slept till one in the afternoon and woke feeling the rottenness that comes with tampering with one's biological clock. Two cups of coffee and a cheese Danish each got us on patrol again. Mid-afternoon I got in touch with Whitcomb's lady lieutenant. I stretched the truth and said I was working with him. I asked her if Olga was in the cooler. She wasn't. Back to the streets we went.

Through the next fifteen hours we found three almost-Olgas and heard two barrages of curses. By now my impatience and concern were soaring. I sensed Nicholas was going to be sent out of the country any moment, possibly Father Alexander with him as a willing—or unwilling companion. As we turned corner after corner I began to think we were too late, that chasing Olga now was closing the proverbial barn door. Maybe—based on the discovered I.D.—Nicholas was long gone to foreign lands.

Finding him for Ludmilla wasn't the only ball game now either. There was the monster insurance policy that GNL, by way of looking after its own interests, wasn't going to honor because Nick had apparently left the country. Proving that he hadn't left, even if we didn't find him, meant tens of thousands of dollars for the Markov family. Finally, the sooner this business ended—one way or the other—the sooner I'd be able to begin work on mending the serious breach between me and Tatiana, the woman I wanted to spend the rest of my life beside.

Charity it seemed had different ideas about Tatya's and my relationship. As we drove and searched, we talked. During the first day she never came straight out with her opinions of my Russian love. She took indirect shots by way of teasing me, talking about my "hothouse flower" and my "nun." I found that teasing a bit irritating because, like my increasing understanding of Tatiana's flaws—specifically withdrawing from conflict and her unreasonable expectations—it further spoiled the perfection I chose to see in her.

I let Charity know she was annoying me. Unlike Tatiana, however, she was as happy in disputes as an Angora in a catnip patch. "I know we have a tacit agreement to stay out of each other's emotional fields, Yuri—"

"But you've decided not to. Tatiana's too much to pass over, isn't she?"

She nodded. "Friends have serious problems when they see people they care about going unwise ways."

"Who's to say—"

"What's wise and unwise?" She grinned, eyes on the traffic. It's judgment. *My* judgment in this case. Suppose you drank too much, were getting to the point of having a real problem. What should I do? What would you want me to do?"

"Speak up. But Tatiana isn't a case of Stolichnaya vodka."

"Trouble comes in all shapes."

"She's not trouble."

Charity drove on in silence, four left turns. Finally she said, "If I were a matchmaker for Yuri Nevsky, I wouldn't pick a pious, exotic lady with social skills as shaky as Emily Dickinson's. *She* never went out of the house, either."

"Tatya goes out."

"You know what I mean."

"She's on a religious retreat."

"OK. OK. I'm not going to argue with you, Yuri. I'm just trying to make some points. I'll save my debating for the courtroom. To come right to the point, the way she's handled her life, never mind her relationship with Father Alexander, isn't healthy—for you."

"How do *you* know?"

Traffic came to a halt. Charity looked at me. Instead of showing the exasperation I had earned, her expression was warm, almost tender. A breath of a smile blew about her lips, "We've drunk a lot of coffee together. We've worked together. The only way I *don't* know you is in the biblical sense. Even if I did it wouldn't change what I know about the essential Yuri Nevsky."

"Described how?"

"A basically unafraid guy. Bright and imaginative. Zany and pleasure-loving. Nicked here and there by life. Good solid ego. Very social. Very . . . special." Traffic started up and Charity turned back to driving.

"And you don't think Tatiana and I are a good match."

"I know it."

"Could your jealousy be talking?"

Color crept into Charity's neck. "I told you before—that's not *fair!* Yuri, I'm taking all kinds of risks in saying what I am. Don't punish me for revealing some of myself. I care about you very much. I don't want you to hurt yourself. That's all. I think we should drop it."

"You have more to say."

"I do. And I'd *love* to have a knock-down-drag-out with you about her. But this isn't the time or place. And we have to work together for a while. Not against each other. OK?"

"OK."

I scarcely slept that night and woke too early on the morning of Day Three. I felt as compulsive, as obsessed as Ahab chasing Moby Dick. By now I didn't care whether Charity and I were right or wrong. We were going ahead anyway. Megalomania had set in.

At 2 A.M., when the night life of Gotham was at its peak, we spotted Olga—negotiating with a carload of college boys right in front of us on Eighth Avenue almost to 48th. The discussions were long. Olga rested her folded arms on the roof and peered down at the six eager faces. If I made a move toward her, she'd be scared halfway to next week. It was chancy, but we had to wait.

We clenched our teeth and exchanged whispered curses. Our aching eyes were hooked by the seemingly leisurely pantomime.

After a wide drop of sweat made its long journey from my right armpit to my belt line, the car zoomed away—leaving Olga behind. A break at last! I eased ahead and waved her toward the door.

Besides a good shape, the only thing she had to sell was her youth. So the Snakeman had dressed her like a high school junior in sneakers, a short skirt that showed her legs, and a faded denim jacket, blouse under. The only make-up she wore was a bit of mascara around a pair of suspicious brown eyes set in a face too heavy to be pretty.

"My wife and I want to have a party," I said. "Wanna come?"

She leaned over and peered in at us. Her eyes passed from me to Charity. "You don't look the type, lady." Her voice came out husky. It smelled of cigarettes and crème de menthe. "Him, he looks like he'd do *anything*. But *you*..."

"We came all the way from Wichita Falls," Charity said. "For us it's a regular once-a-year thing. You don't wanna come to our party, we'll find some other girl. Go ahead down the street, Harry."

"Wait..." Olga was torn between greed and what seemed uncertainty. No doubt something to do with Snakeman's ground rules. I had a chance to study her face. I saw weakness there in the resemblance to her father, a real sweetheart of a guy. As a friend of mine says: "Everything is hereditary." But there was more there. I didn't get a chance to concentrate right then. "...how much and for how long?" Olga was saying.

"Maybe three hours. Three hundred bills," I said.

"Four hundred. There's two of you."

"Three fifty." All I had, squirreled away in my money belt.

"Let me see it," she said.

"I've *got* it, honey," I said. "And you'll see it before the party starts. Think you're a vice-president of Chase Manhattan or something?"

She hesitated, hanging there in the car window. I felt like a man who had to depend on a skittish mare for a dangerous gallop to freedom and prosperity. I wanted to grab her silly head and drag her in.

"No kinky stuff, hear?"

"What's kinky?" Charity said.

Olga told her. My partner worked bravely to keep the disgust off her face. "We... won't be doing those things," she whispered.

I pulled the little post that unlocked the back door. Olga slid in and I pulled off. The car filled with the scent of her perfume, right off the sale counter at CVS. Negotiating the traffic and the turns on the way to her hotel, I studied her face in the mirror. Some of it was turning hard. Why not? So many of the dice that each of us rolls every day had come up with the wrong spots for her. They came up different. She goes to college and has a career. Marries a nose and throat man. Goes to the Bahamas every winter on the H.M.S. Earache. Her face told me, too, that deep down she hadn't quite given up. The craft of her future was on the rocks, but definitely could be safely floated off. Yes, I saw some character under a tart's toughness. What else *was* there to life but the hazard of those tumbling dice, and character?

The Hotel Tropical ranked one-and-a-half short steps above the Hotel Moskva. We went in a side entrance and trudged two flights smelling of disinfectant. It was nearly five in the morning, at the end of four rough days. I was tired and slow. I wanted to find out where in New York Nicholas was. I didn't want a hassle.

At the turn of the hallway was a small lounging area. A sprung couch had been shoved under a corroded chandelier with one bulb in it. Sitting in the gloom was a big man in a Stetson and oddly patterned boots. Closer, I saw they were finished with rattlesnake skin. So was the belt of his jeans, his vest and his hatband.

Snakeman got up and raised his palm. "Hold it, Olga-shugah. What you got heah?"

Snakeman's voice, rising from under his blond handlebar moustache, sounded with the soft tones of the Southern Crescent. A stone set up shop in the pit of my acid stomach.

"They're just a couple from out west want to have a party. Everything's straight, S-man. Everything's OK."

"I told you you ain't ready for trios."

"Listen, mister, we made a deal," Charity said.

Snakeman sauntered close, his boot heels clicking on the ruin of a once-gleaming hardwood floor. "Ain't no deal 'less I *say* there's a deal. Y'all heah me?"

"S-man, they're all *right*. They're from Wichita *Falls*, for Chrissake."

"They are? I been some time in Wichita Falls." Snakeman stood almost chest-to-chest with me. "I don't like yoah looks, beard-boy. And beggin' yoah pahdon, ma'am, you look a l'il cold to me. Like, somebody say, 'Screw or die,' you'd *die* on account of it'd be *easier*. Dig it?"

Charity stood close behind me, so I heard her indignant gasp. I knew the red spots were rising in her cheeks.

"S-man, it's three fifty for *three hours*." Olga was whining.

"I don't smell a party. I smell *cops*. Y'all better name me three streets in Wichita Falls. Right quick!"

He was a big man, crowding close and abrim with menace. A bribe would quiet him. A couple hundred for him, $350 for her, and they'd have half a grand without Olga undoing one button of her High School U.S.A. blouse. I didn't have the cash. Instead I had trouble. "We want to talk to Olga," I admitted.

"You *are* cops." Snakeman's blond brows rose in alarm. "This some kinda bust?"

"No. We just want—"

"Goddamn cops!" he screamed. Then I knew his wits were only half together. In that instant of screaming and wild glance I smelled Nam jungle, sharp stakes with shit smeared on them, fungus and ugly, senseless death.

"We have money here!" Charity fumbled in her purse.

Olga's control dissolved into anxiety. "Snakeman, don't get one of your *mads* on!"

"I'm gonna *kill* me a cop. Oneuh them pestering god*damn* cops!" With a twitch of his forearm and wrist fast enough to take any quick-draw contest between Mississippi and San Francisco he pulled a Bowie knife.

My reflexes were slowed by fatigue and surprise. I knew he was going to gut me bad—real bad. He stepped in to do his dirty work. Charity's arm shot through just below my armpit. Her blurred fist touched him in the meat where his knife arm joined his shoulder.

A muffled pop not much louder than a party snapper sprayed Snakeman's blood and tissue against the wall. He howled as the Bowie hit the floor. His left hand flew up reflexively to cover the oozing wound. His eyes filmed over with agony. He howled again and staggered. I heard dead bolts sliding closed along the hallway. He caught his balance and ran. The unadorned walls echoed his footfalls.

Charity dropped the heavy two-shot derringer back into her purse. She was pale and her hand shook. She jammed her powder-burned knuckles into her mouth. "I didn't know you had one of those," I said. "Or know that a point-blank shot hardly makes a sound."

"I wouldn't come to *this* town without a weapon. And I took a long course on handguns through the firm."

"Good thing."

She looked down the hall at Snakeman, who was diving down a stairwell. "Rather die than screw you rednecked bastard!" I was forever seeing new sides of my colleague.

I turned to Olga.

She was gone.

"Oh, my *God!*" I ran down the other deserted hall, cursing

my carelessness. I hadn't heard a room door open. I had to gamble that my unfocused attention hadn't betrayed me. An exit sign marked another stairwell. I shoved open the door—and heard the thump of sneakers on metal stairs. I ran and stumbled down the two flights and caught Olga just before she escaped into the street.

"Leave me alone! I hate all you cops!" she wailed.

I grabbed her arm. I wasn't taking any chances now. "We're not cops and we're not going to hurt you."

She burst into tears and collapsed against me. I sensed the rugged months in the big city crushing down on her this moment. And she had lost her only "support" figure—scabrous as Snakeman was.

"Get out your room key."

"Who are you two? Whadaya want?" she wailed.

"The key, Olga. The *key*."

She dug in her denim jacket. We went back upstairs. Charity was waiting at the top of the stairs. I gave her the key. She found Olga's room, opened the door wide. Olga was clinging to me and crying loudly. I half carried, half led her in. I sat her on the bed.

I heard Charity turn the dead bolt. She wet a handkerchief under the ancient porcelain sink's only spigot and began to wipe Olga's mascara-smeared cheeks. For a moment Olga's hands rose to resist, then she let Charity finish with her sweaty brow and leaking nose.

Finally she sniffled and straightened her spine.

This moment was a long time coming. I drew a deep breath and let it out slowly. Then I said: "Tell me all about the night you left Russian Slope with Nicholas Markov."

18

"I don't know what you're talking about," Olga said. "And I don't know who you are."

"Olga, goddamn you!" My fatigue and short fuse were showing.

"Yuri, be *still*." Charity waved me into silence. She explained who we were, that we were working for Ludmilla Markov and that we were looking for Nicholas, not Olga.

"You went through all *that* to ask me where Nicholas Markov is?" She waved toward the hallway. "You shot my Snakeman, the only guy who's ever given a fart for me, to ask me where *Nicholas Markov* is?" Her voice was rising. "I don't *know* where Nicholas Markov is. And I don't *care*. Now get out of here and leave me alone!"

Charity and I exchanged dull glances. Fed by my fatigue, my despair whispered: dead end.

Charity wasn't about to be easily discouraged. She got the ball rolling. "We know you left Russian Slope unexpectedly the night of the murder. We know somebody came to the door of your apartment and got you. We know you cashed a bank check earlier that day for five hundred dollars. Father Alexander said you came to him that night and asked for money——"

"He *what?*"

"He said you came to his study sometime after nine fifteen. The way time and people worked out, it was possible."

"A golden cross was stolen from St. Basil's," I said. "Somebody broke into the church, broke the case. Father Alexander said he thought you stole it."

Olga frowned. "He *did?* He lies! And after all the trouble I went to for him—and for Nick. What the hell's got into the hairy dude? I helped them both by helping get Nick out of trouble."

"To help him get away from the Eleven-to-Seven after he murdered Dixon," I said.

"What the *hell* you talking about? I don't know anything

about any murder. You must have it wrong. Nick wouldn't go to a place like the Eleven-to-Seven on a bet. Nick wouldn't murder an ant. He's so straight his pee doesn't curve. Anya probably had to tie him down drugged and smashed for him to get her pregnant."

Now it was Charity's and my turn to cry "What?" We leaned forward in our shabby chairs.

In Olga's face we saw backing off. We had gone at her helter-skelter. Bits and pieces shoved at her from all angles. We had been so confused she didn't even know what direction we wanted to lead her. And the rough stuff had terrified her. It was time to step back and start right. I wet the handkerchief and gave it to her. She touched up her face. "Try to relax a little. We're not out to hassle you *at all*," I said.

"After what you did out *there?*" Her brown eyes again flashed fear.

"He pulled a knife. He was going to kill Yuri," Charity said. "I could have just as well shot him in the heart. Right?" Olga nodded.

"The money's yours," I said. "The three fifty. We'll pay you for your time."

"Oh." We had said the magic word: money. Olga really started looking better.

"You talked about doing Nick and Father A. a favor. Want to talk about that?"

Olga got up and padded in stocking feet to the grimy window and looked down at the street. "You been on the Slope, you must know how I felt about Nick. He was the class of the crowd. I wasn't. I was the un-class. But I had a thing for him. A real, crazy thing."

"You weren't the only one. He had so many followers he coulda started a religion," I said.

"Don't I know it. Anya was one of them. She wanted him. She pushed hard, hard, hard. I wouldna thought she'd have a chance. But she scored..." She smiled. "...and so did he. He got her pregnant."

Olga's words fell like wood blocks on my ears. Not what I wanted to hear. "Yeah? How'd you find out?"

"It was a secret. Nobody knew except Father Alexander. He's the one who told me. The two of them had gone to him for help. They talked it over this way and that. A lot of soul-searching, prayers, counseling, blah-blah. Their decision—the three of them—was that Anya should get an abortion." Olga

204

laughed harshly into the grimy window glass. "Tough T-bone for old Anya. She thought she had it sewn up. Thought Nick would do the 'honorable' thing. Thought he'd fall right down into that old pipe-and-slippers shit. She shoulda known. Nick wasn't like *any*body else. He wouldn't marry her, so *she* had to decide about baby or no baby. She decided no baby."

"Father Alexander told you all this," Charity said.

"Yeah. When he came asking for help. And to make a deal, really."

Olga raised the hair on the back of her head and let it fall back on her neck. She did it several times to cool herself and gather her thoughts. Her neck was long and white, like my Tatiana's. I ached to look into Tatiana's almond eyes again. I resented the wedge between us.

"Here was the deal," Olga went on. "I had been talking to Father about leaving town for here, for New York. He kept saying don't do it, try to work things out with Dad. I should move out but stay in town, he said. Then I told him how old Lev wanted me to spread my legs for his pictures." Olga's laughter fell on my ears like so many ice cubes. "That seemed so wicked then. Now look what I'm doing. That what they call irony, Nevsky?"

"Something like that," I said. "Tell us about the deal."

"Father A. told me that Anya's trip to the abortionist was scheduled. He would take her there. It wasn't far from the Slope. There were a lot of reputations to protect, he said. Anya's, Nicholas's and his. He knew I needed money, so he made me one of those offers you can't refuse. He wanted to use a rented car. He would drive it in street clothes. Anya would be down in the back seat going and coming. After the abortion Father Alexander would drive her to a 'religious retreat' where she would stay for a while until she felt better."

"What about Nicholas?" Charity said.

"Father said Nick and Anya had had words over his not wanting to marry her. Everything changed. Now they couldn't stand each other. Nick was to leave town. Head out west. Get it all behind him. Very hush-hush."

"So you rented the car," Charity said.

"So would you, lady, for five hundred bucks. I took buses out to the South Hills Plaza, rented the car—"

"Blue Chevy Nova." I added the license plate number.

"Yeah. I guess it was. Hey, you been around that deal."

"Better believe it."

"I parked the car about a block from St. Basil's, found my check under the stone where Father Alexander said it would be. That weekend I planned to come here. I cashed the check right away. That was more money than I ever had in my life. Until I met Snakeman, of course."

"How'd you feel about Nicholas going out of your life forever?" Charity said.

Olga turned away from the window, her face stony. "I never meant nothing to him. Woulda died for him, too. How'd I feel? I did it for him first and for the money second."

"Don't feel too bad about Nick and you," Charity said. "We have reason to think he was gay."

"Huh? What—"

"Now, what happened that night?" I said. "And make sure you get it right. We want our three fifty's worth."

She plopped down on the saggy bed. "Sure. What's to tell? I got a surprise. Father A. came to the door and offered me the car to go to New York right away that night. Turned out all the excitement was too much for Anya. She miscarried. Just the same, Nicholas had split for L.A."

"Oh, God," Charity said. "We're on the wrong coast."

"Jury's still out," I said. "Keep talking, Olga."

"Father said he wanted Nick to be safe in a new life. I knew Nick meant a lot to him, that he was helping him, as a sta-rets . . ." Her eyes brightened. "If Nick was gay, maybe there was more to those two than everyone thought."

"More to it than you'd ever dream, Olga." I made a hurrying gesture. "Go on."

"To help make Nick's getaway completely clean, Father gave me two things and told me what to do with them."

Charity gasped. She raised her hand and ticked them off on two white fingers. "One was a letter addressed to the chief of police—Polsky. The other was a bag of Nick's clothes with his wallet on top. He told you to mail the letter in New York a.s.a.p. and dump the clothes at J.F.K. by International Departures."

"Holy Jesus! You *do* know, don't you?"

"He also told you to leave the Chevy by the rental office with money on the front seat," I added.

"I don't think I was a block and a half away from Avis when I met Snakeman." Olga's voice cracked.

"Lucky you," I said. "One last question: how did Father A. say Nick got out of town?"

"He drove him out the parkway to the turnpike. He started hitching west."

"You went back inside, got your purse and met Father A. in the car outside. You drove him back to St. Basil's and swung the wheel toward this here Big Apple."

"I was so happy! I was still singing when I passed the New Stanton Exit."

A lot of pieces had tumbled into place for me. Synthesizing information, once I had it, was one of my strengths. My mind was busier than a five-year-old in a pile of Lincoln logs.

"You gotta tell me about Nick's killing somebody," Olga said. "How did that happen? *When* did it happen?" Now she was leaning forward. I told her. When I finished, I added, "And that's why the last stuff you told us doesn't wash."

"Hey—"

"From our point of view, not yours. Because it doesn't wash, it's not likely the first part about the abortion washes either."

"I'm confused," Olga said.

"I'm still a little confused myself. But not enough not to be nervous." I got up quickly. "Let's go!" I said to Charity.

"Go where? You know where in this big town Father Alexander and Nicholas are? J.F.K., ready to fly to Russia and the Valley of Promise?"

"That makes sense. But it made just as much sense last week and the week before."

"I don't understand."

"And for that matter, it's Greater Pittsburgh *International* Airport, isn't it?"

"Sure, but—"

"If that's where it all was going—toward Old Russian mumbo-jumbo, fanatics and the family Markov, why wasn't Nick sent weeks ago right out of Pittsburgh? Connecting flights from London or Paris to northern India or someplace."

"I see."

"He may be in California. At least that's a real possibility."

"How do we find out?"

"The answer to that isn't here. It's in Pittsburgh. Father Alexander, I'm guessing, never left town. And he has *all* the answers. We're going back." I headed for the door.

Charity hung back and held out her hand to Olga. "Come back with us. There's a lot people can do for you. You don't have to handle everything by yourself."

To my surprise, Olga looked uncertain. All along she had sounded brighter than I had expected. Her emotions had been bent far out of shape. I hoped she'd say yes: she was redeemable.

She shook her head. "Too much back there for me." Lev, her father.

"Too much here for you to handle, cookie," Charity said. "This is Tough Town, U.S.A."

"Thanks, but no thanks."

We left her sitting on the bed, frowning. I ducked into the first phone booth I found.

"Calling?" Charity said.

"Tatiana. To warn her that Father Alexander's likely in Pittsburgh. And likely to be more erratic than ever, considering the ploys he's trying."

"If the California bit didn't happen, he may already have flown out with Nicholas. Maybe whatever's been delaying the departure—the Holy Order of the Caucasus, or whatever—has been straightened out."

"The imported giant was the order's ace," I said. The connection to St. Basil's went through. The ringing signal sounded in my ear. "The order played it when they thought we were catching on. I think we were right about the double dip last Sunday. Father A. *was* going to kill you while the Bald Bruiser took me—and Tatiana. That was the plan."

"Bloody."

"You know who I think gave Father A. orders?"

Charity shrugged.

"Maybe high-ups in the order. But more likely . . . Nicholas, from wherever he is."

"You figure for sure he's bought in *all* the way, huh?" Charity fingered the blouse collar by her throat. "Father A. would probably have killed Ludmilla, too. Stan Pokora saved our lives," she said weakly. "And I sent him home saying there wasn't any sense in our meeting again. I wasn't being fair to him."

That sounded like good news to me. The unanswered fifteenth ring sounded like bad news. Right there in that phone booth on Ninth Avenue a hard knot of dread began to bind my stomach. It didn't slacken in the least on the USAir flight to Pittsburgh we caught at seven that morning.

Charity and I put together some of the pieces on the way back. I used my Coop notebook. She had a legal-sized pad.

208

There were a couple of big gaps left. We would make Father Alexander and Nicholas fill them in after they were warming Polsky's new cells. *If* they were still in town.

And we had to warn Tatiana. I had tried her number again from J.F.K. No answer.

We rushed to my car, leaving the luggage behind. Another call to St. Basil's. Same result. By now my dread, like a beast, prowled back and forth inside me. I hadn't slept. I hadn't rested. Charity and I were both running on nervous energy—and anxiety. We wheeled out onto the parkway. "Floor it, Yuri!" she said.

We set some kind of speed record getting to St. Basil's. The heavy door to the priest's home was locked. We pounded the crucifix knocker until the walls throbbed. No response.

I forced a ground-level bedroom window. Charity and I scrambled in. She drew her reloaded derringer. Tatiana's bedroom was deserted. So was Father Alexander's. The kitchen was still and mealless. No one was in the cellar or the hallway.

In the study we found Tatiana lying amid her own blood—too much of it. I felt her pulse. She was still alive. Charity ran for the phone. I knelt by her and began to turn her over. Then I saw what had been done to her abdomen. I whimpered and released her shoulder. I got up and fought back the emotions. My love dreadfully wounded! I took a half-dozen deep breaths. When I pushed through to calm, an icy lucidity came with it.

One of Father Alexander's heavy old books lay open on the table. I saw the items that had led to Tatiana's wounding by Nicholas or the priest. The papers had been hidden in there. I opened the blood-matted airline tickets. Their date was six weeks ago—well after the murder. Flight was Greater Pittsburgh to London to Istanbul. Travelers: Father Alexander and "Brother" Nicholas. The second item was a U.S. passport. For Brother Nicholas. Nicholas's photo had been taken with him wearing priestly garb. The last item was Igor's letter, stolen or bluffed away from the Markov home.

"Why didn't you leave the country?" I howled at the ceiling. I threw the sticky documents on the floor and screamed again in rage and anguish over my wounded love. *"Why didn't you leave the country when you had the chance?"*

On the priest's desk was an open folder of his personal papers. I noticed an envelope marked "visa." It was empty.

Charity finished with the phone and hurried to my side. "Yuri, the ambulance is coming right away. Oh, God, I'm so *sorry*." She put comforting hands on me, not seeing the rage in my face, not knowing what an icy, murderous grip seized my innards. Tatiana horribly wounded. Cut down by one of two fanatics. I intended to pay them back—in the same coin, if I could. If I couldn't, it would be because I had been killed trying.

I lifted Charity's hands away from me. "I'm going to find them both," I said.

"Yuri. You don't know where they *are!*"

"I have an idea. But I don't know just how." I picked up the phone. P.Q. Antonelli was at work. I had a chance for two ringing tones to draw in the ragged edges of my voice. When she answered I was Mr. Coherence.

"P.Q., Yuri Nevsky."

"Well. Nice to hear from you."

"As your matchmaker, I called to find out how you like Lucas Vokoffsky."

Charity said, "What the *hell?*"

"Dynamite, Yuri!" P.Q. said. "He likes spring and takes walks, too."

"Great! Hey, I'm in a rush and need the answer to one question."

"About Nick?"

"In a way."

"How's it going? I'm not over him yet, you know."

"Get over him. He's almost found, but I need a fact from you."

"As always—anything."

"You used to go to Father Alexander's youth meetings at the Moskva. They still going on?" I held my breath. My heart pounded, thumping at my rib cage like a jackhammer.

"Nah. He canceled them about a month ago. Easter's coming and he said he couldn't keep it up. After the holiday he—"

"Thanks, P.Q. Gotta go." I hung up and headed for the door.

"Charity, stay with Tatiana till the ambulance gets here."

"Where you going?"

"Hotel Moskva."

"But you said Nicholas wasn't there. Polsky said he wasn't there. The place is searched every other week."

"He's there. Somewhere. We should have made more of Rastokov being from the Valley of Promise long before now."

Call Polsky and tell him that's where I went. But wait twenty minutes."

"Why, for God's sake?"

"I want that much time with the three of them—alone."

"Yuri, I am not going to needlessly—"

"Do it!" I had never raised my voice to her. I had been, up to now, pretty much of a gentleman.

I aimed my Datsun down the Slope. My mind was icily clear. All the pieces had come together save two. First: Why had Father Alexander been so increasingly upset if he knew all along where Nicholas was? And second: Why hadn't they left the country, now that the heat was pretty much off?

My mind was clipping along like a computer. Its memory bank fussed with information about the Moskva—searched room by room, basement and attic by Polsky's men a few days ago—yet again. Anton Rastokov's aristocratic Russian hummed in my brain, words from our first meeting. *"... And such drinking! It was said only at the Hotel Moskva did wine flow as it had in the court of the czar! ...* And then that wonderful machine inside my skull served up my first view of the wretched hotel. Its keystone read 1923. Nineteen twenty-three meant Prohibition. The only kind of wine a European would serve, particularly in the "Russian" style, was European wine. French, most likely. That meant large amounts of wine had to be delivered without arousing suspicion. And Rastokov had designed his own hotel ...

I burst into the lobby. I saw the fright wig of white hair behind the desk. I expected Rastokov to bolt up and try to chase me away. Instead he only nodded. "Welcome, Yuri Vladimirovich."

At that moment I saw everything hung in the balance. Fired up as I was with rage and will for revenge, it would be too easy to tumble down the card house of the situation by roughing up Anton. I clamped down an iron control over my emotions. I had the sense to search for a cue in the old man's grizzled face. I found it.

Madness.

His leaking eyes were wild, his jaw wobbling and oozing drool. The last thread in his old wits had been parted by ... I saw his hand pressed against a sodden spot low on his jacket. Blood smeared his fingers. He had been stabbed.

Intimidation would get me nowhere here. I needed some of Ludmilla's peasant cunning. Instead of raising a fist, I sank to my knees. I looked up at the wild eyes. "I hope Father Alexander told you that I have accepted the divinity of the Wonder of Holiness," I said in Russian. "He ordered me to help him take the Wonder of Holiness back to the Motherland. He ordered me to come to you. He said I was to order you to take me to the tunnel to the river."

He nodded dreamily. "The tunnel. Yes, the tunnel *and* the storage vault. They served me well, Yuri Vladimirovich. Large shipments of wine came from Canada, always by night. By barge in silence they came. My storage vault was as large as my bribes to the police. Such parties we had! They danced all night—"

"The holy one said there was haste. He said he needed my help quickly."

Again the dreamy nod. "The holy one is impatient now that time for departure draws near." He looked down at his oozing wound. I noticed a puddle of blood on the floor. The old man was bleeding to death. Religious fervor and madness kept him alive. He said, "I overstepped my bounds. I asked to walk with the Wonder of Holiness out of my hotel—he, the greatest of all my great and famous guests. I was punished—"

"By Father Alexander or the Wonder of Holiness?"

"The holy one. I failed to remember only he may look upon and serve the Wonder of Holiness. Only he hears his prayers and confession. Only he can instruct him in the ways of the Holy Order of the Caucasus and the family Markov. When the holy one was not there, the chamber door was padlocked. I swore on my soul to avoid the chamber. I was justly punished for my presumption."

I rose from my knees and gently helped the dying man to his feet. "Don't be ashamed, Anton Alexandrovich. It was you who sent word back to the Caucasus that you had found the Wonder of Holiness growing up so near, wasn't it?"

He nodded. "It was God's will that Igor Gregorevich should come to this community after I did. It was God's will, too, that the scoffer never set foot in St. Basil's to see the gold cross, that holy treasure I had saved from Lenin's thugs."

I held the old man's arm across my shoulders and led him, staggering, away from the desk. He was so light! Like a sack of dried sticks. There wasn't much left of him. "We have to hurry," I said. "The holy one needs my help. He has ordered me to serve the Wonder of Holiness. Through me, then, you serve him still. No matter your errors."

The old man turned his skull face to me. His breath stank of age and dying. In his leaky eyes I saw the faintest glimmer of suspicion. He trembled. The wild glow of mad piety swelled—and that doubt was burned away. "I will . . . lead you to the tunnel." He took me on a winding trip down through sixty years of stored hotel furnishings and equipment. The basement was large and cavernous. Shaky wooden stairways joined the various levels of heavy flagstones. The deeper we went, the damper the walls. The smells of mildew and moldering hung in the air with the increasing chill. "I am filled with age and error, Yuri Vladimirovich." He shook his head. "The other night I shot to kill you. The holy one had said you were an enemy."

"You're forgiven. I was a doubter then. Not now. You were serving the Wonder of Holiness." I lied on. "What can't be forgiven to those who serve him?"

He made a keening noise of delight. I thought of the woman who meant so much to me lying in a smear of blood. I gritted my teeth and swallowed the urge to crush his thin neck with my hands. I said, "The holy one is clever. He hides his intents well. He called Tatiana Tamanov and told her he was in New York."

The old man giggled. "He ordered me to shout in Russian. He dropped the instrument, then cut the connection . . ."

In the large room in the deepest basement Anton led me to a wall made of heavy hand-cut stones a foot square. He pointed to a ledge set in the adjacent wall and made a tugging gesture. I left him staggering and tipped the release lever ledge.

Ingeniously counterweighted, half the wall swung away. More dampness and cold hung in the air—along with a sweetish odor. I knew it from St. Basil's: church incense.

"Lead the way, Anton Alexandrovich," I said. I held his arm.

He lurched down the stone stairs. The tunnel was both higher and wider than I expected. And colder. The Monongahela River damp had pushed in over the years. The stones, lit by a strung cord of eight bare bulbs, sweated cold-looking droplets. About a hundred yards down, the tunnel had been bricked up, the way to the river permanently blocked. Fifty yards in I could see the heavy oaken door of the storage vault. Twenty yards in stood a massive bearish figure, black and brown in the shadowy light. He bellowed at sight of us. "Anton Alexandrovich! You fool! You bring *him* here?"

The old man was befuddled and nearly dead. "He . . . serves the Wonder of Holiness now."

The priest howled with rage. "He serves no one but himself!"

I collared the old man and dragged him forward.

Father Aleksander called over his shoulder toward the vault. "Stay within, Wonder of Holiness. A last bit of business has to be taken care of and the way will be clear to the Valley of Promise."

"Taken care of like you took care of Tatiana." My tight voice echoed from the dripping walls.

"She pried," the priest said. "I found her with my hidden papers after I returned to collect my visa. She accused me. She blasphemed God and the family Markov."

"You have no compassion left, do you, priest? You are what you told your giant stooge to call you—an 'anti-priest.'" I dragged trembling Anton with me down the cold, echoing tunnel toward Father Alexander. The sweet stink of incense grew stronger.

The priest's somber voice boomed out: "Anton Alexandrovich, you have betrayed our cause bringing this man here. The Wonder of Holiness has instructed me to spare no effort to clear our way to Mother Russia. And you have put another obstacle in our path."

"Nicholas's mind is as poisoned as yours, priest," I said. We were all speaking Russian now. There was nothing American in what we were about.

Anton was half fainting from fear and loss of blood. I held him up with one hand and pointed at him with the other. "You owe him better. It wasn't easy for him to get word to you a couple of years ago."

The priest shrugged his massive shoulders. We were quite close now. I could see the bright light in his eyes burning with lamplike intensity. Like that of the relentless giant. "The order was waiting. It is as patient as a spider and as long-lived as the Caucasus mountains themselves."

"And you were chosen."

"I knew English well and something of American ways."

"You arrived and started the youth groups to meet Nicholas. All low key. You revealed to him what you wanted, and he swallowed it all, bought in. But you couldn't stand Igor being here. You had to shove his 'broken promise' down his throat."

"He threatened to kill me. I let him put his pistol to my

head, invited him to pull the trigger. And told him that if I died, others would come—that we knew who and where his grandson was. So he killed himself later. Coward and blasphemer!"

"If you had known just a *little* more about how things work with police, you'd have kept right on going the night of the murder the way you planned, in the car Olga rented for you. No matter that Nicholas had just killed a man by accident. You had your first set of tickets, didn't you?"

"Yes. Pittsburgh to London to Istanbul."

"Then across the border and the long trek to the Caucasus."

"The Wonder of Holiness was long awaited. Believers then—and now—wait all along the way to ease his journey."

"It should have worked—if Nicholas hadn't insisted on keeping his rendezvous with Nolan, who turned out to be Dixon."

"I did everything in my power to sway him! To keep him from going to that accursed tavern."

"It must have galled you to know he kept his word out of love for his lover, Nevick. When you wanted to be his lover, Wonder of Holiness or not."

"You blaspheme, Yuri Vladimirovich." His eyes told me I was right.

"When he jumped in the car and said he'd killed somebody you had to think quick. You thought cops would be waiting at every airport and bus station. So you came here with Nicholas, hid him with this poor geezer's help. You got Nicholas to draft the letter to Polsky. Then you went to Olga's apartment and gave her the letter and Nick's clothes and I.D. And finally you gave her the Chevy—after you got a ride back to St. Basil's. After that you decided to lay low, because now the cops *were* watching the airport. Nicholas stayed hidden. You visited him here every chance you got. Before and after every youth and y.a. meeting. And then you canceled them completely to spend more time with him. Other times you took him food—"

"I gave him further instruction in matters of the Holy Order of the Caucasus, his responsibilities to us in these days of the commissars. The time was not wasted. I saw him grow still stronger, more pious, more commanding."

I leaned closer, the failing Anton Alexandrovich drooped over my arm. "About six weeks after the murder you planned to leave again—and didn't. *Why?*"

Father Alexander blinked and said, "The Wonder of Holiness didn't feel sufficiently prepared. We entered a period of intense religious instruction and great meditation on his part."

"And so Charity and I had a chance to come on the scene."

"You didn't fool me, Yuri Vladimirovich. At once I sent for a man from the Valley of Promise. The Bald One. A peasant by vocation, an assassin by avocation."

"And now you *are* ready to leave?" I said.

"Yes."

"Nicholas doesn't have a passport."

"I have had another made. One that shows the full glory of his new beard. We have our tickets. The believers all along the way have again been contacted." He glanced quickly at his watch. "And our flight leaves before too long."

He pulled out his knife. It was still caked with Tatiana's and Anton's blood.

I had been ready for it all along. From the moment I saw Tatiana lying in a pool of her own life, I knew I would have to face that razor-edged metal in the priest's—or in Nicholas's—hand. I felt ready. I had passed the threshold of fatigue and sleeplessness. My stomach was empty. My vision was clear and my reflexes, spurred with edged nerves and the first leakings of adrenaline, felt sharp and quick.

"Anton Alexandrovich, you have to stand now." I kept my eyes on the blade. I let the old man go. Struggle and emotion had pretty much leaked out of him. There was only a little life left.

He stood, tottering. He raised his hands in an effort to get his balance. Father Alexander rushed. I retreated. The priest drove the heavy blade savagely into the old man's stomach. "Betrayer of the Wonder of Holiness!" he bellowed. He ripped the blade up like an enraged bull working his horn. He had done the same thing to Tatiana.

Anton Alexandrovich toppled away with a weak groan and fell twitching to the cold stones.

I was next.

I was also a little tougher cookie than an eighty-six-year-old, half-bled-to-death man. Knife fighting is all counters, reactions to the other's aggressiveness. That's my natural style. I had no knife with which to counterthrust, but I did have two quick and dangerous hands. I figured I had a chance—if I could keep the new, fanatical Nicholas inside the storage vault before he got the idea he should come charging out to help his mentor.

That Father Alexander didn't call for him right off meant the priest was very confident in his horrible knife. That was a break for the Yuri Nevsky team of one. So I had three goals: shove the hasp home, pin it to keep Nicholas inside, then wear down Father Alexander.

I had a thick Rapidograph pen in my pocket. The one I used to take notes. It looked like it would hold the hasp.

Father Alexander called on God for strength and charged. I sidestepped and dealt him a stiffened knuckle jab. Pinned his left ear to his mastoid in a brief, agonizing pinch.

He charged again and I tripped him. He went down hard, kept his knife up and sprang to his feet in a moment. He was quick. But I was past him. I slipped the pen out of my pocket, slapped the hasp home and jammed the pen into the thick arch of the staple.

Then I advanced, doing what I could to protect the sealed door. Over and over I reminded myself to be patient. I would need time to wear the priest down.

But he didn't give it to me. He had a plane to catch. He advanced quickly, swinging the knife back and forth in front of him like a man cutting waist-high grass. He was forcing my back toward the wall of brick that sealed the tunnel.

I had to try something. I made a grab for the blade. His powerful arm broke my grip. There was the briefest instant when I knew I would be punished for my failure. I twisted wildly as the blade came foraging for my gut.

The edge seared across the rib cage of my left side, rasping and gouging at the protective bones. I slammed my upper arm down on his forearm and wrist and got my left hand behind his arm above his elbow. In the instant it took him to shake himself and his knife free, I gouged out his right eye with my right thumb and forefinger.

He howled, the sound echoing and reechoing in the closed tunnel. "Wonder of Holiness, help me!"

I didn't wait for action from within. I aimed a kick at the priest's crotch. I wanted to finish things before I missed the blood pouring down my left side. Too hurry. My toe thudded against a thigh like a bridge column.

He came stalking me still, treading slow and careful. His left palm was pressed against his oozing eyesocket. His right

217

hand gripped the knife rock-steady. "You are a devil, Yuri Nevsky. Sent to torment the family Markov."

"You used that knife on Tatiana. I mean you, not Nicholas."

"Yes."

"I'm going to kill you for that."

An odd smile flashed through his pain. "Good!" he said.

I didn't know what he meant, but in the next moment he overextended his knife arm. I managed to get stiffened fingers into some of its nerve clusters. The knife clattered down to the damp stone. We both dove for it. Still sprawled, I scooped it up.

He scrambled up to bent knees. He was going to spring at me, pin me to the floor with his bulk. I just had time to grip the handle in both hands—icy it was, a breeder of death—and tilt it up.

He growled and his weight slammed down. The butt of the knife handle was driven down against my breast bone. The razor point pierced the priest's abdomen. Not a fatal blow. We were joined by a steel umbilical cord. His good eye and the waste of twisted, collapsed lid and lashes bored into my gaze— wild light and darkness.

His massive arms reached around me. He embraced me wordlessly, as though in thanks. The knife between us scraped and shuddered further into him. Surely he had to faint, I thought, and relax—and so live. But his strength was endless. His will to die relentless. I didn't know why. His arms forced us closer, forced the knife into his vitals. Only when the curving guard sank flush against his flesh did he relax. His head collapsed on my shoulder. Blood and vomit burst from his mouth. I knew he was dying.

I rolled him off me. I was shaking from fatigue and gross assaults on my nerves. I knelt beside him, eyes closed, drawing deep breaths. After a few moments I stopped shaking. I pulled the huge knife out of his gut. I dried the blood-smeared handle in his wiry beard. I stood up, knees trembling.

It was time to deal with Nicholas Mikhailovich Markov, the Wonder of Holiness.

I pulled my pen out and freed the hasp. The sweet reek of incense seeped from around the oak. I got a good grip on the knife and swung the door open. "Nicholas Markov! I'm here to take you to your grandmother," I shouted.

Candles! The vault was ablaze with them. Hundreds and hundreds burned on the floor, on old shelving, in natural niches.

Most were six or eight inches in diameter, and tall. They burned for days. Their flames danced and shuddered in the draft from the opening door.

I saw dozens of ikons set facing the front of the room. Gilt faces in which painted eyes looked forward. Some were worked with hammered silver and gold, others were ancient wood, mellowed and gleaming with age. Bronze braziers on tripods belched clouds of perfumed smoke. They had all come out of the crates stacked against the wall. Ikons and candles were purposefully positioned to draw the eye toward the front of the vault, which I couldn't see from the tunnel.

The incense was powerful, almost enough to take the breath away. Even so I could smell that it was somehow tainted.

"Nicholas!"

No answer. I leaped through the doorway, landing on the balls of my feet, knifed poised. My eyes swept leftward, devouring the hidden third of the vault.

Before me a man knelt in reverence, huge hands folded before his chest. His hairless head gleamed in the yellow candlelight. The giant, dragged from the thicket by Father Alexander the night Anton shot at Yuri, the intruder. The huge limbs had been propped into positions of devotion directed toward the front of the vault. The stiffness of death had turned the corpse into an adoring statue.

In the front of the vault a throne—there was no other word—had been set up before the wall. It was a heavy chair with high back and armrests, a relic from the glory days of the Moskva. A solid crate raised the throne about eight inches above the floor. Onto the throne had been fastened clusters of ancient religious jewelry, clusters of pearls, ruby crosses, golden ikons, mounted sapphires big as eggs. In the chair, hands on armrests, sat Nicholas Markov dressed in sumptuous garments. Their fabric gleamed with interwoven gold and silver threads. Robe, jacket, puffy hat and vest were nearly blinding. His slippers were set with pearls. Around his neck, strung on the thickest of gold chains, hung the massive Slavic cross stolen by Father Alexander from his own church. Beneath the dazzling finery Nicholas Markov was swollen. Not with fat, but with festering rot. A reeking, bloated corpse sat enthroned.

Then I understood the depth of Father Alexander's final descent into madness.

On the floor and kicked into the corner I saw the empty packages and containers of nonprescription medicines with which the priest had tried in vain to stem Nicholas's cold and most certainly the pneumonia which followed it in this damp, cold and dreadful place. Uneaten food was heaped in mold-furred hills. Six weeks he had sat decomposing in the dampness.

I had deliberately not looked directly at Nicholas's face. Now to continue a long, impenetrable ritual which I only dimly understood I had been performing for two weeks, I walked forward. From four feet away I looked at the front of the corpse's head. What I saw was half skull, half face of festering flesh. Its dreadful, gaping eye sockets, when my shadow fell on them, came hideously alive. Swarms of small black beetles boiled from within the rotting head and spilled down the cheeks.

To my dazzled wits it seemed the Wonder of Holiness wept, wept, wept black tears. My eyes were captured by that weeping visage. Such tears fell not for whole human beings. They fell for the ill-formed, the cretinous, the hopeless, the scabrous, the perverted, the deluded, the mad, the doomed dwellers in misery, and for all for whom life was endless pain and suffering.

I could not tear my glance away. My trembling became like palsy. I tottered backward to the rear of the chamber and sank down on a crate, mouth agape. The reek of incense and rotting flesh rose about me like a cloud.

From the tunnel I heard cops' footsteps and Polsky's voice. "This deal's gonna be wrapped up in minutes, Sergeant—I mean *Lieutenant* Whitcomb."

The chief and the lieutenant, enjoying the first three seconds of his promotion, burst into the vault.

"Congratulations, Whitcomb," I said. Then I fainted.

19

I woke up in Columbia Hospital some distance from the Slope, with stitches in my side and a tube in my arm. I had lost more B-negative than I thought; they were putting some of it back. Aside from that and feeling very tired, I was OK. I began to lay plans to get home as soon as possible. I had this theory that so many people brought to hospitals with minor ailments developed major ones because the places mess up biorhythms. Wake-ups at quarter-to-six in the morning, and no rye whisky.

I wanted to know about Tatiana. My questions might as well have been about the number of hairs on a dried yak scrotum for all the response I got from doctors, nurses or candy-stripers. No trouble did I have finding out what happened to me. Polsky and his gangbusters came storming in—and puking out, some of them. They scooped me up, dumped me in an ambulance and off I went. Father Alexander, old Anton and stiffened giant went directly with Nicholas to the county morgue.

They left me under observation for two days. At the end of day two, I finally got a look at Charity, who was leading in a doctor with thick glasses and the air of egomaniacal confidence that only a surgeon really *had* to have.

I sat up fast. "I want to know about Tatiana!" I said.

"There wasn't much hope from the start," Charity said. "She didn't make it." She fought to control her voice. "This is Dr. Santucci..."

He had come along to explain what had happened. He had tried. He had taken eight hours. He gave me the operating procedure. The intestines and many of the vital organs were damaged. He and his team sewed up the guts with little trouble. Spleen came out—fairly common. It was the big boss down there—the liver—that had been mortally wounded. "She was a gutsy lady," Dr. Santucci said. His eyes were locked on mine; he wasn't using standard platitudes. Somehow that made me feel a bit better. "She nearly made it. She was a lovely woman. I wanted very much to have her live." He grabbed my

221

shoulder, rose and walked out. I don't like doctors, but I liked him.

Charity stood close by my bed. "I'm so *sorry*." Her pale eyes were brimming. "She meant so much to you. She turned you away from being a limited Yuri Nevsky toward—I don't know—being a better person somehow."

I nodded. Grief loomed up like an ocean liner in fog. Totally unanswerable. The pitiful homilies by which I guided my life were mercilessly exposed, picked clean by this carrion crow of the death of one I might have grown to love uncritically. Where were my well-reasoned lectures on the total capriciousness and hazard of existence, the unresolved subatomic ambiguities at the very heart of matter? My tears were eloquent testimony to the barrenness of my sophomoric philosophies. "Leave me alone now, Charity," I said.

Noon the next day I checked out of the hospital. The bill—not a small one; they never are—had been paid by one "I. Tschersky." Waiting for me with my receipt was an envelope with Volodya's personal check for $10,000. His short note said the cross had been returned to its home at the heart of St. Basil's. What he described as "the valuable paraphernalia" had been locked into an unused church storeroom to stay.

Charity carefully avoided the worst potholes on the way to 138. Her consideration and my trying not to breathe a whole lot kept the pain in my side at a bearable level. I eased up the stairs to the second-floor entrance to be greeted by a committee of one—Ludmilla Petrovna Markov.

She embraced me gently, then used her weight to lever me down to where she could plant kisses on each of my cheeks. No missing the grief in her eyes; new webs of pain and endurance branched from the old. A tough old dumpling, no mistake about it. I slipped my arms down to where her waist ought to have been and gave her a hard squeeze. Too hard for my side. I whimpered.

"You will go to bed, Yuri Vladimirovich," she said.

"I'm all right. I was just dis—"

"You will go to bed! You will sleep. Hospital sleep is not same as house sleep. *Go!*"

I went.

She was right. I slept half the day away—and the night as well. When I rolled over and sat up it was nearly noon the next day. Summoned by some infallible maternal instinct, Ludmilla

222

showed up at once with a tray. I smelled chicken soup. An envelope was beside the bowl. In it was $2,000 in cash.

"I don't need to take your money," I said.

She picked up a chair and heaved her bulk into it with a grunt by my bed. The Russian poured out. She had no use for money now. Had more than she needed from her share of the huge insurance policy. The money she had put aside for Nicholas's education . . . She shrugged.

"I'm sorry about your grandson," I said. "I'm sure it's all been terrible."

"We will not talk of him."

I wanted to know how much information about the Holy Order of the Caucasus and the priest's obsession had been made public. How much had been said about mad fanatics chasing will-o'-the-wisps down the hallways of sixty years? What about Nicholas, who might have matured as a saint of sorts, instead was corrupted, tempted and fell from his own unique grace to an ugly end? I wanted more: I wanted closure to this near-barbarism that strung back to Old Russia and older ways. I wanted an end to my own ritual odyssey. But Ludmilla would not give me either. "We will not talk of any of it," she said.

I looked into her moon face. Where before I had seen a quaint simplicity, a babushka, a tramper among potato vines and a puller of beets, I now saw an enigma that I could scarcely discern the shape of, never mind unravel.

She heaved herself to her feet. In parting she said, "Tatiana Tamanov's death was a great loss to our community. But she was not the woman for you—"

"Ludmilla!"

"When some misfortune came her way, she ran. She did not immerse herself. Though soiled, she did not soil herself. Despite her age, she was a virgin in spirit. Committed to nothing. Except the small thing of her own happiness. Yuri Vladimirovich, she never drank from the bitter cup of experience. In that cup are poison and power. We all must drink sooner or later. There is no escape. Then we know if we must hide from life for all our years—or are strong enough to shape it to our will."

"I don't think I understand."

"Tatiana was not your woman. For you should be somebody like Zharity."

"Charity?"

"*Da.*"

"I'd like you to leave now," I said.

She did. Charity came in a few minutes later with coffee, cheese Danish, the *Post-Gazette* and Trackman Tolovitch's *Russian Voice*. She held up the *Post-Gazette*'s front page first. Below the usual reporting of international misadventures was a wide-angle photo of the inside of the vault which caught the full sweep of candles and ikons. Nicholas's remains had been removed. The headline read: "Crazed Priest Enthrones Dead Youth." I scanned the article. It was a wonder of incompleteness.

I looked up at Charity. "All the spicy stuff is left out."

"Uh huh."

"How?"

"Polsky provided the information. You can ask him about it. He'll be here this afternoon."

"It says here I discovered everything by accident while looking for Father A., wanting to ask him about some youth group activity. Says he cut me to keep me away long enough for him to kill his hostage, Anton, for psychopathic reasons. Finally he fell on his knife. Suicide. Nicholas died of pneumonia while hiding out . . ."

I shook my head and picked up the *Russian Voice*. Trackman's article was even more oblique. Stuff about strains on the Orthodox clergy, evils of the drug business.

I threw the papers down with a frown and changed the subject. "It took us a long time to catch on to what was bugging Father A.," I said.

Charity nodded. "Six weeks ago he and Nick were ready to leave the country. Then Nick got sick, sicker and died. The one and only Wonder of Holiness dead and gone. And *he*—Father Alexander—was responsible to whatever black-robed, white-bearded weirdos are still in the Valley of Promise. He had failed—without any hope of redemption."

"His mind did a long, slow dive," I said. "For a while he could still think, dissemble and scheme. Teaming up with the old-country assassin was about the last halfway sane thing he did." I readjusted the pillows in back of my head. "You know, Charity, toward the end he really *believed* he was going to take Nicholas back in glowing triumph. He had them send him the jewels and clothes, all the shinies. He made himself *believe* the kid was still alive."

"At least halfway," she said. "You must know he wanted to die. In a way, Polsky was right—suicide."

"It was almost suicide—for me."

Charity pointed an accusing finger. "I want you to know our unofficial partnership is going to be dissolved if you try any more of that hero stuff again. Going down there unarmed to face *three* madmen. You were just lucky there were only two and one was a feeble old man."

"I didn't know how crazy Father A. was. Anyway, I was after revenge, not justice."

"You should know better than *that*, too. And I don't like macho-leave-the-ladies-behind. If you had left me outside Olga's hotel, Snakeman would've cleaned your clock."

"Between you and Ludmilla . . ." I sank down and pulled the covers over my head.

"I'll go," Charity said. "But I want to leave you with one we'll never answer."

"About what?"

"How high does the influence of the Holy Order of the Caucasus go? Someone *very* high in the church sent Father A. here, knowing . . ."

I felt a chill. No, we would never know.

By the time Polsky arrived in the early afternoon I had dressed. He, Charity and I met in the kitchen. He allowed he'd drink a cup of coffee. Then he scowled and shook his head. "What a case you are, Nevsky. I'd still like to find a reason to throw you in my new slammer. I *told* you to keep me informed about what was going on."

"Things happened too fast."

"My *ass*. I got down into that tunnel, I hadn't been around so much blood 'n' guts since the last time I saw *Patton*. I thought you had bought it, too."

"Not that time."

"But next time if he tries it again." Charity was not smiling.

I drank some coffee to wet my throat. I knew what was coming. Out came the chief's Panasonic. "I want *everything*," he said. "Right down even to time and place of your every peepee."

It took two hours. The chief shook his head, tsk-tsked and nodded from time to time. Pretty much let me run on. A couple of limping questions, one or two loose ends, and I was through.

The chief switched off his machine, leaned back and closed his eyes. "Jesus," he said softly.

"Question for you, chief," Charity said. "You going to call in the press and explain everything? All the stuff they left out?"

Polsky poured himself more coffee and smiled slowly, eyes half-closed. "No way. And I have two good reasons. First is, I'm a Russian. I live on the Slope, even if my HQ is in the next town. We have a certain set of values. Religion plays a big part in those values. A priest tumbles into insanity—that's possible. A misguided kid gets mixed up with drugs and gets chilled in a damp room—that's possible, too. But fanatics from another age with knives who hire assassins—then lead us in the matins on holy Pascha—that's *not* acceptable." Polsky shook his head. "A priest who buys into the darker side of the Russian soul doesn't belong in modern Russian-American life. I'll do what I can to hide that part of him."

I wasn't quite so ready to believe what did or didn't "belong" in Russian-American life as I might have been before it all started. I found myself wondering what Ludmilla would think. I kept quiet and Polsky went on. "The other reason is you two. You and your 'information business.' The last thing you need is being in the papers, having your faces on TV. What you want—talk-show appearances? If this got out just the way it happened, that's how you'd end up. Everybody and their uncle would know your faces. And you'd be out of business." Polsky packed up his tape recorder and got up to leave. "I'll follow up those reasons with some advice. On the way in here I told Ludmilla you two were to be protected from callers—media people or anybody else—"

The phone rang. I heard Ludmilla's lumpy tread heading for the instrument. Her language when she picked it up was a thicket of Russo-English that a linguist couldn't have penetrated. Deliberate. "Hello . . . What? . . . No understand . . . No, not here . . . Neither both . . . Impossible! . . . Don't know . . . Nobody here—else . . . Good-bye!"

Polsky grinned and stroked his goatee. "She can keep them away for a while, but my advice to you both is—take a vacation. Beat it for a coupla weeks. Go where it's warm. Get the winter out of your blood. I'll do what I can to soft-pedal the whole deal and keep you out of it. If I were you, I'd leave right after the big service we're having at St. Basil's tomorrow."

Volodya came that evening to inquire after my health. He accepted my thanks for his generosity, then invited Charity and me formally to the coming Orthodox service for the dead. Four of the dead were without kin: Father Alexander, Anton Rastokov, Tatiana Tamanov and the nameless bald giant. Only

Nicholas Markov had family. A group of seniors from the Slope—Volodya included—had chosen to ask the priest imported from across Pittsburgh to lead the service over all five coffins. The priest had gone into conference with his soul and consented. Only Mikhail Markov refused consent. "But in a very short time Elena Markov made *her* views known to him." Volodya wiped at the sheen of brow sweat raised by his second cup of tea.

"She did?"

"As she had not in many years, I gather."

"So all five souls will be prayed for at once," I said.

"Pardon me, Volodya," Charity said. "I don't understand how you can have a service for—well, murderers and victims together. That's not *right*."

"All truly belonged to the community of Russians. And to the greater one of Our Lord and His Son—He who taught us to forgive and offered even the worst of us redemption. We Russian Orthodox are not so—unh, *tidy* about spiritual matters as many other religions, Ms. Day. We do not so quickly draw lines between the saints and the sinners, or the quick and the dead. For example, we feel those called dead are still much with us. And so we pray for them as much as for the living. To us all five souls are still with us. *In* each of us is some of them. You see, *we* make up the church. The lines between us, the laymen and theologians, are unclear as well. As is that between what can be known through our church and what remains impenetrable mystery."

Charity shook her head and laughed politely. "I like things laid out for me. Sharp and clear, without fuzzy edges. I want to know where I stand all around—and that includes with my Creator."

"Then I think Orthodoxy is not for you, Ms. Day..."

To help out our anonymity Charity and I decided to split up for the service at St. Basil's. She was going with Stan Pokora. She wanted to tie up the last of the loose ends with him by thanking him for unknowingly saving her life that Sunday afternoon. She would have to walk carefully around the issue of Father Alexander's intentions. I had some loose ends, too, so I called and asked Betty Ellen Edwards to go to the service with me.

She slid into my Datsun with a polite hello. She wore large round sunglasses and the closest thing she had to mourning clothes—one of the ankle-length black dresses from her act.

"I know you said you didn't want to see me," I said.

"I also shouldn't have said yes. But here I am."

"Thanks for that." She didn't reply, and we drove on in silence. "A couple things you should know about Ray Nevick," I said. "One is that he was crazy in love with Nick. I mean they were gay lovers."

"They were?"

"So much that he went crazy missing Nick. He started doing the worst kinds of dope. And they ate his brain like some kind of cancer. When he tried to kill me he really wasn't thinking at all."

She shrugged. "He slams you with the car, I'd be going to *your* funeral with *him*."

"I want you to understand he wasn't right in the head. If he had been, I'd be squashed."

She shifted a bit away from me on the seat. "Ray was always crazy. That was his style." She folded her arms.

"Betty Ellen, I was happy to see you after all those years. I didn't mean to louse things up."

Her face swung quickly toward me. "I really didn't need that shit you dished up at Volodya's party. I *mean* . . . the one lady was married and lived in a castle. And that P.Q. person is just a kid. I didn't even mind you slipping out that night while I was on stage. I knew you were a busy man—"

"Betty Ellen, I apologize."

She nodded. Her huge sunglasses were like the headlamps on a luxury touring car. "That's nice to hear. But . . . don't try to put it back together, OK? You and I, Yuri, are like a couple of trains that started out of the same yard. We got switched around all over the country for fifteen years. Now we're sitting on the same siding for a few weeks. Pretty soon we'll be on our separate ways again. I didn't think so that night Ray bit your ear. I had a surge of romanticism. It dies hard." She swept off her shades. Her eyes were very dry and cold. "It's all those cheap romantic novels and bad TV shows."

I nodded. "Just the same, I hadn't forgotten how you were fifteen years ago. And I won't forget how you are now. When I'm in the old folks' home in my rocker, peeing through a straw, you'll be one of the memories I'll be replaying on that Betamax in my head."

"Really?"

"You must know that."

She smiled and put her glasses in her purse. "I guess I will, too. What else is there that counts in the end but memories of people?"

"Nothing." I smiled as I remembered Artie Greenberg. "You might want to know how you got un-fired so soon after being fired."

"How'd *you* know?"

I told her.

She giggled and shoved playfully at me. "I'd have paid any price to see his *face* . . . And a *raise* will come in handy. Oh, I always *knew* you were basically OK, Yuri. And I'm sorry Ray got it in his head that you were after making trouble for Nick. After all, by then the kid was in the biggest kind of trouble. He was dead. Who would have thought Ray could go so bonkers?"

There was a crowd outside the church. Mostly Slope people, some gawkers-after-tragedy, and some press. I saw one Channel 4 van. Nobody paid attention to me and Betty Ellen.

I did a double take when I saw Olga Samnesovich. She was surrounded by P.Q. Antonelli, Anya Rok, the Ice Queen, and her fiancé, Ron Sakinoff. They were clearly offering her emotional support. They explained it was Ron who had decided to act on Charity's phone call. She had called P.Q. and told her where Olga could be found—not what she had been doing. And that she needed help in deciding to come home to the Slope. Might do it if some friends showed they cared. The rescue mission would have aborted if it had been left to Anya. Ron—whom I had underestimated—rallied the two women, and they set off on the long drive to New York. Their mission of resurrection probably would have floundered without a vital ally—Lev Samnesovich's liver. It had failed him. Cirrhosis. He had vomited blood all over the bar at the Eleven-to-Seven. He was in the hospital, they explained, and wasn't likely to survive long. Without him Olga thought she could face the Slope.

Olga looked slightly dazed. No wonder. In the end she would be OK. I nodded briefly, smiled and maneuvered Betty Ellen away and into the church. It was packed with standees. I saw Charity beside Pokora. I saw Ludmilla and Sasha and Mikhail Markov. Elena stood apart from them. As I glanced around I saw every person I had talked to on the Slope, from Trackman Tolovitch to Artie Greenberg. Community.

I knew that under usual circumstances, bodies of the dead Orthodox faithful were kept in their families' houses for two or three days. During that time the psalter was read by relatives and friends. Short services called *Panihida* were held. Under these special circumstances, and considering my very limited knowledge of church goings-on, I didn't know what to expect.

There were five coffins. There was a choir. There were prayers and responses, much weeping. The service unfolded, expanding, moving toward a high point as in a Wagnerian opera.

The priest chanted, "'I weep and mourn when I look upon death, and when I see our beauty, created according to the image of God, laid in the grave, formless, shapeless and without glory. What is this mystery that is our lot? Why are we given to corruption and yoked together with death?'"

Finally, the congregation sang, in culmination, "'Come oh brethren, let us give a last kiss to the dead and render thanks to God, for our friends have gone from their kinsfolk and rest in the tomb, and they have no longer a care for the things of vanity and of our much-toiling flesh. Where are we now, their relatives and friends? Lo, we have parted from them to whom Lord, we pray, give eternal rest.'"

The choir replied for the five dead souls. "'We lie voiceless, deprived of breath. Beholding us, bewail us, for yesterday we spoke with you and suddenly on us came the dread hour of death. Come all that love us and kiss us, for never we shall converse with you again. For we depart unto the Judge before whom king and servant, rich and poor, stand together... We beg you pray to Christ our God for us that for our sins we be not bidden unto the place of torment, but be granted the right of life.'"

Toward the last of the recitation I began to cry. I wept for Tatiana, of course, but for mad Father Alexander, odd Nicholas, old czarist Anton and the nameless giant. I wept for my father, my mother. I wept for all of us.

Betty Ellen and I made our way out with the crowd. As we moved across the parking lot, a woman called to me. It was Elena Markov. She beckoned me toward her car.

"Same old Yuri." Betty Ellen dabbed my eyes with a Kleenex and shoved me ahead.

I noticed Elena's car was packed with suitcases and other possessions. She was dressed expensively and looked good. "Mikhail and I have agreed to a trial separation. I'm going to live with my sister awhile." She continued earnestly: "All this business has changed me—in ways I don't really understand.

My Nicholas—gone. My life exposed as . . . trivial. My seeing what a tyrant Mikhail is, how much harm he did Nicholas. And—well . . ." She laughed nervously. ". . . you had some impact on me, too. By just being decent to me. I saw how starved I was for some kind of adult relationship. I want to apologize for having tried a come on. It's not my style."

"I could tell. You're too classy a lady for that."

"I'm taking a risk in all this. In separating in the midst of my grief for my son. I borrowed money from Ogalkov against my share of the big insurance money. I thought and thought about it. I think now's the time to go, if there ever was one."

"Good luck," I said.

"Thank you, Yuri."

I wanted to tell her how dangerous it was out here in what passes for the real world. Rude shocks, danger, money-grubbing, deceit by men and women with the most earnest faces flourished mightily far from the alphabetical spice racks of safe—if stifling—domesticity. Risk-taking can be contagious. But we all have to be infected before we can truly prosper in our hearts, the only place where prosperity has meaning. So I kept my mouth shut and accepted her peck on the cheek. Daring stuff for her with her husband across the lot with others, looking on.

Ludmilla waited by my car. "I bless you a thousand times, Yuri Vladimirovich." She pressed an envelope into my hand. "Read this when you can." She gave me a great hug. She smelled of flour and strong tea. I stuffed the opened envelope into my pocket. I would look it over when I had a chance.

The rest of the day seemed to pick up speed. At 138 I met Charity. We'd both managed to squeeze some extra time out of our schedules for a short vacation. We were both packed. We drove to Greater Pittsburgh and caught our flight to Miami. We changed there for St. Martin. We arrived at sunset. A jeep moved us over the spine of hills to Spiked Cannons, a small hotel high above a private beach. As we traveled my mind tumbled about the events of the last two weeks. Two matters were central to my thoughts. The disappearance of Nicholas Markov, now put to rest. And the uncertain metamorphosis of Yuri Novsky—still very much in process.

I had lost a father, a mother and left a wife and two daughters. I had found a love to help me right my life. But the hazard that rules all had taken her from me. I wasn't sure I would ever forget she died resentful of my reckless accusation. A page forever turned. An error forever unmended. I had been forced to accept myself as a Russian. I was a Russian, squirm as I might, a race about which I knew little. I was a member of a community I hesitated to acknowledge. Uncertainties, ambiguities and confusion reigned over me. I was incomplete, floundering and alone.

Such was my state of mind when I sat with Charity at seafood salad and a bottle of Piesporter Goldtropfchen Moselle. The flagstone balcony where we had been seated was perfumed with the night odors of tropical flowers. Beyond the golf course, the line of palm trees, and the beach with its phosphorescent surf line stretched the moon glade on the water, a silvery promenade to the edge of the world.

The moonlight, though it shadowed the scenery, cast the brightest glare on my inner landscape. In it I saw Charity in fresh detail. I saw a woman who had helped me through tough times, who wished me well, who was willing to risk our friendship to warn me not to be blinded by flawed love. She had shot a man and saved my life. She was without question a tough and lovely lady. How had I never fully realized it before? Grasping these things completely for the first time, I saw it was a better time than most to ask her to marry me. So I did.

20

We sat on the fine white sand amid snorkels, masks, fins, big towels, a thermos and beach bags. Behind us, high on its stony promontory stood Spiked Cannons, cool stone and shadows. Ahead the Caribbean, faultless blue under a sky midsummer Kansans would envy. To our left about sixty yards away were the beach's only other occupants: Mr. and Mrs. Howard S. Racquette of Mink Run, northern Wisconsin. He was in traps and hunting equipment. She was in the Friends of Needlepoint and the Rococo Recorder Club. They loved their lives and their home, but enough winter, Mrs. R. said, was enough. To the right stretched the beach, a long white hook that grew thinner and thinner until it was lost in the blue sparkles of water and sky.

Our first morning had begun with a dip in the ocean's bath-tub waters, a fruit-and-crêpe breakfast and a stroll through a junglelike park populated by birds with outrageous plumage and watered by tumbling falls and freshets bubbling out of clustered boulders.

Charity and I wallowed in small talk. We caught up on the things we hadn't had time for in the last two weeks. The Pirates' chances in the season's opener and thereafter. What was going on in her law firm. The high-grade vaudeville of Allegheny County politics. We agreed I had been lucky when Volodya Tschersky offered to find people to redo my roof. It would be *na-levo*, as the Russians say. That's halfway between under-the-table and moonlighting. Men who worked for a roofing company would wrestle with the slate over several weekends, on their own and to their own profit.

How could I complain? The climate was Eden-like, the Spiked Cannons' chef had been trained by Fernand Point, my side was mending nicely, and I could gloat—in a small way, so as not to tempt Fate—about having escaped death.

However, I was not at ease. My engine refused to idle. My mind refused the order: Vacation Mode. As they say to those who want to get away from it all: You really take it with you. It's all sewn in a sack that goes right along with you. My sack bulged. And I couldn't empty it. Worse, I had added to it.

The first item was Charity. And a nice item she was in about one-and-a-half ounces of Lycra—a strap here, a little vee of fabric there. I didn't know any other thirty-six-year-old who could still wear so little and get so much out of it. A few light stretch marks branching like shallow gullies low on her belly were the only external signs of bearing three children. Particles of fine sand clung like glitter to the blonde hairs and white skin of her forearm.

For the last half hour of heat and glare she had been quiet. I knew she had been thinking of our conversation last night. The one that began in moonlight and ended under the considerably less romantic fluorescent lights of the only all-night coffee shop on the island—four hours later.

I fiddled with the snorkel gear, tested the straps, lined fins and goggles neatly on the sand. Then I poured us each a generous gin-and-lemonade from the hotel's thermos. I waited. Until I couldn't wait any more. "You said—in the end—you'd sleep on it. Think it over," I blurted.

She rolled over and faced me close. She propped the side of her head with her palm. Her face, reddening shoulders and cleavage filled my field of vision. "I have been. Reviewing the two offers. The opportunity to be your wife. Or a moved-in lover. Either on some kind of a long-term basis."

"Sounds accurate, counselor."

"I appreciate your being honest with me about your state— or was it states?—of mind."

"I'm changing in ways I don't understand. For example, that burial service and the five coffins. '". . , What is this mystery that is our lot? Why are we given to corruption and yoked together with death? . . .'" I found myself thinking about death, where we fit into life." I let the thought—and all the attached, complex ones—squirm away to silence. Then I said, "My life seemed so empty, so full. Now . . ."

"You think maybe I can save you."

"I don't need saved."

"You need something from me," Charity said. "Something that I can't give you. In a way we were all over this last night. Not this focused. But it's where we were. And good as I feel about you, wanting to share as much as I do with you, I can't be balm to another one of those tortured Russian souls you talk about."

"But that's not—"

"Listen, Yuri. You've always been a good listener." She raised her palm and laid it on my sun-warmed brow, pressing down and rubbing lightly, as though to iron out the three big wrinkles there. "Look at it from my point of view. I had a crisis not long ago—a worse one than yours. Everyone I loved was torn from me. Now I'm putting the pieces together. One by one, very carefully, because that's my style. So far it's working. I have my profession. I have a nice place to live, thanks to you. I have our information chases to keep my mind off the past. Little by little I'm coming back. I've got the shell up. Now I'm working to fill in behind for strength. So I can be a whole, solid person again. So that some day, when you or somebody else makes long, binding propositions, I can say OK, let's try it. Instead of no—which is what I'm saying now."

"So it's not a forever no?"

"It's a now and immediate future no. If you can't deal with that or having me around a lot, I'll move out. I'd like to stay with our present arrangement." She looked down at me. Her pupils were small dots in the brilliance and heat. "You have a right to think of that as my wanting my cake and eating it, too. I will leave if you want."

"No. It's OK," I said. "Stay. I want you to."

"I'm not slamming down any iron doors. At least I'll try not to." Charity kissed my cheek. Despite the heat, her lips were cool. They smelled of lemons. "I'm very flattered to be thought so much of by a wonderful person like you."

I lay quiet awhile. Then I said, "I wonder when you might change your mind."

She scrambled to her feet. "I'm hot," she said. "I'm going in." She scooped up a snorkel and fins and ran off toward the low surf. Her rolling-hipped woman's run kicked up little sprays of the powdery white sand.

I sighed to see her go. Yes, she was one of the central issues in the sack of my concerns.

And I had also that second new consideration to mull over. I dug in my beach bag and pulled out the opened envelope Ludmilla had given me in St. Basil's parking lot. I had forgotten completely about it. That morning, while cleaning out my jacket pockets, I had found it. I studied the envelope. It bore two postmarks dated early this year. The first, January 14, was from Ankara, Turkey. The second was New York, February 27, after Nicholas disappeared. I had slid out the single sheet of rough paper and read it disbelieving. Now I read again the Russian script, the tiny precise hand.

Pura, Tamyr
September

For Ludmilla, wife of my late beloved brother Igor Gregorevich Markov:

I weep with you at the passing of our beloved kinsman, your husband, my brother. These words of my grief and sympathy are doubly late. Word of his death came by mouth to this remoteness in ways so indirect that only those who live in a closed society can understand them. These words to you must also travel in much the same way.

His death affected me so sadly. Of our entire generation only he and I survived. And, as you must understand, at first for safety's sake, I could not share with him the knowledge that I was, after unimaginable upheaval, alive. Later it seemed unwise to do so. Igor, as you also know, was a reckless and romantic man. Given to doing foolish, dangerous things. Yes, we both survived. He because he went to another land. I because I was born with the cunning so many of us lacked. Sixty years ago, though only a child, I bribed the Evenks who seized me. They scattered my clothes dripping chicken blood, hid me. And told the world they had ravished me and cut my throat. Then we traveled north.

In time I married one of their leaders, a bearded brute of a man who knew nothing of European Russia or the Great Russians, as we are called. The muscles of his right arm and his horses were all he had on earth, and all he needed.

In time we settled here, north of the Arctic Circle. The doings of the commissars mean little to us. The only true government in Pura is Frost. I changed my name. My husband was pleased with me, though we had no children. I thought often of our estate in the Valley of Promise, the holy fathers who linked our leadership with all our prosperities. And very often indeed my mind turned to the profound Prophecies of Father One-Leg. But I knew when—and where—I was well off.

Through traveling friends I learned, over the years, the fates of my parents and my brother and sister. I greeted long-delayed word of the birth of your son, Mikhail, with joy. I lit many candles to your good fortune in bringing to the world the one who might well be that saint-on-earth whom we had been taught to call "The Wonder of Holiness." And in my private breast I lamented my barrenness. Only you were carrying on the Markov line.

For many years I waited to hear word of Mikhail's good works, his bold deeds and of course his return in triumph to the Valley of Promise. When none came, my heart slowly sank. The well-being of our valley and those who still live there is of such great importance to me!

Then a great wonder occurred for which I thanked God a thousand times. A sign—though I did not know it then. Though I was in my fifty-third year, I conceived. I bore a beautiful son with corn-colored hair and wide blue eyes. I named him after my father—Gregory.

As time passed, my amazement increased. My Gregory spoke and walked before his time. Sick animals and ailing plants brought into his presence seemed to heal themselves. He is eighteen now and already a leader and priest in heart and soul. He needs no schooling, no beard or black robes, no estates bearing his name. God is with him. *In* him. As He was with his ancestor, Katerina Ivanovna Markov, who healed in ancient times. He leads in prayers and songs. He gives wise counsel to men thrice his age. Word of his wisdom has traveled a hundred versts in all directions. He lays hands on the sick and often they rise whole again.

I write to ease your grief with the knowledge that, through the grace of Almighty God, I am mother to that one who must surely be the Wonder of Holiness called out in the divine Prophecies. I much regret that this happy news didn't reach Igor Gregorevich before his passing. It would have eased his mind greatly.

When my Gregory is twenty I shall notify the priests of our most holy order that our leader lives. That the Wonder of Holiness walks among us. That the Markov uniqueness marches on through time!

I am giving this letter to a friend bound for the West. If it's the will of heaven, one day it will reach you. Each day I will light a candle to that happy moment.

I shower you with kisses, my sister-in-law. I must share your grief—as you must share our family's triumph!

I bless you a thousand times,
Alexya

The warm breeze that stirred my hair did nothing to dispel the chill that held my spine. Ludmilla had read this letter between the time her grandson disappeared and that rainy March day she had come to ask me for help. How much more she knew—or had guessed—than was written down here I couldn't say. Surely a great deal.

So I had been manipulated. No, that was not the right word. Used was closer. Yes, used. But not only to serve her ends, but somehow mine as well. And possibly those of others on the Slope. After all, other lives had changed recently besides mine. So far did her perceptions and cunning exceed mine that she seemed nothing less than a sorceress—a juggler of time, destiny and human hearts.

My modernized mind quickly mobilized to destroy that concept, that explanation—a fat, web-faced worker of wonders. My rationality might have succeeded but for the letter I held from Tamyr. Among the obvious messages it carried to me were some less so. The precise script spoke of old ways and an old people who endured circumstances and governments like mighty trees. It told me without apology that to serve rationality at the expense of spirit was a popular but destructive arrogance. To weigh everything in terms of the modern was self-deception, for the second hand's swing, like a relentless scythe, chops everything at once into the past.

And finally for me possibly the most important: however I put myself together and struggled toward the best Yuri Nevsky I could be—doomed never to be satisfied—many motives, understandings and behaviors lay rooted in the ancient race of Russians. I had denied my past. Now I needed it to help assemble my future...

Charity stood in the shallows, stooping and scooping up handfuls of water. She tossed them skyward. They sparkled in the perfect sun like jewels embellishing the heat.

I didn't feel heat. My chills had turned to shivers, as though a cold wind blew over me. I saw that I didn't belong amid this tropical pretension. I imagined the wind blew straight from where I might have belonged had the paths of reality split a different way—that land where my people had flourished for more than five hundred years. My chill wind smelled of birches, mud, suffering, black bread, endless train rides, endurance, buttercups, dreadful cold, tea and misery, vastness . . . Russia. Yes, Russia. Russia. Mother Russia!